Scribe Publications
TAG

Barry Heard was conscripted in Australia's first national service ballot, and served in Vietnam as an infantryman and radio operator. After completing his national service he returned home, whereupon he found himself unable to settle down. After twenty years, he succumbed to a devastating breakdown due to severe post-traumatic stress disorder.

Since recovering, Heard has decided to concentrate on his writing. His first book, *Well Done, Those Men*, a bestselling memoir, dealt mainly with his Vietnam War-related experiences; his second book, *The View from Connor's Hill*, also a memoir, dealt with his youth in the Victorian countryside. *Tag* is his first work of fiction. He lives with his family in rural Victoria. His website is barryheard.com.au.

To the nearly one million horses who died during World War I.

In 1926, a granite horse-trough memorial was constructed to mark the contribution of horses to Australia's battles. Originally unveiled in St Kilda Road, Melbourne, the memorial was relocated to the Shrine of Remembrance in 1987. It was erected by the Purple Cross Society of Victoria, a group concerned with the welfare of horses.

TAG

A MAN, A WOMAN, AND THE WAR TO END ALL WARS

BARRY HEARD

SCRIBE

Melbourne · London

Scribe Publications Pty Ltd
18–20 Edward St, Brunswick, Victoria 3056, Australia
50A Kingsway Place, Sans Walk, London, EC1R 0LU, United Kingdom

First published by Scribe 2009
This edition published 2013

Typeset in Dante by the publishers

Printed and bound by CPI Group (UK) Ltd, Croydon, CR0 4YY

National Library of Australia
Cataloguing-in-Publication data

Heard, Barry.

Tag.

9781922247186 (UK edition)
9781921753084 (e-book.)

1. Australia. 2. Army. 3. Australian Light Horse–Fiction.
4. Horse whisperers–Australia–Fiction. 5. World War, 1914-1918–Cavalry
operations–Fiction.

A823.4

scribepublications.com.au
scribepublications.co.uk

I have returned to these:
The farm, and the kindly Bush, and the young calves lowing;
But all that my mind sees
Is a quaking bog in a mist — stark, snapped trees,
And the dark Somme flowing.
— Vance Palmer, 'The Farmer Remembers the Somme' (1919)

CHAPTER ONE

The secret to making a daisy chain was to use the pointy little fingernail on your right hand. That was what the kids at the Doctors Flat school had told Phyllis Wardell. During the flowering season, many daisy chains were worn to school — it was almost the fashion. So here was Phyllis, sitting among the capeweed just up from the creek, plucking the daisy flowers carefully, pushing a small hole in the end of the stem and then carefully threading another through. She picked the flowers slowly — not to protect the plant, but simply because any quick movement would upset the bees that were landing and doing their little wriggles on the bright-yellow flowers. If you upset the bees, they had a nasty way of showing that they didn't like being disturbed.

This daisy-chain necklace would be for her mum, Mrs Ann Wardell. Mum had given Phyllis several days off from school, so she deserved a present. Although her mum had offered Phyllis no reason for the reprieve, making daisy chains beat schoolwork any day.

All of sudden, a piercing scream frightened Phyllis. She rushed up to their log cabin and pushed open the door, only to see her mother on the hardened dirt floor, clutching at her huge stomach. Phyllis stared at her mother. She was obviously in extreme pain. There was sweat dripping off the end of her nose, and a disturbing grinding noise was coming from her mother's mouth as she gnashed her teeth in agony.

'Catch Dimble and go fetch Mrs Carroll … Now!' barked her mother. Dimble was a black pony.

Ann Wardell was on her knees, staring, almost consumed by the pain. Phyllis's mother was about to give birth to her fifth baby. It was seven days early. Phyllis, who normally would have been at school, was her youngest child. Phyllis's two older brothers were at school. Fred, Ann's husband, was at work miles away. Ann had planned for Phyllis to be the messenger — this was the reason for her having been kept home. However, Ann had said nothing to Phyllis. Giving birth to babies was secret, private women's business.

Quickly, Phyllis turned, snatched the halter from the hook behind the door, and sprinted out the cabin door. There was no time to look for the bridle. Dimble was down by the creek. Phyllis threw the halter over the pony's head, pulled the rope tight, and quickly led the horse to the fence. She stepped up the stay, onto the top of the strainer post, and leapt on the pony's back. A sharp kick in the animal's ribs had the nine-year-old Phyllis dashing across the paddock on horseback, out through the gate, and onto the narrow bush track. Galloping with no saddle was difficult. To stay on the pony's back, Phyllis held tightly to a tuft of the mane, her knees locked onto the horse's shoulders. Dimble, normally a lazy, sour pony, was a horse on a mission. The young gelding's unshod hooves slammed into the gravel track as he galloped frantically, perhaps sensing the urgency of the moment.

It was two miles to the Carrolls' homestead, and it was hard to steer a horse with a halter (a single rope), but Dimble didn't need directions — the narrow, winding track through the stringy-bark bush was the same route that Phyllis's two older brothers had taken to school earlier that day.

The bright sun flashed and flicked through the tall trees as Phyllis urged the black pony on. At last, she swung open the gate that led to the cleared country, and a homestead appeared in the distance. There were only two slip rails across the gateway into the house paddock, and Dimble jumped them in one bound. Somehow, Phyllis, with her arms wrapped around the pony's neck, made it to the Carrolls' back veranda. Mrs Carroll was almost ready. The yapping sheepdogs and squawking geese had heralded Phyllis and the pony, long before they reached the homestead.

Ann Wardell gripped at the rusty steel headboard of the bed as it bumped against the dry stringy-bark logs. She yelled with fear, anger, and anticipated joy. Her husband, Fred, a road builder, was a four-hour horseride away, but she still cursed his name, as many mothers do during childbirth. Then came relief: the new, pink baby wailed his arrival. Tag Raymond Wardell's entry into the world was only a short, searing burst of pain for his mother. Quickly, she looked up to Mrs Carroll with large, searching eyes, pleading for a description. Mrs Bill Carroll, from over the ridge, informed Ann Wardell of the baby's gender and condition. He was a healthy redhead with a sharp cry. It was 12 May 1896.

Although exhausted and throbbing with pain, Ann beamed with pride and satisfaction. The birth was a familiar experience for her. Tag had other brothers and a sister, but this baby was special—her precious baby. She clutched at the baby boy and hugged him tightly. It was something that Tag was to experience continually in his formative years: hugs and praise from his mother.

After having a long rest, Phyllis and a tired Dimble arrived back at the log cabin three hours after Tag's birth. She had forgotten all about the daisy chain. The new baby soon blotted that memory out.

In truth, it is a little premature to call the baby 'Tag'—that happened many weeks later. In those early days, he was simply called 'Manny' or 'our little man'.

Months passed. Inside the log cabin, a contented Ann had finished her early-morning chores. The new youngster would spend many of his first years close to his mother's side, watching her making clothes, tending the vegie garden, knitting and, most importantly, keeping the cabin clean and cooking. Ann would glance continually in this new baby's direction. *Just in case …*

Then, with all her immediate jobs done, it was time to have a cuppa, a break. At one end of the log cabin, a heavy chain hooked to a horizontal pipe halfway up the chimney allowed a big cast-iron kettle to hang over the open fire. After several prods with the iron poker, the fire flared up. Once the kettle boiled, Ann made a strong brew of black tea with a teaspoon of honey. Tag was plopped on a kangaroo-skin rug on the floor. He knew — even at this young age — that it was the special part of the day. He rarely cried, and regularly nodded off to sleep.

She put the pannikin of tea on the rough table, and ferreted through the steel trunk until she found the quilting bag. Ann was most at peace when making waggas or quilts. Sitting next to the open fireplace on a crude wooden stool, she reached for her bag of material nearby and, for the first time since daybreak, relaxed. She hummed, swayed, and rocked. Her wiry hands cut out the picture labels from sugar bags, flour bags, and leftover remnants from worn-out men's suits that she'd collected from church bazaars. She then sewed them together by hand. It was her time, and a practical one at that.

Tag was her last baby. His birth finally offered some comfort to her, after the tragedy of baby James. Sweet baby James — beautiful, soft, cuddly baby James — had died a terrible death, several years before.

ANN WARDELL was not a local. Years ago, along with her mum, her brother Ron, and three canvas bags of luggage, she had arrived as a six-year-old called Ann Williams at the Doctors Flat Pub in far-off East Gippsland, Victoria. It was the end of a long, sad trip for the three of them. Her mum, Gloria Williams, had come out unannounced from England with her two children, to be with her husband Jock, a Scotsman. She had written ahead but, as he never replied to any of her letters, Gloria was unsure of Jock's whereabouts. She had missed her husband terribly since he had sailed for Melbourne.

This disruption all started for the Williams family when Jock had burst into their small lodgings in outer London years earlier. Ann was only three at the time. Jock was so excited when he arrived home that night from the Barrington Arms Pub that he had grabbed his wife, danced around the small kitchen, and then told her that their days of struggling in small rented lodgings were over. He told her of a job he could not refuse. It was better pay, a promotion, and would bring them wealth. Finally, he told her he would be sailing to Melbourne alone. It was a wonderful opportunity, according to Jock, but he had to leave immediately. Within days, he was waving goodbye to his family as they stood together on the dock. Jock was so confident. In no time, he promised, he would send for Gloria and the two children, Ron and Ann.

In truth, Jock Williams was a liar, a conman, and a poor father. He had left England to sail for Melbourne in search of a fortune. He joined the rush for gold, but he never made it to the goldfields. Instead, he became a petty criminal in Melbourne, and lived a life similar to the one he had left in England as a shyster and a conman. He had duped his wife. She had always believed he had a good job in England, and was proud of her man. He had put food on the table and paid the rent. When Jock boasted of a make-believe job and promotion in the firm, and set sail, he was simply satisfying two selfish desires: to escape the law, and to pursue adventure and risk. This included, he hoped, more adulterous relationships, just like those he had enjoyed in London. Within months of arriving, he was familiar to the traps (the police); he avoided arrest by bribing them, which was now common in Melbourne. It was quite different from England, where he had tried to buy his way out of trouble only once, before he discovered that those police were men of good reputation.

It was more than two years later when Gloria packed up and sailed to a strange country with an even stranger history. All she knew about her destination was what Jock had said on the day of his departure: that the ship he was about to board was sailing to Melbourne. Now, thanks to her own parents, Gloria and her two children set sail for Melbourne. Her father, who was always moved by his daughter's love and devotion to Jock, had given her his life's savings. It was he who had suggested the idea. After accepting her father's generosity, the family prepared to leave; they were packed and ready to go in three weeks.

On the pier, it was difficult. As the family bunched together, bitter tears quickly swamped sad farewells and promises of letters back home. It was also difficult because Gloria and her children had lived amicably with her parents, and she had worked part-time in her father's pub. Still, Gloria believed in her man Jock, and felt he must have had a good reason for not contacting her. Many times, people had told her that the mail had been slow, and that letters took many weeks to arrive. Gloria had her mind made up; even if it frightened her, she showed none of this to her children or parents. The two children, Ann and Ron, were excited, and saw the trip as an adventure.

On arriving in Melbourne, Gloria went to the police in the hope of getting them to help her trace her husband. As it turned out, their directions were too good: to her shock, she located the scoundrel in the arms of another woman. Jock was annoyed and inconvenienced, as it ruined a lie he had been spinning his girlfriend. Both women soon realised that he was 'nothing but a two-timing mongrel'. Gloria was devastated and went to find an acquaintance in Carlton, an inner suburb of Melbourne. She had an address of sorts, where she managed to find this kind person. They had met and made friends with each other on the slow journey over on the coal ship from England. The woman, Claire, had an uncle at a place called Doctors Flat. Consequently, employment and board was organised at his pub — the Albion — for Gloria, as a cook.

So, within a week of arriving in Victoria, Gloria, Ron, and Ann trundled off to a remote part of the state, east of Melbourne, with few possessions, little money, and without a husband or a father. It was a blunt introduction to wilderness, poverty, and isolation, none of which Gloria had ever faced before. She would remain a bitter woman all her life. She never again considered another relationship, and remained cool to most men. However, Ron and Ann, her two children, soon adapted to bush life, and loved the crude colonial existence offered by the Omeo district in the late 1870s.

After a year at school, Ron, the eldest, moved away as soon as he was able to find work. He was ten years old. Ann stayed on at school until she was fourteen. When Ann finally left the Doctors Flat school, she remained with her mother and worked in the pub alongside Gloria. In those days, it was not acceptable for young women to leave their mother unless they were married. By her middle teens, Ann was an attractive young woman, and caused many a head to turn. Most romances that led to marriage in the 1880s were a brief flutter of chemical energies and physical attraction. There was time for little else. Life was constant, tiring, and demanding for working families and their children. This was exactly the way it would turn out for Ann.

Even as far back as grade seven at school, a small attraction had developed between Fred Wardell and Ann Williams. Fred used to wink at Ann—from a distance, as he was bashful. She in turn would blush, giggle, and quickly tell her classmates that he was making a line for her. However, at home, when Ann's brother Ron heard about this, he warned her about Fred Wardell. 'If 'e gets up ta any funny business, I'll ring 'is ruddy neck.' Ron also threatened to dob Ann in to her mother. That was a worry. Gloria Williams was a severe woman with her daughter in matters of romance. As it so happened, the early-adolescent attraction between Fred and Ann slowly faded and came to nothing. By the age of fifteen they were both in work, and had little time to socialise.

Fred's parents had met back in the early days of the gold rush. Fred's father, Bill, was of convict descent, and had met Fred's mother, Irene, at a gold camp at Buckland 'over t'other side'. She was the daughter of a hotel owner. They had trekked over Mount Hotham to Omeo on foot with meagre belongings and two youngsters, both girls, way back in the 1860s, again chasing the precious metal. Fred was born much later. Sadly, his mother died during his birth, and Bill struggled to raise young Fred and to maintain work as a shearer-cum-farmhand. Communities were close and supportive, and didn't hesitate to assist others faced with such a tragedy. As a result, Fred soon found himself separated from his father and two sisters, and grew up in four different houses in his first ten years. By the age of fourteen, he had had only four years of schooling.

The three local families that cared for Fred instilled good manners in him, as well as the Christian faith and a doctrine of hard work. Fred was a loner. He never fished for compliments or praise. He was a perfect example of 'be seen and not heard' as a child. His tight, red, curly hair was quite common among boys at the time. Like most redheads, from a young age he continually wore a hat and suffered with skin problems from the harsh sun.

Fred's first job was at the makeshift butter shed at Swifts Creek, a small town about three miles up the road from Doctors Flat. He was a quiet, withdrawn young man, with a warm grin and blue, welcoming eyes. At fifteen, Fred was tall and strong. He had to be, as lugging cream cans filled to the brim was a bugger of a job that few men would stick with. There were a couple of tricks of the trade: he wore a heavy roll of leather over the shoulder that he carried the cans on, and he would also tie a rag around his forehead to stop the sweat from getting in his eyes. Quickly he muscled up, and threw the cans around as if they were empty. But, although he worked as hard as he could, he was never able to satisfy the bullying foreman.

To Mr Bourke, the boss of the butter shed, Fred was his best worker—but, like most bosses of the era, he never told Fred, or hinted at this opinion to his foreman. Fred felt uncomfortable with the men's talk at meal breaks, and hated the abuse he kept getting from the foreman, so he started to look around for another job.

When he was aged eighteen, a road builder approached Fred. There was a job for him on the road as a maintenance man. Fred was pleased; he would be alone from Monday to Friday, camping out. He took the job and liked it, and stayed at the Junction Pub at Swifts Creek on weekends. His interests away from work were footy and fishing.

By the age of sixteen, Ann Williams had risen to cook's assistant at the Albion Hotel in Doctors Flat, where she shared a room with her mum, Gloria. Ann was a popular young woman who hummed and smiled all day. Her delicate, white skin was unusual, but it was typical of kids who had spent their childhood in England. Her beautiful, long brown hair, continually worn in a bun, and never cut, was a pest during the long, hot summers. She ignored the flirting and whistles of the customers at the pub;

there was no time for that nonsense, according to Ann's mother. Ann was mature for her age. Like Fred, she had seen nothing but the tough side of life, and the experiences had strengthened both their characters. Ann was attractive, intelligent, and capable of embarking on a far better career than was available to a cook's assistant. Nevertheless, women such as Ann had little choice. It was either the church or marriage: they were the decent things for a young woman to do. Most chose marriage, as there was an abundance of nuns.

Occasionally, during brief trips into Swifts Creek with the horse and jinker, shopping for the pub kitchen, Ann would leave the shopping list at Sandy's store and wander out into the street. She found some time to look in front yards, admire the flower gardens, and catch up with a few old school friends. These trips were usually on Saturday morning; it was her only day off. The first time she saw Fred—while he still had the job at the butter shed—Ann was surprised. He was seventeen. Her memories of him as a skinny redhead at school received a pleasant jolt. He had filled out into a rugged young redhead. The other thing she noticed was his height and powerful forearms; he was well muscled and had a thin beard. Suddenly, her original schooldays' interest in him was again aroused. She smiled and said hello. Fred simply touched the brim of his hat. Later, when she met her friends, she asked about him, and found out that he worked at the butter shed.

From that day on, whenever she did the shopping at Swifts Creek, she attempted to find Fred and engage him in conversation—not in a flirtatious manner, but simply by making polite, friendly enquiries. Fred would respond with brief, awkward mutterings. This never worried Ann too much.

One day, she saw Fred at the Doctors Flat Pub. He had come to look at a horse that the pub owner wanted to sell. Fred needed a horse for his new job on the roads. Ann organised a quick visit out the back so she could accidentally bump into Fred. She rushed out the back door, struggling with a basket of wet washing. It was only a brief meeting for the two young adults, but it had a profound effect.

Fred spoke — only three words, admittedly, but he spoke first!

'G'day. Howya goin'?'

He bought the horse, a quiet half-draught, and called her Molly.

The meeting worked wonders on both of them. Ann suddenly became particular about her appearance away from work. Fred took an interest in his attire as well: he regularly cleaned his boots, and shaved every Saturday. Up until then he was almost oblivious of Ann's presence; now, suddenly, he looked out for her on Saturdays in town. Ann noticed the glances and was thrilled.

Months of accidental meetings passed. Come the winter, when Fred played footy for 'the Creek', Ann saw her man every Saturday afternoon. She became infatuated with Fred, the fullback. He was tall and, like so many men from the high country, he wore striped tights and a matching cap. On those same Saturdays, his polished, hobnailed work-boots became footy boots by being built up with strips of leather across the soles. On Saturday morning before the match, using a foot last, he would nail these on. After the game, the strips came off and out came the boot polish. Fred was handy and rugged, and refused to wash, bathe, or brush his hair before a game. This was his commitment to the game. With wild, tangled, ginger hair, an unruly beard, and several front teeth missing, he looked 'bloody ugly', according to his team-mates, and 'bloody frightening' to his opponents. However, it was Fred's granite-like attitude that won Ann over. He would jog onto the ground, shake the opposing full-forward's hand, and then he would niggle the poor bugger for the entire match. No talking; that was another rule.

'Ignore the opposition bastard,' the coach preached, 'and you, young Fred, stick to the full-forward's side like glue. Got that?'

Fred, a well-built sod, as the locals described him, would go through many a full-forward at steam-train pace and force, usually leaving his opponent winded, in agony, and quite pale. The full-frontal assault—commonly called a 'shirt front' (it was heard all around the oval)—had the locals, including Ann, cheering and heartily applauding Fred's fearless crunching of the hapless full-forward. Then, mission accomplished, Fred would simply stand on the goal line with his back to the crowd and hands on his hips, or clearing his nostrils with his thumb, and spitting. These were well-honed rituals for hardy full-forwards. He would ignore the cheer squad, and was oblivious of the crowd's approbation. Footy was a serious business.

Ann, only feet away, would chant primitive mutterings like, 'Onya, Fred!' or 'Bewdy, Fred. You showed the ugly Omeo blighter.' Both sayings were ritualised chants of adoration bestowed on stoic full-backs like Fred. He naturally ignored the praise, staring straight ahead, while at the same time treading with as much force as he could apply all over the full-forward's boots. This primitive behaviour melted Ann's heart. She told all and sundry what a fine man he was … well, not quite all. The only problem Ann faced was convincing her mum that Fred was a good man. That took some time until, finally, with her mother in tow, Ann made several neat dresses in which to go out and ply her courting wares.

Whatever attire she was wearing, Ann was a beauty. Her eyes were large, soft, and hauntingly brown-grey. They could give a glance that matched a Labrador pup's, a fleeting look that melted anyone's heart. Her long, brunette hair shone with a soft sheen. She regularly brushed and fiddled with her locks, and had a habit of twisting the wave of hair that continually hung over her forehead. It was the first thing that Fred noticed one day, after the footy at Swifts Creek. The young adults had gathered at the pavilion, and were enjoying a sandwich and cuppa. The young male footballers were still red-faced and flushed. It took a lot of energy to get through the game, which usually left them with many bruises and temporary limps as they sauntered from the dressing shed to the crude lean-to referred to as 'the pavilion'. Instead of the cursory glance that most girls got from Fred when he was in their presence, he hesitated and watched as Ann softly twisted her beautiful hair and talked to a friend.

Fred noticed her rich, warm, mottled-brown eyes, which appeared larger the longer one stared at them. And, somehow, Ann was aware of Fred's attention. Her face, which was always eye-catching in a fresh, healthy way, flushed mildly. Fred was absorbed. Ann's open smile and warm demeanour indicated to anyone that she was a nice person. Of late, she had made every effort to get to the footy or a dance where she hoped to find Fred. Today, to confirm her curiosity about Fred's goggle-eyed staring, Ann glanced from the corner of her eye, as she 'sort of knew he was eyeing her off'. She said as much to her friend, Maggie. They both giggled and ignored Fred, who would have blushed had he been aware of the tapestry of the courting ritual that was beginning to develop. He was a very private young man, and not the sort who could walk up to a girl and just start 'chattin' 'er up', as it were. Ann looked beautiful in her homemade dress and borrowed bonnet. Her neat figure was barely discernible under the layers of petticoats and long, thick bloomers. Fred gave a nod of approval; just a slight nod, mind you — Fred would have been horrified if he knew someone had seen him. It was just a nod, reported to Ann by one of her spies. Ann was smitten; Fred was her hero, her man.

For the next twelve months, a slow, steady courtship developed. They spent several hours alone on the riverbank, on the bench on the pub veranda, and after sport, having a quiet talk and getting to know one another. Once, Fred held Ann's hand and helped her to her feet. They both maintained the grip for those precious moments longer than usual. It was a defining moment.

IT WAS AT A WOOLSHED DANCE that Fred finally popped the question. He didn't rush into it. One might expect he would go somewhere quiet to rehearse his lines—but no, not Fred. His first duty had been to get mildly drunk with the full-forward he had 'ironed out' that day at the footy against those Omeo blighters. Strangely enough, there was never a mutter between the two rivals during the match on the ground. Fred had drawn blood on the poor bugger at least twice, and had screwed his heel so severely on the bloke's boot that he had snapped the laces. Yet now, after the game, they were mates. This was typical behaviour—automatic friendship after the game.

Once this men's business was over, Fred sauntered over to Ann and said, 'Can I speak in private, like, for a moment?' They both ventured away from the crowd into one of the holding pens behind the wool bins. Fred took off his hat, held Ann's hand, and burst out with, 'Want ta get 'itched, Ann?' He put his hat back on and looked at the floor. That had taken a lot of courage—far greater than what was needed to flatten the odd full-forward.

Ann was rapt. Her smile and brief hug conveyed the answer. So Fred took her home to Doctors Flat that night in his dray, and there he asked her mother for the hand of Ann. Mrs Williams was quietly pleased, but maintained her cool demeanour towards Fred. Her response was, 'You look after my Ann, my boy, or you will have me to deal with.'

They were married four months later, in January 1885. It was a typical rowdy wedding with boisterous football mates, school friends of old, and some family. Fred and Ann, who were both well liked and highly thought of, soaked in this wonderful day, which was more a party than a wedding. Tin cans, old boots, horseshoes, and a rough sign wishing them good luck adorned the covered dray. Molly the horse was wary of the raucous goings-on as they mounted the metal step onto the front seat of the dray. Then, cheered away, Mr and Mrs Wardell headed off as Molly paced out a slow trot in the direction of Tongio West, where they were to spend their honeymoon visiting friends and relations around the district.

The owner of the Doctors Flat Pub, Herb Wilson, was disappointed when Ann informed him that she was leaving to marry Fred. He liked her wit and conversation. Ann didn't chatter as some of the other female workers did; she just got on with her job. The newly wedded young couple had a wonderful honeymoon visiting friends and some of the other towns in the district like Ensay, Tambo Crossing, Reedy Flat, Brookville, Long Gully, Tongio West, and finally Cassilis. Molly the horse was the proud escort, and strutted off every day with her head held high. She had never seen so much chaff, grain, and grass.

Their honeymoon was typical of the times. The average newly married worker never had enough money to go off and spend time at a guest house or to stay in a pub for a while. They generally stayed close to home, and put what little money they had towards furniture and household goods for their new accommodation. Kettles, pots and pans, blankets, chairs, and a sturdy table were the priorities. Newlyweds would spend a night with family or mates, and would usually leave with a nice gift. In fact, for Fred and Ann it wasn't a honeymoon; it was more like a break from hard work. At some places they had to sleep in separate beds, and Fred often found himself on the veranda or in the shearers' quarters. After ten days of these dutiful visits, they rushed to their new home and set about tidying up the log cabin on Sheepstation Creek. Naturally, a bed was the first piece of furniture brought into the cabin. Then sugar-bag curtains were hung up.

The cabin was located about fifty yards above Sheepstation Creek. The roof was made of stringy-bark. With the benefit of the odd repair, it didn't leak; but then again, it didn't rain very often in the Tambo Valley. The roof was also the home of spiders, rats, snakes, possums, and 'bloody cockatoos', as Fred called them. These noisy birds would attempt to tear the roof slowly to pieces early each morning, or whenever the cabin was vacant. Ann, upon hearing the squawking at dawn, would hit the sapling rafters inside the cabin with a broom to scare the birds. She hoped this would also deter the snakes and the spiders—Ann called them 'bloody spiders' under her breath. It made little difference. They called the bark roof their home; over time, these pests got used to Ann's bashing, and simply ignored the thumping broom.

After a few months, the log cabin had become a home. Ann's pride lifted every time she brushed the floor with the horsehair broom. Edna Gale had shown Ann how to make a marble-like floor by mixing ox blood and red clay. It hardened, and was easy to keep clean. The log cabin belonged to the Carrolls, sheep farmers who lived over the ridge, towards the Tambo River. Ann and Fred were its first occupants for many a year. It was located on the Carrolls' bush block about two miles from the main coach road, the Omeo highway. To get to the cabin from the highway, they had to use a small, rutted dirt track that followed Sheepstation Creek.

The cabin and a small shed had both been erected originally for old Mr Carroll on a small, five-acre paddock that had been used as a stopover by bullock wagons some years back. The wagons would spend a night on their way to or from Haunted Stream—the cargo would be dropped off from the wagons, and would then be delivered by horse and cart to the Doctors Flat

Pub and the other farms nearby. The log cabin and shed were built in the early 1850s, and were the Carrolls' first home; Bill Carroll's father had built it when the family first moved to the area. Old Mr Carroll had set up the small business for the hungry bullocks and tired teamsters.

The Wardells' rent was cheap: two bob [two shillings] a week. The cabin was set in a tight valley of stringy-bark trees. The surrounding mountains were over a thousand feet tall, and the sun rose late and set early on the cabin. The creek was narrow and fast flowing. In most places, a running jump was all that one needed to get over the stream. Small flats surrounded the creek. They were home to dozens of wombats, the odd kangaroo, and a few emus. Occasionally, rabbits skipped across the flats, but they were hard to see and preferred the cover of ferns.

The Wardells' closest neighbours were at Doctors Flat, where Sheepstation Creek ran into the Tambo River. They were the Wilsons, and they ran the pub. This was where Gloria Williams and her children had moved to fourteen years earlier. Since their move, nothing much had changed: Mrs Williams still lived in a spare room and paid no board, as she helped around the pub. It was an hour's walk downstream from the cabin to the neighbours. The pub or staging post was one of many stopovers for the stagecoach from Bairnsdale. A quiet pub, its one claim to fame was the occasional visit it had received from the Kelly gang. They had stayed there on their way to Tambo Crossing.

In those days, everyone knew the story of the Kellys. It wasn't because the Kellys were considered heroes, or because Ned had been hanged recently. It was because people simply didn't trust the traps, often having seen them abuse their power, and knowing of the corruption that prevailed within their ranks. The Kellys weren't an isolated case; many locals told stories of the traps' bullying and rapacious behaviour.

CHAPTER TWO

The years rolled by. Babies were born, and Fred still had his job on the highway. He built a new cow bail and a vegie garden, and turned the old shed into a chook house. It was a busy time. Fred would be away from Ann and the kids all week, camping on the job. Fred worked for a contractor from Buckland, a settlement over the other side of the Alps. He did small repairs, filled potholes, and emptied drains. Whenever there was a storm or strong winds, he would spend long hours removing branches and sawing up trees that were then snigged off the road. He still had Molly, his half-draught horse, a small horse-drawn carriage called a dray, and a scoop. The scoop was a large, shovel-like contraption that Molly pulled along the road. It was like a crude grader, and Fred had to struggle to hold its two wooden handles. He cursed at the constant jarring and jolting as the implement slid over the road surface, but the scoop was good for big jobs.

Fred enjoyed the work and the isolation, but couldn't get home quickly enough to be with Ann and the kids on the weekends—although he would head for home in a roundabout way, partaking of some liquid refreshments at Tongio West on the way. After each weekend break he would leave the log cabin early Monday morning on the dray, and head for the Tongio area.

His job required him to maintain ten miles of road. He still enjoyed his own company and liked camping out. Sometimes, a local farmer would have him in for tea; other times, there would be a swaggie 'doing the road'. They would bed down in Fred's humpy for company. This didn't bother Fred, as he now liked a yak occasionally. He had three such humpies along his ten miles of road. They were permanent tents with a chimney at one end. Inside each tent, a stretcher-like bed of two wheat bags strung between poles took up one side. A packing box did for a seat, and the table was a large, up-ended log, neatly sawn off with a sharp crosscut saw. The table was in the middle. The tents were comfortable and clean, and provided good shelter for Fred and his dog in the unpredictable weather that occasionally rolled in without warning over those high mountains. Molly didn't have a shelter on such days, but instead wore a large, lined canvas rug that kept out the cold wind and the rain.

Most nights during the week, it would be just Fred. Well, not quite—he had his mouth organ, and Buster the dog, and Molly was usually hobbled close by. Buster loved the mouth organ. With his ears laid back and his nose pointed skywards, the dog would howl long, gruesome whines totally out of tune with Fred's playing, but with such enthusiasm that Fred never had the heart to say what he thought: *Shuddup, ya ugly bastard!*

After Fred and Ann's marriage, the Wardell children arrived regularly. Their first child was Harold, born in November 1885. By 1892 their family had swelled to Harry, Albert, Phyllis, and James, who was still a small baby. The stringy-bark log cabin was a large, one-roomed, comfortable home to Ann and Fred Wardell and their four children. For most of the early years, it held nothing but fond memories for them. Albert and Harry slept under their parents' bed; Phyllis, in the other corner; and James the baby, in a basket—or with his mother, really, as his dad Fred slept under canvas on the road during the week.

The Omeo shire, located in the far east of Victoria, roughly four days' travel from Melbourne, was a thriving area due to the gold rushes and the presence of several large farming settlements. Considered the most remote area in the state, several large sheep stations had been settled there by the early 1850s. All were now well established: Bindi station boasted a shearing shed with thirty-two stands for the shearers; nearby was Tongio station; and, further down the Tambo River, the Ensay station was just as big. However, it was the discovery of gold that woke up this sleepy settlement and saw its population boom. By the end of the century there were fifteen schools within twenty miles of the Wardells' home, and several of these had over one hundred pupils. As with every gold rush, the area attracted many nationalities, particularly Chinese. This racial mixture sometimes ignited outbreaks of violence. But, as so often happened, law and order didn't make it into the remote area until the town was developed and the goldfields were well established.

By 1893, FRED'S DAD had died and his sisters had moved to Melbourne. Consequently, Gloria, Ann's mum, remained as the Wardells' only grandparent, and Ron was the only close relation to Fred and Ann's kids.

After Christmas, Gloria Williams stayed with the Wardells for a week, sleeping in the back of Fred's dray. Located near the creek under a weeping willow tree and covered in canvas, it provided a suitable shelter. This didn't deter Gloria, though. As usual, she complained about how hot Christmas was, and about the flies, the squawking cockatoos, the ants, 'whereas, back home in England, we have daffodils, and snow ...' Fortunately, Fred was a patient man and had warmed to mother Williams.

It had been a dry year, and the Tambo River had dropped considerably. There had been bushfires behind Cobungra, up

Omeo way, and a wind change was all that had stopped the fires from heading for Omeo. The calf sales in January 1894 were down in numbers, and most of the stock was doing it tough. February was a very hot month.

It was a Tuesday. A harsh, dry day greeted the Wardell family. Fred was working on the crossing at Bald Hills Creek, and school had just gone back the previous week. By now, the children were back into their early-morning routine after the holiday break. During that time, the boys and Phyllis had found some precious time for camping, fishing, and visiting friends. This Tuesday, like any other day, Ann was always the first up. She was an energetic mother and, like any mum, satisfying her baby's hollow tummy came first. James, the baby that they all loved, was almost fifteen months old. With the bub's belly full, Ann lit the open fire. This was an easy task, since Fred had given her a set of bellows for Christmas. It only needed a few shreds of stringy bark, dry leaves, and small sticks, plus the bellows puffing away, to have a good fire flaring up in no time. Then it was time to wake the kids.

Harry went off, grumbling, to milk the two jerseys. It was always the same request from Ann: 'Time to milk the cows, Harry. Make sure you wash your hands first, young man.' The two cows, Goldie and Myrtle, were standing patiently near the cow bail, as Harry was always late. Two years younger than Harry, Bertie went around the snares and collected the rabbits, as he did every morning. He hated the task. This morning there was only one motley rabbit. Then he gathered firewood and fed the chooks. The chook house, originally an old shed, was an elaborate affair completely covered with wire. It had to be checked daily for any holes around the perimeter. Foxes, snakes, kookaburras, and goannas were all partial to the odd egg or chook. Most weekends, Fred had to attend to repairs, as the predators never gave up.

Then there was Phyllis. Almost seven years old, she would fetch water from the creek, help prepare meals, soak her father's clothes ready for washing, and collect the kindling wood. Ann, usually occupied with baby James, had Phyllis make the beds, clean up, and tend the fire. She rarely sat still for long. Upon entering the cabin after doing their chores, the males rested, talked, and never lifted a finger. Phyllis served, washed up, and cleaned. She could cook oat biscuits, dumplings, and porridge.

This Tuesday, she returned to the cabin with a large armful of dry stringy-bark twigs, which she shoved into the grate beside the cabin. Scooping up three cupfuls of crushed oats, she started to prepare the porridge, while Ann worked at the table packing mustard-and-egg sandwich lunches for school. Both females would talk to James. He almost demanded attention, having been plopped unceremoniously on the floor, where he played after his early-morning feed. When Ann and Phyllis started their kitchen duties, James tried to spark up a conversation in baby talk, as hunger had yet again set in. Nevertheless, he had already worked out that complaining to his mum about his growing hollow belly would get him nowhere. His turn would come.

This morning—as on most weekdays—the commotion began after breakfast. The shouting was necessary to get the three children herded together and pushed off to school, which was an hour's trot down the track and over the Tambo River. The two boys mounted up on Tom, the old, bay gelding, and Phyllis rode Dimble, the young, dark pony. Ann stood at the gate and watched as the horses trotted off along the gravel track. After a final wave, she turned and wandered slowly back to the cabin. With the busy, chaotic part of the day finished, Ann turned to James.

It was only 7.30 a.m., and for a brief moment, with the kids plodding off to school and the chores finished, Ann could relax, play with James, sing him a song, and wallow in his warm smiles and cute, alluring little giggle. Her routine was to head outside and put him in the crude swing that Fred had made in the apple tree near the vegetable garden. Pushing him gently, Ann would chant ditties that her mother had sung to her all those years ago in England. Then, with James waddling by her side, clasping one finger, Ann would head for the garden. The vegie garden was her pleasure, and Ann enjoyed the rewards of the endless weeding and pampering of her plants; they produced many tasty meals. This Tuesday, she shut the rabbit-proof gate behind them, and left her little man James to his own devices.

Lovable baby James had just started to walk. His swaggering little efforts, with his hands in the air, while giggling, were a delight. Ann was in the vegie garden weeding her new carrots. Humming to herself, she took her eyes off the little tacker for just a moment. He was walking with more confidence and speed, a fascinating new skill for him. He stopped abruptly, sat backwards without bending his knees, and plopped on the ground. Something had caught his eye. Reaching down with his fat, awkward little fingers, he poked at the little black creatures and disturbed their minute world. The jumping ants attacked James with vigour, stabbing violent pain into his tiny, stubby fingers several times. When he screamed and shoved his throbbing hands into his mouth, several ants found themselves locked inside James's oral cavity. They attacked with a vengeance.

When Ann snatched her precious, screaming baby up from the ground, she saw the ants all over his bare legs. She frantically slapped and brushed off the evil creatures, while continually consoling James. He screamed in horror and fright. His hands were still in his mouth. Rushing inside, she swabbed his tiny limbs with vinegar, a remedy recommended by the local bush nurse for bites and stings. James cried out even louder with terror. His little soul was unable to convey, even in baby babble, that it was not his legs, or arms, but his throat that desperately needed salving. It throbbed, it swelled, and it choked sweet little James to a silent death.

Ann clutched at her prized child with gasps of horror and grief. She pleaded to James, to God, to no one in particular, to help her and her baby. Her feeling of hopelessness would haunt her in the months that followed. Then, almost to spite her, a jumping ant crept out from between the dear boy's dead lips. Ann screamed. She cried, knelt down, put James gently on the clean tablecloth, and tenderly kissed his petite forehead. Humming and swaying, Ann took her dear, adorable, sweet baby James, changed his nappy, and put him to bed—her bed.

When Phyllis and Bertie arrived home from school on their horses, Ann demanded in a sharp voice that they do their chores immediately, with no cakes or a bikkie. They were confused, even frightened. Holding back tears, they both ran outside the cabin. Albert consoled Phyllis; but to Ann, for the present, these two young children did not exist. She stood in the doorway of the cabin, turned to the two bewildered children, put her finger to her lips to indicate quiet, and went back inside.

Harry, the eldest child, arrived an hour later on foot. He had a job at the Doctors Flat Pub every afternoon after school, cutting firewood. Harry, as usual, dawdled home after his errand at the pub. He enjoyed the time alone; of the four children, he was the most like Fred. However, this Tuesday afternoon a sharper-than-normal growl greeted Harry. Why today? He was always late. His mother's behaviour puzzled Harry. He wasn't sure what it was, but he knew that something was wrong. He couldn't tell his younger siblings, as he didn't understand what was going on himself, but something was amiss. It had to be …

Then, every afternoon and every morning for the next three days, they saw their sweet little brother apparently wrapped up asleep on Ann's bed. She said nothing. Mind you, the children could only see little James's tiny nose, as the blanket almost covered his face. The household functioned in almost complete silence.

At the end of the working week, poor Fred came home with his stupid Friday-night grin that indicated he'd overindulged in the amber fluid. As usual, he had swung by the coffee parlour at Tongio West for a few ales with a couple of old mates. He had left, slightly merry, and had taken a short cut by heading up Powers Gully. At the log cabin, his good humour on these nights was usually most welcome. He would rouse the kids affectionately, and then have toffees for them and a special liquorice treat for Ann. Finally, he would cuddle and tickle James with unbridled love. Privately, James was Fred's special little man. Most parents have one special child. Wisely, like most good parents, Fred kept this to himself.

On this fateful night, he was too merry to notice Ann's cold, removed behaviour. Fred looked about for his little James; then, having noticed that his special baby was all wrapped up, he assumed he was asleep. Poor Fred. When Ann broke the news about his precious little man, he reacted as if he had swallowed a pannikin of boiling-hot water. His reddened, contorted face pleaded in disbelief, he roared—bellowing like a calf just branded—and clutched at his stomach. His eyes stared with fear and hopelessness … he grasped for comprehension. Even sadder was the fact that this was the first time the children had been told of the tragedy. They did not run to their mother, or to Fred. Both parents were preoccupied with their overpowering grief. Harry consoled the children; instinctively, he took on the mantle of their carer. He took them out the back to check on the new chickens that had hatched recently. There is something consoling about touching a small, soft, warm, yellow chicken. It was half an hour before the children returned inside. Their parents did not notice.

It was an agonisingly long night for pitiable Ann, befuddled

Fred, and their lost children. The death devastated the Wardell family. Where do you go in a one-bedroom cabin after such sad news? It was a sombre, hollow night of knees against chins, shivering, staring. There was no fire and no meal prepared, nor anyone there to support this torn-apart, isolated family. Fred went into the male mode of total silence and feeling the need to find solace in powerful alcohol—preferably, spirits. He headed for Wilson's Pub early the following morning. Gloria, Ann's mum, pumped him for the reasons for his appearance, but Fred offered only a strange, frowning grimace. He conducted his drunken swill at the Albion Hotel in complete silence, except when he ordered another ale. The blokes at the bar thought he and Ann had had a quarrel of some sort. It was not until Sunday, when Ann told the Catholic priest, that the district became aware of what had happened.

Naturally, on the news of James's death, the locals rallied with food, love, and support. Gloria came over, and Fred's boss offered him a week off with pay. Fred, not out of allegiance to the job but needing to be alone, went to work straight after the funeral on the Tuesday, drunk. The kids changed. Harry became the man about the house through the week. He took a lot more control of Bertie and Phyllis. He did not dawdle after work at Wilson's Pub anymore. After he finished his chores he came straight home, almost jogging. In the space of a month, the three children became strongly independent. Bertie and Phyllis turned to Harry for support. Ann changed. She withdrew from the family, not in a supportive sense—they were well cared for—but, emotionally, there was nothing left.

Gloria, a sensible woman, who had toughened up after her ordeal with her errant husband Jock, tried to offer support. She rode to the cabin every morning, early, to help her daughter. She could only keep this up for a fortnight, though, as Ann's cold demeanour and distant bearing confused her. Finally, distressed,

Gloria chose to grieve in silence in her small room at Wilson's Pub, still smarting from her daughter's request to 'just stay away'.

For Gloria, the change in her daughter Ann's behaviour was too much. Trying to take stock, she turned to a man for support and advice, for the first time in years. It was Fred. Poor Fred, he was an unfortunate choice as he was not capable of consoling Gloria, let alone connecting with his wife. Fred, too, was baffled by Ann's changed demeanour. He was at a loss. He loved his Ann, but this strong feeling failed to direct him in the ways that helped express love and support for his wife. Fred simply felt hopeless. His job denied him the time to spend with those he loved, but when in their presence he was ill at ease and remote. Ann began to detest the weekends; she looked forward to the weekdays, and secretly welcomed Fred's absence. It allowed time for her to shed tears and burst forth with erratic outcries and a wrath that sometimes conjured up mindless ranting about disbelief in God, Jesus, and the Church.

Physically, Ann distanced herself from Fred. Initially he understood. Then after some time — months, in fact — Fred frequented the coffee lounge at Tongio West again. For the first night in a long time, he came home smiling and beaming with a false, alcohol-induced affection and a need for sexual satisfaction. Poor Fred, it was not surprising that this behaviour drove Ann into a cold seclusion. Unfortunately, Fred referred to her in his drunken overture as 'a barren bitch'. Although it was out of character for Fred to act in this manner, it put up a barrier that never really went away.

Two TRYING YEARS had elapsed. The Wardell family remained unchanged. It had become dysfunctional at an emotional level, but to the outside world they were the same happy family. Harry was almost twelve years old, and the three children had become very close. Even after all this time, James was a name never mentioned. Fred and Ann were polite, but their earlier desires and affection for each other had all but disappeared.

Then, suddenly one day, a confused Fred found an amorous Ann hinting at a desire for sexual union. Naturally, he obliged — is there any other way for a husband? Sadly for Fred, this expression of physical desire from Ann was all too brief: nine weeks, in fact. When Ann realised she was pregnant, she reverted to her withdrawn, familiar behaviour almost overnight. This new tiny life-form, conceived from a yearning on Ann's part to fill a void, didn't quite replace the hollow left by the death of baby James. Her overtures to Fred had had nothing to do with a desire to have sex with him. Where possible, Ann had ensured he was pretty drunk when they did the deed. She had hopes of success as quickly as possible, and she was right: Ann fell pregnant, and her time spent carrying this new swelling of wonder in her body was a joy. She regularly rubbed her tummy and spoke to her precious baby. She knew he was a boy. Before he was even born, Ann was warning him about hot camp-ovens, snakes, and ants — especially ants.

When the time for his birth came, and she screamed at Phyllis to catch Dimble the pony and go fetch Mrs Carroll, Ann welcomed the knowledge that the old woman would stay while Fred was away. Once this little baby boy arrived, he was to Ann as baby James was once to Fred. He was her precious little parcel, the special one. After the birth, Ann warmed a little more to her other children, but it was too late. Their period of imposed independence simply made the three of them very close. However, the new baby was a burst of sunlight in the lives of the entire family. The three kids fussed over Manny, the unnamed baby, and Fred played with him at any given chance.

Although Fred and Ann would not admit to it, initially it

was hard to name the new little man. Once you name a child, if tragedy steps in, as it did with James, that name will haunt you forever. Forlornly, for every name that came to mind, both would recall a sad event in the district for some little tyke called Bill or Bob or John. Young deaths were common in remote areas. Just over the hill, the cemetery at Cassilis was testimony to this, with one in three graves marked, *Here lies … infant son of … sweet daughter of …*

Hence, for a time, the Wardell's new baby came into the world with no real name. Many nicknames like Manny, Bibby Boo, and Bub were used, but nothing permanent. Finally, Phyllis, frustrated by this, turned to Fred and demanded, 'What's the baby's name, Dad?' Fred, enjoying a cuppa, and avoiding the answer as he always did, replied bluntly, 'Tag along, Phyllis. Just tag along. Find Bertie, and tell him to go around the traps.'

Phyllis stormed outside to her mother, Ann, who was hanging clothes on the line and growled, 'Daddy is really annoying sometimes.'

The following day, just after Fred had left for work, Mrs Bill Carroll arrived to enjoy Ann's company for a day. By late afternoon, the children were back home from school and enjoying a bikkie and cordial when, somehow, the topic got around to the new baby's name. Mrs Carroll was somewhat surprised by the answer to her constant enquiry of, 'Have you named that beautiful baby boy yet?'

'Not yet. In time, Mrs Carroll, in time,' replied Ann. Suddenly, and totally out of character, Phyllis, who was sitting quietly listening, butted in.

'Just Tag is his name. That's what Dad says, Mrs Carroll. Just Tagalong, or something. A funny name, I reckon.' The silence was broken by a frowning Ann, who quickly made the connection and, in a fit of teary giggles, said, 'Yes, we've called him Tag.'

Amazingly, the little baby with no name, who was almost three months old, now had a new name: Tag. An unusual moniker, it caught on very quickly. Funnily enough, Fred loved the name. A passer-by had told him about it before he got home moderately drunk on the Friday. He told Ann what a lovely choice it was, but he had never heard it before. Ann kept quiet, and never offered an explanation.

CHAPTER THREE

Tag was eighteen months old when he went on his first official outing. It was the Omeo hospital auxiliary sports day. Being during school holidays, all the kids were home, and Fred had been given a week off. Christmas had just passed. Molly, hitched to the dray, was anxious to leave. The dray was full of food and blankets. The Wardell family piled in, and Fred gently slapped Molly's rump. The horse, which knew this was an adventure of sorts, strode off with an air of excitement. Molly was pulling quite a load; fortunately, the four-wheeled wagon was big enough, and it boasted a canvas cover. The plan was to slowly ride to Omeo, a comfortable two-day walk for the wiry horse, while stopping at one of Fred's camps overnight.

The high plain country was like a plateau, with wide, flat plains and many creeks. It always fascinated Fred that the creeks flowed the wrong way, as he often pointed out. Having just passed over the high alpine range, it was only natural that water flowed down the other side, towards the north, but it fascinated Fred that this happened over a distance of only ten miles. Back in the Tambo Valley, all the streams gravitated south to the ocean. By late morning, the family pulled off the road, only five miles from Omeo. Fred had the billy boiling in no time. Sitting on a blanket, enjoying scones and jam, they watched many locals pass by, all on their way to the Omeo sports. Some were on horseback, others in drays, and the more affluent trotted past in smart, lightweight jinkers.

The township of Omeo, which was located in a small valley, was a hub of activity, and a testament to the benefits of gold mining and farming. A beautiful town, it contained many majestic brick buildings, as well as many hotels, stables, hardware shops, dentists, doctors, and numerous small businesses. It supported the local mining industry and an agricultural community, and was the last major town along the highway.

Its meandering, steep, wide main road was very busy as the Wardells trotted downhill into town. Tag stood looking out the back of the dray, and clapped with excitement the whole way. Finally, they reached the Omeo showgrounds. Numerous events, ranging from pushbike races and horse races to novelty games, were listed in the well-decorated program that was handed out to every new arrival. Inside, a band was playing in the middle of the arena. It was all very exciting: the showgrounds were full of horses, drays, jinkers, and many small camps set up for an overnight stay. Bertie was sent to buy a bag of chaff for Molly the horse, and Fred busied himself unhitching and then brushing the tired half-draught as she drank from the trough located just inside the gate. Ann and Phyllis remained with the dray, and started to set up the camp.

The oval was large. At one side of it were the lanes, marked with string and flags, that held the running events—the highlights of the day. The winner of the Omeo Gift went home with a ten-pound prize in his pocket. The grandstand on the side of the oval held over two hundred people and, as usual, was full. The Wardells were always keen participants in as many competitions as possible: Ann with her quilts; Fred, the wood chop; and Harry in the junior sprint. He came fourth in the finals. There had been three heats, and only the first four went through. 'Well done, boy,' was Fred's comment. Bertie had three hits from ten throws at the wicket-hitting competition, and won a toffee apple for his efforts.

Then Fred, who always enjoyed sport, strolled onto the oval and took up his position as the anchorman for the Doctors Flat tug-of-war team. Each team had to weigh, in total, less than one ton. In fact, Doctors Flat had poached Fred from the Cassilis team. Somehow, weight for strength, Fred was the strongest team member in the district. He not only had strength, he instilled a primordial chanting ritual that saw his team grunt and heave in unison. They were never beaten. Fred's payment for deserting the Cassilis team was a generous supply of the amber fluid whenever he ventured to the Doctors Flat Pub.

Thrilled with a line of men grunting while pulling at a rope, Tag warmed quickly to the tug of war. He clapped and cheered along with the locals. Then he ran and hugged Fred when it was all over. Fred had Tag on his shoulders when they presented the trophy. Phyllis and Ann were spectators. Later that same afternoon, Ann got an honourable mention with her quilt, and Fred, after celebrating the tug-of-war victory, withdrew from the wood chop. Actually, it was Ann who banned Fred: anyone could see that he had already had one too many. The family camped that night within the showgrounds, where they were able to visit many camp fires, greet friends, catch up on news, and show off Tag.

Tag's toddler years were a delight. It was as if Ann considered that every moment might be his last. She clothed him in new garments—most of which she made herself—whereas the older children had always had hand-me-downs. She asked her brother Ron to make a small wheelbarrow for Tag to play with, and to help her in the vegie garden. Ron was now a wheelwright who worked for Burley, the blacksmith, at Omeo. Once, on her only trip to Bairnsdale in a decade, Ann had a photo taken of Tag, and it held pride of place over the open fireplace in the cabin.

It turned out that Tag was different. He had a softness about him that was unusual for a country kid, particularly a boy. Tag loved animals. Most kids do, but he not only loved them: he had a unique connection with them. By the time he was of school age, he had a pet wombat, a cheeky joey, and three very cute blue-tongue lizards — one of them very, very pregnant. The chooks were his friends; the horses and many types of wild birds were part of his menagerie. Initially, it fascinated Ann as Tag spent endless hours with these creatures. They sat on his lap and allowed him to stroke or scratch them. He carefully handled their young, and was sensitive not to upset their mother. His knowledge and understanding of numerous animals was remarkable. He knew their breeding cycles, and watched and noted what food they ate, and the type of nest or bed they prepared when they gave birth. He never locked them in cages — apart from the chooks — or tried to domesticate them completely. Tag spent any spare time he had with these animal friends.

Over time, Tag's constant attention to his furry, scaly, and feathered friends became more than a curiosity for Ann; she was concerned, for these animals were the centre of his universe. She tried to get him to play with simple toys, like a spinning top and the game of quoits that her mother had brought from England. No such luck: the animals won out. Tag would talk to them, knew when they ate and how to handle them, and had most of them sleep together in his bed each night.

Tag's bed was an old Furphy water tank with one end removed. It was outside the log cabin, jammed up against one wall and then covered in dirt. Over the open end, or hole, was a canvas flap. This was the doorway to his secret home. He was almost five when he moved into this cave-like, little added-on room. It was private and warm, and the perfect cubby for a kid. In fact, had Tag's parents checked carefully, they would have noticed that Tag had other room-mates at night—like the wombat, Fred's dog (on weekends), the lizards, and occasionally a chook. Of all Tag's animal acquaintances, chooks were the most unpredictable. Tag always prefaced his remarks to them with 'silly chook'. Then there was Joey, the little kangaroo; however, he grew too quickly and did not quite fit, so he slept outside with his head on Tag's feet. In fact, one morning Tag nearly gave the secret away when he informed his mother that Joey purred like a cat when he slept.

When he started school at Swifts Creek—the better school, according to Ann—Tag rode the little pony, Dimble. Both Bertie and Phyllis changed schools as well. For their transport, they doubled up on Fred's other old half-draught, Dommy. By the time Tag started school, his eldest brother Harry, now going on fifteen, had left, and was working for Winter's General Store in Omeo as their delivery boy.

At the Swifts Creek school, although all the kids had seen or heard of Tag, he quickly became a curiosity and was immediately considered different. The talk and stories that students had heard about this new tyke were confirmed by his actions. His gift with animals fascinated them. His mother, Ann, had worried that kids would pick on him for his strange ways; but, fortunately, the students reacted in a positive way.

However, there were other subtle reasons for Tag being put in a special category. Many people treated the arrival of the Wardells' new baby as a blessing and a joy, and a way of starting up conversations after sweet James's death. Until Tag came along, Ann had remained in a world of silence for over a year. Then, like a match that lights a wick and brightens a room, the new bub elicited pleasant chats, smiles, and joy. When he started to grow up with his special characteristics, it was like an added treat—so much so that people often spoke to him encouragingly, with comments such as, 'How's our special little man?' and 'How's Greg, your happy goanna, Tag?'

Tag didn't surprise anyone when, each day, he came to school with one of his animals as a companion. The lizards were his favourite — he kept them under his shirt. At first, the wombat and the little kangaroo trotted and jumped behind him a few times, but Tag ended up leaving them at home, as a few stray town dogs chased Wally the wombat with intentions of killing the furry beast. Joey was never to be seen again after his third trip to school: he cleared out after McCoy's dog chased him.

Tag's first two years at school were fun. Doing finger painting, counting beads, singing songs, and playing games all offered new experiences. However, as Tag got older, his love for his animals put him through painful trials that brought him misery and grief. In the bush, turning eight didn't only mean that you were allowed to use the axe for the first time to cut firewood, or use the sledgehammer and wedges to split a gnarled log; it also meant that same axe could be used to remove a chook's head. And the plucking ... To Tag, it seemed so brutal. A hammer took the life of young unwanted pups; his pet rooster chickens found their way into the oven. It was very traumatic for Tag. He was dreading the time when Bertie would leave home and it would be his chore to kill a chook or rabbit. Quickly, Tag learned not to make friends with animals that were destined for the chopping block or the butcher's knife. His bed beside the log cabin — the Furphy tank that originally boasted a menagerie of animals — now housed only lizards and Fred's dog on weekends. He let Wally wombat and Joey-the-second go bush. Apart from his lizards and his magpies, Tag stuck with the domesticated animals.

However, this didn't stop him feeling affection for animals, or curb his desire to see that all of them were looked after. He took spare leads to school, so that during his lunch hour he could halter the horses ridden to school and offer them a treat. Because the school horse-paddock was too small for the sixteen horses ridden there each day, he would tether them out the front or in the laneway — anywhere there was a bit of grass to pick at. Over time, he erected a temporary fence around these grassed areas.

Tag's interest in animals didn't totally exclude him from human contact. He was seen as just one of the kids, though admittedly he was quieter than most of the boys. He participated in most games. Tag was okay at knuckle jacks, tiggy, and blindman's buff, but he had no interest in football — much to Fred's disappointment.

But in the classroom there were very few happy moments for Tag. He was bright, keen, and well behaved but, unfortunately, he was also left-handed. The education system refused to tolerate such a breach of nature, common though it was. It resulted in Tag bearing the brunt of taunts from his teachers, and being slapped, beaten, and strapped by his early educators until, finally, he wrote untidily with his right hand. He got strapped for that, too. He pleaded with his mother to intervene, but to no avail. Teachers were citizens of high repute; their advice and instructions were never questioned. Consequently, almost every day from the age of ten, Tag begged his mother to let him leave school.

Thankfully, at school he had the benefit of mates. He had a friend called Golly (Golly had been a left-hander also); they shared a desk in the 'slow learners' section'. At an early age, both these boys had decided to leave school and get a job. After their parents rejected this idea out of hand, Tag and Golly came up with another plan. Between them, they concocted a way to leave school within the year. They wanted to impress their parents that they had good reasons for leaving. The first to attempt this new approach was Golly. He wanted to be a jockey, he said. His dad, a baker, was stunned: 'You silly boy. Don't you realise you'll keep growing? I bet Tag put you up to this!'

Golly didn't even answer. Golly's dad had gotten to know Tag really well, and liked the boy. Tag, on the other hand, told his parents that he wanted to train racehorses. Fred just laughed, and Ann gave Tag a five-minute lecture, ending with 'you silly boy!'

In the end, Tag and Golly resigned themselves to school. Tag started to mix a little with some other boys as well and, in time, the group turned into a little gang. Tag now had a collection of mates that were like his pets at home. His friends were different. Like Tag, they weren't footy or cricket fans. Yet, like Tag, they loved horses, the bush, and camping out. Tag's mates' names were Charlie 'Chatty' Bills, Reg 'Tiger' Tompkins, Andy 'Bucket' Banks and, of course, Greg 'Golly' Elliot.

Chatty, *Tiger*, *Bucket*, and *Golly*.

Add the name Tag to this juvenile collective, and their nicknames alone were enough to put a smirk on anyone's face. They hung out together at playtime and lunchtime, knocked round together when they had a chance away from school, and visited one another's homes regularly. All of them were keen on horseriding, and they often planned short ventures together. Perhaps the most unusual thing about these lads was that occasionally they would confide in one another — a rare attribute for young country boys. Away from their little gang, they were quiet, heads-down boys. Together, they were like magpies, and Tiger was the gang leader. He normally directed conversation, and encouraged the larrikin behaviour that was starting to emerge among the lads.

In fact, the way that Tiger and Tag teamed up was unusual. Tiger warmed to Tag the first time he watched him as a mere youngster feeding the horses at school during the lunch-breaks. Tiger admired the young lad, and that was it. After two years at school, Tag had his horse-feeding routine down to a fine art: prior to the lunch bell, the horses would be at the school-paddock gate, awaiting his appearance. This particular day, Tiger, on his own as usual, stood in the shade of the peppercorn tree, and watched Tag leading the horses. He had seven in tow, and Golly had three. Tiger heard a sharp yell. He turned, and suddenly one of the Anderson lads threw a pebble at a bay gelding, which shied and pulled Tag over. The Anderson lad thought this was hilarious, and started to pick on Tag. He called him a sheila for being such a horse-lover. Tag was more concerned about the horse: he spoke to it in a calming voice, maintaining strong eye-contact with it. The Anderson lad continued, 'They reckon you even eat horse shit for breakfast.'

Those watching all laughed. Except for Tiger. With a deep frown on his face, he stepped in: 'Hop it, Anderson, ya m-mug. P-p-pick on m-m-me if ya want to p-p-pick on s-someone.'

Anderson hopped it very quickly. No one picked on Tiger or gave him cheek. Yes, Tiger had a stutter, but no way would anyone say a word about that. Apart from his old man, that is … He was the reason that Tiger was tough. Tag, wiping his dusty pants and brushing the bay at the same time, thanked Tiger. Then, totally out of character, Tiger responded, 'You're o-o-okay, mate. I-I like w-wotcha d-d-doin.'

What followed from that brief conversation soon turned in a permanent friendship. Tiger not only warmed to Tag; he enjoyed his company. Sometimes, after school, the three boys — Golly, Tiger, and Tag — would venture up to Tiger's home, just over the bridge in Swifts Creek. His mum, Mrs Tompkins, was a kind person and welcomed the fact that Tiger had a couple of new friends. Naturally, she had to ask where their strange nicknames came from.

Sadly, most of the time, life for Tiger at home was cruel and hard, for Tiger's dad was an old bastard. He was a drunk. Fortunately, he was rarely about after school. Mrs Tompkins, or Mrs T as the boys called her, always had a blackberry cordial waiting when they ran across the veranda and let the back door bang shut. Mind you, if the lads had deviated via Golly's place, they were in for a feast, as Golly's dad was a soft touch and always saved day-old cakes and bikkies for them. Was there a better combination of parents: one, a cordial maker; the other, a baker?

Many a time you could find the lads with a mug of cordial and a cake, sitting on the bank of Swifts Creek. Here they chatted about camping out, horses, the future and, sometimes, girls. The visits to Tiger's house were usually only short get-togethers before they had to go about their chores or head for home.

The Tompkins' house was on the banks of a small creek, Swifts Creek, which passed through the edge of the town with the same name. About two hundred yards past their house, it entered the Tambo River. The boys often sat on the banks of the creek under a huge rivergum. It was here they would yak, chiack, and laugh. Although they came up with many ideas for camping, exploring, and fun, few came to fruition. Being in their early teens, the opposite sex weren't paramount for them in these get-togethers; what small interest they had in girls was never reciprocated. Most girls thought their gang a bit odd. Apart from Tiger, the most common attribute these young boys had was shyness in public, and with girls. The boys simply enjoyed each other's company and were in a world of their own. Tiger wasn't shy, though—just very quiet.

FEDERATION HAD COME and gone. It was no longer on the front page of every newspaper, or boasted about by political leaders. By 1905 there was a new butter factory up and running in Swifts Creek. It had replaced the butter shed.

There were many other changes as well. Education now emphasised several things: strict discipline; reading, writing, and arithmetic; adherence to the flag—that is, the new Australian flag; and honouring King Edward VII. The latter intrigued Tag and many of his schoolmates. Until Federation, there had been little emphasis on royalty and the flag. Victoria had become a state in 1851, and its citizens generally considered themselves Victorians. They took great pride in the knowledge that their government, in this small, isolated country, was the first to have introduced the secret ballot for elections. Now, after Federation, marching became a permanent part of any organised movement around the playground or quadrangle at school, and the flag was at the centre of any assembly. Increasingly, the Victorian education department encouraged the formation of cadets at schools. They provided uniforms, and training was almost obligatory. This was 'in preparation for any imminent conflict', according to the new federal government.

All schools had been issued with a funny Union Jack-type of flag, as the locals described it. With a fair amount of pomp and bluster, the flag was carefully unfolded and hoisted up a high flagpole every day. This was an important event: the flag held a prominent place in the Swifts Creek schoolyard. At the first assembly every Monday morning, the girls stood to attention, and the boys saluted. Finally, the headmaster, who never smiled, demanded that the students vow: 'I love God and my country, I honour the flag, and I will serve the King and cheerfully obey my parents, teachers and the law.'

To conclude with, they gave three hearty cheers for the King to acknowledge their loyalty. Any students caught not making this patriotic vow with fervour found themselves singled out and strapped in front of the whole assembly. The students soon accepted the changes and enjoyed the rituals. However, away from school, they only aroused curiosity and questions from many of their parents.

At home, over a meal, warm sentiments about the flag were

not so forthcoming. Many of the parents had knowledge of what had happened on the goldfields or to the convicts, when both groups had been treated harshly by those in power. This led to pointed retorts, such as 'Strewth, yer bloody granddad got flogged and sent to Port Arthur for liftin' a flamin' saddle!' or 'What about Ned Kelly's mum? They locked her up in Pentridge—and for what? For being a bloody mum, and an Irish-Catholic one at that!' Often, it left the children confused and groping for answers. However, the more coherent and strict education system won out.

CHAPTER FOUR

The year was 1905. It was a typical spring morning: a fairy-like fog hid the Wardells' log cabin as cockatoos heralded a brisk start to a fresh day. There were grunts and snorts all round as Tag mounted up on Dimble, the pony, along with his new young puppy, Jess the beagle. The three of them departed quietly. The frost season had recently finished, but at five in the morning the temperature was still only just above freezing. With Dimble trotting quickly, it took all of thirty minutes for Tag to reach the meeting point they had arranged, just below Cole's hut on the Tambo River. Jess's nose never left the ground for the entire journey; she was not yet brave enough to wander off on her own. She was oblivious to those around her, for the beagle's nose, once on a scent, is consumed by the smell — any awareness of the outside world or of any other existence disappears. For the time being, still a big puppy, she only deviated ten yards from Tag and Dimble.

This morning, Dimble was not impressed. Then again, the black pony was not impressed with anything at such an early hour. Tag had to continually prod him in the ribs to maintain a brisk pace. Dimble snorted long, steaming gusts of vapour from his nostrils, and flicked his tail in anger. He laid his ears back for the entire trip: a sure sign of sulking.

Tiger, Chatty, and Bucket were waiting with their ponies

at the Tambo River when Tag arrived. Clouds of heavy steam burst from their mouths as they greeted him. Quickly, they told him that Golly couldn't make it, as he had to help his dad at the bakery. The three boys had left Swifts Creek much earlier, and had lit a small fire to keep themselves warm while they waited for their mate and his new dog. When Tag dismounted, the beagle got a warm welcome, with many pats and a belly scratch from Chatty. He loved dogs, and Jess was beautiful.

For Tag and his friends, today would be an adventure centred on the tiny township of Ensay. After mounting up, the boys burbled away like magpies as they trotted eagerly along the riverside track southwards. The low fog still hung over the Tambo River this early. As usual, several water-jacks, little lizard-like creatures, were active. Once disturbed, the funny-looking lizard would dash across the grass with its scaly head held bolt-upright. Then, with a huge leap, it would launch itself off the riverbank and shoot out into the water, landing with a large, belly flop-like splash. Wriggling its tail vigorously, the lizard would swim to the other bank.

Normally, the boys saw a lot of wildlife. Not this time, though: most likely, the creatures were frightened off as the lads chattered and laughed, enjoying their precious freedom. As the track meandered along the riverbank, Jess's nostrils almost became clogged with the scents of the numerous animals that had visited the river overnight for a drink. Her nose skidded along the ground sniffing vigorously. Then, that sound! It was the first time that Tag had heard the unusual howling yip made only by beagles. They make a peculiar shrieking noise once they are on a strong scent. Today, it caused a lot of laughter among the lads.

It was unusual for Tag to have ended up with a beagle pup. It had been Ann's decision, which she had made after hearing a story of how a beagle dog had saved its master in Queensland. Apparently, the man, attacked by a swarm of wild bees, ended up with his eyes swollen to the point where he had no vision. The faithful beagle, with the man's belt threaded through its collar, led him eleven miles through scrubby bush to his back door and his distraught wife. That was enough to convince Ann, and she went to some trouble to get Tag his first dog for his thirteenth birthday. He was thrilled to receive the cute and cuddly pup.

Today the Ensay Pony Races were on. Getting to the tiny settlement took roughly two-and-a-half hours of trotting along the Tambo River track from Cole's hut. Along the way they passed the Pride of the Valley flour mill, and then deviated around a long bend to see the beautiful swing bridge that crossed the Tambo River. Both the flour mill and the bridge had been recently completed. Then they were finally at the Ensay sports ground. The lads dismounted, gave their mounts a drink at the river, and entered the ground. Like many ovals in the district, the ground had many uses: footy, cricket, annual sports, gymkhanas, athletic races, and a variety of other events, including the monthly pony races. During the week, it served as a paddock for Harman's sheep.

Bookies worked all the races in the Omeo shire, and large crowds attended; they took the horse racing very seriously, as money was involved. It was the same at Ensay, where the races had up to twelve horses entered in each event. The riders, mainly locals, wore bright uniforms to identify their mounts. Between the races there were novelty race events, and ponies like Dimble entered for free — the winner's prize was a ribbon. It was a guaranteed good day out.

The boys all understood the routine, and in no time Tag had Dimble entered in two races. Chatty also entered a race; he managed a place, and proudly wore the red ribbon on the horse's neck for the next week. However, Dimble's results were nothing to write home about: he got sixth in his first race, and last in his second.

Tiger had gone to Ensay for the ride, as well as to indulge in his other hobby: he liked looking at people, fine animals, and the wide variety of life that turned out on such days. Tiger walked around quietly, his hands jammed in his pockets, looking at the jinkers, coaches, and spring carts that surrounded the oval. He was fascinated by the sophisticated apparel worn by the wealthy graziers and their children. Many of their horses, still in their traces, were magnificent beasts that were well fed and beautifully groomed. Near one group of people a chestnut mare stood out, with a cluster of feathers attached to the top of her bridle. She was still in harness. The jinker was beautiful—the coachwork, leatherwork, metal buckles, and swivels were perfectly polished—and Tiger stood for ages admiring the rig.

The Ensay Pony Races were a festive day for most, as well as providing an occasion for some in the district to display their affluence, and to reinforce the social strata that were well entrenched in the area. Farmers or graziers were the community leaders. Several dozen of these wealthy people clustered at one end of the oval—the women with parasols, the men with expensive fob watches adorning their pin-striped waistcoats.

The lads had planned this day for months. Bucket and Chatty had saved some pocket money, and intended to spend it on fairy floss and toffee apples. They went from one food vendor to another. At colourful stalls, gentlemen in striped aprons and bowler hats boasted that their food and wares were the best. No matter, the first booth saw both boys parting with their pennies and scoffing down sugary treats. They often bumped into kids or families they knew, and had a quick chat with them. A dapper gentleman on an elegant horse would interrupt this gaiety every twenty minutes to announce the next race through a megaphone.

Then it started—possibly with a whisper, some pointing, a nudge. Who knows? Today, there was an unusual distraction.

Between races, people noticed a young boy and his black pony — a very special pony. The word had spread around the sports ground that 'this young fella's got a horse like a dog'. People turned to look, and smiled. The young boy was Tag. Dimble, who wasn't yarded or hitched to a rail, was free to wander, but he would follow unless Tag ordered him to stay. On that command, Dimble would stand motionless. However, with a sharp whistle from Tag, Dimble would come trotting over. There was no tangible reward for doing this, just a 'well done, mate', or a pat.

Dimble, Tag's sulky pony, had his reins attached to the pommel on the saddle. Never had the Ensay locals seen a better-behaved horse. Kids started to follow the pony and Tag about the grounds, simply to see this very obedient pony in action. Dimble had the skills of a good sheepdog. Naturally, they thought that he was very unusual. On the other hand, perhaps someone had spent endless hours training this ordinary-looking nag. It became the highlight of the day, and several people stopped Tag to ask him the breeding of the pony. That was a laugh: if ever there was a mongrel-bred pony, it would have been Dimble.

The long day was a lot of fun. The boys arrived at their homes at dusk; however, the adventure didn't end there for Tag and Dimble. Their day at the Ensay races had aroused so much attention that Dimble starred in the next edition of the *Omeo Standard*, with the bold headline: 'Freak horse entertains crowd at Ensay Pony Races'. Tag got a brief mention — enough to generate some talk at school, and for his father to ask, 'What's all this about, young Tag?' Tag provided a vague answer. It didn't satisfy Fred, but Ann knew what was going on, as did the kids at school.

Tag had a special touch when it came to animals. He had an ability to relate to them and to elicit behaviour or habits that would normally take an average horse handler hours of training.

In fact, what the article in the *Standard* should have been about was Tag's way with animals, which separated him from others. The article focussed on Dimble the pony, but Tag was the real story: he was different. Some claimed it was almost a gift. Others believed it had a lot to do with Ann and her adoration of her precious son. From the day Tag was born, most conversations she had with her wonderful baby boy ended with: 'Such a clever boy', 'What a smart young man', or 'My, what a handsome lad'. It had made him sensitive, self-assured, a lover of nature, and a very likeable boy.

Whatever it was that Tag possessed, he somehow managed to form an intimate bond with his charges — not just with Dimble the pony, but with all his animals. This ability showed itself in many ways. Ann, for example, had her best crop of lettuces for years, thanks to Tag. With his small gang of blue-tongue lizards, he kept the snail population down to zero in the vegetable garden. Ann would ask her son, 'Tag, can you get rid of the snails in the garden? There's a good boy.' Tag would let his little army of lizards loose in Ann's garden. Then, snap, crunch, the defenceless snails were quickly gobbled up by Tag's lizard warriors.

Another instance involved the apple tree in the middle of the small orchard. It had at last produced a good batch of Jonathans, thanks to Tag. He had built a nest for his magpie family in the fruit trees beside the log cabin. After accepting some bribes in the form of small pieces of meat, the magpies happily called the apple tree home. These aggressive birds were powerful protectors of their new territory. Many visitors to the log cabin could vouch for that — particularly the parrots that normally gorged themselves on apricots, apples, pears, and quinces. Tag's magpies were ruthless guards. They squawked, swooped, and worked with team-like precision to petrify intruders. The parrots kept well away from the Wardell fruit trees, and never again would a cockatoo attack the stringy-bark roof.

Fred, Ann, and the other kids thought nothing of the way that Tag was able to encourage his pets to do useful chores. Tag's animals had assignments inside the log cabin as well, much to Ann's delight. At times, an eyebrow would be raised when a visitor asked why there were lizards in the roof.

'Oh, they're Tag's. He feeds them up there; they keep the snakes and rats away,' Ann would assure the startled caller.

'Haven't had a bloody snake in years, I can assure you,' Fred would vouch.

Often, during school holidays, visiting friends would ask, 'Why's the beagle locked in with the chooks at night?'

'That's to keep them bloody foxes away. Works a treat, ya know,' Fred would boast. Consequently, for those who knew Tag, it was no surprise that he was capable of training Dimble to obey complex commands.

By the age of thirteen, the only things that Tag as a schoolboy looked forward to were going home at the end of the day, and school holidays. It was during these times that the boys occasionally got together and went camping overnight in the bush. They had done this a few times over the years. However, this year would be their first big venture into the bush; they would be camping out for six days. The boys were all turning fourteen, except for Tiger. He was fifteen, and would not be returning to school next year. He had a job lined up at the butter factory at Swifts Creek.

A lot of planning had gone into this camping venture. Most of it involved conning parents and other siblings to ensure a longer-than-usual break from home. Tag did a sterling job on his mum, and gained an extended leave pass. The plan to con his mum had centred on Jess, the beagle bitch.

This beautifully marked, attractive little dog fascinated Tag. She, too, was unique, but in a more frustrating way. Jess would never come when called, never sit when instructed, and usually found her own way home from most of the adventures that started out with her, Dimble, and Tag. Initially, her waywardness frightened Tag, as he thought he had lost her for good. Inevitably, the beagle would wander off, disappear, and re-appear many hours later at the cabin. Jess was a cat in a dog's body. Tag hoped that the young dog would improve as she aged, but it was a forlorn hope. In fact, what had happened was that Tag had found another singular animal: a dog that ignored attention, affection, rules, and rewards. Well, that's not quite true — the beagle did respond to food.

'Useless bloody bitch-of-a-thing,' was Fred's description whenever he spoke of Jess. Nevertheless, the fact that Ann believed in the beagle enabled Tag to go camping out for a week at a time — she believed that Jess would lead the boys home, no matter where they ventured. Tag let his mum believe this, although it was only partially true. He had painstakingly trained Jess to do one thing: return home. This was quite a feat, as people who have owned a beagle will tell you that it is almost impossible to train the breed. However, Tag had devised a cunning method, even if it was simply to satisfy Ann's belief in Jess's homing abilities. He knew that beagles had an insatiable appetite and a powerful nose for finding the scents and trails of animals. With this in mind, he devised a special treat for Jess that he called a wad, made up of dried kangaroo meat, bacon, and fat, forced into a sausage sleeve made from a sheep's guts. Tag had taught Jess that when presented with this sausage — the size of a large cucumber — she could only eat it at the door of the Wardells' log cabin.

This was his plan: he started on small ventures with the beagle into the bush, only a few miles from the cabin. Naturally, before they left the cabin, Jess knew that Tag had the wad in his saddlebag, so powerful was her nose. She cunningly refused to venture too far from Tag and Dimble. Then, several miles from the log cabin, Tag would dangle the wad in front of Jess's nose, and bingo! The moment he dangled this succulent sausage, she would tear off for home, knowing it could only be eaten at the door into the log cabin. Unfortunately, the first few times he did this, Tag couldn't keep up with his dog on a mission with tunnel vision—Jess would arrive home twenty minutes before Tag. Ann was not impressed, as Tag, Dimble, and Jess were supposed to arrive together. Luckily, it being not too far from the cabin, Tag knew his own way home. However, Tag worked out other ways to curb Jess's enthusiasm and to completely frustrate both Dimble, the loyal pony, and Jess, the recalcitrant beagle—he put Jess on a long lead after he produced the wad, and she would head for home while tugging on the lead. The important thing for Tag was that his mum was finally convinced, which meant that he could go camping with his mates.

CHAPTER FIVE

It was just past lunchtime. After a hearty plate of sandwiches, the five boys gathered outside the Wardells' cabin. They were very excited. They had six horses and the dog, Jess, with them. After saying their goodbyes to Ann, they headed up Sheepstation Creek in a long line. The bush in this area was open, dotted here and there with large stringy-bark trees. Smaller wattles and the odd kurrajong tree, with its smooth, dimpled bark, added to the beautiful vista. Along the way, cockatoos peered from gum trees, lifting their yellow crests and twisting their heads to one side. Wary of any stranger venturing into their territory, these large, white birds screeched warning sounds that were regularly ignored. The monkey bears, or koalas, who also called these same trees home, simply slept through the birds' protests. The lads prodded the fresh ponies into a steady walk along the ridge, and then followed the bullock track that headed up to the Angora range. This track, used weekly, served the Doctors Flat area.

It was already hot, and the March flies were bothering the horses, who continually swished their tails and shook their heads. The March fly is as big as a bee and has a savage sting. This afternoon, they were so bad that the boys finally stopped and snapped off long, thin, green branches from a wattle tree. They used these to flick and switch the horses' rumps and necks, and to keep away the annoying grey flies. The horses immediately felt the difference, except for Dimble, Tag's pony, who plodded along at the rear, riderless and sulking. Dimble was the packhorse; there was no one on his back. He had to carry all the camping and cooking gear. Chatty led him, riding another horse and holding Dimble's halter. The horses walked in single file. Occasionally, a faint, barking howl in the distance indicated that Jess was on the trail of something. She rarely stayed with the boys. The scents that she detected consumed her entirely.

About an hour's ride up from the cabin, they dismounted and tethered the horses to trees on top of a ridge. It was time for a rest, although the local birds had hours earlier finished their early-morning duty of heralding in a new day with a variety of songs and squawks. The parrots continued to babble. They were arguing in the wattle trees, as crows made their doom-like, evil sounds. The crows kept watch on the gang of boys through their wicked, vivid, yellow eyes. These ugly creatures twisted their heads and surveyed the lads from high up in the tall trees. In the bush, any living thing is prey to a crow.

The boys decided to move on. They led the horses, moving several feet apart. In front was Tiger, his eyes darting left to right looking for snakes. It was common to see several snakes once the weather warmed up. It wasn't that the snakes were a great danger; it was simply a habit that bush kids developed from a young age. Rarely would a snake bite, as it is a timid creature; the most common time for snakes to attack was when someone stood on them. As they walked, the boys chatted about school, other horses, and the bush—their shared interests. Even Tiger was talkative. This was no surprise to the boys, but anyone else outside their tight little circle would have been amazed. Everyone knew that Tiger didn't talk a lot. He was a young man of few words, and the words he did mutter came out in the form of a stutter. However, once he was with his gang, 'the blighter gasbagged all day', according to Chatty. Tiger was bigger and older than the rest of the gang. A thickset, tall youth with tight, black hair and hard, brown eyes, he was quiet, serious, and tough. He had to be; his old man was a drunken bum and a bully. Tiger cherished his small group of friends because they were good company, understood his family, and asked no questions.

Teachers often thumped this young man for his silence and slowness at studies. They ignored the fact that it was hard for Tiger to attend school regularly, as he had to fill in for his father who worked down the road at the mine. If Tiger didn't replace his father as he slept off yet another drunken splurge, there would be no job, no income for his family, and further problems for his mother, who also suffered in silence. His teachers, only partially aware of Tiger's domestic turmoil, simply responded with indignation, and belted the young lad for gaps in his learning. This didn't help Tiger's affliction; instead, the stuttering got worse. At home, his old man was frustrated that Tiger gibbered, or stammered, as he called it. As far as he was concerned, such behaviour by his son was unmanly. This meant more beltings for Tiger, particularly when the old fool was drunk.

Now, at the age of fifteen, almost sixteen, Tiger still wet the bed, and was belted for that, too. However, for all this cruelty, he refused to cry. Sadly, this really riled Ted, his old man, and the shaving strop was often lashed across Tiger's back. The fact that Tiger would never shed a tear really 'pissed the old bastard off', as Tiger described it. Ted would belt Tiger savagely with the strop; Tiger would flinch only slightly and never cry. It was a vicious circle: no tears would further ignite his old man's fury, and Tiger got another flogging. Strange as it may seem, there was a bonus for Tiger: he feared nothing and no one. Mind you, he rarely had to prove this characteristic; people just knew. Even though Tiger rarely spoke, he had an air about him that said, 'Stay your distance. It's not worth the risk.' Well, just about everyone — his teachers and his bloody father were exempt.

However, under this exterior of strength and a steel-like demeanour was a soft, intelligent young man. His irregular school attendance prevented him from realising his academic potential, although at home his favourite pastime was to go into his own room and read. To his friends — Tag, Chatty, Golly, and Bucket — Tiger was a young man you could trust and rely on. He enjoyed his self-imposed leadership role with the other boys. They, in turn, welcomed his presence, particularly at school where, without Tiger, they would have been the targets of the bullies.

THREE-AND-A-HALF HOURS from the cabin, the boys reached the top of the Angora Range, a beautiful, long ridge of Australian bush that is part of the Great Dividing Range, over fifteen hundred feet above sea level. Looking down from high up, they could see the tiny dot of the log cabin below. It had been a steady climb. The views from the high ridges were magnificent: the entire Tambo Valley was on display. Although it was only early in the evening, they would set up camp here for the night.

The boys had a routine that was well practised, but it still took at least an hour to set up. The horses, hobbled except for Dimble, had their saddle blankets removed and their bridles hitched to low branches. Dimble, as the sixth horse, had plodded along behind, carrying the stores and cooking gear. The boys had ridden their horses bareback. Well, not quite: in place of a saddle, they each had a surcingle (a large belt that goes around the horse's belly), which held a folded collection of two blankets, a large sheet of canvas, and a few spare clothes if the boys got wet. All the horses had to be geldings because, if these young lads had ridden mares and come across wild horses when they camped on the high plains a short distance away, the stallions would have attempted to steal their horses.

The lads started their camp routine. Chatty set up the canvas ground cover and blankets that had acted as the saddle blankets for each rider. Then he collected the firewood. As usual, he wandered off talking to the beagle, himself, and anyone else within earshot. Golly described Chatty as a drunken parrot, 'He never stops gibbering!' Hence the name Chatty—it really suited the young lad, who'd originally come from Benambra, and then Tongio, just up the road from Swifts Creek. In no time, he'd collected a large pile of twigs, small branches, and heavier logs. The larger logs were from the grey box trees. They burnt slower, had more heat, and left good coals for cooking. The camp always had two fires: one to cook on, and the other for sitting and yakking around.

Golly, the baker's son, was the cook. He undid the pack on Dimble's back and, before unpacking the swag, brushed the pony briefly, under instructions from Tag. The swag contained a bag of onions, a sack of spuds, a bag of flour, and a camp oven. Another bag was full of fruit—mainly quinces—and a loaf of bread. A leather pouch held some matches, bullets, a tin of golden syrup, a bag of mixed fruit, and salt and pepper, along with a tin of lard for cooking. Finally, there was the billy, plates, eatin' irons, and the camp oven. Golly loved his job as camp cook. Even before they had left for this adventure, he had worked out a crude menu and made sure there were suitable ingredients. Golly was meticulous and said little: for him, cooking was a serious business. The quietest of the group, he was embarrassed by the others' mild swearing and shenanigans. He still blushed when they talked about girls; his strong Christian upbringing had taught him that such conversations were like talking to the devil.

Golly was the smallest of the group; like Tag, he was fair skinned, but his hair was sandy and neatly trimmed. During their conversations, while wandering up the ridge earlier in the day, Golly had trouble hiding the fact that he found some of the descriptions of Tiger's dad quite rude, but also humorous. At times like this, the occasional smile crept onto Golly's face; if one of the boys noticed this, they would tease him and encourage him to laugh or join in. However, on this magnificent night, Golly was keen to show his culinary skills. As well, he decided he would disobey his father's wishes and put off the Bible reading until tomorrow night; in fact, he had almost left his Bible behind.

As Golly wiped the camp oven with dripping, Tag looked after the animals, and Tiger headed off with a rifle slung over his back. He would return with tea. Before he left with the .22 calibre weapon, he heard the usual comments.

'No bloody monkey bears or possums. Got it?'

'Sick of ya bloody monkey bears, ya slack bugger!'

'Get us a young roo, mate,' said Golly the cook. He knew he would cop the most flack if he cooked a monkey bear, or koala. The boys were tired of being served up koalas as a meal. They were still plentiful in the remote ranges at the foot of the Alps, and didn't present a moving target for Tiger like a young roo did. As well, they were easy to find, as they only fed off certain trees that were dotted about in the bush. Further south, in the more populated areas, the slovenly behaviour of the koalas became their own greatest danger—to such an extent that, in 1898, the Victorian government had legislated to protect the native bear, as they called it, because professional trappers and shooters were hunting it to oblivion. However, this night, the boys decided that flavour, not legislation, would be their guide. Tonight, neither monkey bear nor possum was on the menu: kangaroo was the better meat, and Tiger was on a mission.

Bucket was the water boy. Although they camped on top of a ridge, the camp was always near water. They had fixed on this spot from their last venture into this beautiful area. Bucket led the horses to the waterhole and sat patiently while they had a pick at the fresh grass around the banks of the permanent soak. Each animal drank in turn at the small pond, which wasn't much bigger than a large bedroom. Paperbark trees surrounded the waterhole; and, as Chatty knew, paperbarks were one of the monkey bears' many homes. But Golly and the others had warned Tiger off them ...

When all the animals had had their fill, Bucket would bring back enough water for cooking and for several brews that would be made to perfection in the billy by Golly, and some for a wash and a clean-up in the morning.

Andy, or Bucket, was the son of a dairy farmer whose property was on the edge of Swifts Creek. The Banks' farm, which supplied the Swifts Creek area with fresh milk every day, had thirty cows, all milked by hand into galvanised buckets. That was where Bucket got his nickname. His dad, Bill Banks, his two sisters, Maude and Jean, and his older brothers, Frank and Jim, all worked on the farm. Apart from Tom and his mother Matilda, the rest milked the cows every morning and evening throughout the entire year, except during calving time. After finishing work each morning, Bucket delivered milk in a light dray around town and up as far as the Walnuts. On the back of the wagon was a large milk vat. Bucket would stop, run, and get the milk container from each house, and ladle it full with fresh milk. His special brother, Tom, came along for the ride and waved to all the customers. Tom was three years older than Bucket. He was a simple young man, full of life, and loved by all.

Bucket was a character. He walked, talked, and answered slowly. He had a wonderful, wide grin, and rarely uttered a mean word. He was Tom's favourite brother, and was kind and compassionate to him. Although Bucket appeared happy with his lot, fewer jobs were more demanding than working the long hours required on a dairy farm. There was no time for holidays, sport, or a day in bed. On the rare occasion that one of the family was unable to work, Mrs Banks stepped in, and the housework and cooking suffered. Consequently, Bucket was aware that this brief holiday into the bush with the boys was a rare treat.

Tonight, after the fresh meat that Tiger would return with, the second and final course in this bush banquet would be damper—a very special delight for the boys. Golly was a fussy cook. No one interfered with his routine or offered advice; they simply obeyed any orders he gave. He cleared an area and spread out the canvas mat, which was the size of a small table. It was a thick, padded mat that Golly had designed and that his mother had sewn on her Singer machine.

First, he organised the sweets or damper. He measured out two cupfuls of flour and a pitch of salt into a metal bowl, and placed it to one side on the canvas, nodding to himself and muttering, 'That's the damper prepared.' Then he cut up two onions on a small board, diced up four big spuds, and placed them in the greasy camp oven.

The oven was heavy, made of cast iron with a bucket-like handle. It was the small, one-gallon size. Suspended over the fire by the handle or, more commonly, twisted deep into the hot, glowing coals, it worked a treat once the cooking fire had died down. Then Golly covered the lid with coals as well.

By now, Chatty had collected a large pile of wood and was about to light the cooking fire. It was hard to light a fire in the damp of the evening. However, he was experienced. First, he cleared a large area for both fires, to prevent them from spreading. The boys knew that lighting fires in the open bush was a serious business. It would be terrible if they were to cause an out-of-control inferno; the guilt would be unbearable.

The first fire was for Golly, the proud cook. Chatty, reciting a bawdy bush ballad that he had heard outside the pub window one night, set about a routine that had been used for thousands of years in the Australian bush. He stripped a long, red, stiff piece of bark off the northern, dry side of a stringy-bark tree. Rubbing it into a small pile of fluff-like fibre, he carefully lit a match and teased the burning bark as he blew small puffs of breath on it while squatting on his knees. The fluffed-up bark was the perfect firelighter. The only difference from the method used by the Aborigines was that Chatty had matches at his disposal instead of a firestick. Slowly, he added small sticks and then larger ones until a healthy, strong fire burnt freely. No more wood would be added: Golly would take over this fire and tend it carefully until a hot bed of coals was all that was left. Then it would be ready for his culinary skills.

Greg, or Golly, was the odd one out in the group. His dad enjoyed seeing the enthusiasm with which Golly took on baking, especially of pies. Golly, although only a lad, was in charge of all the meat pies baked at the Tambo bakery. Although he needed few skills to do this, Golly enjoyed the praise from customers, who often complimented the Elliot bakery on its pies.

Tiger returned with three rabbits that he'd already skinned and gutted—he hadn't spotted a roo. Golly carefully chopped up their pink bodies and put them in the camp oven with the vegies. Then he added a bit of hot, homemade plum sauce, put the lid on, and wriggled the oven deep into the hot coals. It would take about thirty minutes to roast the meal to perfection.

Golly then turned his attention to the damper. He rolled and kneaded the flour, salt, and water until it had a plasticine-like feel, and then put it to one side.

An hour later, they had finished eating the main meal.

'Strewth, that was a bloody good feed, Golly,' Tag said. The others nodded their approval.

'Bloody oath. Nothing better!'

'Seconds anyone?' asked a proud Golly.

The boys settled down for a good night's yak and another

helping. Tiger produced a tin of Herbert's blend tobacco, and proceeded to roll a fag. He was the only one who smoked, although the others were keen to try. The fire glowed with a welcoming warmth. Earlier, Bucket had dragged over a large log for a seat, just the right distance from the large, roaring fire. The lads ate with a spoon from their tin plates, and scooped up the gravy with some bread from the Tambo bakery. Not a lot of conversation filled the air — just the noise of slurping, slopping, and the odd 'ahhh' as the meal went down. Jess the beagle was on her best behaviour. She sat on her hind legs with her front paws clasped together. The look on her face, best described as pathetic, worked: she got her scraps, and licked all the plates spotlessly clean, which saved on the washing up.

Time for the damper: the lads loved Golly's damper. With the camp oven wiped clean and washed out with water, Golly threw in the flour mixture. He walked back to his saddlebag and came back with a small bag of dried fruit, mainly sultanas, slowly scattered two handfuls over the dough, and carefully mixed it together. With the lid off the camp oven, he placed it back on the hot coals and watched until the damper turned a golden brown. Golly slipped it out onto a plate and poured golden syrup over the lot. They all munched up the warm, crisp, damper, making grunts of appreciation.

With the hearty meal finished, Chatty did the dishes. It was his turn; the boys always knew whose turn it was to do the dishes. Jess was rather browned off, as there were not a lot of scraps from the damper. So much for begging and forlorn looks; this time, it didn't work. Naturally, she had already forgotten that Tag and Tiger had given her a very generous feed earlier that evening, plus the scraps from the camp oven and the plates.

However, there was yet another disappointment for Jess: she found herself tied up for the night. She hated the idea. Her tail, which normally stuck straight up like a ship's mast, now curled backwards. Her long face displayed the saddest look that a beagle could muster, but it made no difference: she had to be tied up, and that was that. So, just to irk Tag, Jess walked as slowly as she could towards the chain.

'Hurry up, ya bitch-of-a-thing,' muttered Tag, mimicking Fred, as Jess walked even slower. Jess's appearance of complete devastation didn't bother Tag. It had in the past, when she was a young pup, but she had been putting on this pathetic act for months, and the novelty had worn off. Now her solemn display was a source of amusement for the lads. Little did the dog realise that everyone enjoyed her grumpy demeanour and ever-so-slow walk. To an outsider, Jess looked like a dog who had a lousy master and a terrible life. In fact, it was the opposite: Jess had it made. The only reason she found herself at the end of a chain was to pacify the horses. With her powerful nose, she could detect a dingo and many other animals some distance from the camp. Hence, during the night she would howl at any intruders, and the horses enjoyed this early-warning system.

With the dishes done and things put away, the boys settled back on the log for the best part of the evening: yarning around the camp fire. There is something about an open fire in the bush — it conjures up honesty, camaraderie, gaiety, and peace.

Tiger usually spoke first at these camp-fire nights. Although the poor bugger had it tough, and was normally a private person, it was important for him to get things off his chest with the boys. He took a drag from his cigarette and started.

'The other night, mum bashed the old man with the back of the flaming fry pan. That made the old bastard sit up and pay attention.'

Golly giggled. Then he asked, 'What happened, Tiger?'

'The old bastard blew half his week's wages at the pub, and mum's about a month behind with the rent. Anyhow, he'd stormed into the house with a skinful, demanded tea, ate like a pig, got halfway through his feed, and flaked. His face fell into the plate. Hell, it was funny! Anyhow, mum got the fry pan and donged the old drongo on the flaming head. Made my day, it did!'

They all laughed. Tiger enjoyed re-living the moment. Over the last year, he had shared many a tale about his bad-tempered, drunken father with these mates. They liked Tiger, not only because he stood up and copped endless abuse — he suffered horrendous floggings — but also because of his caring nature. This was his special gift, which the lads admired. Tiger supported his mum and her other kids. He knew how to handle the old man when he came home in a drunken rage. Tiger knew how to deflect the violent anger from the others and towards himself. The boys remembered one horrific story in particular.

It came about during a screaming, ranting, alcohol-induced episode, when the other Tompkins kids had slunk off. Tiger stayed, and his mother, petrified of the old man's temper, remained to cop the abuse. If the old bastard moved towards his mother, Tiger would deliberately stutter — he knew the words that were hardest to get out.

'F-f-f-fl-l-l-l-lam-m-m-m-ming …' That's all it needed. The old man would turn to Tiger in a fury. 'Ya stuttering, fuckin' fairy fool,' he'd roar, and Tiger would be beaten. With luck, the old man would be so drunk that there'd be little strength in his blows, and he'd miss every second swipe. Nevertheless, the pain of the belting and the screaming was insignificant when measured against the disgust that Tiger felt for his cruel father. Fortunately, it didn't make him bitter; it only made him feel more protective towards his mother, and determined never to be like his father.

The camp-fire banter was a bonus for Tiger. He enjoyed the laughter of the boys as he told them his stories about the old man. He also knew that they would keep it to themselves. Most people in the district reckoned that Tiger's dad was a good bloke. If only they knew. Perhaps the other thing the boys never mentioned was that during these delightful nights in the bush, around a camp fire, sharing secrets, Tiger never stuttered—not once.

The fire started to die down, the stars above were brilliant, and the barking owls were in full chorus. Jess howled briefly, but the owls ignored the beagle. To a newcomer, the barking owl's weird sound—a piercing, sobbing screech, like a woman in pain—would have been frightening. But to Tag and the others, it was another of the evening's pleasures. Occasionally, a monkey bear barked to a mate. Two months earlier, at the peak of the mating season, the boys would have heard a chorus of calls as the male monkey bears boasted of their appeal.

There were many croaking, squeaking, and hollow noises coming out of the bush, but there was only one sound that the boys didn't like—the noise made by dingoes. It sounded like a person choking to death. A chilling, cutting wail of agony, it spooked the horses, and it frightened the boys. At the first hint of a dingo, Jess went berserk. She was good for something, at least.

Just before the fire died down, Golly walked out into the dark and returned with a large log from Chatty's pile of firewood. He threw it on the fire, and the sparks twisted and streamed like liquid fire lines towards the sky. He sat and poked at the fire with a long stick until fresh, licking flames started to flash and twirl. The orange flashing light from the fire warmed their faces, and each of them stared at the wonder of the camp fire. Golly was the next to speak.

'Saw a beauty at the bakery the other night. Dad and Jack were rolling out the bread dough, while Jeff and me had the mixer going, ready for the biscuit run. When the mix was ready, I gave a thumbs-up to Jeff, who took a deep breath, and then heaved to tip the mixture onto the wheeled table. Anyhow, Jeff lost his balance, fell sideways, and plop!—the damn mix all spewed out onto the floor. Thank heavens, Dad didn't see.'

'Whadya do?' asked Chatty.

'Oh, Jeff just scooped it all up with the shovel, threw it all back up on the wheeled table, and went on as if nothing had happened.'

'Hell, ya went ahead an' cooked 'em, dirt and all?' asked the stunned Chatty, horrified, as he loved the Tambo bakery's biscuits. Golly used to save broken ones for him.

'Yep, we baked them and then I went to bed. Next morning, I ate one — tasted just the same. In fact, I gave you some, Chatty, and you didn't complain.' Golly smirked.

'Stone the crows, that's the last flamin' time I'll eat your bikkies, ya bastard.' They all laughed, knowing it would take more than that to put Chatty off. Disgusted, he replied, 'I'll get ya back, ya Christian bastard, you'll see.'

Golly enjoyed the attention, and the fact that he got a laugh was a bonus. Like Tiger, Golly was quiet and shy, but for completely different reasons. From an early age, Golly knew he was in a very Christian family. Any luck, good fortune, good health, or pleasant times they enjoyed were all due to the presence of the Lord. Time was set aside before each meal, before bed, and for two hours every Sunday to thank this eminent benefactor for His blessings and grace. There was no alcohol, swearing, or blasphemy allowed in the house or at the bakery. Any worker heard swearing faced instant dismissal. The result was that Golly was a reserved, sheltered lad with impeccable manners and few friends. He never swore; his cussing was limited to using words like 'golly', 'gee', 'gosh', and 'holy smoke'. That was why the other boys called him Golly, and his nickname stuck. Chatty had invented it, as he occasionally boasted. Golly didn't mind, but it infuriated his dad, who for the life of him couldn't see the relevance of such a stupid name.

MOST YOUNG PEOPLE had endless chores to do and little free time after school. Their fathers worked long hours, often away from home for days at a time, and their mothers were unpaid workers with little or no choice: a large family and endless housework was their lot. Golly was the only one among his mates who got to spend some time with his father every day. His dad was fortunate that Golly enjoyed the bakery; without his help the business would have struggled. This was a familiar pattern. From a very young age, children had to work or pull their weight.

Chatty was the opposite of Golly. He had grown up in the company of rough, hardworking men. His dad, who used to be a drover, now managed the butter factory on the edge of the small township of Swifts Creek. Both Chatty's dad and mum worked at the factory all day, every day, except for a brief respite during calving time. The butter factory ensured a steady income for Chatty's family.

The factory, in a large, weatherboard two-storey building, turned rich cream into butter. It was still quite new. It employed twenty-five other workers, all men, divided into two shifts. They had sharp, rough tongues, and acted like larrikins — it was their only way of surviving the boring, repetitive, heavy work. A group of local graziers owned the business. The wages were poor, but at least the factory provided permanent work for some of the older workers. The goldmine had been the main employer for the past twenty years, and it mainly required young, strong, energetic workers. The mine, just up the road at Cassilis, was booming.

From the age of twelve months, Chatty often found himself alongside his mother as she walked along the factory floor counting containers of butter. The workers responded favourably to this little bloke, and continually tickled his chin or ruffled his hair. As he got older and started to talk back, the first crude words he learned were 'bugger', 'bummer', 'hell' and, of course, 'bloody'. To his mother's disgust, 'bummer' was the first audible swear word that burst out of Chatty's mouth. Naturally, a proud, mischievous grin accompanied the word. So Chatty, or Charlie Bills, grew up with a sharp sense of humour and a barrow-load of pranks. He was skinny and gangly, and walked with long, swaggering strides like a drover. The droll Tiger often told Chatty, 'Ya walk like a drunk emu, mate.' Never mind; regardless of his elongated, ugly face and slow amble, Chatty had a wonderful sense of humour. He often tried out new pranks on his mates, and bored them with local tales and legends. However, the reason for his entry into this small clan of unusual boys was different from the others. Chatty had dark skin: he was part-Aboriginal.

Then there was Tiger: he was perhaps best considered fatherless because his dad was nothing but a drunken fool. Tiger was the real head of the Tompkins household. Without making any fuss, he helped his mum keep the other six kids in line. This last year, Tiger had worked part-time alongside Chatty at the butter factory, cleaning milk cans after school.

Chatty's mum, Lilly, had lined up the job for Tiger. This was lucky for him, as they lived just across the road from the factory. Mrs Tompkins was very grateful for the extra money; it put food on the table on many occasions. Bucket Banks, the dairy farmer's son, was also a hard worker. He grumbled about milking, but he was a fit, strong young man, and knew he was better off than many men at his age — he had a stable life.

THE BOYS MOVED CLOSER to the fire as the evening grew late. The chill in the air was much sharper than that found in the lower country. Somewhere in the dark, they could hear the hobbled horses shuffling about and snorting through their cold nostrils. The fire popped and crackled. Occasionally, there would be a long hiss as a pocket of sap, hidden in the dry wood, boiled and then ignited. All of these sounds were familiar to these young bushmen. The night went on with jokes, laughter, and some talk of girls, mainly from Tiger. Then came the ballads. Chatty, like many young people of the era, had had to learn the poems and work of Australians like Banjo Paterson and Henry Lawson; and, being the extrovert that he was, Chatty loved to recite poetry. The most popular was 'The Man from Snowy River', whose lines Chatty recalled with gusto and waving arms. This ballad was popular in the shire for many reasons, the most important of which was the fact that the Snowy River was just over the ranges in an easterly direction—about fifty miles away as the crow flew. The two areas were very similar. For the boys, *their* bush abounded with wild horses, too. It boasted excellent horsemen and rugged mountains like the ones Paterson described in his poem, as well. Chatty's rendition was so good that it drew a small round of applause from the others.

They turned in at about one in the morning. Their beds, which had been laid out earlier underneath a large, dark-green canvas, were warm and welcoming. Jess howled just once during the night.

CHAPTER SIX

The magpies gave their early-morning call. The kookaburras simply laughed with the joy of another dawn. There were smouldering coals left from the overnight fire; in no time, Chatty had it going, and the billy was soon on the boil. Tag had let Jess off the chain, and already they could hear her somewhere out and about, on the scent of something or other, howling and yipping. If the boys were lucky, they would see her once or twice through the day. That, of course, was ignoring mealtimes. Jess was punctual — never, ever late — at mealtimes. She would turn up panting, with a grin across her face that would melt the heart of any dog lover. It was all part of her charade to ensure that the boys threw a few scraps in her direction.

This morning, they had toast and golden syrup for brekkie. It was just on daybreak. Jess returned briefly. She did well — several generous crusts were thrown her way — and then disappeared when she reckoned there were no more handouts to come. Golly did the dishes while Bucket and Chatty packed up the gear. Tiger fetched a bucket of water and carefully doused the fire, raked out the coals with his boot, and watched for any signs of smoke. Tag prepared the horses. He brushed their backs, scratched their ears, and had a chat with them. Dimble followed Tag around during this ritual. The blokes reckoned the pony wasn't happy — 'totally browned off' — as he felt he should have all the attention. For Dimble, it was a simple matter of liking to be near his best mate Tag. Dimble enjoyed nudging Tag affectionately, as Tag would cackle and snatch at Dimble's soft nose.

This all changed, though, when Tag slipped the halter with the long lead over the pony's ears, and started to arrange the swag on Dimble's back. The horse was not a happy little chappy. Dimble probably reckoned it was the other horses' turn to lug the gear. Whatever the reason, the tired pony laid back its ears and sulked for the remainder of the day. Dimble was getting on; he was the senior horse, at twelve years of age. Although this wasn't old for a pony, he might have felt that he deserved some privileges. In fact, the easiest job for any horse on the trek was being the packhorse. Tag had been good to Dimble, but it seemed that the pony wasn't convinced. His sour behaviour got many laughs, much to the horse's disgust.

By 7.30 a.m. they had mounted up, and the fresh horses walked off briskly. Their destination this morning was Mount Baldhead. It was easy going along the undulating ridge with its knolls and small gullies, through open bush and the odd patch of clear ground where beautiful tree ferns were common. There were occasional huge trees, which towered skywards. The boys craned their necks and looked up at these magnificent, majestic beauties of nature. Already they had seen a lot of wildlife — mainly rabbits. They were everywhere, and a pest.

For this holiday, their plan was to get to the Dargo high plains and to camp for at least two or three days. They had ventured there earlier in the year. On that brief visit, they had seen evidence of wild horses — old hoof marks and a pile of dung left by a stallion. But when they returned home from that trek, the locals reckoned they had it wrong. 'Probably roo dung, I reckon. No brumbies on the Dargo high plains, mate, betcha,' said Alex the drover. Now that it was mid-summer, there would be an abundance of grass on the plains. If there were any horses, the boys were determined to find them.

They turned their horses down from the main ridge, and headed along a narrow shoulder leading down to Haunted Stream. At its head, this fast-flowing, noisy creek, which finally flowed into the Tambo River, was narrow, and boasted many fine trout. There was dense, low scrub here; it was heavy going and steep. The boys slipped one hand under the surcingles and held on, to stop themselves from sliding down the horses' necks. As they almost reached the bottom, there was a small, flat gully. It housed a stream that would supply fresh water: time for a brew.

After watering their horses and having a cuppa, the boys all mounted up. Eagerly, they headed up and along another ridge, until they reached the Bairnsdale-Bullumwaal road. It carried mainly bullock wagons and drays, and was an alternative route into the high country. Along the way, there were many turnoffs that led down to other settlements and small towns. The road ended at Brookville. It mainly serviced the Haunted Stream goldfield area of Baylis Flat, Stirling, Dogtown, Dawson City, and several other small mining settlements. In all, over two thousand people lived in this large, spread-out countryside. These small locations around Haunted Stream were all involved in the hunt for the elusive metal, gold. The boys avoided these small villages; they preferred the excitement of the bush.

The horses broke into a trot along the road; it was only five hours to the high plains. By early afternoon, they had turned off the road, struggled down a steep ridge, and reached the head of the Wentworth River: it was time for lunch. Hurriedly, Chatty got the fire alight and Golly had the damper mixture ready. Out of nowhere, Jess appeared. Panting vigorously, she was very pleased with herself. Somehow, she knew it was lunchtime. This apparently uncanny ability always bewildered Tag and the lads. Little did the boys realise that she would have circled close to them about every twenty-five minutes on a long trip like this. Also, she could smell the smoke and, more importantly, the camp oven, from a distance of over half a mile.

After giving Jess affectionate pats, Tiger and Bucket headed excitedly for the river with handlines, in the hope of catching sand trout or tupong. These small trout, no longer than the span of an adult hand, were a succulent delight when cooked the same day. On the way down the hill, Tiger stripped a piece of bark off a dry log and collected some witchetty grubs, which were ideal bait. After Golly finished the damper mixture, he placed it in the camp oven. He would cook it when the boys returned with the fish, which could take some time. Tag had attended to the horses and then joined Golly; both were keen anglers. They raced one another to the river. Tiger greeted them with, 'For God's sake, keep the bloody noise down, ya bloody drongos.'

Chatty was already at the stream. He handed his line to Golly, excused himself, took some old newspaper out of his pocket, and headed back up the ridge. Nature was calling—that's what he told the others. He wandered off, reciting Banjo Paterson's 'Mulga Bill's Bicycle':

He turned the cycle down the hill and mounted for the fray.
But ere he'd gone a dozen yards it bolted clean away …

The boys had recently learned it at school.

There was quiet excitement at the river. In no time, they had caught several trout, certainly enough for their evening meal. Quickly, the boys gutted, scaled, and wrapped the fish in a damp cloth. Golly returned to the campsite and placed the camp oven on the coals; twenty minutes later, the damper was ready. It was to be a healthy lunch of fruit, a cuppa, damper, and golden syrup. They were all yakking away, with their mouths full, when Golly noticed that Chatty wasn't eating the damper.

'Not hungry, Chatty?'

'Bloody oath, but I wouldn't eat that damper if I were you blokes.'

The boys all looked at Chatty for an explanation. Between them, they had eaten most of the damper. There was only one piece left for Chatty if he wanted it. They waited for an answer, and then Chatty replied, with a grin as wide as a lyrebird's tail.

'While you buggers were down at the river, I crushed up some dry wombat droppings and mixed them in the damper!'

The boys spat and coughed, and Tiger rushed at the talkative larrikin. Chatty was putty in Tiger's hands: he ducked, he ran, he laughed, he choked. However, his choking, caused by laughter, was infectious. The others joined in, and they rolled around tickling and thumping Chatty.

'I was only joking, ya dopey buggers. Crikey, it was great to see the expressions on ya dials!'

They settled down. Occasionally, Chatty would start giggling again, and Tiger responded, 'Shuddup, or I'll biff ya one, ya smart-arse dark bastard!' Chatty ate the remaining piece of damper. It was a long, slow lunch. The horses had worked hard to get to the head of the Wentworth, and Tag wanted the animals to have a good rest. As well, there was a good pick of grass here, and the horses took the opportunity to fill their bellies.

Slowly, the lads gathered their horses and started on the next leg of the journey. Jess jogged along in her unusual manner: out in front, tail vertical, nose on the ground … sniff, sniff, sniff. The fact that she seemed to close down all other sensory functions fascinated the boys. They all had dogs at home, the most common being kelpie, or other breeds used on farms or for droving sheep and cattle. The one thing their dogs all had in common was obedience, whereas Jess was oblivious to any other commands in the bush: her nose became her entire world. She was in her element.

It was the perfect picture: the lads chatting, a beautiful day, and full bellies all round. Jess, for the moment, was leading the gang. Suddenly, she started making those familiar yips. Her tail went as stiff as fencing wire. Her short, stocky, little legs carried her in a zigzag motion until she started to run in a straight line. This meant the scent was warm. She almost vibrated with excitement, her jowls drooled, and her stubby legs went flat out. Then the dog stopped abruptly. The boys, who had not long ago mounted their horses, now trotted behind the frenetically yipping beagle. Suddenly, the enemy came into view — it was a wombat. Startled by the raging beagle, it ran off at a great pace towards the river. Frantically, the lads tried to keep up. Then, just as suddenly, the wombat disappeared down its burrow.

The opening of the hole was large enough for a young boy or girl to crawl inside. However, encouraging a dog to go down a wombat's burrow was not wise. Many children had been frightened by yarns told to them around dining tables of dogs that entered a wombat burrow, never to re-appear. Once down the burrow, the dog would bite and attack the wombat, and try to get its head to turn so it could force the creature back out. But many a time, a frantic dog owner had dug down where he had heard dull barking and grunting, only to find that the dog had been killed. Apparently, the wombat crouched down and allowed the dog to crawl over its back. Then the wombat forced the poor dog against the roof of the burrow, and the dog, unable to move, was crushed to death.

Tag was the first on the scene. He sprinted towards the opening. He could read Jess's mind.

'No! Stop! Don't go there, you stupid dog!' Jess turned, panted a smile, and looked at Tag as if thinking or maybe paying attention. Mind you, this thought was only a fleeting clash of neurons that lasted a split second. Like the fox, the dingo, and other predatory animals, Jess went in for the kill, without caution.

Down the dark tunnel she raced, yipping for all she was worth. Tag, along with his mates, rushed to the opening. They called, they begged, they almost went hoarse, and then they stopped. Listening quietly, they could just hear a muffled howling. It was Jess, a long way down in the burrow. What to do? Tag looked at the others frantically.

'What …?' All of a sudden, it went quiet. Nothing: there was no noise at all, except for a bird somewhere. After several minutes, Tag looked away; he had guessed the dog's fate. He stood up, kicked at a stick, put his hands in his pockets, and walked towards the river.

Golly heard the first rumble. He jumped backwards and—would you believe it?—said, 'Shit!'

Suddenly, there was a lot of noise, especially grunting and yipping. Then, like a ball out of a canon, the wombat burst from its burrow. Jess appeared within a second, and the chase was resumed. The boys all cheered, and both the wombat and Jess disappeared over the ridge. Ten minutes later, Jess returned, with no wombat. The dog looked like she had run a marathon. Perhaps she had.

Never before had this proud beagle received so many pats and scratches and so much adoration. Jess was their hero—for the day, anyway. Finally, after much talking and fun, the gang slowly headed back up to the ridge. It took ages for Tag to work out what had happened in that burrow. Somehow, the beagle had survived the attempted crushing. It was amazing. He looked at the beagle many times that day and simply shook his head.

But there was a simple solution to the mystery. Of all dogs, beagles are the most powerfully built. This is their one outstanding characteristic. With short, powerful legs, a strong brisket, and a small, barrel-like body more like a draught horse's, it would take more that a wombat to crush a beagle. Jess had performed this feat on many occasions; it was only by chance that the boys had witnessed this latest escape.

After crossing the sharp ridge and at first leading the horses along an open knoll, they were again among the magnificent mountain gums. Their plan was to reach the first of the Dargo high plains by sunset. Being December, the days were long. On the night of a full moon there was almost enough light to read by for the whole twenty-four hours; certainly, the twilight would last until ten at night. It was just on five o'clock when they reached the Birregan Range, the last of the steep ridges and heavy bush. They were now in the high country.

The long trip so far had revealed a large variety of trees that had changed from stringy-bark in the low country to grey box, a common Australian hardwood which was excellent for fence posts and firewood. Next, at one thousand feet above sea level, the majestic blue gum appeared; this magnificent tree was a medium-sized hardwood that grew as straight as a gun barrel. It was a good timber, used for bridge making. In the heads of these trees were monkey bears in their hundreds. They were always sleeping, and it was rare for them to come down. Most bears slept up to fifteen hours, and travelled for brief periods in a day. When they did move, it was just to stroll to another blue gum or wattle, the odd yellow box, or manna gum, their preferred diet.

By now, the horses had a decent sweat up; they grunted and heaved their way up the last steep rise. They were climbing the steep Birregan range. Here, the bush changed to the mountain ash, an imposing hardwood giant of the Australian Alps, and one of the tallest trees on Earth. They were huge, some measuring fifteen feet in diameter at the butt, and dotted along the sides of the ridges, with low ferns and kangaroo grass in between. It was a steep climb, with the timber thinning out just before the plains. Suddenly, there they were — it was like riding in a wonderland — on the Dargo high plains. A chill on the air greeted the tired horses and their riders as they finally reached the edge of the first treeless plain. Apart from local graziers, few white people had ventured into this area. The Treasure families were early settlers, and recently Jack Treasure had been born during a snowstorm on the plains.

Once they entered the flat, wide, open plains, the boys yet again enjoyed a new vista. The trees had changed abruptly to low snow gums, so called because they indicated the start of the snow line in winter. The country was almost flat, had few trees and, it being summer, hosted many animals. Most ignored the humans among them. Small wallabies hopped about regularly. They were curious little animals with a dense, dark-brown fur and the same build as a kangaroo, only smaller. If something interested them, they would squat on their hind legs, rise up, and peer about, with their tiny front paws clasped together in prayer-like fashion. There was an abundance of kangaroo grass over an open area measuring a hundred acres. A few kangaroos could be seen dotted here and there, and a small bunch of emus lifted their heads out of interest, but there were no horses.

The five boys had been to these plains earlier in the year during winter, when the wide plain, covered in a thin layer of snow, had looked like an oil painting. It had been exciting for the boys; the clean crispness of the snow presented every scene as a postcard vista. The wide-open, white blankets of snow and the eerie quiet had held them spellbound. They had hoped to see wild horses on that trip, but didn't realise that there were two reasons why this wouldn't happen: first, there was a shortage of grass in winter; and also, as the boys found out, the horses didn't enjoy the snow, because it packed up inside the frog—the hollow under their hoofs—and was painful for the horse. It was worse if the horse was shod, and if the rider had to constantly dismount and dislodge the compacted frozen ball of ice with a pocket-knife. Consequently, the wild horses kept well away from the snow. But the boys did find a mound of horse manure.

Now, on this latest venture, the summer presented them with an aura just as impressive as the winter snow: the wild flowers. They were abundant across the high country, particularly on the open plains, and their colours were vibrant. Most flowers were small in size — particularly the orchids, which were mainly white with a slight splash of colour in the middle. These wild flowers were unique to the high country. It was the first time the boys had seen a panorama of such delicate beauty. They were more familiar with the bright egg-and-bacon plants, the pungent, prickly boronias, and the bursting wattles of the lower country. Here on the plains it was quite different, yet still a stunning display. Was it any wonder that these young lads loved to explore, camp, and venture into these isolated areas?

That afternoon, they hobbled the horses and walked ahead, looking for a place to set up camp. Ideally, it would have water, a small clump of bush to provide protection from the wind on the open plain, and plenty of firewood. Bucket was the first to spot the waterhole. He was thrilled. Then he turned to the others and yelled, 'Crikey, take a look, will ya? Bloody hoof prints, and plenty of 'em.'

Tag was very excited. This was what they had come for: the brumbies, the feral bush horses that had escaped from farms or been let loose. They seemed to adapt to the high country, not in huge numbers, but in a mob of up to a dozen with a single powerful stallion in the lead. The waterhole, which was on the edge of the treeless plain, was more like a soak than a hole. It provided clean, fresh water, and was the size of a small suburban house. On the western side of the soak, low snow gums grew right up to its edge. It offered a good spot for a camp, and provided an abundance of firewood.

The waterhole teemed with a life of its own. Bulrushes grew near the edges. Within the soak, thousands of tadpoles fed and pulled at the roots of plants, sending up small clouds of mud.

On the strong stalks of the rushes were dragonflies, swaying in the gentle breeze; others were flying, their wings just tipping the water as they hovered in search of food. Then, joined at the rear and flying in unison, the mating dragonflies darted this way and that. Kookaburras sat quietly in the trees along the edge, their sharp eyes detecting every small movement. Like a propelled spear, a kookaburra could swoop, retrieve a snake, and then, with a snap of its beak, break the reptile's back; any remaining life was crudely thumped out of the snake by the bird smashing it against the tree. The snakes, usually in abundance around a waterhole during the warm weather, were catching frogs. Frogs, in turn, ate the small, wriggling life-forms that grew in plague proportions. Some of these microbes continued to grow to the point where they sprouted wings and flocked out of the swamps in swarms on warm evenings. Smaller birds — willie wagtails and wrens — guarded their territory with twittering might. They gorged themselves on the abundant insect life. Nature was in balance, in harmony.

Finally, there were the local animals that simply stopped by the waterhole for a drink — a long, cold, fresh drink of crystal-clear mountain water. Most drank at dawn and then headed into the low shrub for a day's sleep. The kangaroos left long, three-pronged prints in the mud, while wombats and dingoes stamped a more familiar paw-like print. Nevertheless, the horses' marks were what excited the boys. The hoof marks were fresh, probably made earlier that day. The waterhole was certainly a busy place.

The boys decided that they would only light a small fire tonight — just enough to cook the trout and some damper. Jess had arrived with panting enthusiasm and a large appetite. The look on her face was still that of a superhero. Her minute wounds from the wombat encounter were covered in dirt and dust from rubbing on the ground. Tag was pleased that Jess appeared the moment they lit the fire, as she would warn off any snakes. They had seen two already, and Jess would have her work cut out. The snakes were mainly small browns and copperheads; they were venomous, but not lively or aggressive like the tiger snake, which could move with lightning speed. The snakes were only a danger if you accidentally trod on them, and Jess would see to it that this didn't happen. Then, as the sun went down, the snakes, being cold-blooded, would return to their logs and holes to sleep off the day's food-gathering and sunbaking.

The boys had made their plan of catching fish in the Wentworth River days before they headed off on this adventure. They wanted their arrival on the high plains to be quiet and unannounced—devoid of rifle shots and a blazing fire. They were determined to see the brumbies.

Quietly, the camp was set up, the meal prepared and, as usual, the compliments directed to Golly. The fish were delicious; the damper, perfect. Finally, sitting around the small fire, the first conversations started. All of them had heard their parents and other adults speculate about a new subject of interest in the Omeo district. Chatty wanted the other blokes' opinions about the new mail car that had just completed its first run up the Omeo highway from Bairnsdale to Omeo. It was a Hudson fourteen-seater petrol sedan with large wheels and no windows, and it had become a highlight up and down the entire valley. Most locals made the effort to be near the road as it passed.

Chatty was the first to comment.

'Dad reckoned the bloody thing frightened the horses and spooked the calves his brother was drovin' down the road. Bloody thing runs on petrol, they reckon—whatever that is.'

Bucket, the dairy farmer's son, hadn't seen many trucks, but had heard them described on many occasions. He was sceptical.

'What happens when the damn thing gets bogged? Ya can't unhitch its engine and pull the damn thing out. It'll never work, I reckon. You'll never stop the horse and coach!'

However, Chatty was worried.

'Dad reckons they'll have calves for passengers some day, and that'll be the end of the drovers.'

'What bulldust,' said Tiger. He had the knack of cutting off a discussion that didn't interest him. He wanted to change the subject and talk about leaving the district some day. 'You know,' he started, 'I reckon we should all take up shearing or somethin' like that. Work as a gang, you know.'

'Yeah,' was the chorus — except from Golly.

'Then we could head off up ta Queensland or somethin'. You know, travel a bit. Whadaya reckon?' They all agreed, except Golly: he wanted to help his dad, the baker.

'Dunno, fellas. Me dad wants me to bake, and I like the idea.'

Golly was a family boy. He enjoyed working with his dad. He took pride in filling the pie shells before baking. Then, afterwards, he would often ask the kids at the school if the pies were okay. Golly's dad was a good man, and a non-drinker, which was unusual. He slept during drinking hours, and worked through most nights. They were a close, happy family. There was no baking on Saturday night, which allowed the entire family to attend church at least twice on Sunday. Golly never tried to keep up with the other boys, whose swearing and wild ideas increased every year. Then again, Tiger did enough cussing for Golly and the others as well. Chatty, Tag, and Bucket were very keen on the idea of leaving the area. Bucket, about to turn fifteen, had had enough of 'milkin' flamin' cows'.

'Hell, just about every day of the bloody year, it's a bastard of a job. Fair dinkum, nothin' bloody worse. Then the old man expects me to deliver the town's milk before I go ta bloody school, and then I get into trouble for being late! Strewth, ya can't bloody well win.'

'Yeah.' They all agreed with that statement; they knew he did it tough. Bucket never played after school or at weekends.

This break with his mates came about after much whining, and support from Bucket's mum. She had offered to step in and give Bucket a break.

Tiger pushed on with his ideas. He came up with another idea: buck jumping. Excitedly, he put his spiel to the others.

'Good bloody money, plenty a travel, and a good way to pick up sheilas, eh?'

'Yeah.' All of them had been to the rodeo at Omeo, a nearby town, and had watched the gun riders from Victoria and the other states. The competition was always keen, and the prize money as high as anywhere in Australia. For all that, it was usually a local who won the best 'rough rider' award.

'We've got some bloody top riders around here, you know,' said Tiger.

'Yeah,' Chatty said. 'No wonder Banjo Paterson wrote "The Man from Snowy River" about a local. They're the best, ya know.'

Local gossip had it that the man from Snowy River was from Omeo — one of many similar claims from the myriad small towns in the high country. However, Tag wasn't happy with this idea. He reckoned that rodeos were wrong and 'bloody cruel'. What followed was an intense argument, and Tag lost the battle. Finding himself shouted down, he took no offence, and the conversations bubbled along quietly.

About ten o'clock, just on semi-dark, the boys headed for their beds. They looked out from under their canvas, feeling privileged and in awe of the flashing of the southern auroras in the sky. Added to this was the thrill of seeing constant falling stars that faded out just before the horizon. At this higher altitude, the sky seemed clearer, sharper, and more dramatic. It was a moonless night, and the heavens put on a fine display.

For once, Jess wasn't tied up; she'd been invited to spend the night with Tag and the others under the canvas. She dived under the covers, not to be seen until daybreak. No way would she desert the warmth of Tag's body for a pee or any other distraction. Tonight was a rare treat for the beagle, although Tag would have a restless night while Jess snorted, twitched, and made short squealing noises. However, there was a reason for the excited beagle finding herself a guest in Tag's bed. He knew that, if she was tied up outside, Jess would bark the moment that she smelt the wild horses. Under the canvas, snug and content, Jess would put aside her sentry duties for the night. Dimble and the other horses remained tied up with halters. They would be hungry by the morning, but the boys didn't want the horses to wander, even if they had been hobbled.

CHAPTER SEVEN

The next morning, Tiger woke to a weird yet familiar noise. Like a deep throttling sound, it broke his slumber. Rising quietly, he could see a black stallion about fifty yards away in the early-morning fog. Twirling tunnels of smoke-like mist shot out from the horse's nostrils every time it snorted a high-pitched squeal that was instantly recognisable as a brumby's. The animal sensed something different, but seemed curious rather than alarmed. It thumped its front hoof quietly on the damp turf as a caution. Tiger blew a soft whistle, mimicking the honeysuckle bird. The boys stirred. Tag held Jess's muzzle and demanded silence in a quiet, firm voice. In no time, five eager faces (not including the beagle) were peeking out from under canvas. At least fourteen horses were around the waterhole. They seemed content to drink and graze, except for the stallion — he guarded his flock. Slowly, over a period of twenty minutes, the mob's leader calmed slightly, walked up to the edge of the spring, spread his front legs, lowered his head, and took a long, slow, soothing drink from this crystal-clear pool. One of his mares wandered towards Tiger, on the far edge of the canvas. Then another horse sniffed at some riding boots warily, within inches of Chatty and Bucket.

It was exciting. No one moved. Suddenly, a rumble of guttural sounds cleared the air. They were the low grunts and snorts of the magnificent black leader with the white blaze on his nose. The mares, startled, spun and trotted to their leader. Chatty got up quietly. Kneeling behind a low bush, he admired the stallion. The amazing thing was, the stallion just stood back and observed them all. Finally, with a short whinny, he called his herd together, and they all wandered off towards the far end of the wide, open plain. Horses other than stallions don't have a strong sense of smell, and even then the stallion's main use for its sensitive nostrils is to indicate if a mare is in season and ready for mating. Aware of this, the boys knew that they would pose more of a curiosity than a threat to the wild horses. They simply had to remain low and under cover, keep quiet, and enjoy watching these untamed creatures.

After a hearty breakfast of damper and a cuppa, with their horses hobbled for a feed, and Jess sulking when Tag tied her up to a chain, the boys headed off on foot across the plain in an easterly direction. They carried a sack each, and a walking stick or staff to ward off any snakes found sliding around in the long grass. There were two large mobs of kangaroos feeding on the eastern side of the plain, having their last quick snacks before heading into the low bush for their daytime naps. They, along with the platypuses and wallabies, were mostly nocturnal animals. Then, in the distance, less than a quarter of a mile away, the boys spotted the black stallion and his herd. The shining animal lifted his proud head and snorted a warning, but the other horses in his clan merely looked about casually before continuing eating.

Tiger led the boys at right angles to the horses and directly towards the edge of the plain. The low snow-gum trees offered good cover for them to move closer and observe the mob. Tag was interested in the quality of the horses. They were average size, and the straightness of their backs and the strength and width of their chests showed some good breeding. Few had hollow backs and sagging stomachs. It being summer, they had clean coats, and several had small foals skipping and kicking about in fun.

The boys followed the horses for two hours. Occasionally, Tag would show himself for brief periods. Initially, the stallion objected by half-heartedly rounding up his herd, rearing on his hind legs, and thrashing the air. The third time he did this, Tag walked quietly onto the plain and sat down. Several horses came within twenty yards for a sniff. Quietly, Tag reached into his bag and produced some segments of quince, a pear-like sweet fruit that all horses loved. Back at the log cabin, Ann had two quince trees: one for quince jellies—a delight on toast—and the other for the animals. At home, Tag used them to catch his horses. Always, the milkers stood every morning at the crude dairy waiting for their quince treat.

Tag, crawling quietly, put several pieces on the ground, and then crawled about ten yards away. He crouched and waited. It didn't take long: the horses crunched the sugary fruit with delight. Being curious, the wild horses started to look for more surprises. A bay mare with a strong foal behind her walked towards Tag with her head down, nostrils flaying as she sniffed the ground—so he put another sizable piece of fruit about an arm's length from where he was squatting. Craning its long neck, the mare muzzled the fruit in its soft, hairy lips. It snapped and ground the firm fruit, and then looked for more. Slowly, Tag slid out his hand. Calmly, or perhaps under the influence of this rare, sweet treat, the mare reached forward and softly took the fruit from Tag's palm. The boys, some distance away, looked on in amazement—only Tag could have performed such a feat.

An hour later, Tag stood, feeding the trusting mare. The only horse not in his immediate vicinity was the black stallion. Nevertheless, it didn't snort or protest. Probably, his male pride stopped him from moving closer. The other boys had stood out in the open, but didn't interfere with Tag until, finally, after an hour of feeding the wild brumbies, the boys headed back for their camp. The horses followed until the black stallion screamed a high-pitched whinny, warning his mob to go no further.

Back at the camp, with Jess let off, the lads busied themselves collecting wood and tending their own horses. Tiger wandered off to the far side of the plain to collect the evening meal. He went deep into the bush and returned with a small kangaroo. Golly set about tea and sweets. Later, over a large camp fire, the boys talked about the day, the horses, and school.

'Ya think Miss Gerber will marry Mr Barnes?' asked Golly.

'Hope not. She's a good teacher and she shouldn't go.'

'Come on, Tag. If she gets hitched, then that's it—married women can't teach,' answered Tiger bluntly.

'That's bulldust,' Chatty added. 'She's okay—stupid bloody rule, if ya ask me. All that friggin' learnin' and trainin' that's friggin' wasted. She talks German, ya know.'

'Her big brother knows my old man real well. Dad's trying to get him a job on the roads—anything would be better than that bloody mine,' added Tag.

Finally, the talk got around to the subject of girls.

'Sally Sandy is the best-looking sheila in the school, I reckon,' Tiger said. 'Gunna ask her to come fishin' down on the Tambo soon.'

'And what else, Tiger boy?' smirked Chatty.

'None of ya business, smart arse. When are ya gunna get yaself a sheila, ya ugly bastard? Poor woman would need bad eyesight to like you, Chatty boy.'

In no time, the boys were wrestling and giggling. As usual, Chatty had managed to stir all of them up, and he would have gotten away with a lot more if he hadn't been such a giggler—he had an uncontrollable giggle. He always hoped to upset Tiger, but there was nothing violent about it; in fact, most rumbles ended up with the boys ganging up on Chatty and tickling him. Several times, he had had to plead and make ridiculous promises to stop the probing fingers.

The comment directed towards Chatty about girls was the one he could not normally cope with. However, coming from Tiger … well, it was okay. Every member of this group of young men was unusual. Tag was there because of Tiger. Both Chatty and Bucket were part of the group because of the constant teasing they had endured at school for years. Tiger attracted such loners. They were the strongest-bonded group at the school; each had a cross to bear. However, Chatty copped the most slander. As a part-Aboriginal, he always had to cope with snide comments and subtle jibes, often muttered within earshot.

His mother, Lilly, was from outback New South Wales. Chatty's dad, Dave, had met Lilly on one of his droving trips. She had been working as a cook's helper on a big station. Because she was a half-caste, both her people and the station owners treated Lilly poorly. Lilly had known her mother only briefly, before the station people took her away from the native camp. Her father … well, she had no idea who he was.

It had been very wet on one particular droving trip. Dave had come down with a cold of some sort, and had been quite ill. The head drover reckoned it was some sort of fever. Whatever the illness, Dave had to leave the drovers and return to the station, where they had picked up four hundred heifers two days before. Lilly, the only woman left at the homestead, answered the kitchen door when he knocked. The mistress had gone to the town for a week, and the boss cocky was spending some time away at an annual show. Lilly was relieved when she saw that it was Dave riding into the homestead; the barking dogs had alerted her. Had the rider been a stranger, there was a good chance she would have hidden. Instead, she offered to help Dave using some herbal plants commonly used by the Aborigines.

Dave recovered quickly, so that what would normally have been a two-week confinement to bed only took four days. In that time, he got to see and understand what a special person Lilly really was. He found her kind, intelligent, very feminine, and serene: a wonderful woman. Immediately, this normally quiet, shy man took a shine to Lilly and asked her to come away with him. He was disgusted by the way she was being treated. She had been a cook's helper since the age of eight—thirteen years without a wage, a holiday, or respect. That's what irked Dave the most: no respect. He returned to the homestead after the droving trip, and took Lilly back to his hometown, Tongio, just up the road from Swifts Creek. His family had a farm there.

Chatty was Dave and Lilly's only child.

THE HIGH PLAIN's cold evening air had the boys moving closer to the soft, glowing fire. Golly was the first to exhale a long, deep yawn. It was time to hit the sack. With the fire doused to save wood, they put their hats on top of their boots in case it rained, and to prevent the heavy morning dew from leaving its watery deposit. That night, Jess sat with dignity and charm, looking at Tag as he slid into his warm canvas bed. How could he resist? Jess dashed into the opening when Tag lifted the canvas. Tonight their horses were hobbled, and were free to wander and fill their bellies. A mopoke made an eerie, solemn, bugle-like call, which was answered by a mate some distance away, and a fox gave a barking squeal, but Jess didn't respond. In no time, they were all sound asleep. For the boys, this was a perfect, rare holiday.

Shafts of bright sunlight slashed the sky as the boys woke to enjoy their last day. The Australian Alps put on a beautiful dawn display for the campers. The morning started with the familiar warble of magpies, and at the same time Jess found herself crudely shoved out into the cold air. Her foul farts had caused her expulsion from paradise — she had gorged herself the night before, and had become very loose in the bowels.

Today was pack-up-and-head-for-home day. They had been away for four days. There was a heavy, damp fog covering the plain: this was a good sign as, once it lifted, a pristine day usually followed. Bucket, as was typical of a dairy farmer, was the first up. He soon got a fire going. It was a cold, fresh morning, not quite a frost; it was quite common to have temperatures close to freezing early in the day on the high plains in summer. Within an hour, the fog had lifted to a clear morning, bursting with birdlife and bright sunlight. In the hazy dawn, just out from the waterhole, stood several wild horses. The stallion was apparently missing, but there was no doubt he was lurking in the trees on the edge of the plain nearby, watching every move.

The hobbled horses hadn't moved far from the camp, and the wild horses simply stared with curiosity at these domesticated animals. Tag, after putting on his boots, wandered slowly towards the inquisitive brumbies. They didn't move as he approached. When the wily old bay mare moved forward slowly, Tag was prepared: he held out his hand with a large piece of quince, tempting the beautiful horse. She took her time. Then, with her ears forward and her neck stretched out, the animal softly removed the quince from Tag's hand and crunched away with delight. The other horses started to move in, but it was too late: what little fruit remained would be for the boys' own horses that night. After a big day of walking up and down steep hills, the fruit would be a welcome bonus.

The adventure was at an end. Jess would lead this merry gang directly home: no deviations. Tag's training of her with a wad had done the trick. Once it was dangled in front of her snout, she would try to make a direct beeline for home, even if it were a thousand miles away. However, much to Jess's disgust, it was not that simple: a team effort was required. Dimble was Jess's teammate — though he wasn't too happy with the arrangement either. Tag would put a long halter on Dimble. Then Jess, with a long, sour face, would find herself attached to the horse's lead. Poor Dimble: he would be led by this single-minded beagle on a mission for food. After the boys had packed up camp and headed off, the antics between Jess and Dimble became hilarious. Objecting to Jess's constant pulling, Dimble would prop, and Jess, pulling hard, would almost choke. Then Dimble would get frustrated and canter after Jess, trying to lash out and kick the dog with his hoofs. After two hours, they somehow worked out a satisfactory agreement. Both animals plodded along, with Jess sulking, and Dimble disgusted with Tag and the world at large.

It took two long days for the boys to reach the head of Sheepstation Creek. Back at the log cabin, Ann knew they would be home that afternoon, as she had spotted the large signal fire that the boys had lit on the top of the Angoras the night before. When the excited campers returned to the holding paddock that surrounded the Wardells' log cabin, a strong smell of rabbit stew and fresh bread tickled their noses as they walked through the crude wooden gateway. A large hot meal greeted the adventurers. They were hungry, and bursting with tales of their travels.

That weekend, Fred was intrigued by the yarn about the wild horses. He had heard Tag's claims earlier in the year, and had secretly dismissed them as a childhood fantasy. It was common knowledge that there were no horses on the Dargo high plains. There was no arguing now, though, as these boys had seen the proof. There had to be a reason, and Tag reckoned it was the bushfires. Fred agreed, as the wild horses from behind Cobungra — a large cattle station on the edge of the high plains — had gone missing after the severe fire of 1897. Most thought that the horses had perished, but it now appeared they had taken fright and, led by a young stallion, had travelled for days to the Dargo high plains.

Fred informed the Kellys and the Faithfulls—high-country families who regularly mustered potential stock horses from the Cobungra mob—of the find. The Omeo horsemen were pleased when they finally heard of Tag's and the boys' discovery. The horses took some finding, but they were eventually rounded up and driven back to the main mob behind Cobungra. A little while later, a beautiful, handcrafted stock whip arrived for each of the young adventurers, courtesy of the grateful brumby men.

CHAPTER EIGHT

With the holidays over, school was a drag—as usual. Lunchtimes for the boys meant sitting around and yarning about their trip, or planning the next one. This year, both Tiger and Tag worked at the butter factory after school. Later, after milking the cows, Bucket and his older brother Tom came over as well. Between them, they cleaned all the empty cream-cans so they could be returned the next day to the farms. Lilly worked with the boys, and they loved her company. She seemed to be always happy, and treated them as 'her boys'. They didn't mind that she preferred to walk around in bare feet, or continually hugged them as her way of saying thanks. Most of all, it was her way with Tom, Bucket's brother, that was special.

Tom, like Lilly, was an outcast. He was three years older than Bucket. Somehow, during pregnancy or at birth or who knows when, fate had paid the youngster a blow. Tom appeared to have entered into the world as a healthy, robust, little baby boy. Then, over a period of several months, his mum came to realise that there was something wrong. By the time Tom was three years old, the family knew that he was profoundly different. The doctor proclaimed him mentally retarded; but, undeterred, the family kept the little tyke and treated him as normal. This included going to school. He went to school for three years, and never moved out of grade one. Tom loved school, and appeared oblivious of the fact that his classmates moved on each year. He just loved company. This was a relief for his mum because, until he started school, Tom would refuse to leave his mother's side. It was a heavy responsibility for her.

Then came a day that would be pivotal in Tom's life — when Bucket attended school for the first time. Tom and Bucket sat together in grade one. Bucket was proud of Tom. Although Tom was much bigger than the other kids, he was a kind, gentle boy and a model student; but, academically, he learned nothing. The following year was a nightmare for Bucket. Tom wanted to go up into grade two with his brother. With some hesitancy, the school agreed. There were two classes in the one room, grades two and three, and very soon Tom found the classroom too difficult to handle. At the beginning, he shot up his hand to any question the teacher asked. Naturally, the correct answer was rarely forthcoming. Within weeks, Tom had become a nuisance, and soon he found himself removed back to grade one. He protested, and became angry and loud. It was an unhappy situation. Bucket was the only person at school who could calm him.

Tom started behaving erratically, frightening the much younger students in the room, while older students teased him. Bucket couldn't win. He understood his brother's frustration, but it was hard to defend Tom's behaviour. The teachers seemed to ignore the fact that Bucket was an innocent seven-year-old boy; they continually referred to him for help, instead of to the boys' parents.

Finally, when the school bullies sorted out a bewildered, sweet Tom after school one afternoon, the problem came to a head. Naturally, the simplest solution was for Tom to be taken from the school. As a result, Bucket's lot in the playground was fixed forever: he became the butt of endless name-calling and insults directed at his brother Tom.

It seemed only natural that Bucket drifted towards Tiger: they were both outsiders. Tiger, just as he had with Tag, stepped in one day to stop the school bullies in their relentless hounding of Bucket. However, the problem for poor Tom Banks remained. At many a mealtime and gatherings in the district, Tom was discussed to the point of boredom. There were too many opinions. Tom came out of all these discussions as a bad-tempered, erratic, and moody dill. At home, Bucket's mum was lost. Tom couldn't be left alone; he couldn't follow instructions or milk a cow.

That was when Mrs Banks had a visit from Chatty's mum, Lilly. This wonderful woman became Tom's saviour. Lilly asked Bucket's mum if Tom could help her at the factory, and she agreed. It was to become a wonderful union of two special people. Somehow, under the guidance of this barefooted, dark-skinned, kind human, Tom became a very enthusiastic worker when given a simple task. His job was to mop the floors and help Tiger after school. Lilly was kind but smart. Tom's language skills improved, he learned to count to five, and he developed a brilliant memory for names and numbers. He could tell Lilly how many cans of milk the Taylors had dropped off the Friday before, and he was never wrong. Tom had no numerical concept of this number; it was simply a sound to him. Over time, Lilly had him count to twenty-five. Yet, if he was asked to count backwards from three, he would be lost. Surprisingly, he became an important part of the business, and a highly valued worker. His only request was for Bucket to work there after milking on the farm had finished. Bucket couldn't get there quickly enough.

FRED WARDELL ENJOYED reading the local newspaper, the *Omeo Standard*. A big paper, it carried local and national news. He would take it to work to read, and then use it to start his fire or to wipe his backside after performing his ablutions.

This year, the paper was paying a lot of attention to the subject of rabbits. The pest, which had arrived in the continent with the First Fleet, had been in Victoria — via Geelong — for over eighty years. It thrived in the mountains and the open plains, and had no problem living in the harsh desert environment. Even at the Wardells', on the small, kangaroo-grassed flat across from the log cabin, twenty or thirty of the furry buggers grazed openly of an evening. The consensus was 'multiply that figure by ten' — that's roughly how many were actually there. Regular reports on rabbits in the newspaper and from the government gave rise to many changes in the district, and in the whole of Australia.

The year was 1909. Every week, there were dire warnings about the rabbit problem in the local rag. Much earlier, in 1900, when the 'rabbit plague' problem had first emerged locally, the Omeo shire had formed a committee called the Omeo Rabbit League. This committee appointed a full-time rabbit hunter called the Rabbit Destroyer. After experimenting with traps, snares, and dogs, the Destroyer bagged 625 rabbits in his first year. The council, acclaiming the result as an outstanding success, declared that the rabbit was under control. Proudly, the *Omeo Standard* headlined the result: 'Swift action by local council averts potential rabbit plague'.

By May 1910, when Tag turned fourteen, the rabbits were in plague proportions again. They were a menace that almost crippled the farmers financially. But, for local workers like Fred, the rabbit was a bonus. Rabbits provided a free feed, replacing the kangaroo and koala. This meant that when Ann prepared supplies on Sunday nights for Fred's week on the road, she no longer cooked meals and prepared sweets. She still cooked bikkies; but now a bag of spuds, a bag of onions, some vegies, some flour to thicken the stew, and several home-grown herbs were enough to get Fred through the week. With a camp oven and half-a-dozen traps at his disposal, he had rabbit stew for dinner nearly every night. Occasionally, Fred would have a sand trout. Admittedly, when he first set the new rabbit traps, he bruised the end of many a finger. It was a common accident suffered by first-time users. Fred's furry mate, Buster the dog, had once put his foot in the wrong place, and had ended up with a permanent limp. Consequently, Fred became adept at setting traps, and Buster became wary. However, Buster loved rabbits. He lived like a king on the stew scraps and rabbit innards. The dog's bowl was always full.

It wasn't the first free feed that was easily attainable in the district. The first had been the monkey bears. These tree-bound animals squatted in the high branches; normally asleep or moving very slowly, they were easy targets for anyone with a rifle. Originally hunted for pelts, in no time they became a source of food. Their numbers quickly diminished in the areas where humans dwelt. Unlike rabbits, monkey bears weren't prolific breeders, and they soon disappeared.

IT WAS MONDAY, early, the start of Fred's working week. Molly the horse, harnessed to the dray, and near the gate to the house paddock above Sheepstation Creek, was loaded and ready. An assortment of items were neatly crammed in and covered with canvas: the local paper, along with the spuds, tomatoes, and onions, some spare clothes (in case Fred got wet), and two bottles of ginger beer. Every Monday, Ann packed these essentials carefully into the pine box under Fred's seat. Buster was excited and raring to go. He had completed his morning duties of urinating on every post within a hundred yards of the cabin. It was daybreak—six o'clock in the morning. The kids were up, Bertie ready to milk the cows, and Tag collecting kindling wood. Fred said his goodbyes and called Buster, who was sitting on his haunches while Bertie squirted milk into his mouth from the cow's teat.

Fred put his foot on the serrated steel step and heaved himself up onto the bench seat of the four-wheeled dray. He slapped the reins on Molly's rump. The horse and dray crunched off down the dirt track, and Fred whistled as he reached into his pocket and produced a tobacco pouch. With precision and concentration, he rolled the stiff, dark tobacco and then filled his pipe. He would spend ages trying to keep it alight. Good, fresh tobacco was hard to come by. Buster, who was some way ahead, was tearing around on the trail of a rabbit.

Most Mondays were like this. The trip to Fred's camp near Bald Hills Creek would take over two hours. Fred had three camps along his ten-mile stretch: one at the base of the Gap, a steep road that led to the high plains; another at Holland's Flat; and a third at Bald Hills Creek. Two of the camps were on the Tambo River. Each had a small yard to hold Molly, and a canvas tent that was Fred's room for the week. He always headed for the camp first, unloaded his gear, and put Molly in the yard. He then set a couple of crude fishing lines in the stream, which usually produced small sand trout once or twice a week. Next, he would set fresh rabbit traps and attend to his tent. He would unload the provisions, and put a clean sheet on the bed or stretcher that was a jute sack suspended over two saplings. Next came the jam, honey, and butter, all carefully placed in the Coolgardie safe. This water-cooled metal cupboard was for storing condiments that soured or went off in the heat. Best of all, it kept the ants and insects at bay.

Buster always rushed into the tent first. This didn't worry Fred, as often a snake, goanna, or echidna would flee from under the flap. A canvas water bottle hung on a nearby branch. Fred refilled it from the river. At one end of the tent was a neat rock fireplace used for cooking, light, and warmth. Just outside the entrance flap was a smoothed, round dry log; it acted as a seat, and was big enough for Fred and several guests, if need be. The camps were several hundred yards away from the road, all in picturesque places, and acted as a home-away-from-home for Fred. He worked from dawn to late afternoon, allowing just enough time to get to camp, hobble Molly for the night, and then check his traps and lines. Before cooking tea, he would sit on his log, with Buster at his feet, and would roll his tobacco and load his pipe. Fred was a good, reliable worker. Once a year, the big boss from Buckland would come over and check things out, and then they would both head to Long Gully for the remainder of the day, yakking over a beer. Fred never said much.

On this Monday, Fred arrived at the Bald Hills Creek campsite at 8.25 a.m. He set his traps, baited the lines with worms, and quickly cleaned the tent: a fox had paid a visit over the weekend and had left a turd at the entrance. Fred then unhitched Molly, except for the collar, and put her in the yard, ready to harness her to the scoop. As always, before anything else, Fred headed down to the riverbank with a few old pages of the *Omeo Standard* in his hands. Squatting in among some ferns for privacy, he grunted and cussed. Normally, this was a ritual: a crap, and then work. However, poor Fred hadn't had a decent bog for days. He had sat on the long drop behind the log cabin at Sheepstation Creek for half an hour on Saturday: nothing. This morning, again, nothing. So, hitching up his moleskin pants, he slowly walked to the yard.

He ambled along with a forward stoop, not feeling too well. Suddenly, there was a sharp pain in his right lower abdomen. He had been constipated for five days, and hadn't said anything about it to Ann—she would have made him drink that vile castor oil. He would rather be silent and constipated than drink that stuff. Gritting his teeth, he opened the yard gate. It was time to put the scoop on Molly. Fred was about to attach the trace chain to the collar hook when the chain fell to the ground. Reaching down and stretching forward, he grimaced as a hot, piercing pain suddenly shafted from his groin to his rib cage. He fell forward, clutching his stomach. His teeth ground together in a gnashing protest. He knew something was wrong—something really bad. Slowly, he tried to get up. He got to a kneeling position on the dry gravel, bellowed in pain, and fell again. Fred struggled while kicking at nothing, which caused his face to bleed as it rubbed and thumped along the rocky, dry earth. The confused Buster ran in circles at first. Then he stretched out on his front paws and barked at Fred. The dog was frightened. Although his master had never behaved so strangely before, the animal knew that these screams meant pain and disaster.

Fred was facing death; he understood that much. He called out to his Ann, to Harry, Albert, and Phyllis. He called out to Tag several times. Finally, weeping, his warm tears washing away some of the blood and dirt, Fred pleaded to a higher spirit. He didn't ask for the pain to go away or for his life to be preserved. No, quietly, he called out to baby James. It was the first time that Fred had uttered his name since the funeral. As he started to fade and drift into unconsciousness, he started to speak to James, his precious one, 'I'm coming, my little mate. I'm coming ...'

Poor Buster was frantic—he barked, he ran around his master—until, finally, after Fred had died, Buster just lay down facing him, whining softly.

Later, the doctor told Ann that appendicitis occurred mainly in males but that, by the age of twenty-five, there was usually no risk of it flaring up. Fred was thirty-four when his useless, little-finger-sized appendix ruptured and perforated, spilling its poisonous contents into his abdominal cavity, causing peritonitis—which is always fatal unless there is immediate help. None of the medical details offered by the doctor helped Ann. He had known Fred and Ann all their married life and, as usual, he used jargon to cover his own grief. However, something else made Fred's death even more tragic: he wasn't found until the following Saturday, by which time he had been dead almost six days. This had given the dingoes plenty of time to have their fill of both Fred and Molly. Molly had died of thirst, they reckoned. What was never told was the whole story of what poor old Dan Hogan found when he stumbled across Fred's corpse. Crows—the lowest form of life on earth, according to local opinion—had attacked poor Fred's body in a hideous manner.

It is a vile creature, the crow. Many a farmer-cum-bushman would agree with this. During lambing time on a farm, the crows will pick out an eye from a ewe trying to give birth. As the lamb emerges from the ewe, they will nip the end off its tongue to doubly ensure that the little blighter can't suckle. They will nip the top off the mother's teats so the lamb will find it hard to drink. Then, as if possessed with evil, they will peck out the lamb's eyes. That is all they will have to do with that mother and her lamb. No, they don't linger and eat the carcass. The eyes and teats are their fill. Then, as if bored, they will simply move onto another victim. Bastards!

Early that Saturday morning, Dan Hogan had been walking along the banks of the Tambo River collecting blackberries, heading roughly in the direction of Fred's camp. It took him two hours to fill his billycan with the berries. Afterwards, Dan reckoned that Buster must have barked and attracted his attention, although he never saw the dog. Then again, curiosity might have been the reason that saw Dan wander up to Fred's camp. This was a Saturday, after all, and Fred should have been at home.

Dan found Fred's body in the yard, next to Molly the horse. Dan stood for ten minutes, stunned with shock at what he saw. Fred's eyes were missing, and his tongue was partially removed—undoubtedly the work of those black, feathered devils. Half of his left leg had been gnawed off—Dan guessed that there was a well-fed pack of wild dogs nearby. The same dogs had eaten quite a bit of Molly as well. Poor old Dan, one of the district's confirmed bachelors, took it badly. 'A fella was badly shaken, in fact,' is how he described himself later that night at the pub. Dan had taken ages to move from the sight. He knew there was nothing he could do to help, except find Buster perhaps. Then he quickly walked the three miles to Swifts Creek and contacted the local policeman. By early afternoon, following a brief autopsy, there were hasty arrangements to have Fred's body nailed in a coffin. Then the pace slowed to allow a dignified funeral to be held—without a viewing.

THE BEAGLE WARNED Ann of visitors approaching. As they got close, she recognised the two women in the moonlight—Mrs Carroll and Mabel Pollard, the wife of Bernie, the policeman. She waved briefly to them, and then clutched the neck of her blouse as the colour from her face drained rapidly. Neither woman had waved back. They both dismounted. Mabel walked towards Ann, and they hugged tightly.

'It's your Fred,' she said. 'He got sick and died.'

The particulars were essential, but irrelevant. As humans are not used to such news, no one can prepare for or easily cope with the outburst of anguish that usually follows.

'No … no … no. I thought his horse must have gone lame!' Ann screamed.

Tag ran out. Mrs Carroll beckoned him towards her. He sobbed bitterly.

'Get some more wood, Tag,' Ann yelled in a voice that quivered and shook.

'Come in,' she said to the visitors.

Tag and Phyllis sat on the bed as the three women pulled the chairs to the table. It was uncomfortable. Phyllis wanted to placate Tag, but she had no reserve or strength. There was an awkward silence. Ann, desperately wanting questions answered, instead simply twisted her handkerchief, looked down, and shook in fear. Her questions were too hard for her children to hear.

Mrs Carroll took over.

'Grab your pyjamas, and we'll all walk to my place,' she said to the children. 'I've just cooked a new batch of biscuits. Mrs Pollard will stay the night, and we can come back tomorrow or later. Move along now.'

Ann nodded. Within minutes, the frightened children and Mrs Carroll left. Mabel had packed her own bag before she'd left home … that was a smart move.

What followed was a night of tears, hugs, cups of tea, and unimportant comments made by Ann. There were moments of silence when she lost track of time. By dawn, the tears had slowed, but the grief had consumed poor Ann to the point where Mabel realised that she should tell Ann what to do over the next few days.

'Tell me what chores to do. I'll stay until tomorrow, then we'll go past the Carrolls, pick up Phyllis and Tag, and attend dear Fred's funeral. You are not to worry about the money. It has been taken care off. Bernie will let the district know the sad news. Does that sound all right, Ann?'

Ann nodded. So often when Mabel had spoken during the night, Ann had nodded.

At the funeral, which was well attended, many spoke of Fred in glowing terms. Even Bernie spoke, which was unusual for a policeman. He echoed many when he mentioned the tug-o-war team, the footy, and Fred's commitment to family and work. That night, Bernie hugged his Mabel and kissed her forehead. Mabel didn't respond. She sat, cried with a deep passion for the first time, and attempted to picture the Wardells trotting home in

Fred's old dray, pulled by a new horse, courtesy of Mr Bills. For the first time ever, she truly understood why there were times that Bernie hated his job.

CHAPTER NINE

At the tiny log cabin on Sheepstation Creek, the Wardells' world had plunged into the unknown. However, this time, unlike when she had lost her sweet James, Ann took control. Having gathered strength from the wonderful words that were spoken with so much sincerity at the funeral, Ann swamped her children with love, strength, and all the care that a child could ask for in such a sad situation. The following day, she welcomed her mother Gloria with open arms. She left her grief to private moments and cemetery visits and, in time, was able to share it with other people who had suffered a similar loss.

Next, for Ann, came the reality of day-to-day existence. They had no savings. It was not well known that Fred had been buying the Wilson house and six acres in the Swifts Creek township. He had paid off fifty pounds, and only had ten pounds to go. As well, Ann had purchased a treadle Singer sewing machine from Mr Collect in Day Street, Omeo, on which she still had ten payments at 1/6d a week left. Ann knew there was next to no money in the bank: Fred used to give any spare money to Mr Wilson to reduce the debt on the house. It was their secret—the kids knew nothing about it. Mr Johns, a bank clerk, and his wife rented Fred's new dwelling, and their rent payments came off the house as well. The Johnses were building their own house, and were going to move into it by the end of the year. Now the Wardells would be almost ten pounds short and, somehow, Ann had to find the money. Then, as so often happens in the Australian countryside, the money problems soon faded: Gloria had a little stash; Mr Wilson stated there would be no payments until Ann could afford them; the Carrolls refused rent payments; and Ann didn't receive a bill from Sandy's Store in Swifts Creek for the next six months. Poor Fred had left behind a wonderful legacy—one not measured in pounds or pence. He was just a good man. The locals paid their respects to him and his family in many ways.

A sad, tired Tag left school a week after the funeral. Almost fifteen by now, he got a job with Sidley and Cooper, the blacksmiths, as an apprentice, where his wage was two quid a week. He gave one pound and ten shillings of this to his mum, and boarded at Golly's place for five bob a fortnight. Albert, Harry, and Phyllis helped Ann with money as well, and their mum moved into Wilson's house with her sewing machine that Christmas.

Buster, Fred's dog, just disappeared—he was never found. Well, that was the story, but the word around the district was that the Murphys knew that old man Hastings had shot Buster. Bill Murphy had seen Buster heading for home a fortnight after Fred had died. The dog, who was spotted by their young Billy, was heading for Mount Flagstaff, across Hastings paddock. They reckoned that that lousy bugger Hastings claimed he had spotted a stray dog, and shot him. He reckoned it was killing sheep!

The blacksmith's shop, Tag's place of employ, was right on the creek, just over the new bridge on the way to Tongio. It was about two hundred yards from the Swifts Creek post office, a stone's throw from Tiger's house, and about three hundred yards in the other direction from the butter factory. The blacksmith's shop had a livery stable for housing horses overnight, and a paddock out the back for holding freshly shod animals. Tag liked the new arrangements, and Golly's household welcomed him with open arms. They gave his payments for board to Ann. It was only a five-minute walk to the blacksmiths' from the Elliot's bakery.

Tag worked six days a week. Straight off, he liked the job. At first, he coked up the fires in the small furnaces used for shaping the new horseshoes and any minor tooling jobs. He also led the freshly shod horses out the back, and brought others in for shoeing. Bill and Sid, the owners, were tough, hardworking, hard-drinking smithies. Bill, a big, strong, wild-looking man, with a full, tangled black beard, had an angry streak in him. Sometimes, Tag found himself holding moody horses that wouldn't stand still when tethered to the rigging pole. He didn't like that part of the job; Bill had a quick, foul temper. Tag had never come across an adult with such a bad temper before — he felt for the horse. Tag would turn away if a horse he was holding tried to pull away or rear up while Bill was attempting to shoe the poor animal. The foul-mouthed Bill would thump it in the ribs as hard as he could with the rasp; sometimes, there would be blood.

When Tag led the animal to the holding paddock, he would offer quiet words and encouragement to the animal. Sid said nothing; it didn't pay to comment or interfere when his partner was in one of 'those' moods. Often, after one of those outbursts, Sid took note of the horse and its owner. If possible, he tried to get the horse shod elsewhere, pathetically suggesting to the owner, as they collected the animal, 'Look, mate, your horse gets spooked when he comes here. Why don't ya take him up to Burley's in Omeo next time?' To which the owner might reply, 'Crikey, mate. Burley's sent me here — they reckoned me horse was scared by the chaff-cutter's noisy machinery next door.'

Over time, this led to a new sign hung out the front of Sidley and Cooper's: *Hacks 3/6d. Buggy horses 4/6d. Special horses 5/-.* The 'special horses' were the ones that Bill had had 'a run in' with.

With Tag at work and Golly finishing his last year at school, the five boys saw little of each other. For a time, Tiger worked seven days a week at the butter factory to cover the debts that his old man had created at home. Although Chatty worked in the same building, there was little time for talk; ten-hour days were common.

By the end of that year, Golly had left school and was working happily in his dad's bakery. Tag left Golly's family, and moved in with Ann at the new house next to the Catholic Church just on the edge of town. Some Sunday evenings the five lads got together at Tag's and yakked for hours. Laughter was the other sound that filtered through the lounge-room wall while Ann sewed in the kitchen. She loved the boys, and kept them satisfied with scones and cordial. On most Monday mornings they would regret the frivolities from the night before, as it was hard to get out of bed.

Each boy was doing a man's job. Their adolescent frames and lack of hardened muscles left them weary and aching every day for their first months of work. Bucket now worked full-time on the dairy. His day would start at 4.30 a.m. He milked, separated the cream, fed the pigs, and wearily walked into the kitchen at 7.00 a.m. for his first break and a meal. Then, at 8.00 a.m., he would start his town deliveries. Returning home, he would put the dray on the horse and work hard repairing fences that had been washed down by a bad flood of the Tambo River six months earlier. Of an evening, Bucket simply fell into bed—every day, every week, for those early years.

It was twelve months almost to the day before Tag shod his first horse. A small pony, about the size of Dimble, it was a chestnut with a white blaze. Sid had spent a lot of time teaching Tag the skills; he was happy with Tag, who was slow but thorough. Tag looked kindly at the small chestnut horse. It stood beside its owner. 'Four new shoes,' the work sheet stated.

The horse's owner, who had been waiting, leaning on the hitching post, eyed Tag suspiciously. The man had a reputation for giving endless advice. An hour later, Tag had finished. It had been a difficult exercise, as the pony had somehow sensed Tag's lack of experience. The wary horse had pulled and struggled, and wouldn't settle. It had taken twice as long as expected. Bill made a snide remark when Tag finally finished: 'About bloody time, ya bloody slowcoach.'

Over time, Tag got faster, much stronger, and more skilled. In a blacksmith's shop, the time taken to shoe a hack varied. This was due to the speed of the smithy and the temperament of the horse. The latter became Tag's challenge. Unlike Sid or Bill, Tag had a quiet chat with the horse before the shoeing started. He would pat the wary horse and scratch behind its ears, remove the saddle, and check for any saddle sores or girth burns. If needed, Tag applied a smear of lanolin paste with a rag to any tender parts. Once it was tied to the hitching pole, Tag's first chore was to give the horse a small handful of oats, which he paid for himself, or Bill took out of his wages anyhow. Bill reckoned Tag's attitude to horses was soft, and bred bad habits. Bill seemed to enjoy giving Tag a hard time, but that was about to change.

There came a day in Tag's second year as an apprentice that would remain etched in Bill's mind forever. A few spectators were around, but Bill was the one moved deeply by what he saw — almost to tears.

It was a Monday in winter, and early. The stagecoach from Omeo via Cassilis had arrived. Not only were the coaches rotated with fresh horses; today was shoe day for the two stagecoaches. Bill, as usual on a Monday, was in a foul mood. His team had been beaten at the footy — unfortunate, maybe — but that hadn't stopped him from getting a skinful at the Junction Pub. Then he'd done his dough on the races at Omeo. This was not a good way for bad-tempered Bill to start the week.

Sid waited for the stage driver to unhitch the traces and lead the tired horses out into the backyard. He knew from experience that it would be a difficult day. Not only was Bill a pain in the arse on Mondays, but there was another major problem: two of the stagecoach horses were almost impossible to shoe. Last time, Bill managed to shoe one of the coach renegades, but the horse still carried a scar from where Bill had thrown a red-hot shoe at the unfortunate animal. Sid knew it would take almost a miracle to get the horse into the shop this time. The problem was growing more acute, as Bill's temper appeared to be getting worse. Then Sid did something he had been thinking about for weeks. He asked Tag to come out the back, away from Bill, where they discussed which of the horses Tag could shoe. Tag didn't hesitate: he vividly remembered the attack on the poor piebald hack on its last visit. At the time, he'd almost called Bill a bully, but that might have meant a red-hot shoe thrown in Tag's direction as well.

'I'll take the piebald,' said Tag.

Sid frowned and looked puzzled.

'Ya sure, Tag?'

Tag nodded. The two men walked back inside and greeted Bill with the new arrangements. He roared with laughter.

'This I'll just have ta see — Tag the sissy, shoein' the friggin' piebald!'

'I'll do it in the paddock behind the shop,' offered Tag.

The piebald glared at him as he reached for and took hold of the halter. The horse's nostrils flared and quivered. It stamped its front hoof, reaching out and trying to lash out at Tag. With its ears laid back, it rolled its eyes, showing a large, white ring of evil: it was time for the fight to begin. Given the slightest chance, this horse would do as much damage as it could to Tag with a hefty kick delivered from one of its powerful hind legs. But Tag, ignoring the horse's bad-tempered display, pushed his hand into his pocket, held out a handful of oats, and spoke quietly.

'G'day. We've got a job to do, piebald. But first, I wonder if ya got a name?'

The piebald sniffed at the oats. Softly, he pursed his lips and picked up about three seeds. Nibbling warily, the piebald twisted his head sideways as if to get a better look at this wily young human with a soft face. The piebald made a low, honking noise through his nostrils. He reached his long black-and-white nose towards Tag as if to double-check his human enemy. Then he gave a sign—a sign that says to any horse handler, 'I'm interested'. The piebald flicked his ears forward, which was a horse's acknowledgement of consent. Tag swelled with excitement. Temporarily, one ear flicked back, then both went forwards again. Tag turned his pockets inside out and poured the oats onto the ground.

'You eat the oats, and I'll let ya think about me,' he said.

Tag walked backwards, then turned and strode into the shop. He put on his leather apron, collected his rasp, hammer, and pinchers, put some nails into a pocket, and then turned to Sid.

'Sid, has the piebald got a name?'

'Patch.'

Finally, Tag took off his felt hat—which was out of character—filled it with chaff, and picked up his currycomb. He whistled softly as he walked out the back. Bill, who been standing watching Tag, snorted, 'We'll be here all bloody day at this rate. Pull ya friggin' finger out, boy.'

Tag ignored the remark and walked quietly up to the horse. It didn't jump back, shake its head with anger, or blurt a warning. It stood warily, trying to sum up this young man.

'Hi, Patch. Feel like a brush?'

Patch snorted, eyed Tag warily, and didn't move. Tag put his hat on the ground. Then, with an open palm, he beckoned the piebald towards him. Patch took a small step forward, twisted his head, turned sideways, and then, stretching his neck as far as he could, managed to snatch the brim of the hat and pull it towards himself. All this time he didn't take his jet-black eyes off Tag.

'You have a snack. I'll give you a brush.'

Patch, engrossed with the chaff, didn't even flinch as Tag quietly brushed his long, black-and-white, straight back. Very few horses will turn down a good brush, and Tag had the best currycomb that money could buy. Even after Patch finished the chaff and had a play with the hat, he still didn't acknowledge Tag's presence. Mind you, his jet-black eyes still held Tag in full view. Then, like a cat, Patch arched his back and lifted his head high, making a soft, purring grunt. He loved the comb. He didn't quite close his eyes; he opened them slightly to show a white moon-crescent, and then half-closed them again. They were drooped like a drunk. In no time, Tag was the centre of Patch's attention; the currycomb was bliss, perfect.

'That'll do, mate. Let's get these shoes on.'

Patch turned and nudged Tag gently with his long, mottled, black-and-white nose — a nudge of affection and trust. Tag responded, 'Hi Patch, I'm Tag. You've got a beautiful coat, old fella.'

Sid, engrossed in this almost magical connection between man and horse, turned and saw Bill watching through the slats of a rear window. Bill walked over to Sid, and the two men stood and watched in awe as this quiet, unassuming young man shod the horse — the horse with the reputation of being moody and sour-tempered — that no one could shoe. However, here, in a paddock, stood two connected animals, calm together. One had its halter untethered; the other was talking gently and adjusting a shoe to fit the rear hoof. The piebald called Patch now stood quietly as Tag Wardell did an excellent job of shoeing. Sid's eyes swelled and wetted to the point where he had to wipe them with his dipping rag. He turned and looked at Bill, who was simply nodding his head. When this powerful performance was finished,

Bill, totally out of character, walked over to Tag, put his arm around Tag's shoulder, and said, 'I take my hat off to ya, son: that was bloody worth watchin'. I wouldn'ta believed it, except I seen it with me own eyes. Bloody good job, me boy.'

Tag put his put arm over the horse's neck, turned to Bill, and said, 'Oh, he just likes a good comb.' Sid's face displayed the widest, warmest smirk it could produce. Bill ruffled Patch's ears, which were both laid back.

Sid told everyone at the bar at the Junction Hotel later that night, 'Bill, the bugger, had tears trickling down his face and, bugger me, that bloody rogue horse just stood quietly.'

From that day on, Bill had the deepest respect for Tag. In fact, the change in Bill was remarkable. He always offered Tag the rogue horses, the feisty, savage stallions and the first-timers. The two men had a cuppa together regularly, and Bill offered Tag good tips on many occasions. Then, one day, Bill walked into Tag's workroom and sat down. He had two pannikins of tea.

'Take a break, Tag.'

'Thanks, Bill, just finished anyhow.'

'I see that,' answered Bill. 'I's been meaning to talk to you about something for a time, Tag.' He handed Tag the mug of tea. 'You know, a few years ago, your dad, Fred, called in here. He wanted to have Molly shod. We were having a yak while I worked — good bloke — when, just like that, Fred, ya dad, got up and walked out the back, which was unusual, you know — not like him. So I called out to Sid, and he took over.

'Bikkie, mate?' Bill handed Tag an oatmeal snap, then continued. 'Your dad was walking out the back slowly. I followed him, and I found him sitting under the lemon tree, bawling 'is bloody eyes out. Poor bugger — ya brother James had been dead only a month. Fred was a good man, mate; a bloody good man. I felt privileged to know him. Anyhow, he tried to talk about James and Ann, and ya family. Poor bugger was really hurting like, really sad. He was one of the best men I've ever met, ya dad. You're just like him, Tag. I'm real sorry, me lad. I know I've been a crabby old bastard towards ya at times.'

Bill went quiet. Tag looked him in the eye.

'Thanks, Bill.'

The awkwardness that would have normally prevailed returned. However, Tag and Bill always had lunch together from that day on—a quiet lunch, for sure, but they enjoyed each other's company.

The word soon got around about Tag's unique abilities with horses. People called it a gift; others referred to it as legendary. But whatever the reputation bestowed on Tag, Bill Cooper and Sid Sidley's business boomed. Other blacksmiths didn't hesitate to send their rogue horses down the Gap or up the river to the smithy's at the Creek. The extra work led to a new apprentice being put on: Jack Murey was his name, and Tag was his mentor. Tag worked solely on shoeing. People would walk down from the post office, then stand and watch, or tell others that Tag was about to shoe another 'ugly bastard' or 'brute' or 'bad bugger'. They didn't clap or respond openly. However, in pubs and halls you could hear things like, 'He's bloody unreal, mate!' or 'Ya gotta 'ave a gander, mate—he's the bloody best, no kiddin'!'

Back in the smithy shop, Tag was now the head farrier, while Bill spent most of his time making gate hinges and sharpening picks, mattocks, crowbars, and other mining equipment. Sid allowed Tag to allocate all the horses, as by now Tag was very quick and strong, although he only used his strength to work tirelessly, and not to force his will on the horse. He had powerful shoulders, sinewy arms, and sturdy, well-built legs. He had grown to five foot, eight inches in height, and still wore his hat all day, every day.

Given the task of training the new apprentice, Tag had Jack simply brush each horse and carefully tend to saddle sores. Saddle sores irked Tag. Brushing the horse, providing a clean saddle blanket, and occasional sponging were the answer. Mind you, Tag didn't hesitate to tell the owners if he saw neglect. Although it was out of character for Tag to 'speak up', his reputation was such that any advice he gave received a nod and a smile.

Ann had well and truly settled into the house at Swifts Creek. It was up on the hill, just past the Bouchers' house. From the front veranda she could see the post office, the pub, and most of the township. By now, her new house had the Wardell touch—a fine vegie garden, a good chook run, magpies guarding the fruit trees, and a five-acre backyard, with stables that held eight horses. They belonged to Tag. A brickie mate of Chatty's dad from Tongio had built the stables. According to Archie, a traveller for Raleigh's who stayed at the Creek Pub regularly, Tag's stables were better than a room at the pub.

Tag had set up a new business—although his mum argued that it was just a hobby, because he really enjoyed doing it. Tag bought horses. It was the agent for Goldsborough Mort, a stock and station company, who first approached him with the idea. Each week, horse sales attracted many buyers at Benambra, Omeo, Cassilis, Bruthen, and Bairnsdale. It was the agent's job to get a background on every horse, so that, before the auctioneer started, a brief history of the horse—such as its age, breeding, and background—could be given. Good horses were in high demand. Sales were big and well attended, and usually bidding was lively until the crowd reached the yard that contained a rogue or 'glue' horse. Rogue horses were usually young, poorly broken-in, and unmanageable, or had been mistreated. Glue horses were sometimes old and past their working days. Glues were for butchering; the term referred to the horses' hooves, which were melted down and turned into adhesive. However, not all glue horses were old. In some cases, their owners had just given up on them as too lazy, slow, stubborn, or moody. Rogue horses, on the other hand, were usually referred to by two words: 'mean bastards'.

The deal between the agent and Tag was simple. The agent bought the rogues and younger glue horses for Tag. They were very cheap, because who wanted them? Only the butchers were interested and, generally, they wanted them for almost nothing—the horsemeat would go to Melbourne, mostly, for pet meat.

The agent had up to three horses a fortnight delivered to Tag's paddock. Very soon, Ann became involved. She fed the horses, rugged them up at night and through the day, and followed Tag's highly specific instructions. Some horses required two brushings a day, which seemed to settle them a lot quicker. Others were led on special walks devised by Tag: up to the mines at Cassilis, and down near the machinery, so they would be free to smell strange smells. Some horses found themselves at the footy, or down the street shopping; and all the horses, no matter what plan Tag devised for them, got lots of pats and scratches.

Every horse had a turn in harness—Tag used Bucket to trial them once they had settled down. Bucket, like Tag, loved horses, and because he delivered milk around the town for three hours every day, it was excellent training for the horses. Like Tag, Bucket had a placid nature that worked in harmony with the animals, and he enjoyed the privilege of helping Tag. In turn, Tag saw Bucket as a valuable member of his team, and paid him for his troubles. He paid Ann, his mum, as well. She was thrilled with getting some pocket money of her own.

Tag's results with these horses were amazing. Rarely would a horse fail to improve under Tag's guidance—so much so that most horses would be valued at five and ten times their purchase price. Tag by now only worked at the smithy's shop for five half-days a week, and spent a lot of time with his horses on the flats, where Ann had bought some acreage. Tag had up to four good horses a month for sale; however, there were unusual conditions placed upon the potential buyer. Tag had to watch the owner handle the horse, and each horse sold came with a kit. It included a rug, a currycomb, at least three woollen saddle-blankets, and individual instructions from Tag. If Tag was happy, the buyer got a good horse. Tag never sold a horse unless he was satisfied.

Sometimes, Tag would get a special horse: one that wasn't fast enough to race, or strong enough to stride down steep hills while mustering, or the type of horse that tired easily whether in harness to a dray or plough. When they had spent enough time to move on from Tag's holiday camp, as Ann called it, the horse usually went to deserving owners. In his first year as the proprietor of Wardell's Horse Centre, Tag gave twenty horses to schools in the district. These went to kids who normally walked for hours each day to get to school, as they couldn't normally afford a horse. For local families who were struggling to manage, it felt like an honour to get a horse from Tag.

Tag felt like his life couldn't get much better. His mum gushed with pride when she heard Tag's name mentioned and held in such high esteem—that was *her* son. Tag was no longer just Ann's special boy or her precious parcel; many people thought the world of him. In fact, Ann's bragging about her son was typical of a doting mother. Recently, local tongues had been set wagging when Tag, along with 'those mates', were found drunk, as a result of their first try at alcohol. Mr Adams, the local copper, caught the lads down near the riverbank, dressed them down, and sent them home with a stern warning. By now, like most young men, Tag smoked, had started swearing, and looked a little longer at the fairer sex. However, Ann was unmoved, convinced that his drunken misdemeanour was a one-off. To Ann, Tag was special. Even when the local priest admonished Ann for not enforcing the rules of the Sabbath with young Tag, she made excuses. He was not a church-goer; instead, he went riding with the lads on most Sundays. Well, not quite all the lads: Golly still went to church.

By now, all the gang had rifles, and they usually came home with a few rabbits and the odd roo. They weren't reckless shooters — unless they saw a crow. Tag, in particular, hated crows. Now, come Friday night, they all had a quiet sarsaparilla at the pub, Golly included. They were still under drinking age, 'and the police weren't to be crossed'. After the pub, they went up to Ann's: time for a cup of tea, a game of cards, and a smoke. By now, Tiger had a girlfriend of sorts, Mary Boucher, but he only went out with her on Saturday nights. There was a woolshed dance at Dan O'Brien's, and both Tiger and Mary liked dancing. The other lads, although interested in the opposite sex, were thwarted by their own shyness.

Life, although simple, was good for the Wardell family. Harry Wardell was now married, with three cute little boys. He had set up his own firewood yard in Cassilis, selling firewood to locals. It was a good business. You would think that living among the mountains in the bush, there would be an abundance of fuel. Yet, in every direction looking out from the goldmining town of Cassilis, the hills were bare. It was the mountains within miles of Tongio West, Cassilis, and the like that provided timber for fuel. This had led to denuded hills as far as the eyes could see, decimated by the wood-gorging steam furnaces that powered the mine machines. Harry's team had to go up into Brookville, into the hills, to secure wood — which was a good ten miles away. A long, slow, steep pull to the top, it was very hard on the horses; and the downhill slopes on the return trip were just as difficult. Harry, on Tag's advice, would rest the horses by jamming a log under the wheels to take the weight off the animals.

Harry, like all Ann's kids, looked after his mum. He had the paddocks around her house fenced in with the new wire-netting to stop the rabbits. Phyllis married a butcher from Omeo. And

Albert … well, he was never in any job for long, but he was never out of work, and had too much fun to consider marriage.

Ann chose to remain a widow. Sure, there were suitors. But Ann, for many reasons—secretly, it was the loss of her sweet James—never encouraged any of them. Like many working families, Sunday was roast day. For the Wardells, this included the whole family and Tiger. Tiger was a regular, as Sunday roasts were not part of the Tompkins' household routine. Tiger's dad, the old bastard, had put a stop to those years ago. Every second Sunday, the five boys got together at Ann's house with her family.

However, roast day was different on this Sunday. It was well into the year of 1914, and Ann and the young adult children were talking about the overseas problems they had heard about that might lead to war. The newspapers, including the *Omeo Standard*, were publishing many articles about a conflict that was rumbling on the horizon. It sounded like a big war was looming—a world war—with hints of participation in it by Australia, a new, young nation. This Sunday night, there were many opinions aired in the Wardell house. It was a heated discussion. Ann had strong opinions about her home country, England, and the Empire. Nothing—not even articles about heroism, bravery, and the nasty Hun—would change her mind on the subject. She had no time for the Union Jack; she had heard too many sad stories from descendants of the convicts. Harry and Albert agreed with their mum, but they thought that the papers made some good points. Phyllis, nursing her first baby, agreed with Ann and was emphatic: 'What has England ever done for us? No man of mine is going to fight for them.'

Harry reckoned that was because she didn't want her man, the Omeo butcher, to sign up. Around the Wardell table the talk went back and forth, until they reached Tag. He was discussing riding drills with Sally Sandy. She worked for her dad at the local grocery shop, and spent a lot of time helping Tag with his horses; they were just good mates. Tiger, having finished with Mary Boucher, followed by a brief fling with Judy Ward, was now keen on Sally. Ann, waiting for a break in their conversation, asked Tag what he thought about the upcoming war. He frowned.

'I can't see what Swifts Creek has to do with a damn war. Where the hell is Europe anyway? I still haven't been to Melbourne.'

The lads all joined in; their reactions and opinions varied, but generally, like most younger men they kicked around with, they felt more patriotic about the Crown. All of them had been students in a system that championed the flag, the king, and the home country. The meal ended with the consensus that the bloody British should fight their own bloody battles.

Then came a day, several months after the enthusiastic arguments at the Wardells' house about the war, that made people stop, consider, and work out what they thought.

First, there were reports of a commotion that had to do with the local road-maintenance man, the man who had replaced Fred Wardell as the 'repair bloke'. It had all started with the early arrival of the petrol-driven mail car from down the line, from Bairnsdale. Being earlier than usual didn't raise any eyebrows — it was just on its normal mail-and-passenger run. However, this time, an official-looking man in a smart military-police uniform stepped down from the Hudson motorcar and was greeted by the local policeman. He was holding two strong, well-bred horses. After exchanging several quiet words and a few nods, the military policeman cantered off in the direction of Tongio, leading the other riderless horse. The gossip soon began, and people awaited his return. Two hours later, the official reappeared, trotting towards the Swifts Creek lockup. He was still leading the other horse, but now the local road worker — Werner Gerber was his name — was in the saddle, arrested and handcuffed. It caused quite a stir. Apparently, just as Werner was putting the scoop into the traces on the horse at the Bald Hills camp, the uniformed man had arrived, read out some gibberish, and demanded that Werner give himself up.

This all happened at the same camp where Fred's mutilated body had been found. Like Fred, Werner was a good man, widely respected, and capable of working honestly, without supervision, alone on the road. According to locals, the only difference between the two men was that Fred had been a champion footballer and Werner didn't even play the game — more's the pity. Upon Fred's death, a hole had been left in the Creek's back line.

The arrest of Mr Gerber, a man of German descent, caused a lot of confusion at first. Then it changed to a feeling of unease and friction around the town and district. Several days later, there was a noisy gathering outside the Creek jail one night. Many questions were asked, like, 'What's going on? We know Werner—he's a good bloke.' The answer was silence. The whole episode put the local constabulary in an awkward position. It was all very perplexing.

After all, Mr Gerber was married to a local, they had two young kids, and his younger sister was a teacher at the school. The questions kept coming and, initially, there were few answers. Then, by the weekend, the community got the message: according to the newspapers, the government, the graziers, the Masonic Lodge, and the fine, upstanding citizens in the district, it was because Mr Gerber was a Hun.

Over the following months, there were further arrests made within the shire, so that Mr Gerber became only the first of many Germans who were harassed and finally interned. The war had reached the Creek in more ways than one. At the tender age of eighteen, Tag's life was about to change, dramatically and forever.

CHAPTER TEN

Tag, at eighteen years of age, had filled out to twelve stone, was five foot eight inches tall, and still had red hair. His life was very full. Apart from his mornings at the blacksmith's, he spent the rest of his time with his horses. Footy, cricket, or athletics didn't interest him as they did most young men. He reckoned there was no time for that stuff and, anyhow, he enjoyed his horses more. Now a smoker, he never took off his hat unless a lady walked past, or when he was inside the house. Wearing a hat was a smart thing for the fair-skinned redhead to do; but then again, every man, whatever his complexion, wore a hat. Mill workers, miners, and labourers wore the bowler style, whereas horseriders like drovers and farmhands wore a bigger 'cowboy type' called the Stetson. The brim was usually pulled down over the forehead most of the time, being the only way to keep it on in a strong wind or a gallop. In fact, bald drovers looked strange when they 'dipped their lid' in the presence of a lady, as a bright white dome of skin like a bowl of cream greeted the female as the wearer lifted his hat. It stood out in sharp contrast to the heavily tanned and rugged face.

Tag still lived with his mum. The two of them got along well, and enjoyed each other's company. In the quiet of the evening, they played cards — particularly cribbage — and at least once a week there would be pontoon with the lads at the kitchen table in Ann's freshly painted house. The card games were fun, dominated by laughter, mild swearing and, where possible, cheating. Ann enjoyed preparing a sumptuous meal and cake to follow. She loved all 'her boys', as she called them, and had a similar bond with the lads to the one that Lilly enjoyed. Golly was the card sharp — his parents would have been horrified if they knew that the boys gambled, even if it was only with matches. Tiger told jokes and Chatty, as usual, tried to stir the others up. Tiger always took the bait, and invariably they would end up hurling insults at each other. These were memorable evenings of laughter and companionship in the welcoming Wardell home.

Tag had an infectious smile, which shone through the freckles scattered all over his face, and a wrinkled grin that revealed four missing teeth and a larrikin demeanour. Tag's humour was most evident when he was around his horses. He would play chasey with them, and throw fruit in the air and teach the horses to catch it. He would tease the horses to frustration by hiding bits of apple in his pockets, under his hat, and high in a tree so that the animals had to stand tall on their rear legs to retrieve them.

Tag's generation had grown up in a different era from their parents. They were now Australians. For the first time in the country's history, almost every child had been given the opportunity to attend school, to learn how to read and write, and to learn a little history, literature, and arithmetic. Tag's parents were not so fortunate. When they were growing up, it took wealth to acquire an education, so that pastoralists, businessmen, and the titled dominated universities, governments, and the offices of power. Both Tag's parents could at least read, but that was only because their own children's schooling had encouraged them to hone their skills in both reading and writing. When the Wardells' eldest child, Harold, first attended school, both he and

Fred had developed a wonderful relationship learning together. This was quite common for most adults with children in the late 1800s. The children and the parents learned together. With most adults then able to read, the newspaper became a window—the only window, in fact—to the outside world.

By 1913–14, Australia was emerging with a new-found sense of identity. Suddenly, it was a nation, it had allies, and it had responsibilities on the world scene. Interpreting this to the people of this very young, diverse country was the responsibility of the government and the press. Hence, readers and listeners were learning that there was more to life than attending school, going to work, and being a parent. They had obligations to the mother country, which meant they had a duty to perform—and an honourable one at that. Those with influence were preparing the Australian population for war. For the first time in this tiny nation, a looming military altercation was presenting itself as war on a global scale, between countries that were being described as either intrinsically good or bad. It was a daunting, emotionally stirring prospect. Even in Swifts Creek, people wanted information and news.

The pages of the *Omeo Standard*, which often reprinted articles from the Melbourne and Sydney dailies, reflected the press's none-too-subtle support for the war. Australia, *a good side,* was obliged to take part—no question—and the war was portrayed as a grand adventure, a true test of manhood and sporting prowess. The youth of Australia might miss the experience of a lifetime if they didn't join up. Slowly, the propaganda machine, supported by journalists operating under strict censorship rules once the war was imminent, enticed young men like Tag, Tiger, Chatty, Bucket, and Golly. Yet, even though they were persuaded, they didn't react by rushing to join up. At first, the whole saga fascinated them, but that was all. Their get-togethers at Tag's place now led to animated talks that concerned Ann.

Tiger was the only one considering enlistment. On one particular evening, he was extolling the virtues of joining up to the others. A concerned Ann took him to one side.

'Tiger, I understand you wanting to join up and travel. But what about your mum, the poor woman? People admire what you're doing for her, and she still needs you, pet. All of us need our boys at home.'

'But what about the Hun, Mrs Wardell? That beggar could take over the world.'

'I think you would do better at home. If they attack Australia, then we'll all fight the Hun. But I'm worried, Tiger. War is such a waste of life. I'm sure it's different from what the papers say.'

'Oh, Mrs W, you're just like mum — you two been chin-wagging.'

'No, Tiger, you're special, very special, and I'm worried that if you join up they'll follow you.'

Ann turned and looked at the others.

'They're big blokes now, Mrs. W. They'll make up their own minds, I reckon.'

Tiger wasn't listening, and what hope did Ann have against the persuasive press? She went back to her quilting, and Tiger rejoined his mates. Golly was bragging about his bedroom. On its walls he had stuck articles and pictures about the pending war, as well as maps of where it would take place.

'They reckon the Australians will fight on horses. We're the best horsemen in the world, the paper reckons.'

'Yeah, just like the man from Snowy River, eh?' Chatty said.

Their conversations became more excited. In the other room, Ann rocked and swayed. Her eyes misted over, to the point that she had to put down her sewing and hum softly in an attempt to block out the fever pitch of enthusiasm that accompanied the lads' discussion of the looming war. They weren't even considering the fact that it could involve death, loss, grief, and destruction. This was not part of their idea of battle. But mothers like Ann thought of nothing else ... nothing but unimaginable horror and loss.

Even at home, Tag had one of Norman Lindsay's posters in his bedroom, which many of the young men had collected from a supplement in the Omeo paper. It featured an evil-looking Hun snatching a baby from the arms of a sweet, young European mother, her face distraught with fear and anguish. Like most of the cartoons posted in the *Bulletin*, the Huns, the filthy swine, were monsters. The message, put simply, was to hate the Hun.

Initially, the local response to the pressure to join up for the war was poor. There was no rush to enlist, despite what the press and the government claimed. Nine out of ten eligible young men chose to stay at home and not don the uniform. Throughout much of rural Australia, where most of the men worked for low pay on farms and in the mines, or in small family businesses, this trend continued. Many of the workers were of Irish or convict descent, and had no time for mother England, the establishment, and local law and government. As far as they were concerned, there were people with power and political inlfuence, and there were the workers. In some ways, it was a mirror of the old Dart—them and us.

But the press and the government were persistent. Already, they were hinting that those not willing to enlist weren't patriotic. The pressure, the persuasiveness, the fervour, and the excitement was a powerful mixture in a one-sided argument, and it gradually enticed the doubters. In fact, this subtle grooming had started long ago, at school, since the birth of this tiny nation: young Australians received constant messages about the virtues of the Crown, their allegiance to Britain, and their duty to help the mother country in its hour of need.

Eventually, Tag, along with many young men from the area, volunteered. Those enlisting included Chatty, Bucket, Golly, and Tiger; they all signed up with Tag. Afterwards, they held a small celebratory party. Other enlistees ended up in a drunken revelry that required police to quell the excitement; but, for once, there were no arrests. The press told those joining that they were signing up for a noble cause, and that to volunteer was the ultimate deed a young man could perform for his country. To top it all off, the conflict brewing in the Middle East would be *an adventure*.

The government extolled those already signed up as fine, upstanding young men, doing their country proud, and thanked them for the patriotic passion they showed.

At the start of what was to become World War I, Tag was still in his eighteenth year. At this young age, his successful horse business had already been running for two years. He was a good blacksmith and an outstanding farrier. Sally Sandy was wheedling her way into becoming his girl; the relationship was just starting to take shape. At his age, Tag was more interested in his horses; but some nights, when Sally leaned on him softly and rubbed his leg, bits of his anatomy throbbed with desire. Had it not been for the war, there was a strong chance they would have married when Tag turned twenty-one.

Unbenown to both Ann and Sally, Tag had been ruminating about the war and the idea of signing up for quite a while. Years earlier, as a youngster, he remembered his dad, Fred, talking about the Boer War. Fred had followed the heroic deeds of the brave soldiers in the Boer with interest and a touch of excitement. Nevertheless, even back then, the papers avoided reporting the casualty figures that came with major campaigns. They instead emphasised the small, single-handed heroics of Aussies saving mates and winning on the day, and noted 'what great shots' the Australians were. When Tag was a kid, Fred had read out bits of the paper to him, bragging about how 'the blokes from over here' were better than the British, whatever that meant …

127

However, what finally moved Tag and his mates to sign up was the promise of adventure in a foreign land; it sounded like the opportunity of a lifetime. As well, Sally Sandy and some other young women had started to hint that real men went to war.

First, there was an immediate problem to tackle: it was time for the boys to break the news to the family. All of them except Golly had signed up on an impulse, and hadn't consulted their parents. Admittedly, there had been mumbled hints and dire warnings from their mothers. Now the cold reality of what they had done had to be announced.

It was a hollow, awkward night in the Wardell house that evening. Finally, Ann's precious son spoke up.

'I've signed up, Mum. In fact, we've all signed up.'

That was how Tag broke the news over an evening meal of lamb's fry and bacon. Sally, his mates, and the entire Wardell family were present. His friends had told their parents before they wandered up to Tag's for tea. The silence that prevailed after Tag's announcement hid powerful emotions that were too strong, too painful, and too hard to put into words for Ann. The lid on the boiling, black cast-iron kettle rattled like a warning. Ann stood, clutched the bottom of her apron, and lifted it to the side of the stove. A small gush of water blasted from the spout and hit the top of the stove. Small round rivulets of hissing water bounced and then burst into a puff of steam. Ann had tears in her eyes as she watched the small eruptions — transfixed, consumed, by the burden of being a mother. Then, like a reaction to the snap of a magician's fingers, she blew her nose and turned.

'When are you going, son?'

'In August. We catch the coach to Mossiface, and the Tanjil to Bairnsdale, and then onto Melbourne.'

'We?'

'Yeah — Tiger, Golly, Chatty, and Bucket.'

'Oh.'

It was July. Sadness fell like a Benambra fog on the house that night. Ann busied herself with muttering that she needed to pack a useful kit for Tag to take when he left. After doing the dishes, she swept the house with her new straw broom. Sally chatted gibberish while she wiped the dishes, which was out of character for her. Sally was a sensible young woman. Now, as the reality set in, she was suddenly doubtful about the boys leaving: that was confusing for her. Perhaps a flashing thought of Tag, or any of those young men, dead on a battlefield somewhere made her feel uneasy. Then again, by all accounts, it was an honourable way to die: the ultimate sacrifice. That was what the politicians and the papers had said about the Boer War.

Tag had encouraged Albert, his brother, to come home and, with the help of Sally and Ann, run his horse business. Jack Murey was by now a qualified blacksmith, and Sid had employed two new apprentices. Both were fifteen, fresh from the Tongio West School.

On the day of the local volunteers' departure, there was a large gathering out the front of the Swifts Creek Post Office. A reporter from the local paper was there, along with some shire dignitaries, the families, and onlookers. All of them were dressed up. The Elliots, proud of their son Greg, huddled together and said several prayers for him and the other boys. After saying a loud 'Amen', they shared their son around like a new puppy. He went from one hug to another, looking more bewildered than excited. Bucket's family was quite proud, although his dad was at a loss as to how to replace his son on the farm. Tom had a big grin on his face one moment, and then tears the next. The crowd confused him completely. It was too much. Before he arrived at the send-off, no amount of explanation could satisfy his concern or distress at the thought of losing his other favourite human being, Bucket. Tom was devastated. Added to this, the revelation that all the other boys who had been good to him were leaving also left him frightened. Now what was going on? People were cheering and clapping. Tom joined in. He was happy.

Then there was Tiger. He stood alone. His mum was too distressed to attend after he had said his goodbye to her earlier. He also realised that he would be a stuttering mess if he were required to talk. On occasions like this, Tiger preferred being alone. Finally, there was Chatty. He was excited, but confused by his mum having spent the night outside sitting in the open, sobbing. She had lit a small fire, and simply sat, staring at the flames for hours, while singing and tapping two sticks together. When Chatty asked her about the ritual, Lilly talked about smoking his spirit, to protect it on its journey. The answer confused her son. Yet, standing next to the mail car, stirred and giggling with excitement in his youthful way, Chatty parrotted the wisdom of the newspapers to his sweet mum, telling her of the fun it would be.

'I'll get to England with a bit of luck, mum.'

His dad wasn't there; he was busy. They had shaken hands earlier. Like the dairy farms, the factory operated every day of the year.

Tag shook Albert's hand, kissed Sally on the cheek, briefly hugged his mum, and then joined his four other mates and headed towards the mail car. There were no theatrics, tears, or flag waving—just, 'Be seein' ya.'

The night before, there had been a celebration that included a lot of beer, singing, and bawdy yarns. Tag, along with the others, had 'bloody disgraced himself, well and truly'. He still smelt and looked terrible. Ann was quiet and reserved, and ached with confused thoughts of support and mixed feelings towards her Tag. The vagaries of why her son was going … it was all too much to take in. Poor, sweet Lilly was distraught, and her tears flowed uncontrollably as she hugged each young man in turn several times. It moved the others to see such an emotional display. It also shook poor Tom, Bucket's brother. When Lilly realised this, her heart went out to him. Tom was very confused; so was Mrs Banks, as she was the only parent there who totally supported what the boys were doing.

The lads mounted the step and jammed into the back seat of the open mail car. The crowd cheered briefly, and a photograph was taken. Smiles predominated; but above it all could be heard the sobbing gasps of simple Tom Banks. Bucket, flabbergasted with Tom's mixture of bewildered cheering and tears, leaned out the window and growled at him.

'For Gawd's sake, stop blubbering, Tom. We'll be back before you know it.'

Golly's dad glared when he heard the blasphemous remark. A goggled driver, who looked as if he should have been flying an airplane rather than driving a motor car, cranked the engine. He shoved the handle downwards vigorously, and it started first time. The crowd stood back a step, dogs barked, a horse shied, and kids started clapping. Ann looked around, hoping that the rest of her family would turn up. Tag's older brother Harry wasn't there; he had too many wood orders to fill. Phyllis was too busy with a new family, which was understandable. The war would be 'just a quick affair' — that was the consensus being talked up already by the press. The mail-car engine, now running smoothly, suddenly revved up, and a plume of blue smoke filled the air. The families stood back even further. The final sack of mail from the post office was thrown in the back, and the mail car was ready to leave Swifts Creek for Bruthen. Just as they were about to drive off, Ann handed Tag a small parcel, reluctantly. It was one of her most treasured possessions.

The gearbox grated and the engine revved up. The vehicle jerked and bumped until a slow, uniform momentum and less jerking prevailed. Another, higher gear crashed into place, and the mail car gathered speed. The waving was frantic, and the chooks in front of the pub scattered. Tag had done the trip once before with his mum in a horse-drawn coach. He was only a baby then, so this was all new to him. The motorised vehicle, a big seven-seater car with a large box and parcel rack on the rear end to carry mail and luggage, swayed down the main street. It had a petrol engine that scared horses and other animals as it chugged past. Tag saw a spare seat in the front; he jumped over next to the driver who, squinting through semi-fogged goggles, was gripping the steering wheel with a grim determination. But once the vehicle gained a steady momentum, he turned to Tag with a grin; immediately, a conversation about horses started up. This usually happened to Tag: people respected his ability.

'Ya know that bloody piebald ya shod? He's a different horse now. Good horse, easy to handle. We use him on the mail run now with the coach out to Glen Wills. Tho' I still got a scar on me arse where the blighter bit me a coupla years ago!'

Tag laughed heartily, although he could hardly hear the driver over the roar of the engine, the groan of the gearbox, and the high-pitched whine of the differential. It was a pleasant, exciting trip. The mail car got up to speeds of thirty-five miles an hour on some short strips. Mostly it was much slower, though, as the road was in a bad state; it would take a lot more than men with a shovel or a horse and scoop to repair the damage these new vehicles were doing to the road. The young lads pointed, yelled, giggled, and shouted.

The dirt road followed the Tambo River most of the way until it meandered off into the dry bush, disturbing a few roos and many a rabbit. Apart from Ensay and Tambo Crossing, there weren't many settlements in this rugged part of the journey. Then the vehicle drove out of the mountainous bush and into the open flats that announced their arrival at the town of Bruthen. From there, it was only a small distance from where they would transfer to a boat.

The jetty at Mossiface was exciting. The lads sat and watched as wheelbarrows used to load coal onto the vessel were rushed up and down the decking. Then two young boys pulled small handcarts with tee-shaped handles over the rattling planks of the busy jetty as the boat was loaded with the mail and luggage. The new passengers received gruff orders from the captain of the vessel, who was attired in a uniform and a peaked cap. He smoked a pipe, and looked very important. Tickets were checked, and then another man in uniform rang a bell, announcing to everyone who wasn't a passenger to stand clear, as the boat was about to cast off. He proceeded to rattle off the numerous names of places where the boat would be stopping before it reached Bairnsdale. This would be the first ride on a passenger boat for the lads from Swifts Creek. Not that there weren't opportunities for a boat ride in the Omeo shire — the boys had often promised themselves that they would go up to Lake Omeo at Benambra and have a row in a dinghy, but had never gotten around to it.

The young men clambered to the front of the *T.S. Tanjil*. It chugged over the calm, wide waters, disturbing various ducks, swans, and cormorants. Then, skidding across the water, a pelican landed and surged to a halt. The boys were impressed. New bird life, broad waters, and adventure: this was exhilarating. The wooden boat chugged along the river and passed by beautiful flats and undulating hills. Finally, it reached the open water and the magnificent Gippsland Lakes. With waves chopping at the bow, the boat seemed smaller in this broad expanse of water. The small, attractive boat then headed to the mouth of the beautiful Mitchell River; an hour later, after two brief stops, it reached the jetty at Bairnsdale, just near the tannery. The boys walked along the gravel road that led to the large rural township. There were motorcars everywhere.

They slept overnight in a pub, and joined another thirty-five men at the railway station early the next morning. The train trip was like a party. The young men carried alcohol on board, as well as cards and enthusiasm. It was already true of these young Australians that, if you put them together in a situation like this, without supervision or restrictions, they always had a good time — a bloody good time.

The five young lads from Swifts Creek were together; that was important to them. Back home, the next edition of the *Omeo Standard* proudly printed the names of those from each town who had signed up and would be travelling to Melbourne that week. After a preamble about local support and pride, it provided a long list of names, including:

Reginald Tompkins: son of Tom and Molly (a worker at the butter factory).
Charlie Bills: son of Bill and Lilly from the butter factory.
Greg Elliot: the baker's boy, son of William and Bertha.
Andy Banks: the middle son of Matilda and Bill, the local milkman and dairy farmer.
Tag Wardell: blacksmith son of Ann and Fred (Dec.).

The paper went on. These fine, upstanding young men were all from Omeo and the surrounding districts, and were about to do their country proud. An article on the successful call-up included a section mentioning the five lads from Swifts Creek. The reporter who wrote the article noted that:

the lads in fact had talked earlier in the year about going to the war together. Because they all liked horses and were very involved with them, they wanted to join some sort of horse mob, as Greg Elliot put it. Their work around Swifts Creek saw them regularly involved with horses.

It was a large article covering almost half a page.

It was true. The boys—particularly Tag and Bucket—worked with horses on a daily basis. Bucket, who used the horses in harness on his milk run, was the only young man who helped Tag with his horses; the rest were women. Of late, many of the horses entrusted to Tag had been rejected racehorses, particularly from Omeo, a popular race venue that held meetings twice a week. With other handlers, these horses were the sole domain of men. However, Tag preferred to use women to work in the rehabilitation of his horses. The young women who rode them were Sally Sandy, Megan Crisp, Daphne Adams, and Beth Boucher. All worked after school and on Saturdays. His best worker, and no doubt the best with a rogue horse, was Sally, Tag's mate. Sally Sandy, if the truth were known, was probably one of the best 'horsemen' in the district. She had to be called a horseman, because there was no other word for it.

CHAPTER ELEVEN

The vast army camp was located at Broadmeadows, just twenty-five minutes from Melbourne by train, in an area of countryside made up of paddocks with poor soil and no timber. A city of pointed, circus-like army tents now dominated the landscape. Upon arriving at Broadmeadows station, the lads were told curtly which part to move to: 'Gippsland blokes, down that bloody end.' Looking out from the platform, they could see, apart from many tents, men marching everywhere. Soon, to the tune of barked orders, the new arrivals were lined up on the platform and marched to an official area. The paperwork and signing-up formalities were brief, and finished with the statement, 'You're in the army now.'

At the end of their first day, having been constantly screamed at for their lack of discipline and coordination, the lads sat down for a meal of crude, cold army food. Then, issued with uniforms, the men from the Omeo district found themselves in the tents that had been set aside for men with experience in dealing with horses. Their training would be different from the other new recruits'. After fulfilling the initial requirements of marching and rudimentary drill, the remainder of their training, they were informed bluntly, would involve horses. The whole day had been organised chaos.

It was a rude awakening for Tag and his mates from the Omeo shire. That night, they sat in their tent and said very little. Too much was happening at once; it didn't feel special, or as though they had signed up to a great adventure. Already, they had been abused, insulted, physically shoved into a straight line, and made to feel embarrassed in front of others. The nicest term they had heard used to describe them was, 'You're nothing but a dopey, dingo-eating pack a' drongos.'

Tiger summed up the general state of things: 'Just like being 'ome with the old man—nothing ya do is good enough. Bastards.'

Each tent had a hurricane lamp. Golly trimmed the wick of theirs and filled it with kerosene; all lamps had to be out by ten o'clock each night. A straw-filled palliasse on the dirt floor in the tent, along with three blankets and no sheets, was their new bed, apparently. This would be their home for the next few weeks. A tall brute of a soldier informed them that all ablutions and toilet needs were to be carried out in an area set aside near the west gate. It was an open-air compound that offered no privacy, and the wash and toilet section looked like a long horse trough. Chatty, who had much of his mother's dark skin, didn't go near the long washbasins for two days. He was one of only a handful of dark-skinned lads.

Their tent held six blokes—the sixth was a fellow from Corryong, just over the hill from Benambra. The boys inspected the strange uniforms and webbing they had been issued with, and were quite surprised when they opened a dark-green tin with an arrow stencilled on the top. It contained soap, shaving gear, foot and flea powder (recommended for lice also), and a sizeable issue of tobacco and papers in its own smaller tin. There were matches and a small candle. It was probably the only highlight of their first week.

Tag struggled. It wasn't until the eighth night that he

remembered — he had forgotten or been too busy to keep in mind the very special gift that his mum had handed him on the day they left. He had tucked it in his swag as they hopped into the mail car, and had promptly forgotten it was there. For the first time, he relaxed a little and thought about writing a letter home. This was encouraged by the army. He reached into his swag and pulled out the satchel that held some paper and a pencil. Initially, he felt the odd shape, which was small and square, and slowly undid the string that held the brown paper-wrapped parcel. Inside, he found two books and two pencils. The first book was new, never used—it had faint ruled lines. The second book stunned Tag into a silence that was quickly noticed by the others. Finally, Golly spoke.

'What is it, mate?'

'It's a diary—me Dad's diary … I never knew.'

Tag looked away. He wanted to be alone, but there was nowhere to go. Tiger guessed that something was powerfully wrong.

'Let's go outside and try this new tobacco, fellas. It smells good.'

Tag flicked through the thick diary. There was the odd page torn out, which he knew Ann would have done. He turned to the first page. The handwriting was simple and crude. It would have copped a tongue-lashing at school—but Fred had never attended a school. He had learned to write with Harold and Albert. The first page started:

This is me third diary. I have to start a new one on account of the death of sweet James … it was terrible. Part of me heart was lowered into that grave with me young James. Just one softer warm cuddle would have been enough to get me threw that day. Me poor Ann, who would want to be a mother, I didn't know what to say. I feel useless sometimes. Bloody useless!

Tag's heart ached; his whole being wanted to go home to his mum. He couldn't read any more. As he lent forward on his bed to place the diary in his pack, a piece of paper flipped and drifted to the ground. He picked it up, unfolded the single page, and read:

My dear Tag

Write to me when you can. Please keep a diary. Through your Dad's diary, I have learned that he was a truly remarkable man.

Love
Your Mother

Tag reached for the new blank book. He made his first entry:

Today is my first entry into my diary. Thank you Mum for Dad's diary. Thanks dad for writing it.

The next morning, they were screamed out of bed by a big bully with a fiery red moustache. His first words were, 'Get ya arse down to the mess and be back here in twenty-five minutes — fed and clothed, ya ugly pack a' bastards.'

The food was cold porridge, and a brew. The cup of tea was most welcome. Later that night, Tiger reckoned the breakfast had been the best part of the day. He coped better than the others did with the endless shouting and swearing—it was one of the few benefits that he could directly thank his old man for. He rallied and helped the others.

The next week seemed a relentless repetition of endless abuse, marching, and more marching and rifle familiarisation. Being from the bush, Tag and his mates were familiar with rifles. But Golly, trying to be polite and offering such advice to the sergeant, only brought abuse upon himself.

'Okay, smart-arse, see if ya can run around the paddock with it over ya friggin' head!'

Poor Golly: of all the lads, he had to learn quickly. It didn't pay to be polite. Uttering words like 'gosh' or 'gee whiz' only singled him out with both the regular soldiers and the instructors. His mates kept quiet, having realised that was how things were and would be. In the ninth week, though, the routine changed. Now allocated horses, the lads spent most mornings on horse work. Finally, the lads had their wish: they had joined a light horse squadron.

Tag wrote only one letter home during his initial training. He either didn't have the time to write any more, or was too pre-occupied with all the goings-on when they were given their first pay and leave. The lads, taken with the aura of Melbourne town, were gobsmacked. Wherever they looked, there were pubs, shops, winking women, and crowds standing on street corners waiting for a policeman to signal when they could walk across. Down the road at St Kilda, a unique fun parlour called Luna Park, which was only two years old, already boasted huge crowds. The young men from the high country were dumbstruck by it.

Broadmeadows was only a short train-trip from Melbourne, the capital of Victoria, so selected pubs quickly became meeting places. Soon, young women in for a good time and a few shillings frequented the bar doors and lounges. Tiger and Chatty were in their element. On their second official leave, having worked out where the 'hot' spots were located, the two lads encouraged Golly to let his hair down. Golly, drunk after his first two beers, found himself led upstairs; when he came back he was grinning, in love and guilty all at the same time. Bucket and Tag went to the races—Bucket to bet, Tag to admire the horses. Both had their full share of grog, but there were no women at the track. Tag did well with the bookies, and sent Ann ten quid in a letter home that simply said, 'Had a bit of luck, Mum.'

Both Ann and Sally wrote to Tag regularly. One of Ann's letters brought news of the arrests of more foreigners around the shire and throughout Gippsland. As well, there were the names of a smattering of young men who had signed up, including the Faithfull boys, Jack Campbell from Ensay, and other well-known lads in the district. Tag wrote in his diary every day when he was in camp. Already, the Melbourne papers were trumpeting a coming glorious victory over the Hun, using language that was more colourful than that of a coach of a winning footy team. The words were emotional and enticing, and rallied the nation. Tag and his mates looked forward eagerly to completing their training, having their final leave, and taking their part in the conflict.

On 6 October 1914, Tag's diary read:

Melbourne is great, real big. Been to the races on leave, had some luck. As we walk around in uniform, strangers come up and say 'Good show, good onya' and stuff. Still can't work out that business with the road worker at home, Mr Gerber, I reckon the good Germans must have left that country and come out here, don't you think? Still can't work out why they arrested him. He's a good bloke. Ask anyone.

The remainder of their training was well organised and strict; it shaped the men into a tight team. When they finally marched out, mounted on their horses, they beamed with pride and soaked up the atmosphere, which was mainly produced by a large army band and a dais that held a very senior army person covered in medals and looking very important. Then it was off for a final leave in Melbourne, which would allow the boys to blow their last accumulated pay on endless beer and good times. They rushed for the station after the parade.

On their final parade, they were also told that they would

be sailing to London. Their orders to report to the docks in Melbourne were issued on the same day.

THE LADS ARRIVED early dockside, chatting as they looked in awe at all the huge ships. There was no way that were they going to miss this adventure. Their ship, the *Wiltshire*, steamed out of Melbourne on 19 October 1914. The men were excited, but the horses, secured in stalls just below the deck, were very unsettled. It was cramped, and strange creaks and noises spooked the animals for the first few days. Tag was horrified by the prospect of them having to stay in their stalls the entire time they were at sea. He suggested to an army sergeant that they put straw mats along alley walks and long passageways, and lead the horses a bit—anywhere, in fact—to ensure that they got some exercise. The sergeant ignored his request. As Tag had guessed, many of the animals fretted, scoured, and played up in their stalls. He became part of a team that had to attend to bad cuts and gashes caused by the horses rearing. Six badly injured horses were shot and tossed overboard before the ship reached the heads.

The Wiltshire went via King George Sound, where it joined a fleet of fifty vessels that carried over 30,000 men and 12,000 horses bound for the war. Tag was disgusted that the horses weren't let out for a day or two, ridden, groomed, or even led around the docks. Again, he asked the sergeant. Again, no luck.

On 1 November 1914, the fleet left West Australian waters bound for England, or that's what the troops had been told. Suddenly, a new course was announced—and Egypt became the destination. Back in Australia, as the troops left, one of the newspapers reported in large bold letters on the front page: 'Off On A Great Adventure.'

In Tag's opinion, every episode of his life since joining up had been one adventure after another. His only complaint had been about the way the horses were treated. He had his mates, a total different way of life from Swifts Creek, and hearty meals; and he'd made visits to exciting places like Melbourne, with its tall buildings and too many people, its trams, its trains, its busy streets, and the zoo. He'd bragged about all these things in a letter home to the family. There'd been so much to see, to do, to talk about, and they were even doing some army training.

Even the crowded boat trip was fun. The command had set in place a rigorous exercise and sporting regime on the long, slow, ocean-going journey. There was, however, one strange order that came down from the top that confused the Aussie soldiers:

The following strict disciplinary measures are in place:

Every soldier will receive a Brown's diary. One entry a day permitted.

No private diaries—offenders will be charged.

Where possible, all ranks will learn semaphore.

The army then issued every soldier with the designated Brown's diary, which was the size of a playing card. Barely one sentence would fit in the designated space for each day; every page represented a week.

That afternoon, Tag visited the quartermaster's store (known as the Q-store), where he got hold of some strong cotton and a small piece of canvas. He then set to work sewing a pocket big enough to hide the two diaries in the bottom of his backpack. He intended to keep his diary.

On board the ship, there were lectures on army matters every day. Once, a brief talk was given on the perils of venereal disease that used a strange language with lots of big words like 'genitalia', but it went over the heads of most of the troops. Tiger reckoned that 'copulate' was what a copper's wife said to him if he was late for tea.

The ship had been at sea for several days when it first experienced foul weather. The horses were petrified, and suddenly there was a problem of rearing horses, severe cuts, and the odd horse dying from what appeared to be stress, but the army did nothing. On the third day of the inclement weather, Tag stormed back into his quarters and blasted at Tiger, 'They've got no friggin' idea. They expect the poor bloody horses to obey orders like bloody soldiers.'

Frustrated by the treatment meted out to the horses, Tag spoke to several of the senior handlers, but it made no difference. So he went higher up. The result was that Tag's attempt to exert his equine knowledge on one of the boss horse handlers met with a full disciplinary backlash from the army: he was given extra kitchen duties for being insubordinate. A sergeant with years of experience with men, but not a lot with horses, took an immediate dislike to Tag. He was severely dressed down when told of his extra duties. Unfortunately, the army didn't tolerate independent thinking—particularly from young country hicks with no rank or education, who had grass growing out of their ears and their arses.

Tag was furious, as most of the horses continued to display fear, and refused to stand quietly in their stalls. The army's answer was simple: they fed and watered them, but left the animals locked up, and otherwise ignored them. The horses would often fret, shake, and rear in the stalls. Many started to scour and pass soup-like manure—a sign of stress common in any animal, including humans. The boss handler, an army sergeant, would usually instruct his men to solve the problem by using either force or a blindfold. The result was that the petrified animal would thrash its legs and hooves while the handler used harsh language and a whip to persuade the frightened animal to settle. It reminded Tag of Bill the blacksmith when he had first started his apprenticeship with him.

'And these blokes are supposed to know about horses — what bullshit,' was how he described it to Tiger.

Again, Tag returned to the stalls and, again, politely suggested to the senior sergeant that perhaps they should try another way. Yet again, an intense argument ensued. Tag was dressed down for insubordination, brought before his immediate commanding officer, Major Brent, and put under guard. Tag, a private soldier, was well out of order. The army wasn't a place for discussions; orders were there to be obeyed. He had insulted Sergeant Bond, a career man in the army, who had rank and was in charge of the horses. Tag soon regretted his outburst. The major gave Sergeant Bond two alternatives: he could have Tag charged, lose a day's pay, and put on extra duties; or he and Tag could sort it out in the boxing ring. Boxing was a good form of entertainment and discipline in the army; as they said, 'It sorted the men from the boys.'

For decades in the army, many disputes had been resolved in the boxing ring. It suited the organisation's hidden agenda to promote violence. The fact that the sergeant was given the choice also predicted the result: in the army, most boxing disputes were foregone conclusions before the first blow was landed. By chance, Sergeant Bond, a heavier, fitter-looking man, had a reputation as a champion boxer. Naturally, he chose the ring as his method of inflicting punishment on Tag. Who could argue with that logic?

With the time for the fight declared, a notice was posted on the main bulletin board, and the word soon got around. The soldiers eagerly awaited the event — the boxing match would be fun, and it would provide a distraction from endless exercise, and a chance for a wager or two. The blokes in Tag's platoon offered him endless advice and encouragement. This didn't give Tag much heart, though; he thought he was in for a thrashing.

All the Light Horse boys had gathered. The fight had created a lot of interest. Sergeant Bond, who was considered a bully and a brainless bastard, wasn't a popular leader with the troops. The blokes wanted his block knocked off.

Bond guessed as much, and couldn't have cared less — he had rank, he was in total control, and he was keen to show the scum 'just who was in charge around here'. Orders were to be obeyed and not questioned.

Tag received pats on the back as he pushed his way through the crowded room that was abuzz with excitement. He looked odd, with his white torso and bronzed arms and face. Words of encouragement echoed around the large room, but most of them were simply rash comments aimed at getting right up the noses of those with rank.

'Slaughter the ugly prick, mate.'

'Smash his flam'n face in, eh!'

That brought cheers and laughter. Then Tag saw Chatty, who spoke to him just before he entered the ring.

'At least leave a few bruises on 'im, mate.'

'Bite the bastard if ya can,' added Bucket, thumping Tag on the shoulder.

'Bite his friggin' ear awf!'

The boys had had a few too many. The contestants entered the ring. Bond had his own personal gloves, gown, and boots, and looked like a pro. Tag looked like a country bumpkin. He had on a pair of army boots, no socks, and a huge pair of army shorts rolled up and held in place by a piece of rope. However, the stark difference between the two men was Tag's skin. It normally looked as white as snow; but now, as he pushed through the crowd, it looked anaemic, and almost glowed. Years back, Tag had given boxing a try at school. His mates had considered him hopeless at it.

Tiger was in Tag's corner. Chatty, Bucket, and Golly were his close and handy assistants. Between them, they had no idea how to fight within the rules, how long the rounds were, and what tactics to employ. They all looked very worried. Certainly, the last thing that Tag wanted to see as he approached Tiger was the forlorn look on his face. Tiger glanced to the other corner where a trainer was giving endless instructions and geeing up Sergeant Bond, who was hopping and prancing about, punching the air and making hissing noises. Unsure as to what to say, Tiger leaned over to Tag and said, 'Good luck, mate.'

Tag was flabbergasted. '"Good luck"? Is that all you can bloody well say?'

A sailor rang the hand-held bell vigorously. The two combatants shook hands, and pranced around the ring. It was an eight-round bout. Tag had pretty poor odds with the bookies: five to one was quoted for a knockout by Bondy, and ten to one for a win by Bondy. However, the crowd were obviously on Tag's side when it came to the cheering. The first time he made a half-hearted effort to plant one on Bondy, the mob roared its approval. Bondy, though, looked the part. He feinted straight punches, and ducked and weaved while punching Tag with scoring jabs. Early on in the first round, he dropped his guard, tempting Tag to have a go. Then, twenty-five seconds into the round, Tag was on the canvas, down for the count. Bond had hit him with a stunning blow to the side of the head. Tag got up gingerly, and did all he could to avoid a thumping from his taller, heavier opponent.

The bell rang; fortunately, Tag had only received two nasty punches. He turned to see where Tiger was, and wandered back to his corner with a bewildered look. Tiger, Bucket, Chatty, and Golly were offering advice—Tag appeared to have four trainers. This was against the rules, but no one had noticed. Golly was really worried. Tiger, who just shook his head, finally suggested, 'Ya gotta cover up, mate. Wear the bastard out. He's not strong enough for five rounds, let alone eight. I reckon he's soft, couldn't do a decent day's work. Just let him hit ya!'

It was quite a speech, for Tiger.

'Hell!' said Tag. 'Easy for you, mate, just sitting there sucking on a blimey fag.'

The bell sounded. Bondy pranced out, with hardly a bead of sweat on his brow, and a smirk on his dial. Tag covered up, his hands protecting his face, and his elbows pressed tightly against his chest. Bond teased him with a few jabs and dances, again lowering his arms by his side and beckoning Tag to 'Have a go, ya mug!'

However, Tag trusted Tiger, a good boxer in his own right. Tiger hadn't had many wins in the ring; but, around camp, well, you didn't mess with Tiger. Already, he'd had two stoushes since joining the army — one of which he'd taken on to stick up for Chatty, his dark mate. The word had soon got around that Tiger was tough. 'Watch 'im,' a solder had been overheard to say. 'He's as tough as nails, and fights like a mongrel dog.'

By the end of the third round, Sergeant Bond was already panting heavily, and Tag had a bad cut to one eye and a swollen lip. So far, Tag had taken the beating very well. What few of the men on board realised about this quiet, shy redhead was that he had mastered a profession before joining the army that had led to his muscles being as tough as iron. Tag the blacksmith had spent hours swinging a ten-pound hammer. This alone had produced small, tight, well-proportioned arms that were rock-hard. Five rounds of pounding from an ex-bank clerk, now a sergeant with boxing skills, were never going to hurt Tag's arms.

Finally, Tiger intervened. His advice before the start of the sixth round was simple.

Not a lot of cheering came from the officers and other ranks when, halfway through the round, Tag lent forward and, with the force of a sledgehammer, drove Sergeant Bond's weary chin vertically towards the cabin roof. The rest of the room erupted into an uproar never before heard on the ship. The men jumped, yelled, and chanted. They clapped with their hands above their heads, and no amount of shouting from a senior staff member could calm them down. It was the perfect morale-booster.

It was Tiger who had given the signal to sink in an uppercut. That had been his message to Tag: 'Wait, I'll give ya a signal next time the smart-arse drops 'is arms. Be quick, and thump the prick under the chin as 'ard as ya can!'

At that instant, the crowd was stunned. In fact, there was silence until the scene sunk in; then came the almighty roar. Most of them had lost their dough—but, stuff it, this was a terrific result. 'Up yours, army!' was the chant that started and continued for some time, sounding for all the world like the crowd at a football grand final at the Melbourne Cricket Ground.

Tag returned to his corner. Tiger was cool and calm, and glowed with pride. Golly burst into tears briefly. And Chatty was bragging loudly to anybody who would listen that the four of them had all put their money on Tag.

Bucket had a smoke rolled and lit, ready for his mate when Tag collapsed onto his stool. After a lot of towel-flapping and his face being doused with a cold bucket of salt water, Bondy finally staggered to his feet, walked slowly over, and shook Tag's hand. Then he offered a painful smile and said, 'Let's talk about these bloody horses, ya tough little bastard.'

When the fighters left the ring, the crowd clapped with appreciation—of Tag for his strength, and of Bondy, who had at last discovered what common sense meant. It took ages for the reaction to the fight to simmer down; even the next morning at breakfast, Tag found himself cheered heartily when he walked into the mess. The news had already spread via semaphore and signals to the other vessels in the fleet. Although the details were sketchy and slightly confusing, the gist of the message was understood: young Tag was a hero. Not so, the signallers—all of them had relayed the news illegally, without orders, and enjoyed doing it. In fact, it was only when others in the fleet requested more information that the signallers on Tag's ship were caught. Fortunately, they suffered only mild repercussions.

So it came to pass that Tag gained respect for several reasons—mainly, of course, because he had punched Bondy's lights out. This was a dubious honour in Tag's mind, though, because he reckoned it was Tiger who had won. However, in time, it was the horses that really won, because Tag quickly gained a different kind of respect: the hierarchy acknowledged him as an expert with horses. From then on, Sergeant Bond referred to Tag whenever horses became distressed, needed a new routine, or were difficult to handle. Given this rare opportunity to show his depth of special knowledge, Tag's career as a rifleman with the Light Horse was about to end. By now, he had a special title: 'Senior horse handler' (with no rank, or extra pay, attached—naturally).

Consequently, the horses now got a lot more attention from all their handlers on the ship. They sorely needed it, because these Walers were like frightened little children. Their fear was of the unknown. On board, the earth moved under their feet, and it made strange protesting sounds. Where was the familiar grass, and the sun? Even horrible things like barbed-wire fences were missing. The movement of the ship petrified the horses. The groans and grinding of the metal walls and floors were strange sounds they'd never heard in the paddocks around Broadmeadows and other training grounds. Creaking doors with large locks on them that had to be bashed shut sounded like a rifle shot. To the horses, the boat trip wasn't an adventure—it was an ordeal, and they turned to their handlers for affection, calm, reassurance, and strength. The last thing a horse needed in this environment was a bloody blindfold or a flogging with a switch. It frustrated Tag that blokes like Sergeant Bond (now called Chesty Bond) couldn't see this. It resulted in blokes like

Chesty and many others coming to think the world of this quiet, young man. To them, Tag's ideas appeared unique; and then, after they were implemented, they seemed obvious.

Tag said little. He led by example. Like Bill and Sid years before, it was common to see men standing, shaking their heads in admiration, while watching Tag calm a horse or lead it through a narrow steel doorway during an exercise routine. By now, almost all the animals participated in a routine that required the horse to walk along a zigzag of passageways and decks during its morning fitness program. The horse had priority during that hour; men stepped back or tried to avoid the walk area. Once back in the cramped stalls, every horse was brushed, its mane and tail was combed, and talking to it was encouraged. Tag's boxing reputation quickly faded, but his title of horse handler was never questioned.

However, for Tag, the biggest problem was that some of the horses refused to lie down and rest in their cramped stalls. Admittedly, only a few horses were reluctant, but it wasn't until Tag actually slept alongside one highly strung Waler that the horse relented and laid down. Nevertheless, for all the attention now devoted to them, over two hundred horses were lost before the convoy reached its destination, Egypt. Certainly, the initial losses at the beginning of the journey had taken the highest toll. Tag noted that the few that died after those early deaths were highly strung, very nervy and, according to Tag, 'should never have been put on the bloody ship anyway'.

CHAPTER TWELVE

The voyage was almost over. The troops, now allowed on deck, wallowed in the air and sunshine. Egypt was only a day away. Surprisingly enough, the first thing that impressed the boys from East Gippsland was the mighty Nile River. The ship entered where the Nile ended its long journey and drifted into the sea. At its mouth was a huge silt jetty similar to the one found at the end of the Mitchell River just south of Bairnsdale. That, though, was where the comparisons ended—the mouth of the Nile was so wide that it looked like an ocean. Crammed together leaning on rails, the boys from the Omeo shire were in awe. They laughed, pointed, and all talked at once, soaking up the fresh, salty air and warm, tropical weather. Primitive craft with triangular sails busied themselves along this magnificent waterway, their owners all wearing blankets and sheet-type clothes—at least, that's how Tag described them in his letter home. The ship steamed further up the river. The sight of huge, ancient buildings and primitive dwellings led to talk among the boys of them coming back to visit this beautiful place if the opportunity arose. At last, the ship docked at Alexandria.

The soldiers had to be goaded by abuse, shouts, and threats similar to those they had first received when they joined the army to set up their first camp. The heat, biting insects, sunburn, and searing winds all took their toll. Finally, three days after disembarking, with the horses settled, and the tents organised and allocated, order prevailed. Their first camp at Alexandria, located close to the mighty Nile River, was a challenge. The heat they had enjoyed towards the end of their journey on the ship was now oppressive and overbearing; there was no sea breeze on land. What amazed the visitors most was the desert at the backdoor to their camp. There were abrupt changes in the landscape from the river to the camp. First, there were small green flats and then, behind the camp, desert. It stretched inland as far as the eye could see.

Egypt was another world to the young Australians. It was a circus, a party, and an explosion of history all rolled into one. The freedom to move around was most enjoyable after the cramped conditions of the ship. What's more, the lads from the Omeo area were still together. It was fortunate that they were part of the Light Horse and that Tag had a high reputation. During the trip over, he had convinced the authorities that each company should have the same horses, right down to a horse permanently allocated to its rider or soldier.

With the camp constructed and the animals organised, the army turned to a program of drills and training to occupy the troops. However, the Aussie boys were very toey, having been locked up for such a long period on a ship. On the first night, naturally, a large contingent of soldiers went absent without leave. This was followed by a swift, blunt reaction from the British command, who were in overall control of the Australian contingent. The British were disgusted by the Australians' behaviour. Quickly, the Aussie soldiers gained the reputation of being 'an unruly rabble'. When rounded up by the British military police and charged, further insult was added to injury when the Aussie blokes threw hilarious salutes and some even dared to argue their case: 'Come on, hell, we'd been at sea for ages.'

'Even the horses'd started to look pretty,' Golly reckoned. Golly had absconded with his mates, gotten terribly drunk on some vile spirit, and had fallen asleep in a ditch. Chatty and Bucket were charged with being in a state 'unbecoming to His Majesty, and a disgrace to the uniform'. Whatever that meant. Tiger and Tag were placed on a more serious charge. Tiger had decked a British corporal, and Tag had flogged his fancy hat—very serious stuff. The British, initially shocked at this appalling lack of discipline, decided they would re-shape these colonial larrikins, and show them who was in charge of this outfit. How naive: the Australian troops continued to abscond, snuck grog to their mates in the slammer, continued to throw half-hearted salutes, and carried out every childish prank they could think of.

After three frustrating days, the British charted a new direction. At the command posts of every Australian company headquarters, the following directive was posted: 'All charges will be dropped; however, in future, severe penalties will be imposed for any misdemeanours.'

The Brits had no choice, really: about 60 per cent of the ranks were on charge, which would have been a nightmare to deal with. However, being true Aussies, the boys ignored this directive as well. The fun continued. Initially, the British command tried endless drills, training, and exercises with pretend-enemy forces. But the Aussie troops were bored; they were learning nothing new. They wanted adventure—any adventure. The Christmas celebrations relieved some of the repetitiveness, but the Australians wanted action—a bit of fun, and not the sort that the historians recorded.

After the Christmas break, the army got the message, and granted an extended leave of several days. Excitement was in the air. This would be the lads' first real leave in a foreign land. The troops were abuzz with eagerness and anticipation as they were bussed to ancient cities that were full of strange shops in mud-brick dwellings and tents. There were wide boulevards as well as narrow, winding streets filled with people and animals. Everybody in the streets seemed busy, on a mission, and everything seemed so primitive. It was a spellbinding wonder for the lads. Most things that they saw, touched, or tasted were different. The coffee was like mud. The food was hot and spicy, but very edible, which was quite a change from repetitive army tucker. Hunks of meat and vegetables were cooked on skewers. The food was great. However, the locals were a constant source of bewilderment. Their clothes were odd-looking, and the people were timid — until they tried to sell you something. Then, money spoke all languages. Bartering, which was a new experience to the Aussies, was quickly mastered, and many heated, abusive battles began. Nevertheless, the greatest curiosities were the women. Only their eyes were visible in the body-length garbs they wore. They looked downward, and refused any contact with these foreign men.

But, in narrow passageways behind beaded doorways, there were other women soon located by the desperate Aussie soldiers. In these scented, dark places, these very different women bared their soft, olive skin, performed belly dances, wore trinkets, and giggled. That was Tiger's description; he was a regular visitor. It was a shady part of town that held the ladies of ill repute, but it was like heaven to the blokes. A lot of the women wore silky pants and veils, with their faces partially hidden. A mass of jewellery covered their fingers, toes, and ears. Bare bellies were a feature, and some women had a stone or jewellery in their belly buttons. The older women controlled the business side of things while muscled young minders looked on. Mind you, there was a smattering of girls from Europe, particularly France, who wore *normal dress*. But the Aussies went for the girls with beads and trinkets. Dark men with wild beards and what looked like tea towels on their heads were the organisers of the entertainment, which consisted of dance-type halls, bars for drinking, and young women waiting on the clients. The Arab men smoked black cigarettes with a rich, sweet smell. Always, among the giggles, the smoke, and the raspy, high-pitched music, there would emerge a shrewd, English-speaking local who had quickly picked up the Aussie lingo, and was keen to offer the lads a good sheila 'welly cheap'.

Naturally, alcohol can be found anywhere in the world that has soldiers on leave—even in this city where, to the Aussies' amazement, alcohol was forbidden. Sore heads, a sense of sexual satisfaction, and lurid yarns were brought back to camp. The boys from the high country wanted to join the army for life! Soon, camel trips to historic places became a regular event, as the army decided that the best way to manage the troops was to rotate their leave. Letters home from the lads described what they saw of this ancient land.

'Incredible.'

'Really flam'n huge.'

'Big as a mountain.'

'Blimey, Mum, wish you could be here …'

And, finally, 'You got to see it to believe it!'

The pyramids stunned the soldiers; most stood and admired them in silent awe. However, back in camp, the other half of the Light Horse regiment, the horses, were oblivious to all this human excitement; they just wanted open air, a feed, and stability. They, too, were satisfied to be on a flat, steady surface. Every horse was exercised at least twice a day and then brushed, and had a swim in the river. Slowly, the horses' strength and trustfulness returned.

The camp out of Alexandria was set on gravelly sand that got in the horses' feed, and in the men's clothes, beds, and eyes as the hot, dry wind became a constant annoyance every afternoon. Tag, now singled out to look after a large section of the horses, came up with an idea to shield the horses against the wind. He needed to, as many of the animals had red, weeping eyes that the flies then infected. He solved the problem simply by making up a lace-like leather headdress attached to the head strap of the bridles. This was a common device at home, and it worked: it stopped the flies, and the horse still had good vision.

Another problem that started to show up was saddle sores, the like of which Tag had never seen before. The design of the army's new saddle, with just two narrow bars supporting it, was the problem. Back in Australia, the underneath of the saddle was broad and well cushioned. To overcome the problem with the narrow padding, the men were using two saddlecloths, but the sores persisted. With the full support of the Australian command, Tag initiated daily parades of mounts, in which a fresh saddle blanket and fly-lace were compulsory gear on the horse. Yet still the saddle sores remained. Tag thought that a thicker saddle blanket might be the answer. On the other hand, maybe it was the searing heat that caused the excess sweating. Or maybe they should take away the blanket — or use a different material. Tag was frustrated. There were no animal ointments, no routines for regular sponging, and no suitable saddlecloths. He felt that the ones they used might be too thin, as they would often bunch up under the saddle.

Tag approached Sergeant Bond, who by now was called G.J. — glass jaw — by all and sundry behind his back. Tag wanted some help. Unless the saddle sores received proper treatment, and better saddle blankets were used, Tag predicted a plague of sick horses. Already, many of the sores were infected with maggots. Accordingly, a trip into Cairo, which was the base for all medical supplies, was organised. Hoping to procure a large amount of provisions, Bondy ordered a supply truck, which he and Tag were dropped off from at a major hospital. Set up by the Allies, the hospital was in a magnificent old building with fine columns and marble steps. Sergeant Bond introduced himself and Tag to a sombre-looking lady called the Lady Matron, then left Tag and the woman alone as he headed off into the city for the day. Tag awkwardly explained his needs to the busy matron; she eyed the young man warily and then, after a time, offered help.

That was how he came to meet Miss Jill Hunter, a nurse who had just come off her break. The matron ordered Sister Hunter, who was still wearing her red cape and starched collar, to escort Tag to the quartermaster's store. Before receiving these new instructions, Sister Hunter had planned to go into town with two other nurses and do a bit of sightseeing. Naturally, that meant she'd need to be escorted by an officer. Now, having just finished a fourteen-hour shift, the tired Jill found out that there was a change of plans. Consequently, a cold glare greeted Tag when he first met Miss Hunter. Tag avoided any eye contact, and stared at the ground. He was always clumsy with strangers; more so, if they were female. After a brief inspection of the sand at his feet, Tag started talking the moment that the matron left. Not a lot of what he said made sense. Jill gathered that he liked horses, and that some of them needed something. Quickly, she warmed to Tag, and she gave a soft, pleasant laugh that broke the ice. The conversation started all over again.

'Where ya from, Miss?' Tag asked.

'Please, call me Jill. I'm from Benalla, Victoria.'

'Kelly country? Heck. I'm from just over the other side at Swifts Creek — you know, Omeo way. So you're from Ned Kelly the bushranger's country, eh?'

'Yes. My oldest sister knew Harry Power's family, before he took up with Ned.'

Tag was amazed.

'Crikey, didn't hear many good things about Harry Power. He come over my way, ya know — Swifts Creek, Doctors Flat, and down to Tambo Crossing. Stayed there a while, ya know.'

So a pleasant, cautious friendship began. Tag was thrilled to meet an Australian woman; Jill simply wanted to talk to a man who wasn't in an officer's uniform. For nurses, even on the ship coming over, meals and polite conversations took place only in the company of officers. This meant that Jill's only chance to meet the other ranks was when they became ill and required medical treatment. There was nothing wrong with officers, but their environment was too stiff and regimented; there was little laughter or gaiety in their presence. It was the same once they reached Egypt: only an officer could accompany a nurse. Whether it was back in her quarters, or during a visit to the city or to the Q-store, an officer had to be there. The only time she had on her own or with her fellow nurses was in their dormitory — with its prison-like environment. Duty officers guarded the doorways, and bed checks were undertaken every night. This was futile; by the time nurses reached their beds, sleep was their main priority.

Oddly, as these two young people chatted light-heartedly, Jill's first serious enquiry was about Tag's face. It was a mess. Being a redhead meant that Tag had layer upon layer of burnt skin on blisters over dry skin on raw skin. The desert sun and wind played havoc on his face. Tag wore a slouch hat that never came off his head till the sun went down, but it didn't protect his face. Jill, concerned by this, suggested two things. The first — some cream to clean up his skin — sounded okay. However, the second — for him to wear a veil like a fly screen or a beekeeper's net — was impossible for Tag.

'Ya gotta be jok'n',' he said. 'The blokes would rib me to death.'

Jill laughed. 'It's for the best, but that's up to you.'

Jill was the same age as Tag. She had the brisk walk of a nurse, and somewhere under all that regalia Tag thought that she probably had a good figure. She had been a nurse since leaving school.

It was a long trek to the compound. They continued to chat and, after a twenty-minute quick walk, Jill led Tag towards the medical-supply depot. The medical Q-store sergeant smiled as he listened to Tag. Intrigued by the requests of 'this young bloke', as he continually called Tag, the sergeant could see what Tag was getting at. He remembered saddle sores from home on his dad's farm.

'Ya reckon stuff with lanolin or sump'in like that'll do the bloody trick, eh?'

'Yeah.'

'I got just the gear, mate. Whack ya bloody pork pies on this stuff.'

In the sergeant's hand was a round tin of Rawleigh's ointment. On the back of the tin, as the sergeant pointed out, was written, 'Suitable for man or beast.'

'Beat that, me boy! That'll fix ya saddle sores, and ya own bum as well, betcha!'

Tag managed to wheedle ten cartons of ointment out of him. He and Jill then headed back to the main complex, where the transport that had been arranged to pick up the supplies and take Tag back to camp was ready. After they waited for twenty minutes past the designated time, there was still no sign of Sergeant Bond, who was supposed to have met Tag at 1500 hours. The two young people stood and kept on talking, with Tag taking the opportunity to explain the problem of the saddle blankets and sores. He wondered whether Jill had any ideas about it. They were both relaxed.

Then the driver said he had to be off. Awkwardly, Tag took off his hat and reached for Jill's hand, then blushed and muttered something inaudible. Jill smiled.

'I hope we meet again — oops, not in the hospital, I hope,' she said. They both laughed.

SEVERAL DAYS AFTER their trip to Cairo, Bondy took Tag to one side. The sergeant was grateful to Tag for having spun a yarn about why he hadn't made it back on the truck. Importantly, the higher-ups had been convinced. Bondy had, in fact, spent the night in the arms of a most obliging companion, and had arrived next day trying not to look too guilty. He spoke to Tag.

'Thanks for the other day, mate. I might add, I went to find ya and bumped into that sheila, Jill. She's a bit of all right, I reckon. Ya made an impression, ya cheeky bugger.'

'Really?' answered a surprised Tag.

'Yeah, anyhow, that's not why I wanted ta see ya. She said she had an idea for ya saddle blankets. Some surplus army blankets, from England or somewhere, eh. They got little use for 'em — too bloody hot, ya know. Anyhow, she said she'd send some down. And then I reckon you and me should organise another trip. Wotcha reckon, eh, mate?'

Tag agreed wholeheartedly.

SUITABLE FOR MAN? Tag couldn't vouch for that; but, for the horses, the ointment proved to be the answer. Slowly, the saddle sores healed. And, thanks to Jill, he was able to issue a section of a unit with larger saddle blankets. The rubbing that used to cause the sores showed an improvement for the first time; although the blankets still bunched up, they were far superior to the old ones. It was time to organise more blankets … many more.

Tag went to Bondy, who got in touch with the Matron — and Jill. She would be the contact, naturally. Unfortunately, their next trip into Cairo was a rushed affair, as a bloody officer came with them. Tag and Jill treated the meeting as business. Bondy returned at the arranged time, and the way he winked at Tag on the way back made it clear that the allotted hour had given him enough time to satisfy his needs.

Jill was great. She organised the cutting and sewing of the thick army blankets, and sent a message to Tag whenever they were ready. On the strength of this, Tag once again scored a trip. Well, Tag didn't really organise it. He pleaded with Bondy, now a mate, that he should go, once a week, to collect the blankets and supervise the whole business. Bondy not only got things rolling, once he had the plans in place; he desperately wanted to speak to Jill on another matter. Unfortunately, a week later, he found himself in hospital with a venereal disease—thanks to his frequent visits to his lady friends, the belly dancers.

The project of having thousands of saddle blankets made was now underway. Both Tag and Jill were pleased with the arrangements. They saw each other once a week: he would let her know well in advance when he would be coming to collect the saddle blankets and ointment, and Jill would make sure she had the same time off. Slowly, a quiet friendship began to develop between them. Then, one time, Jill appeared in a light uniform—it had taken the army months to organise a replacement for the heavier one, despite the fact that it was sorely needed in the stifling heat—and Tag's heart pounded much faster. To Tag, Jill looked perfect, the most beautiful woman he had ever seen. Most others probably saw her as an average brunette with crooked teeth; they might have thought that her legs were too skinny, or that she was trained above their station, or that she was too quiet. Yet, suddenly, Tag was more interested in her as a woman than as an acquaintance.

Unfortunately, on every occasion that Tag met Jill, she had an escort—an officer again, of course. Rarely were the two of them alone. Consequently, they could only talk business, with some light chatter thrown in as they organised more blankets and ointment. Occasionally, Tag gave Jill some cheek, and she flirted with him, ever so slightly. For both, their meeting was the highlight of the week. After most visits, Tag returned to the sandy camp and opened his diary. He had already written about ten pages, most of it like a travel log for a holidaymaker. Often, he wrote about Jill. This was a typical entry:

> Met Jill again today. She's a cracker. Her full name is Jillian Hunter from Benalla. Could ride over there in three days once this stint is over. She's pretty smart too.
>
> Flying things are bugging the horses.

BY NOW, IT was late March. Tag had drawn out the blanket ritual as long as he could, but he knew it couldn't last much longer. The horses had settled, the saddle sores were under control, and a good routine had been established. The army had stepped up troop training, restricted leave, and hinted that something was in the air. However, although the horses were coping better, there were problems among the soldiers. Sickness had started to seep into the camps. Insidious diseases such as malaria, pneumonia, and influenza were prevalent. Hygiene had become a problem, and the beds were riddled with lice. The men started to complain.

By far the number-one disease was venereal disease. Over two thousand men had left the country already because of it, and three per cent of the force was constantly sick with it. Bondy had the unfortunate reputation of having been one of the first stricken with the disease. The British, disgusted with the statistics, enforced new laws: any soldier reporting with VD was deemed to have committed a crime; they were to be charged and punished for it (Sergeant Bond was demoted); and, for the guilty parties, pay would be stopped for the duration of the infection, and the details would be entered in the soldier's pay book (so all and sundry would know).

The result was that the men put up with the problem in

silence. VD turned into a hidden disease, and sick men were prepared for imminent conflicts with a swollen, dripping, sore sausage. Some men lost complete self-respect and led reckless lives. The trained volunteer medical officers wanted a different approach—based on education, advice, and a more diplomatic solution—but they were only doctors. The regular officers were the real army; naturally, the army's way prevailed, and venereal disease was soon rife.

JILL AND TAG saw each other only briefly over the next few weeks. Tag was growing in confidence, and could laugh heartily in Jill's company. By now, he had many spare saddle blankets. His attitude towards the opposite sex had changed. In the past, Tag had always been shy around most girls—apart from Sally Sandy and her mates. But not only did he feel at ease with Jill; he found her desirable. Regrettably, though, their meetings were becoming shorter or didn't happen at all. Jill's obligations at work forced her to cancel many meetings with Tag. It wasn't her choice; she had simply become too busy. Her shifts were now usually twelve hours long, with four hours on standby, seven days a week. The hospitals were barely coping with camp sicknesses.

Tiger, Golly, and Bucket had the pleasure of meeting Jill several times. Let's just say that Chatty met her in hospital with a very sore groin. Once, the six of them went for a meal together in Cairo; their escort, an officer, was decent enough to spend time at the bar and to leave the gang alone for over an hour. For Tag, with his visits in jeopardy, at least there were letters. He wrote regularly to Jill, but she only answered twice. He continued to write in his diary, which was now a running commentary about Jill:

Jill is a truly sweet person. I hope to see a lot of her after this so called 'stint' is over. I'm missing her already.

This was the last entry he ever made — not because Tag decided to adhere to army orders which stated that 'diaries were banned', or because he lost interest in writing. There was a different reason. The war was about to intervene and to confront these innocent young men with its sharp realities. Tag, like so many, was simply unable to write the truth about it in his diary. Nothing could have warned him that his life was about to change so dramatically in the next few weeks. It shocked him to the point that his mind and soul could hardly comprehend what he saw, let alone record it. Even more to the point, every time he opened his diary and read that last page, he realised what a naive, fanciful life he had been living up till then. Yet some men kept writing; they wanted the truth told … eventually.

There was a reason, all right. It was called Gallipoli.

CHAPTER THIRTEEN

There came a time, a date, and a place when Australia, as a young country, found herself immersed in a powerful historical event that would remain etched in her memory. The time was early dawn; the date, 25 April 1915; the place, Gallipoli. In no time—by early May—hundreds of wounded were being sent to the hospitals in Egypt. It was obvious that a horrific battle on a massive scale was taking place. Word rushed around the hot, sandy, partially vacated Australian camp that was now as big as a large rural city. The stories were met with stares, frowns, headshakes, and expressions of disbelief. The soldiers remaining at Alexandria were only vaguely aware that a contingent had gone to Gallipoli, as the army never kept the troops informed. Then, scant, scary reports filtered back from the hospitals—nothing official, of course.

'Did ya 'ear that several hundred wounded blokes were shipped back for medical treatment? They had the hell kicked outta them.'

'Fair dinkum?'

'They reckon it's a total stuff-up.'

A quiet descended on the Australian camp. Gossip had it that the first troops to land were told to 'land on Gallipoli and give the Turks hell'.

Then, by 3 May, another story filtered through Tag's camp.

There were eight thousand casualties ... total confusion ... a lack of leadership ... a lack of support for those fighting ... no organisation ... chaos during the removal of the wounded.

Surely, this gossip was bullshit.

Sadly, it was the truth. By 10 May, at Gallipoli and in Cairo, the medical services had broken down completely. It stunned those back in Egypt attending the wounded. Belatedly, the army blurted out some vague figures, and pronounced imminent victory.

Instead of asking questions, the men went quiet, drank heavily and, suddenly, their families back in Australia became important to them. Men started to write letters home. They weren't informative letters—that couldn't happen—but, even heavily censored, at least their families received something from them. For the soldiers, contact with home became a priority. Everyone was about to face changes.

JILL WAS SHATTERED and appalled at the carnage on Gallipoli. Even more telling, she was disgusted by the army's lack of preparation or concern. Her hospital at the Heliopolis palace in Cairo had six hundred beds. Within a week, it was caring for over 1500 non-complaining souls. These unfortunate men, more than anything else, gave Jill the inner strength to continue. Now she was working up to nineteen hours a day, then dropping exhausted into bed. That was her lot; there was time for nothing else. Suddenly, saddle blankets and socialising seemed unimportant. Still, Jill desperately wanted to see Tag—not to giggle or flirt, but to warn him, at least to tell him the truth. She knew that a letter, even a brief one, was out of the question. Censorship within the army, the press, and the government had reached the point of paranoia. She knew that she couldn't get away or send a secret message, even if Tag found his way to Cairo. No visitors were allowed in the hospital, and the army had put a curfew on the nurses and their quarters.

A curfew. They had to be joking. All Jill wanted to do was sleep. It was a waste of time putting a guard on the nurses' quarters. Those days were past. Quickly, the nurses decided that this war was crazy, a slaughter on a scale almost impossible to comprehend. For the nurses, sleep became a precious commodity. A very sad Jill resigned herself to the fact that her chances of ever seeing Tag again were very remote.

FINALLY, SOME INFORMATION was provided. A notice was posted on the bulletin board in the Australian lines: 'An 'O' [Orders] Group at 1600 hours—ranks of Captain and above to attend.'

Then, two hours later, with the Australian officers fully briefed, it was time for the men in the ranks to hear the new orders. Tag's company, the Light Horse, gathered just on the outskirts of the camp in a large area set aside for drill. It was a typical desert sunset of vibrant colours as the men sat, swatting biting insects and smoking. The five young lads from the high country listened with interest as the orders were read out, loudly and clearly. In summary, the soldiers' destination was Gallipoli. There were to be no horses; just the men. The Light Horsemen had become riflemen. Their horses would be left in the care of older soldiers, called Remounts—Banjo Paterson's boys—who had signed up. Although too old to fight, they were certainly old enough to look after the animals.

This left Tag confused. All along, he had imagined himself and his mates on their horses, charging here and there, bellowing battle sounds that they'd made in their training, defeating an enemy and driving it into a state of disarray—due to the superior strength and skill of the Aussies. That was what they imagined the war would be for them: a panorama of magnificent horses, an exhibition of their horseriding skills, an array of daring battles, and being in a state of constant excitement.

The gathered soldiers were very quiet. Tag sat next to his mates, who now included Sergeant Bond. Yes, Corporal Bond had his stripe back. As usual, there were no questions; they were receiving orders. They felt excitement mixed with confusion as they stood and wandered back to their tents. There was also talk of it all being a bit rushed ... these Light Horsemen weren't trained infantry ... and what was happening at the front, at that joint called Galloppoli or something? The troops were anxious to hear about the war, how it was progressing, how well the Aussies were doing against that hopeless, poorly trained enemy, 'the Turk'. It was too much to comprehend. Now the men hoped that the reports of appalling casualties on both sides were simply pieces of gossip being filtered out of Cairo or Alexandria.

The army provided no information — especially about casualty figures. With new infantry backpacks and no horses, the Light Horsemen had a restless night that consisted of not much sleep and endless questions. The next day, it all happened very quickly: new webbing was issued, and they were told how to set up theirs packs with bedding, dixies, and spare clothes. Now the rifle had a sling, not a pouch next to the saddle.

The following day, they left Egypt well before sunrise on a ship packed with wide-eyed men. The crackle of nervous tension and bizarre jokes filled the air as the ship cut through a moderate swell. Then, nearing the peninsula at Gallipoli, the shock of pounding shells, cracking bullets, and general mayhem quickly dampened their talk; they hadn't even landed, and already the Turk was blasting his well-honed artillery towards them. Fear consumed the soldiers. It required blunt, crude, loud orders to bring them back to reality. Whatever that was.

Blindly, they leapt from their landing barges into the waist-high water. It was still semi-dark, and the shelling, now quite accurate, took a terrible toll. Then, just as suddenly, the shelling stopped.

The bewildered men staggered onto the beach. Suddenly, their nostrils and stomachs reacted violently to a smell. For Tag, it was a familiar smell.

It had overwhelmed him at O'Brien's boundary fence, years ago. Tag would have been about five years old at the time. A large buck kangaroo had its hind leg hooked in the top wire of O'Brien's boundary fence; it must have been suspended there for at least a week. When Tag came across the dead animal, two large goannas were tugging at a hind leg. It came away easily; the green and grey rotting flesh ripped like wet paper. The two large lizards rushed off, dragging the leg frantically. As Tag got closer, the putrid smell overcame him. It caused the youngster to gag and then vomit; it would have caused any human not familiar with such smells to react similarly.

Now, on the beach at Gallipoli, that smell blasted into his and everyone's nostrils. Many of the young soldiers vomited.

Perhaps it was fate. Who knows? But for Tag, a young soldier, a lad with young mates from Swifts Creek who had joined the Australian contingent bound for Gallipoli on 24 May 1915, a stark, eerie event was about to unfold. Admittedly, the new soldiers were curious when they first landed on the beachhead. The artillery had stopped.

Somehow, the remainder of Tag's unit were gathered together, heads down, on the beach. Immediately, they were given orders in a sharp, shaking voice to move directly towards a secluded area at the base of a sand hill. But no one moved. Mates looked out for mates ... some were missing mates ... mates huddled into groups. There appeared to be an overwhelming sense of shock or bewilderment. Even the officers were briefly quiet. It appeared that, amid the terror of seeing so many wounded, and the smell and mayhem, it was all too much, too soon. Then, like a delayed reaction, the order registered. Suddenly, everyone moved, and they were shown their area of responsibility. Within thirty minutes of landing, they made it to their allotted trench. The sun had just risen above the horizon. It was quiet. There was no shooting, no shelling—almost no noise at all.

So often, in the years to come, those who survived that day from that particular landing would ask themselves, 'Why that day? Why us? Oh God, why us?'

The day that followed contained scenes that would haunt them forever. In time, these would become the fodder for countless nightmares and sudden flashbacks that would burst into their poor heads at the most unexpected times. It would become an appalling legacy for them to cope with for the rest of their lives. At the very least, a peaceful sleep would become a thing of the past.

The 24th of May 1915 turned out to be the first agreed day of an armistice. It had to be. After the terrible carnage of the first month, something had to be done with the bodies.The higher-ups on both sides decided that a day was required to bury all the dead.

That seemed fair, as the bodies were in a place called no-man's-land. It wasn't a large stretch of land—just a barren area located between the two battling armies. Above and below this narrow battlefield were men, hidden in trenches, ready to shoot, charge, and retreat, and to repeat this pattern every day. The dead stayed where they fell, because it was practically impossible to recover a wounded mate from no-man's-land. The snipers were deadly ... on both sides.

On this day, though, *all* the soldiers would lay down their arms and attempt to bury their dead. The war was postponed—for a day.

Soldiers on both sides were given a day to do a task that required a month, allowing only the barest of rituals, and dignity, to be observed. There were over three thousand bodies to be dealt with. On both sides, many had been there for over three weeks.

In one long, hot, stinking, degrading day, Tag, Tiger, Chatty, Golly, and Bucket became old men, never to experience youth again. If there was a God, he didn't provide those young men with enough of that substance called inner strength.

Misty-eyed, the men rose as one. The morning started with orders to move out and retrieve the dead soldiers, and to bring them to a central point, but even the army couldn't cope with the situation. The normal shouting stopped ... orders disappeared ... quiet, hushed requests were made.

Some bodies had been there almost a month.

Attempts to lift them led the remains to fall apart, the limbs to come adrift, and hissing gases to blast from swollen bellies.

Some bodies had been there almost a month.

Bodies farted when moved. Maggots had infiltrated the dead young men's shattered, rotting flesh in plague proportions. Eye sockets moved with wriggling masses of them; ears were the most common point of entry for these disgusting, slimy things.

Artillery had been the main killer. Bodies had their heads missing, or were blown apart or, worse, bits and pieces of them — a boot with a foot still inside it; an arm, the hand still clutching a rifle — were found scattered, belonging to ... who could possibly know? In any case, many of the shattered bodies were missing their dog tags — which was the only way a dead soldier could be identified.

In time, a letter would be sent home, giving a family the wrong message. The Unknown Soldier numbered in the hundreds.

All of this in one day; one long, daunting day. How could countless bodies be buried in one day? Surely, for all this slaughter, the poor buggers deserved to be buried with dignity, a word, or at the least a prayer.

172

But where would they be buried? How would they be buried?

As usual, the army chose the most practical method. As there was little room, no time, and nothing had been organised, the dead were laid in the fighting trenches. There was no other room for them. Laid side by side, they would have needed at least a mile.

The soldiers had to start again: they had to stack the bodies, cover them with lime, hack some soil from the wall of the trench, put it on top …

The men treated the dead with dignity — what little dignity was available to them. The lads stuck together. Tiger was the only one who spoke.

'Give us a friggin' 'and 'ere, mate.'

Then they ran out of sacks for the bodies.

An officer responded to this blunt request from Tiger with a blank stare.

'Well, lay him in there careful, like.'

'Jesus, at least put 'im on 'is fuck'n back, Bucket. Let 'im look up, poor bastard.'

Tiger was always the leader. This was a job that required men of character and strength, not officers. That evening, Tiger grudgingly accepted the odd compliment for the courage and strength he'd shown that day. But ask any man who was present about his most vivid memory that day, and he would say, 'The Turks' or 'the niggers', the slang term created for the enemy.

The Australian soldiers were generally known not to display much emotion. But the Turk was the opposite. He wailed, he cried, he muttered prayers, he knelt, he swayed, and he gibbered. His actions haunted the Australians. The Turks wandered among the dead, side by side with the Australians. If a friend or family member was located, the Turks became distraught with overwhelming emotion. Many blokes became deeply saddened when watching the Turks. These were truly sad soldiers, the Turks. They were distraught young men, just like the Aussies, but much more expressive.

And there was no bloody hate!

There were nods of greeting, brief smiles, cigarettes passed around, and occasional assistance offered. How bizarre, how painfully pathetic, that these men found themselves in this position at the whim of men in power, away on some far-off shore, seeking revenge and planning to win the war—whatever the cost.

Late that night, the men of 22 Platoon, Tag's mob, sat in their trench. There were no jokes, no talking or conversations—just statements.

'Poor friggin' Jenkins found his brother out there today, poor bastard ...'

'Not even a decent fuck'n burial ...'

'Yeah.'

'Too bloody right. Arseholes! Friggin' arseholes!'

'They stop to bury the dead. Why don't they just friggin' stop—full friggin' stop!'

'Jesus, those Turks took it bad!'

THE NEXT MORNING, with yesterday's horror still etched in the tender minds of these instantly aged young men, the fighting resumed. When the shelling started, the memories of the day before disappeared in a flash. The noise would have shattered the average house window. Some shells went overhead, and then a telltale whistle would indicate devastation somewhere else, further down, for the moment. The trenches were adequate, provided they didn't take a direct hit. The only protection was provided by the short tunnels dug into the hill towards the enemy.

The injuries from shrapnel were appalling. Men stared at mates who sat with their stomachs in their arms. Others had metal bits the size of half a sandwich wedged into their torsos, heads, and legs. Initially, the newcomers, experiencing shelling for the first time, were terrified. Most soiled their pants, and continued to wet themselves for the next hour. The wounded screamed with pain, and pleaded for immediate help. Others were lost. It was all too much to comprehend. What to do? There was too much noise for orders to be heard or to be made sense of; there were few orders anyhow. Then there were frightened orders — uttered by young officers who believed they had to give some orders, any orders, amid the mayhem.

First, there were orders to mount the bank and shoot at the Turk. Then there were orders to get down. Then there were orders to undertake a short sortie into no-man's-land to capture an enemy trench just twenty-five yards away; it would take place in fifteen minutes. There were too many orders. Sadly, every man, regardless of rank, orders, or initiative, operated in an out-of-order, automatic trance. It was chaos, havoc, hell. Many men died due to following wrong orders given in panic.

That night, the new soldiers sat and shivered, even though it was the middle of summer. That night, men vomited; not from horrific sights, as was the case the day before, but from fear. They stank; many of them had soiled their pants several times. For tea, on their first night after that action, Tag, Tiger, Golly, Chatty, and Bucket had a fag.

Sleep? What was that?

The platoon was located on the south side of the fighting. Lone Pine was a part of their area.

By the third day, the men had experienced shelling, shooting, and mass burials. Then an order came down from the high command: they were to advance, over the trenches, to gain valuable ground. This was to be a well-planned attack, organised to the minute by the higher-ups. All the soldiers received the briefing, and the men of 22 Platoon stood at the ready. The instructions were: *At a precise time, a barrage of shells directed at the enemy trenches will indicate when to top the trench and attack*. It would be some show.

The blokes from the high country glanced at one another, and wished each other luck.

'Keep ya bloody head down.'

'Good luck, mate.'

'Mind ya arse.'

'See ya back here for lunch, ya ugly bastard.'

But deep down inside, the answers to this madness were already there. They already knew that some of them would die, that others would be wounded, that they would kill another human being for the first time and that, whatever the outcome, nothing would be said about it. The ladders were at the ready. The shelling began, the soldiers rushed up the ladders, and the bullets zinged through the air. But the shelling was ineffectual—it was too far ahead, missing the Turks trenches completely. A message *should* have been sent to the ships to lower their sights slightly; but there was too much noise, so no signal was sent.

After a forty-yard sprint, Tag threw himself to the ground. The enemy trench was only five yards ahead; a Turk briefly lifted his head, and Tag, at the ready, blasted off a large part of the man's skull, including his left ear. The Turk slumped forward, dead.

A brief stalemate ensued.

Then the shelling started to get too close. Screaming, sizzling shrapnel now rushed overhead. A shrill blast from a hand-held whistle indicated retreat. Tag tried to wriggle backwards, and bumped into one of his platoon.

'Sorry, Cocka, but ya in tha friggin' road!'

The bloke was dead. Tag quickly slid over the body and hid behind it for cover. There were ten long yards to go. A brief glance indicated that some of the blokes had made it; many others were dead. Then a head and shoulders appeared over the trench, beckoning Tag to get back.

'Come on!' screamed Golly, frantically waving his hand at Tag.

They were Golly's last words. A sniper bullet removed his right eye, along with the back half of his skull.

'Never, never ever put ya bloody head above the friggin' sandbags, unless ordered—got that?'

These were the first words used to sum up the day's events that evening from the new corporal, who had been promoted only ten days before; already, he was a veteran. He had been there since the twenty-fifth of April. That night, for their first meal since landing, the four mates from Swifts Creek had dry biscuits.

Golly could have joined them had he been alive. However, he wasn't far from them; he was just across the way, with Tiger's greatcoat hiding the body, except for the boots. Their Golly was dead, but they had him sitting up, his head bandaged, his hat firmly in place. The lads had seen to it that Golly was part of their evening ritual. Somehow, he wasn't quite dead ... that was an event that only old people experienced.

What training could prepare young men for death?

A sergeant had told the lads that, at the earliest, the medics would remove Private Greg Elliot's body in a couple of days; the wounded were the priority. The lads didn't even respond. They had their own plans for him, even if they hadn't yet discussed them.

From the outset of this campaign, the preparation and organisation for a soldier who happened to be wounded could be summed up in two words: good luck! Hospital ships would arrive, placing themselves in peril; enemy shelling kept them some distance out to sea. Then, at enormous risk, small boats would attempt to ferry wounded soldiers to the ships, but it was hopeless. The only treatment that most of the wounded received was a cigarette, a bulky bandage to stem the bleeding, and words of encouragement from exhausted medics — most of which were lies, as the chances of survival for the badly wounded were very low. Until a new ship arrived, the wounded were laid out on and near the beaches as if they were corpses — exposed to the elements, not to mention sniper fire and artillery. They were then crudely ferried onto the hospital ships. If, by chance, there was a lull in enemy shelling, there was a frantic rush to the ships. If the shelling stopped, the boats made it. But it was only a brief lapse before the carnage resumed.

Once on board, it was a slow trip. The few medical staff and limited medical equipment on these ships meant that little attention could be given to the wounded until they reached hospitals in Egypt — like the one where Jill worked. And then, whatever little hope the wounded soldier now felt, because he was away from the mayhem and medical isolation of the beaches, was dashed when he reached Egypt. There, he was greeted by overrun, frenzied, undermanned hospitals.

The entire operation was a catastrophe.

BACK IN THE TRENCHES, their Golly was dead. This information was hard to accept for the young men from the Omeo shire. The lads avoided looking at each other. They had already seen many dead in a matter of days, but their Golly was dead ... and he hadn't died fighting. How could they explain that? His death didn't fit the heroic war stories told at home.

That night, Tiger covered Golly's body completely, and yelled if someone walked near their mate, 'Watch where ya goin', ya friggin' drongo.'

The lads wanted to talk, but what words were suitable for such a sad situation? Finally, Bucket spoke up.

'Best we bury him ourselves, I reckon.'

'Bloody oath; good idea.'

That was the end of the conversation.

The next day, there was another charge, and four more killed—none from the Omeo shire, but one from Bairnsdale. Quickly, those remaining were learning skills that enabled them to survive, for a time. *Keep still ... keep down ... move when the arty starts up ... look for hollows in the ground ... keep ya frigg'n head down ... cover ya mate's arse ... zigzag if ya hafta run.* None of this, of course, had been covered in their original training.

That night, with Golly still just across the way, Tiger started the conversation they had to have.

'Ya know that trench we've been digg'n up into the hill? I reckon we should bury Golly in there, correct like, you know.'

Silence.

Then Tag spoke.

'We could dress him up proper, and cover him with a sheet.'

'I'll flog one later,' said Bucket.

Chatty stood up and, grabbing his bayonet, started yet again to gouge into the side of their narrow trench that went into the hill some eight feet. They first decided to dig up further into the hill as protection against the shelling. Three feet high and three feet across, the dirt in the trench was dry, hard, and yellow-brown. The small L-shaped enclave would accommodate Golly's body at the very end. Then Tag and Tiger jammed into the tunnel and relieved Chatty. Bucket wandered off.

'Be back with a sheet or sump'n in a jiffy.'

Chatty kept watch as Tag and Tiger dug away; the army didn't like you taking things into your own hands. Tiger kept filling the sandbags with the dirt from the fresh diggings in the small tunnel—all done secretly, as the bags were always in demand. The crude walls of the trench caves were made of sandbags, which offered safe havens from the shelling.

Gregory George Elliot (Golly), the baker's son from Swifts Creek, rested back into his little grave. It was all done with the utmost dignity and care: he was patted, his uniform was brushed, and there was much wiping of eyes. Admittedly, he was in a sitting or, more accurately, in a kneeling position, as the lads started to run out of time. A rolled piece of cloth under his chin ensured that his head was proudly facing the front. A bandage covered his missing eye. His hands were clasped and sat in his lap, completing the laying out. Bucket had only been able to flog a moleskin blanket from the command post. Carefully, they used it to cover their mate's body. After an absence of words, but a long pause, they filled the mouth of the tiny tomb neatly with sandbags. Then Chatty drove Golly's bayonet into the wall of the tomb, and on it he hung Golly's hat.

The lads sat down in the regular trench—the one with hundreds of Aussie souls buried beneath, with a thin layer of lime and six inches of dirt on top of them. There were no words uttered as they sat, but the entire ceremony had touched them so deeply that efforts to hold back the tears were difficult. Again, it was Tiger who spoke. He offered the first bit of advice.

'If ya can, grab some flowers or a bit of shrub if we go over tomorrow. Golly would like that, eh.'

Tag wrote an awkward letter to the Elliot family in Swifts Creek. It simply said that Golly had died in battle … facing the enemy. A jumble of short sentences told of the burial.

All the lads signed the sad note, and that was that. Their funeral was complete.

But the war didn't stop for funerals or the like—barring armistice days, of course.

Eventually, the letter arrived at Swifts Creek.

CHAPTER FOURTEEN

The weeks, then months, ahead were a repeat of the first few days. Occasionally, a Turkish trench was captured, and then lost. It was like trying to follow the coach's orders at a football game.

Defend ... attack ... regroup ... attack ... rest ... come on, we can do this ... a win ... well done ... a loss ... next time, fellas ... Jim, could you take Bill's place? ... hold your ground, fellas.

The conflict was like a pendulum. It swung with an almost monotonous regularity that saw the Turks struggling to hold their ground, and then the Aussies, along with the other allied troops, facing the same predicament. Nothing was really changing.

Nevertheless, the men had changed. They had a resolve that few humans experience. They had accepted that death was inevitable, and most hoped it would come to them and not their mate. The comfort they offered their wounded or dying mates was touching, sensitive, and done with total compassion. Admittedly, it was usually only for a brief moment. Nevertheless, the times spent with a dying comrade were precious to them. Given a choice, it was always their priority; it came before food, sleep, or their personal needs. *Tend to your mate first*. That was the deal, the bond. Sadly, after this war, rarely would such compassion be shown again. In time, back home, with this conflict behind them, most of the soldiers who survived would turn into hollow men who never spoke of the war, of the reality or the waste of it. Emotion would desert them. They would come to prefer isolation, or the company of their army mates.

For the moment, though, Gallipoli was their whole world. It had been a horrific scene from the day they landed—burying three-week-old corpses—and then the blunt reality had set in that sudden death was a day-to-day possibility. It sounds beyond human endurance and yet, somehow, most of them coped. Certainly, the odd soldier 'cracked up' or happened to 'take a turn', as it was called. It wasn't looked on as a sign of weakness—it just led to a deep-seated horror that the same might happen to them. Invariably, this anxiety would come upon them at night.

Why, you might ask, at night?

Was it because of the nightmares they suffered?

Or because, as individuals, alone and quiet, that was when they found the time to reflect on and to see the insanity of the situation they found themselves in—particularly if the shelling and shooting had not long stopped, and there was finally some silence and then some talking?

Perhaps it was thoughts about home?

No, the soldiers dreaded this time for a different reason. Eerie sounds penetrated their ears and souls during the night—most nights, in fact. It preoccupied the exhausted soldiers.

Were they the sounds coming from their wounded mates, lying and sitting in the trenches, hoping that evacuation would take place the next day, with any luck?

No, these were not the sounds they dreaded.

Some in the trenches would talk in their sleep, cry about a mate, tell the others in their dream the truth of what was happening.

But these were not the sounds they dreaded, either.

What they couldn't bear were the gut-wrenching calls that came from across the top of the trenches every night. They were ghostly sounds—the appalling sounds of the wounded, still out there, screaming out for help in no-man's-land.

So many in the trenches wanted to take the risk to venture back out and retrieve a wounded mate. Some had tried, but they rarely came back. *Maybe there'll be a chance during the next run over the top … the next day—just maybe.*

Yes, what constantly obsessed the men during that campaign and forever afterwards were the haunting evening sounds coming from no-man's-land.

Those poor buggers still out there … wounded, in pain … made such terrible noises. It was a ghastly mixture of pathetic sobbing, crying, pleading, and calling out, naming mates.

Often, a hollow call came over the trenches, prefaced by, 'For God's sake' or 'You there?'

Sadly, attempting retrieval was as good as committing suicide. There was rarely an opportune time, while making an assault or going over the top, to bring back a mate from the day before … or three days before.

THERE WERE GENERALLY two types of assault practised by the Anzacs. The most common was an adrenaline-fuelled rushed charge over the top, followed by a hasty retreat or the capture of a small trench. This assault was simply meant to harass the enemy and to claim kills. A more intense attack or assault, usually supported by artillery, was a 'stunt' or 'push' to reach another well-fortified trench. This included bayonet charges, grenades, return artillery fire from the Turks and, usually, many killed and even more wounded. These planned events happened, at the most, several times a week. The remainder of their time, the weary soldiers in the trenches were on duty or piquet. They became snipers, attempting to 'pick off' targets, or give warning of a charge or anything suspicious.

The so-called stunts were usually not very successful, and were dreaded by the men: casualties would be heavy, and many of those killed and wounded by allied artillery would litter no-man's-land. Once back in the safety of their trenches, the turmoil among the men would subside. Quickly, a head count would reveal casualties, and a crude attempt would be made to administer first aid to those who had made it back. Priority was given to the lightly wounded, in the hope that the soldier could be used again.

Then came the real horror.

The cries in no-man's-land started up. The poor, wounded souls in no-man's-land called for food and water, particularly water. It stunned the men from their platoons, back in the trenches. They could hear the calls, but what could they do? *Do you answer, knowing there is no hope? Do you ignore the special human being who has shared a part of your life and helped you cope with the madness of war? Do you call out lies and bullshit? On the other hand, do you call out goodbye?* It didn't bear thinking about. The one thing guaranteed was that every night, the next night, and the following few weeks, the wounded would cry out in vain. It left an indelible memory, and laid the groundwork for horrific emotional battles in time to come for the rare survivors.

So THERE WERE stints, stunts, and charges. Then it was time to clean up after the carnage. Sometimes, stretcher-bearers were on hand to start the first stage of the long journey to the hospitals in Egypt, but there were never enough of them. What was common was a mate dying in the trenches with his mates on hand. They would promise to write notes home, either from scribbled last requests or by trying to commit the mate's pleas to memory.

Many mums, families, and wives received blunt or brief letters, from men they had never met, that told of last words and last messages of love. It was hard for the soldiers; of all their duties, this was the hardest. Some might question that it was a duty. It was, admittedly not ordained by the army; but, to the men, hard as it was, it was mandatory.

The Gallipoli campaign was a nightmare. To claim that one event or incident was worse than another, to single out soldiers for their bravery, courage, or daring, was the domain only of the officers. Few privates received awards or showed an interest in such things. They simply did their job. Then there was the censor; if you mentioned the censor to an Aussie in the trenches, a flurry of filthy mutterings followed. When they penned a letter home for a mate, only the truth covered the pages; however, the censor's pen found the raw truth unacceptable, and made sure it was muffled. The press and the politicians used a language that muted the truth and exaggerated the glory — a glory that pacified those at home until death notices and the sight of returned troops led to a feeling of disgust toward those in power.

That was Gallipoli.

Finally, another hollow, devastating truth started to emerge. With all the shocking losses, the carnage, the stagnant position of the troops, the lack of even a small advance, it started to become obvious that there was little point to Gallipoli. The Turks, occupying the higher ground, had a distinct advantage. The allies had little or no cover for re-supply, or for removing their wounded. The Turks had full cover. Admittedly, the Allied troops had no idea if the peninsula held any strategic advantage, but the general belief was that it was impossible to take. Morale was low among the troops. As Chatty summed it up, they were 'like lambs to the slaughter'.

Water was still scarce, even two months after the initial landing. Unfortunately, any task that required a soldier to stand or move into open ground and become exposed was dangerous. Water carriers lugging two square four-gallon tins of the precious liquid were prime targets. The Turkish snipers were relentless. Furthermore, the fact that all necessities, including water, had to come by sea was a logistical nightmare, and continually placed those involved at risk. At no time was there enough water to meet the basic needs of the troops; it had to be rationed, and rarely was any used for hygiene. The lack of water was a common source of ill-tempered outbursts and frustration.

Strangely, though, there was always enough tobacco.

During prolonged periods in the trenches — any time longer than a week — the men would dig deeper into their hillside trenches. Some of these excavations had a little bend in them that offered almost complete protection from any shelling that came over between the charges. Amazing as it may seem, after a month at Gallipoli, a man became a veteran … ready for acquiring rank. These men slept soundly during the shelling. They would crawl up into their hollowed-out small trench, almost cover the opening, which dampened the noise and blocked out the shrapnel, and sleep … often, sitting up.

Over the months, by developing clever trenching, better lines of communication were set up. The wounded were more easily shuttled to the beach. Occasionally, men would even be released to have a swim. This didn't stop the Turkish snipers, but it was a chance for a swim — such luxury!

However, by the third month, sickness and disease were rife in the trenches. There was a continual lack of adequate burials, and a lack of hygiene, while an appalling stench, polluted water, and flies, rats, lice, and maggots were ever-present. The numbers evacuated were growing dramatically. Now, almost a quarter of the evacuations were due to poor hygiene and the associated illnesses that went with such conditions. Water shortages and terrible food compounded the health problems.

THERE HAD BEEN no relief for the men in Tag's trench for over two weeks. Mind you, relief didn't mean a return to Egypt for a well-earned rest; it meant time away from the front trenches, and a break in a lower trench or a swim on the beach. By now, it was late July. In Tiger's group, only ten of the original thirty men remained, and most of them had been promoted to corporal and sergeant. Reinforcements were a weekly event. One bloke (those who knew him called him Slops), who had just finished shaking a few hands, having only been on Gallipoli two hours, was blasted to oblivion by a shell as he rushed to get some more ammunition. That's the way it was.

'He should've headed into a hill trench, poor bugger!'

Seasoned soldiers were alert to many sounds and signs. The shells that killed Slops were anticipated seconds before they hit. He had been told to head into a hill trench, but he couldn't understand why, ignored the advice, and continued to obey the order that the officer had given him.

This same day, just on dawn, the lads from Swifts Creek had yet again ended up back in the trench where they'd buried Golly, over three months before. Their uniforms looked like rags. There was little talking nowadays; certainly, no laughter. During these last months, each of them had had several narrow escapes from death, only avoided by luck and an uncanny ability to survive like a vulture or a jackal. Bouts of sickness had seen them laid up for days in a hill trench while their remaining mates continued to rally, storm over familiar ground, and somehow survive. One time, Tiger was so sick that Tag, Bucket, and Chatty tried to force him to leave on the hospital ship. He refused and slowly recovered; that was rare.

Today it was Bucket who was very ill. He had stopped eating, had severe diarrhoea, and smelt terrible. Even with the jesting gibes from the others, he had lost interest in ridding himself of the blood-sucking lice. At seven stone, he made light of his shakes and the blood in his stool. When he had coughed up blood the morning before, Tiger had asked the medic if they could have Bucket evacuated. Bucket, as you would expect, objected.

'Ya look like hell, ya bloody dill!' responded Tiger.

This created a terrible dilemma for the boys, as another stunt was on the go. It would be a charge over the top at dawn the following morning, with artillery support. Later that afternoon, the lads gathered around Bucket. Although nothing was said, they knew that their beautiful friend, their good mate Bucket, the dairy farmer and horse trainer, was dying. They had seen it happen to many others. It was all too familiar.

His death was a drawn-out horror. Poor Chatty, trying to hide his grief and distress, sat with his dear friend, who refused to sleep. He held Bucket's hand, while Tag talked of the good times at home and some of their greatest success stories with the rogue horses that delivered the milk. *We showed the bastards … remember that lanky, creamy mare?* They gave Bucket most of their precious water. Tiger, the leader, the rock, wrapped their thin mate in clothes, and lit a smoke for this special man who was closer to any of them than a mother, brother, wife, or child could be.

The lads took it in turns to talk of the good old days. Chatty talked about his mum, Lilly, and Bucket's brother, Tom. They mentioned the shared times at the butter factory and their love for Lilly. For the first time in ages, Tiger began stuttering, and then stopped talking—it was all too much for him. Tag took over: he recalled the day they had watched the racehorse win at Flemington, and they had got bloody drunk. Bucket smiled—his last smile. The end came when poor Bucket vomited a mass of black blood. His body arched in contorted horror, and his face stretched with total fear. He jerked and sucked in air, and roared. Then, finally, with a sigh, he rested his head on Chatty's shoulder and died.

Quietly, methodically, Bucket was dressed in the cleanest clothes they could muster, and was wrapped in a blanket. Unknown by Bucket, the lads had been digging a small, neat grave to one side of their hill tunnel, next to Golly. A simple, moving funeral by candlelight followed. At least, this time, they honoured their mate with some words. Tag, Chatty, and Tiger spoke of their affection for their mate. After yet another funeral in a hillside trench, they sandbagged the opening and marked it with a bayonet. One of Bucket's dog tags hung off the handle. Finally, as Bucket had requested, Tiger sent their mate's last mutterings home to the Banks family of Swifts Creek. It was a muddled letter of love and simple sentiments, espressing the hope that the cows were milking okay, and saying hi to Tom, his special brother. Oddly, the censor only removed about half its contents.

Along all those Australian trenches, many mates, including Golly and Bucket, were buried in small, uphill graves. They would call this place home ... forever.

THE THREE LADS survived the stunt over the top the next morning, and the troops captured the closest trench further up the hill. That night, they found themselves in another familiar home: they had been in the same trench six weeks earlier.

Ordinary people, back home in Australia, would not have believed that both mindless slaughter and overwhelming affection took place in the hellhole called Gallipoli. To the average Australian, such contradictory things could not have existed side-by-side.

Like a plague, the true horror of war spread as the sick and wounded reached such numbers that stretcher-bearers, mules, and mates could not cope. Beaches were cluttered and crowded with bewildered soldiers, like on the first day that the Anzacs landed on the peninsula in a cesspool of sadness. The overloaded hospital ships attempted non-stop turnarounds to relieve the problem; then, once on board, the wounded and sick were met by tired staff trying to avert mayhem.

The destination for the hospital ships was Egypt. There, the wounded were greeted by done-in local medical teams facing daunting decisions. Nothing had changed.

These medicos received the wounded in a familiar way. They put them in queues — queues of hundreds, laid out like a flattened picket fence in the grounds near the hospitals.

The doctors walked along the picket line and prioritised the wounded: *Ignore those poor buggers who have no chance of surviving, even though they've made it this far*.

Secret signs let the orderlies know which patients to leave and which ones to move to yet another queue ready for surgery or bandaging. A nod from the doctor meant: *That man — leave him to die*.

A rising of the hands meant: *Stretcher that man inside, immediately*.

Was there a worse job for the medics?

The huge numbers of those killed at Gallipoli was only a small proportion of those wounded, and yet the provision of medical services to meet anticipated casualties was not a high priority in the army's planning. The result was that, during the war, health systems failed. The doctors and nurses worked in appalling conditions.

BACK IN EGYPT, in the hospital, Jill Hunter from Benalla was a different woman. She also lived in fear, a waiting fear, that never went away — the same fear that swamped the entire country back home in every house that had a husband, a son, or a brother in the war. The fear was usually ignited by a blunt telegram.

For Jill, there were no telegrams; she just saw the men come in, among whom she recognised the odd face. Many of the soldiers had visited Jill on the trip over with seasickness, sunburn, and other minor illnesses. Usually, the soldier recognised Jill, or nurse Hunter, as they called her. They stated as much, and usually Jill remembered them. Then, later, while attempting to do paperwork, she would come across one of those names … on a list of the wounded from Gallipoli. At times, she wanted to scream with agony at the position she found herself in. She wanted anonymity. Personal contact brought a story and a level of pain that stunned her. Then these same men wanted her to write, to get in contact with their family and mates, to hang around, but … there was never enough time.

'Nurse, see to that man's wounds.'

Doctors felt the tension.

'Nurse, hold him down, for God's sake!'

Time. There was never enough time.

Such demands pierced her fragile world continually, particularly at the time of a man's departure from life itself. All too often, Jill found herself called away from a patient at that precise moment. All she could do was turn and walk away, and obey the order she'd been given.

How could she do this, when all that the sad, wounded soldier really wanted was for someone to hold his hand? He would have preferred a mate, but a nurse would do. He wanted to tell her where he came from, and maybe talk to her about his wife and kids. He wanted to die — amid all this disorder — with some comfort, some peace, some dignity. However, Jill Hunter, one overworked nurse among many, couldn't look them in the face, these poor souls who needed her compassion and time. She would turn quickly, briskly walk to the doctor, and pretend not to hear their pleas for comfort. *Never run, no matter the crisis*. That was part of a nurse's training. It was almost unbearable.

GALLIPOLI: LONE PINE, 6–7 August. General Orders came from H.Q. for Trench Delta, 22–28 Platoons (which included Tag's mob). There was to be another attack: to take the trenches at Lone Pine.

The company commander tapped a crude map, on which crosses marked the position of the Turkish trenches. The entire operation centred on the precision of the artillery and on perfect synchronisation between it and the attack. Tag, Chatty, and Tiger sat, ignoring the ramble apart from the timing; that was critical.

The company commander added, 'Remember, men, when the shelling stops, mount the trenches and attack. It will be at exactly 0600 hours. Remember, that's when you attack, at 0600 hours.'

The lads looked at one another with hollow eyes. Never had one of these so-called well-planned attacks been successful. The company dispersed. The men loaded their rifles, fixed their bayonets, mounted the ladders, and waited.

The shelling stopped, seven minutes too early ... the men waited and waited ... and Johnny Turk realised there would be an assault. Any fool could have predicted that! Johnny Turk had time to load his rifles and prepare during those terrible seven minutes.

The men went over the top ... and were slaughtered. Wave after wave was mown down like wheat being harvested by a scythe. Some made the Turkish trenches, only to find them covered with pine logs.

It was nothing but waste—a total waste. It was certainly not a noble way to die, or the ultimate sacrifice. It was mass slaughter.

A New Zealand battalion was almost wiped out.

Chatty lost the lower half of his leg, blasted off at the ankle by a bomb thrown at him. A mate, Treddy, had managed to lug him back under the cover of heavy shelling. It was a terrible wound, and his leg was severely lacerated—the Turks always used time-delay hand bombs, to great effect. The next day, somehow, Chatty made it to the hospital ship. He considered himself very lucky. Thank God for the stretcher-bearers, those brave bastards. What chaos. Later, when there was a platoon count, back in their original trench, they realised that Tiger was missing.

Tag had received a shot in the right thigh; the bullet, a ricochet, had only penetrated two inches into his flesh. Manny Johns, the company medic, had bandaged his wound and helped him back to a covered-in section of the trench. The smelly trench was full to overflowing with wounded. Few of them would be evacuated that day, or the next.

Day two, and Tiger was still missing.

A week later, Tag's wound had healed reasonably well. He should have been evacuated; instead, he stayed on.

Tiger was still missing.

Then, as sometimes happened, a dazed Tiger found himself in the wrong lines five days later. There was a huge gouge in his bum from shrapnel, which looked worse than it was—a large flap of skin had lifted in a welt. Some codger had cleaned him up and put the skin roughly back in place. It had healed fairly well, so his chances of evacuation were slim. The system to remove the wounded after Lone Pine had all but failed. Fortunately, Tiger's wounds didn't become badly infected. Most of the poor blighters who suffered badly infected wounds died in the trenches after Lone Pine.

When Tiger limped to his own trench, he asked Tag for blunt details about what had happened. It was an emotional meeting.

Chatty was in Egypt.

Tag explained his own bad limp. It was okay, whatever that meant.

Tiger wouldn't talk of the ten days during which he was missing as the only survivor in that short trench. Words couldn't explain some things. He only talked about the rotten food and putrid water.

By September, Tag and Tiger had been there for months; more importantly, they had stayed together. Each had a stiff limp. Fortunately for Tag, his wound had festered, the bullet had popped out and, with a little care, it had healed to form a clean scar.

By now, most of the faces in their old platoon were new. Tiger was now a sergeant; Tag, a corporal. Come October, the weather started to deteriorate and, during the month, continued to turn colder. By November, winter had arrived with force. It began with a severe blizzard that created havoc for both sides. Nevertheless, the Gallipoli campaign continued ... by early December, Tiger and Tag were yet again in their familiar trench. Although they rarely spoke, they stuck together at all times. They shared food and cigarettes. They made no effort to mix with or make friends with the new reinforcements.

They were back where Golly had called to Tag for the last time, and where Bucket had died on Chatty's shoulder. This particular trench was 'home'. It was *their* tunnel, and home for Golly and Bucket. Every time they returned to this part of the tunnel they always extended it further, back up into the hill, stabbing at it with their bayonets and using their bare hands to scrape the dirt back and scoop into a tin, before emptying it in a sandbag. These sandbags were used to build little partitions in the tunnel; they were there to stop any shrapnel. Then, when they stopped their digging, most evenings Tag and Tiger included Bucket and Golly in their brief conversations as they rested in their hollow little cave in the hillside. Bucket was buried only feet away in the main wall. A bayonet still marked the tiny grave, and both lads regularly cleaned the small area.

By now, this cave was quite a size; if he crouched, Tiger could walk from one end to the other of it. There were even small ledges that held smokes, candles, and tins for storing water. Often, conversations wandered back home, and again they would talk as if their dead mates were there, in the dark, listening.

On the odd occasion, they would mention Chatty. There was no question in their minds that he was alive and well. He was somewhere in Egypt — back in Cairo — or maybe he'd been sent home, missing half a leg. It was sad that they had to guess because, despite their enquiries, not a word ever came back to Tag and Tiger about Chatty. He had been gone for over three months. Tiger made numerous pleas for information about him, but heard nothing.

This particular night, after finishing their digging and their chats with their mates, they returned to the main trench and prepared a brew. It was bitterly cold. The twilight hinted at a frost in the morning. The tea was a welcome, warm pleasure that they sipped with quiet sighs and delight. Noise was at a low level. The calls from no-man's-land had stopped. It had been four days; the survivors out there would be dead by now … either from their wounds, or having been finished off by snipers.

A few candles were burning, and a bloke across the way was scribbling a note in a small book. Then something strange happened. A young fellow appeared with a smile on his face.

A smile on his face?

The lads knew this codger: he was young, had rank, and was an original from another mob further back along the trench, Charlie Company. He was a horse handler … and he was smiling.

Briefly, he spoke to both lads. They shook their heads, sure that he was just passing on a furphy that was always circulating among the troops. However, the young sergeant repeated his statement.

'We're gettin' out.'

'Bullshit.'

'Back to Egypt'

'Heard that crap too many times.'

He left, still with a smile on his dial.

Then it came, from high up: the official word came around. They were to evacuate at 0600 hrs. It wasn't bullshit. For the first time, the men's spirits lifted, just a little. It was to be 'a dark, pre-dawn' withdrawal, like their pre-dawn arrival all those months ago. Preparations were made, and then, they heard, they were to 'move out in forty-five minutes'.

It was so difficult to comprehend. Then the time to move out was thirty minutes away.

This wasn't right.

Something was missing.

Then a phenomenon occurred. At a hidden signal, something not rehearsed or imagined began: just before their evacuation from Gallipoli, the men from the Omeo shire acted as one to deal with yet another dilemma.

It was time to say goodbye to Golly, Bucket, and many of their lost mates. They would be leaving these mates behind. No longer would they have almost daily conversations with them. Something had to be said on this occasion, surely?

So, without permission, organisation, or preparation, many, including Tag and Tiger, returned to *their* trench on the final day. During their last minutes on the steep hillside trenches overlooking the peninsula of Gallipoli, sad conversations hung like a cold fog in the air.

For Tiger and Tag, in their familiar cave, in the dark that normally was lit by cigarettes, candles, or shell blasts, the two lads from the high country called out to Bucket and then to Golly.

'What'd ya reckon, Golly?'

Golly was down a bit further, just to one side on this small piece of sacred ground. Tag crouched down, close to the sandbagged wall with the bayonet. The dog tags still hung on the leather handle. Quietly, he started this personal, quiet ritual.

'See ya, Golly, me dear friend ... mate ... I'll be seein' ya ... Bye.'

Tag gagged and put his hands over his eyes. He wanted to say something, but his body and soul refused, emotionally locked. He swayed, similar to the way his grief-stricken mother Ann would have swayed. Tiger, at a distance, was silent. He remained just inside the opening. Similar ceremonies were taking place along the entire length of this fighting trench. Tiger could hear the others. Tiger was still the leader, the strong one, the platoon sergeant, the head of the platoon; he'd been the head of the family way back, a long time ago in Swifts Creek, and he was the head of the family here. He took off his hat, stooped, and walked over, up into the cave-like opening that held their two friends. When he reached Golly, he made a strange sobbing sound, a croaking noise that told of a deep level of sadness that God hadn't provided for in this very old young man. He tried to talk but, instead, fell to his knees. Tag knelt beside his distraught mate.

'Come on, Tiger, old mate. The boys are together somewhere, mate, probably looking over the Dargo high plains, I reckon. They're outa this friggin' hell 'ole, mate. They're okay. I know they are.'

Tiger nodded. 'Y-y-yeah, y-ya right, Tag. Thanks, mate.'

He lent forward and filled a pocket with dirt, and then patted it and turned to the others. 'T-that's me mates—they're com'n with me.'

Again, it was Tag's turn. He hesitated and knelt down in front of his dear friend Bucket.

'Every 'orse I ever own, I'll tell them about you, mate ... the way you used to care for the horses in harness ... you were the

197

best, Bucket. God bless you.'

Then, with a return of confidence in his voice, he turned back and told Golly, 'You were a wonderful mate. Me first kid, mate, if I get outa this hell 'ole and get hooked, me first little bloke will be called Greg … or Golly, and I hope he's a baker some day.'

Tag shuddered after making that statement. Where did those words come from?

Tiger reached down and helped Tag to his feet. Tiger's eyes were streaming with tears. Again, he scooped a small handful of dirt from in front of Bucket's home and put it in his other pocket. Once back in the open trench, they walked quietly away together, an arm around each other's shoulder. Many others were doing the same. Everywhere, men were distraught. They were leaving a place they had called home, a place that held ten lifetimes of terror—a trench that was more familiar to them than any room of any house they had lived in so long ago.

At home, in Australia, a headstone meant a burial spot. Here, it was a cave, a gully, a rock, a bayonet, a half-buried boot, or simply 'over there'. Every ridge, every mound or dip, was where Sammy fell, or where Decks copped it, or 'where I saw Dingo for the last time'. It was a sad day when they left the trenches of Gallipoli for Egypt. It's not that they wanted to stay; they just didn't want to leave. This hollow, inexplicable attachment to the battlefield affected all the men in the trenches, including those up the ranks—even those in the safer head bunkers on the beach were quiet. The only exception was the British command, who were at the top of the hierarchy of all these ranks. The British—or Brittleshit, as Chatty called them—were somewhere else.

One of the enduring changes that emerged from this campaign was the way that the Aussies displayed their dislike for the senior British ranking officers. During their time in the trenches, the Aussies refused to shave, even though there were express orders from above to be clean-shaven every day; the fact that there was a permanent shortage of water was no excuse. Then the Aussies refused to wear the correct uniform. Instead, they wore an assortment of hats, shorts, and shirts with the sleeves ripped out. The sensible Australian commanders simply dealt with the dilemma by saying, 'Choose your own attire.'

On rare visits, the Aussies refused to stand to attention in the presence of a Brittleshit officer. On other occasions, when a young Aussie had to salute a Brit, it was the same action used at home to swat flies.

'I say ... did you see that salute, old man?' the British officer would enquire of his Aussie counterpart.

'Yeah, not bad, eh! Obviously a Queenslander!'

THE EVACUATION TURNED out to be a success. The Turks were fooled; they had little or no idea of the quiet troop withdrawal, which was undertaken under the shield of darkness and with the use of cunning decoys. The men had wrapped their boots in hessian and other materials to dampen the sound as they crept along the familiar ground. As well, rifles were set with strings attached to triggers that fired after a candle burned through the clever delay-mechanism; other ingenious devices attached to very long cords also pulled triggers. Ruses like these led the Turks to think that the trenches still contained troops, ready to rise and charge at a given signal.

And where were they going, these exhausted Anzacs?

'Bloody Egypt, that's where! Bastards should send us 'ome.'

These soldiers would return to their original camp no longer naive, starry-eyed youths on an adventure. These men were now different. Life had been harsh, blunt, cruel, and ruthless. They had acquired wisdom from their survival in such a brutal war. Support for the war among the soldiers did not exist; most of what they had been through had taught them that war was an utter waste. Instead, the feeling of mateship towards one another was total and unquestionable. The Australian soldiers were now a formidable force, and the futility of Gallipoli had beaten out any desire they'd felt before to 'fly the flag'. Many of them now thought of that as 'a load of bullshit'.

This group of weary Aussie soldiers, along with their officers, were about to bring the complete story of Gallipoli and its failures to the British high command in Egypt. Perhaps they thought that their eyewitness reports and evidence of the lack of organisation on the ground would influence those in charge; that the British would learn from the debacle and realise what an appalling tragedy Gallipoli had been.

Gallipoli was a humiliating loss, and an appalling waste of human life. For what? To become an epic battle? This bewildering legend started with military leaders, politicians, and newspapers ignoring the reality, and using terms such as 'patriotic duty' and 'the ultimate sacrifice'. These words jarred for those like Tag and his mates who had seen the war first hand. Those in power didn't mention the men wandering on the beach on the first day, with no ammunition left and at the mercy of the Turkish snipers.

Back home in Australia, nothing appeared in the newspapers for months about the slaughter that had taken place in the landing boats before the soldiers even reached the beaches. The landing was in April; and yet it took until August for people at home to read the first hints in the press about what had happened. Even in those articles, there was no mention of the complete lack of logistical support from those responsible.

The truth was that the Turks had won the battle for Gallipoli. Australia had suffered approximately 26,000 casualties, of whom 7,000 were killed. The press back home gushed about their men's heroism, bravery, courage, and superior skills, and spouted meaningless platitudes. The Turks had won, and there was no mention of the Allies' shattered morale and massive losses, or of the pig-headed stubbornness that had let such appalling carnage continue for almost ten months. Perhaps, in their defence, had both the Australian government and the press told the truth—the whole truth—the repercussions for those in power might have been unthinkable. The Australian public wasn't capable of hearing the whole truth. It would have shattered the young, innocent nation.

CHAPTER FIFTEEN

For the first time in many months, the soldiers were able to wash, put on clean clothes, and sleep in a comfortable bed. It was a rare time when they could have a beer and a rest; a time to chat to the horses. What a sheer joy it was for Tag and the other handlers to meet up with their mounts, and to enjoy the luxury of sitting down at a bench and having a decent meal—well, a meal anyhow. Sleep was curiously difficult; it was too bloody quiet. A mixture of blunt humour and wisecracking conversations returned.

A lot was being said about Gallipoli. It was a constant topic of conversation when they returned to Egypt. After the appalling losses of wounded or killed were revealed, the questions and bitterness began. These seasoned men were close, good mates, hardened to a point that shows of emotion between them were rare. They lived day to day. What hope was there for tomorrow, when the country's leaders incited, boasted of, and didn't hesitate to declare a pointless campaign like Gallipoli a grand achievement—a campaign that none of these decision-makers had ever seen first hand?

The soldiers were hard to handle, and they started drinking heavily. Curiously, the soldiers also started to refer to one another as 'diggers', perhaps because they did two things on Gallipoli—kill and dig. The term stuck.

The irony was that the diggers were good soldiers. They obeyed orders in battle, they respected good officers, and they ignored poor performers. In some armies, poor officers provoked desertions, a lack of commitment, and chaos. But they had no such effect on the Australian army. The diggers could act as individuals, or as a group without rank. They fought ferociously. They stuck together. Once the action started, corporals, sergeants, and officers fought as a team. A soldier's back was always covered; he was were never left behind if wounded, unless it was a hopeless task—like those poor blighters who fell in no-man's-land. There were no heroics in the Australian army: the diggers just did their job.

AFTER THE SUCCESSFUL withdrawal from the peninsula at Gallipoli, and the return to their old camp in Egypt, the Australian command found itself inundated with troops wanting information about their mates. The queues outside the command tent, where a table and paperwork were set up, was a hundred yards long. It was an impossible task for the army to fulfil these requests. Certainly, in the hospitals and medical tents, the formalities of recording such details were a low priority. The date of the injury, and a soldier's name, number, and rank were recorded—that was mandatory—and then there was a brief description of the wound. But that, generally, was the end of the paper trail. The medical staff were exhausted, ill equipped, and in dire need of extra staff. There were few administrative staff or 'paper pushers' to help.

Once settled into their old tent, Tag and Tiger had a new problem. When they first arrived back to the luxury of sand, flies, and three meals a day, they found that two new faces had invaded their tent. Frank and Ted had replaced Golly and Bucket. Chatty's bed was left empty—a good omen, maybe. The new lads had nicknames, but Tag and Tiger called them Frank and Ted. They had been in country for only two weeks. Both were from the wheat belt in Western Australia; one was from north of Esperance, and the other from Geraldton. They were probably good blokes, but they were the unwitting victims of a deep psychological reaction to them. Tag and Tiger were not aware of it, nor were any of the old hands.

New reinforcements, new faces yet to 'be blooded', could find no way to fit in. The same thing had happened back in the trenches. Too often, there were reports of excited new recruits weeping with fear and disbelief. The realisation that they were now part of a world of senseless death was common, but there was more to their distress than fear. Initially, the command thought it was the result of interstate rivalry. But it went deeper than that—too deep for the army to comprehend.

For example, in Tag and Tiger's tent in Egypt, the disquiet felt by the newcomers had its origins in what had happened a long time before they arrived—way back when the boys from the high country had started out on their starry-eyed adventure. As all human beings know, young people do not die. The attendant horrors of the imminent war had never occurred to Tag, Bucket, Chatty, Tiger, and Golly back in Australia—and never would have, even if they had read a hundred books on past wars before they enlisted. Now, though, the brutality of Gallipoli had filled their minds with previously unimaginable sights, smells, and sounds, and the loss of dear mates—mates whom no one could replace. In many cases, the original gang got smaller and smaller; sometimes, it dwindled to just one member. Nevertheless, there was no way that the one remaining soldier would let a new face enter the family or what was left of the gang. The new soldiers had to form their own gangs.

Now, for Tag and Tiger, the new faces of Frank and Ted shone with that starry-eyed look. They were so young, so keen, so patriotic. These young men wanted to penetrate the tight-knit group of war veterans, but there was no way in. Tag could not imagine life without Tiger or Chatty, or vice versa. The idea of having to face such a tragedy in this stupid war was too scary to imagine. Consequently, there was no way that new friendships could be formed. This subtle rejection bewildered the new young men; fortunately, over time, new, small groups formed, but they never reached the deep level of mateship found in the original mob.

Since returning from the peninsula, the lads had started to get into mischief — true to form. The Brittleshit became frustrated with the 'she'll be right' attitude of the diggers in the camp. First, it was the gambling and the copious amounts of sly grog that appeared from ... who knew where.

The response from the Brittleshit was to ban Two-Up, and a longwinded investigation into grog smuggling found exactly nothing. However, more than anything else, the Brittleshit were appalled by the language of the average Aussie and the way he commonly thrived on insults and skulduggery.

The Brittleshit reacted with military aplomb. An official directive was issued by the high command. In a long-winded written request, it asked the Australian command to act upon 'those two beastly words, f___ and b_____,' which were to be banished from the language.

True to form, the diggers responded by moving Two-Up inside their tents, with an unobtrusive guard posted. The word 'fuck' became a descriptive add-on to every uttering.

You fuck'n bewdy!
What the fuck's go'n on?
Fuck me!
Fuck'n oath, mate!
Holy fuck'n Dooley!
Fuck me drunk.

Bill fuck'n Williams, ya mail's 'ere.

Fuck, it's good ta see ya.

To the Brittleshit, it was as if the diggers were now speaking in Chinese. Moreover, as for banning 'bastard', well, any bastard could tell you the outcome of that.

Tiger, a sergeant, and accepted as a responsible leader, was up to his neck in a sophisticated bookie syndicate that would have had the Brittleshit higher-ups, if they had found out about it, 'fuck'n spew'n'. It involved horses, a time clock, and semaphore. At different designated times, a single horse would tear around the camp flat out, through the lines, and down the street, but always on a predetermined track. Then the semaphore flags would flap madly, signalling the next set of odds. With all bets taken, the roadways would clear, miraculously, at a certain time. Then, with the streets deserted, mounted horses would tear past at ten to thirty-second intervals. It worked a treat.

The best thing was, it had the Brittleshit buggered. All they could see, every now and then, was a crazy, bloody digger going hell for leather down the street, urging on his mount, and lying low in the saddle. The only thing the Brittleshit were able to deduce was that most of the riders were small. In fact, what was going on was a well-organised event. Hoppy, from Bairnsdale, calculated the weights: if a horse won too often, the jockey, in a digger uniform with a coloured ribbon on the horse's tail, would be weighed down with extra water canteens full of sand. Part of the reason the system worked was that the Aussie officers were in on the cunning scheme as well.

The reaction of the Brittleshit was curious. They felt that the constant semaphore practice was highly commendable, and were very confused by the Australians' horse-exercising methods. Then, out of frustration or maybe in retaliation, the Brits, unable to quell the Aussie spirit, increased the pointless drill regime.

It seemed tit for tat.

The races continued.

The severity of the drill increased.

The rebelliousness of the Aussies prevailed.

The high command persisted, and finally force-marched the Aussies into the desert sands in an exercise that could have ended in appalling casualties had not a handful managed to make it to the other end and send back supplies, help, and medical aid to the exhausted, dehydrated Australian troops. The insubordinate nature of the Aussies won out. The British simply turned their backs, and let the Aussie command settle these unruly troops.

Back in the main camp, Tag and Tiger became serious about Chatty; they hadn't heard a word about him for months, despite having made many enquiries. Neither would admit that they felt he had met his maker. Their last hope was to get some leave and ask at the hospitals. Tiger organised a trip and, when it was only six days away, Tag read his mail several times — he wanted to be 'full bottle' with the news from home when they found Chatty. He had received over ten letters since his arrival in Egypt, mostly from Ann and Sally. Some brought sad news:

Seventeen young men from the East Gippsland region killed already. However, pleased to hear that from all accounts the war is going well. There is talk of conscription, must be hard up for numbers? Bad drought, 1914–16, need rain, hay and chaff getting scarce. Mr Banks passed on; he took his son's death (Bucket) very badly … a few new cars seen in the district, bushfires a worry.

The news from home was welcome. However, for Tag, there was still nothing from Jill. No re-directed mail … nothing. He wanted to write to her from Gallipoli, but how could you write to anyone about Gallipoli? He didn't realise that he didn't need to try to hide anything from Jill. She was fully aware of the debacle, and a letter from him would have been most welcome. Tag, in fact, wrote very few letters. This is what he wrote in his first letter home on 26 June after a month in the trenches.

Dear Mum,

We have been here just over a month. We have had shells and lost a few men. Poor old Golly has gone, as you know, he died bravely. Bucket hasn't been well. He'll be okay. It's very hot here with a lot of flies. We don't get much news on the war here. Miss your home cooking mum, say hello to Sally ------
[The censor had his way with the next four lines, which praised the attitude of the Turks]

How are my horses? Don't know how long we'll be here.

Love Tag
X X X

Like most diggers, Tag wasn't able to paint the true picture of Gallipoli. Words that showed sorrow and desperation were beyond his untidy hand and limited education. More importantly, he would never reveal the truth; it was easier to let them believe what the papers said. Years later, no diggers wanted to tell it as it really was. How could they? They didn't run newspapers or countries. They just did what was asked of them. Eventually, some of their tiny, hidden diaries would reveal the truth.

LEAVE, AT LAST: the five days of waiting were over. Bearing small, tight grins, Tag and Tiger headed for Cairo. They had been stuck in camp for almost a month. The spring was back in Tag's step — he limped, but it didn't slow him down any more — and there was a glint in Tiger's eye. The ancient city was a welcome change: electric trams, trinkets, markets, and smoky dens with music. Tiger headed for the dens. His priorities were now grog, sex, and a nap, in that order.

The 'live only from day today' attitude that had been entrenched at Gallipoli led to drinking and sexual excesses among the Aussies on their return to Egypt. The local population didn't like the foreigners. With so many diggers about and not enough prostitutes, prices soared; so did tempers. Clashes and abuse followed the diggers. No, they weren't good ambassadors for their country. They had a life-expectancy of maybe twelve months, and recently there'd been whispers — heavy, sad words — about the war in France. News had filtered through the camp, and the diggers knew that was where some of them were heading. The reports came from the mess halls, local people in the city, and the medical staff. It sounded terrible, so why not live it up while you could?

On arrival in Cairo, Tag hoped to see both Chatty and Jill. He hadn't heard from Jill for ages. He guessed she was too busy. At least he hoped that was it — he prayed that she hadn't been posted somewhere else.

An excited Tag had found Chatty, after some persistence and a lot of waiting. Chatty was still in the palace hospital — that was all Tag could find out. However, his enquiries about Nurse Jill Hunter proved fruitless. The man he asked, a new ward attendant, hadn't heard of the woman. At the main entrance to the wing, Tag asked for directions to Chatty's ward and bed. Thankfully, it didn't take too long. Chatty was well known; he had been in and out of the same ward for months.

'Ward fourteen, mate, down the passage and to the right.'

Tag stood at the door to the ward that held Chatty. He hesitated, and felt a strange fear. It was created by the scene itself and by something he had never considered before: what happened after the trenches, once you were carried out on a stretcher? Surely the army provided the best for these brave soldiers? He shook as he walked cautiously towards the lad from the butter factory. The smell in the ward was sickening—a foul stench of strong chemicals and dry, rotting blood. Most patients greeted Tag's nods with blank stares. Many, he noticed, had had amputations. Then he was beside Chatty.

'Ya ugly bastard. Ya still slackin' in bed?'

'Yeah,' was Chatty's flat reply.

'Food good, ya bludger?'

'Yeah.'

'What's goin' on, mate?'

As Chatty was about to answer, a trolley rattled with pans and instruments as it passed. The petrified Chatty ripped the sheets over his head. Then, slowly, a pair of staring eyes emerged, quickly surveying the area for snipers ... enemy ... danger.

'I'm a bundle of friggin' nerves, mate,' he said. 'Not as bad as some of these poor codgers, but all I do all day is jump and then start cryin'. What the friggin' hell's goin' on, mate? Got a smoke?'

Tag looked at Chatty as if he was seeing a ghost. He wanted to bolt, to get out of there quick smart. But, composing himself, Tag took a deep breath and started again. He didn't talk; he just wanted to reach out and cautiously touch this odd but familiar man. His mind would not accept the world in front of him. This wasn't his Chatty; it just looked like him. Chatty was a dag, a laugh a minute—not an old man with the shakes, his eyes flicking everywhere, his lips quivering. Again, reassuring himself, Tag spoke with some hesitancy.

'Sure I got a smoke, mate. Seen Jill?'

Chatty's eyes bulged, and he nodded his head. 'Yeah, mate, She looks ratshit to me; too friggin' busy. Hell of a job, poor beggar. She stopped and talked to me once or twice, asking about you an' all, and got bloody well balled-out by some officer poonce, poor little bugger.'

Chatty had tears streaming down his face.

'Doesn't pay to ask questions about ya mates around here—particularly, ya don't ask the nurses. Poor bastards get to know too many of the poor fellas who come in. Poor friggin' Jill, that's all I can say.'

The hospital was just as Chatty described it. There was no laughter, for sure—you'd expect that—and almost no talking. Unless you had a mate, of course, but that was rarely the case. Poor Chatty: his jerking, awkward conversation went round in circles. He tried to ask how such-and such was, or so-and-so. But, soon, he just groaned, coughed, and stopped talking.

Tag guessed the nature of Chatty's enquiry but, like him, avoided the topic. How do you say the names of so many without destroying what little emotional strength you have in reserve? Then Chatty shuffled in the bed.

'I'll be walk'n on that friggin' thing in a friggin' month, mark my words. I was doing okay, then I got friggin' gangrene, bastard stuff. This is the third time they've had a go, eh. Just when I'm ready to leave, the bastard thing gets rotten again. I reckon it's because I shits me bed sometimes and they don't have the time to clean it up straight away, eh?'

Tag stepped back as Chatty swung his stump out from under the dirty sheet. It was purple, and the end of it looked like a bunch of grapes. Almost cut off at the hip, it looked disgusting to Tag.

'Reckon I'll be able to stuff it in a long leg and boot, eh?'

Chatty looked at Tag with pleading eyes. Tag struggled to look at the mangled leg, or what remained of it.

'A special boot, mate, a special leg and boot. I reckon Bill at McCoy's in Omeo could make me a special boot. He's real good with leather and rivets and stuff.'

The next hour was a sad, confusing time for Tag. It was his first introduction to shell shock. He'd seen many a poor bugger

211

break down in the trenches, but he'd thought they were just 'doing it a bit rough'.

Now, in this room that surely resembled Hades, Tag realised that Chatty was in one of two worlds. In one, he was ever vigilant, checking every nook and cranny for Turks, or for familiar whistles like an artillery shell dropping short. The other world was a mixture of home, Swifts Creek, the pub, and the people. Chatty never mentioned the present. He continually planned how he would manage at home and at work.

'Takes a lot to stop me, mate. Most times I can hop up and have a leak, ya know?'

Then, suddenly, for a brief, heartbreaking moment, Chatty was there with his friend Tag—his mate. Chatty asked him about Tiger, about how things were in camp, and whether they'd be going to France. He even asked after some of the horses. Tag looked down; he'd had enough. Bravely, he said to Chatty, 'I gotta get go'n, mate. Gotta be back in camp by dusk, or I'll be in the shit. See ya soon, eh, mate?'

Chatty stuck his thumb in the air.

'No friggin' worries, mate. I'll meet ya down the pub after work, okay?'

Tag turned, stared at the marble floor, and strode out. Nothing but *Gotta get outta here* buzzed inside his head. The torture of the short-lived get-together with Chatty had sapped Tag of any desire to meet Jill. He just wanted to be alone in some quiet, warm place, away from the army and the war. He walked out into the foyer of the hospital. Everywhere there were blokes asking questions, harassing staff, pleading for information.

'But he was shipped here two weeks ago.'

'You've never friggin' heard of him? Come on, stuff me. Bill friggin' Jensen—he copped it in the guts.'

Tag was horrified. Every one of his senses was affronted by the smell, the panic, the scene in the wards and, finally, the desperation of mates seeking mates. His naive belief that, once away from Gallipoli, those wounded blokes would be okay, was shattered. He sat, exhausted, on the marble step at the columned entrance and rolled a smoke. His first thought was, *Time to get pissed*.

He scratched his head and tried to remember where Tiger had said he was going. He patted his pocket; he had plenty of dough. *Time to get really pissed …*

CHAPTER SIXTEEN

On that same day, early in the morning, Jill was about to begin her shift. She had snatched four hours' sleep and eaten a brief breakfast, and then walked briskly to the hospital. Standing at the door to the ward, what little sleep or drowsiness was left in her body was dispatched by a blunt, cold reality. The scene that confronted Jill was one of foul-smelling, almost unspeakable misery. As always, it blasted her into a wide-awake state as she entered. It was a sight not easily dismissed. Regularly in her dreams, she would enter that same ward, and she would see the devil there — sitting on his throne, high above the patients and medical staff, smirking, and surveying his kingdom.

Sick and wounded men were in beds, some on the floor, and some in passageways. All were missing limbs; many had head injuries. The sounds emanating from them were the saddest imaginable. Kneeling on a filthy, blood-stained floor, a cheerless padre was rubbing a lad's grey forehead with his thumb, muttering words of comfort and peace, and giving him absolution to pass on to another world. Jill shuddered, absent-mindedly tugged the front of her uniform straight, took a deep breath, gave a calm sigh, made a tiny smile, and then strutted like any well-trained nurse across the ward. Most of these men had yet to be treated. Many had been there for days.

Of all the medical staff, the nurses had to remain calm, composed, and supposedly immune to such horror. Like most people who had lived a relatively normal life before the war, Jill had never before seen so many emotionally disturbed people. The poor, suffering beggars kept describing horrendous scenes they had witnessed that flashed in and out of their minds continually. In most wards where she worked during daylight hours, any strange or loud sounds — such as that caused by the dropping of a metal dish — would turn the patients into jumping, tearful wrecks. In time, veterans with this problem were labelled as suffering from 'shell shock'. But the saddest of all were the nights, just when it was time for them to rest their wounded, tired bodies with sleep. Instead, the soldiers' minds went berserk; each night, they were further traumatised by nightmares. Most of these men who came back from Gallipoli would remain emotionally wrecked for life.

The daily routine for Jill and the medical staff involved appeasing or ignoring their distressed patients, briefly administering treatment to their terrible wounds, and coping with continual pandemonium. It was chaos. Because the hospitals were understaffed and ill equipped, and there was never enough space for the wounded, the mayhem was permanent. Naturally, the army, pre-occupied with its next campaign and not the recovery of its wounded soldiers, ignored the problem. Yet, like nearly all nurses, Jill somehow managed. Sadly, some of her workmates didn't: a number of the young nurses were unable to survive the madness of the hospital. They were sent home to mental asylums, displaying severe emotional instability.

A nurse was meant to work, rest, and work, and partake of the odd escorted stroll. The administration's paranoia about how to handle females resulted in nurses being prevented from 'letting their hair down' or enjoying any freedom. This was the exact opposite of the soldiers' regular leave or brief breaks.

With no respite allowed them, some nurses started to crack up. At first, they would cry continually while alone in their quarters, and find themselves unable to sleep, even though they were exhausted. Then they would become irrational, talking to people in their quarters who weren't there, and hiding in wardrobes or cupboards when it was time for their shift. Finally, the nightmares and intrusions started.

There was never enough time for a nurse, especially the time that was most important for her—the time to have a brief chat with her patient. When a patient talked to a nurse, rarely was she able to respond with a reassuring touch, or by putting her hand softly on his forehead, or even by fluffing his pillow. The nurse was too busy. This type of contact was powerful and healing, particularly during a time of suffering; and, more than any of the medical staff, the nurses could sense the lack of this vital personal contact in their work in the wards. For those women unable to cope, it started to affect their innermost souls. They started to break down.

It was pitiful, and an embarrassment to the army. Their treatment of nurses who showed all the symptoms of shell shock was simple: they said nothing, shipped them back to Australia sucking their thumbs and humming, and locked them up in institutions called asylums. These poor young women had succumbed to the madness; the shields they had used to ignore the constant suffering had been crushed. Their normal display of courage in adversity wasn't strong enough to help these nurses cope with the human carnage on display. What they had experienced had the same effect on them as it did on the troops in the trenches.

IT WAS AFTERNOON. The day was like any other. Jill had worked frantically until a rostered relief allowed her time to leave the calamity of the ward and rush off for a quick meal. Walking to the front door of the magnificent Palace building that had been converted to a hospital, she looked for a duty officer to escort her to the mess. Suddenly, there, to her astonishment, stood Tag. He appeared lost—not in his head, but in his heart or soul. Standing next to the magnificent column, outside the front of the hospital on the marble veranda, Tag was staring blankly at the step, and was smoking a cigarette. His shoulders sagged, and Jill was shocked at his loss of weight and the way he had aged so much in a matter of months. His nose, blistered and roughened like a strawberry, looked terrible. There were bags under his eyes. He looked like he needed a week's sleep. His whole demeanour gave Jill a shock.

'Tag?'

Turning, he stared numbly, then nodded in recognition. A short-lived smile rushed across his rugged face, but he looked away quickly.

'Tag, my God. It's good to see you, Tag. It's so good to see you! Tag? Say something, Tag! Are you okay?'

Had Tag opened his mouth, he would have roared with pain and frustration. Looking at Jill, his eyes glassed over. Again, he lowered his head, but this time he held his hand over his eyes. His shoulders heaved several times, and then he nodded.

'You've been to see someone?'

There was no verbal response … just a nod.

'Chatty? You've seen poor Chatty?' Jill asked, becoming distressed.

He nodded, and then, stretching out one arm, had to steady himself against the marble column. He started to shake. It was all too much—too much for this very young but very old Australian man who longed for his simple youth, for his lizards and horses. At that moment, even the sound of a crow would have been all right.

It had already been too much while visiting Chatty. Briefly, Tag had wondered how Jill could cope with it every day. At the time, in a strange way, he hoped he wouldn't see her.

Tag stood up straight, turned, and went to walk away. Inside his chest was a a hurricane that screamed for release. It consumed poor Tag. He was completely exhausted. He wanted to sleep — no, to get drunk, fool around, and then sleep — for days. He had to be alone until he found Tiger. He walked away from Jill, but she strode after him.

'Tag, please come with me.'

Jill took him by the hand and quickly led him along a passage and through two immense doors. In a courtyard outside were medicos and nurses sitting in the sun, enjoying a break. They were still in white uniforms — covered in splattered blood. Jill, with a false, beaming smile, led Tag to a senior-looking gentleman wearing a major's insignia. Jill introduced him.

'Dr Bentley, this is my brother, Tag. With your permission, sir, I would like to show him the parcel I got from Mum yesterday.'

'You're a lucky blighter to have a fine sister like Jill, son. I'll write a note for the duty officer, Jill. How do you spell Tag?'

Tag didn't answer. Dr Bentley scribbled an indecipherable note and handed it to Jill.

'Nice to meet you, son.'

The men didn't shake hands or salute; the doctor was an officer, although not in uniform or wearing a hat. Then Tag, like Dimble his pony all those years ago, just plodded obediently along, quite content to place total trust in the human being leading him. At the door to the nurses' dormitory, an official-looking guard with a neat uniform and polished shoes greeted Jill with a salute.

'Evening, Miss Hunter.'

'Evening, Corporal Grates. This is Tag, my brother. Dr

Bentley has kindly invited him to have a look around the hospital and grounds, and then we thought we'd have a cup of tea in the canteen, eh, Tag?'

Tag nodded vaguely.

'He wrote me a note.'

'Don't you worry about that, Miss. You two young people enjoy yourselves.'

Jill led Tag up the long, winding staircase. She prayed that there would be no one about. He, somewhat stunned, but still horse-like, plodded along. Jill sensed a deep sadness in this exhausted young man, and desperately wanted to comfort him. She opened the door to her shared room quietly and turned to Tag.

'Shhh! I'll wake Doreen and tell her what's going on.'

Since arriving in Egypt, Jill had shared the room with Doreen Haywood, a fellow nurse. She woke Doreen softly.

'This is my friend, Tag. He's staying for a while.'

Turning to Tag, Jill squeezed his hand.

'I can only speak to you for ten minutes, and then I have to go back to work. Would you stay here till I get back?'

Tag nodded. Jill then handed Tag a bed bonnet. She showed him to her bed and held both his hands.

'Dear Tag, I was so worried about you. I couldn't get any sense out of some of your wounded chums … they said there were many killed. I have to go back to work. I shouldn't be here. You shouldn't be here. Lie in my bed. If you hear someone, put on my bonnet and pretend to be asleep. They check our quarters at least once a night. I'll be back some time. Poor Doreen has only had two hours' sleep, but she'll have to get up soon. She's a good friend. Then we can talk.'

The next six minutes of conversation were a one-sided repetition of much the same for Jill. Finally, she nearly squeezed the living daylights out of Tag, kissed him softly on the head, and then breezed down the stairs like an autumn wind skipping and rustling along. Correcting herself, she quickly slipped back into the nurses' brisk-step, and walked with deliberation towards the guard.

'Matron has sent me back; she will show Tag out the east door shortly.'

'Good-oh, Miss Hunter.'

The dog-tired Tag actually fell asleep.

Jill didn't smile as she walked back into the ward, but her eyes did. She had lost her appetite. In the small staff cubicle, she greeted the duty officer.

'I'm back, doctor.'

This evening would be a better one for Jill. Although nothing had changed in the hospital, she had a distraction—Tag. As she worked, she thought of him constantly. She wanted to talk to him without drawing breath. She wanted to have a friend who wasn't wounded, crying, or dying in a bed or in a passage. She wanted a mate who wasn't a doctor or a nurse. Like any person caught up in the war, she craved some moments of sanity.

Later that evening, the doctor and Jill walked into the burns unit. This ward looked different from the others: many of the men in it were under tent-like screens made of cotton and netting. Some of the patients were completely screened, while others had their legs and arms under the fine cotton screens. The ward was too full, and the smell was foul, indicating rotting flesh. But, more than that, there was also a smell which indicated that maggots were doing their work. The ward floor, which felt crunchy underfoot, had been deliberately covered in coarse sand in order to slow down the movement of the maggots that fell off the beds. The maggots were an accepted way of treating burns; they not only cleaned the wound, but also ate dead, rotting skin and flesh.

In fact, the use of maggots constituted a clean, healthy medical treatment for which there was no alternative, but the hospital staff knew that it was unacceptable to have maggots crawling over humans to clean their disgusting wounds. Deception was used to solve the problem: staff hid the evidence under fine cotton veils that were usually used to keep mosquitoes away. Occasionally, maggots would drop onto the floor, and sweepers would tread on them and then brush them frantically into the sand. Perhaps the patients were aware of the little creatures; but, if they were, they said nothing. Back in the trenches, maggots had been an everyday sight at Gallipoli, particularly in no-man's-land. Here, in the burns unit, a digger would complain occasionally about itching or irritation caused by the maggots, but the nurses would rebuff him by replying, 'Burns always itch, old man.'

However, burns, more than most other injuries, left cratered, disfiguring scars. Mirrors were scarce in a burns unit: only the nurses carried them. The quiet doctor and Jill were nearing the end of the first row of beds. The next patient they met with was a young soldier who had had terrible, searing burns to his neck and face. Jill reached inside her apron and pulled out the scissors. She carefully cut across the bandages as close to the skin as possible, then stood back. The doctor, using tweezers, pulled carefully. The young soldier screwed the blankets up and went tense. As the bandage finally gave way, the doctor gulped, closed his eyes, and lifted his head toward the roof. The young man had no hair or face. Even his lips were missing. Jill spoke first.

'It's healed well—very well. We'll have you out of here in no time.'

The doctor, not as strong as Jill, agreed, and added, 'You've done well. A trip home, I would imagine.'

The wound, in fact, was as the doctor had expected. The burns had taken ten weeks to heal, and the process had gone relatively well. The skin was dimpled and pitted, green in places, and very tender. However, the patient had a head like a cabbage.

He had some sight in one eye, and was able to eat. Back home, people would call a person like this 'a freak'.

Jill cleaned up the wound gently, and patted the soldier's hand. Then she followed the doctor to the next bed; in it was a young man of, at most, nineteen years of age. Both of his hands had been burnt off when he had attempted to rescue a mate. Today was the day he was to be told — later, by the nurse — that he had no hands. He thought they were under all those bandages, somewhere.

Sadly, all of this was part of the normal routine in the burns unit.

Three hours after first entering the unit, the doctor turned to Jill and suggested they have a hot cuppa. It was her first break, and she was exhausted. Over tea, they chatted politely and then, suddenly, the doctor spoke.

'I wonder what he looked like before, that poor burnt fellow.'

Jill looked the doctor in the eye.

'I wonder what will happen when he finds out what he looks like now, sir.'

'Doesn't bear thinking about, Jill.'

'Oh, yes it does, doctor. I'll be the one with the mirror, sir.'

He ignored Jill's comment. Nevertheless, it highlighted the reality of what occurred in the hospital: often, the nurse had to break the real news. The doctor would give the initial report, which would be brief and often conveyed awkwardly, and then he would be gone.

'What was that all about, Sister?' a patient would often ask later.

Too often, the buck stopped with them, the nurses. Thankfully, they had a special compassion, a sense of duty that often deserted the men working in the hospitals. The nurses had a strength which equalled that of the soldiers, and at times surpassed it. They, like the men in the trenches, developed ways of coping. They didn't look to superiors for support, comfort, and compassion; instead, they relied on their mates. Jill knew whom to turn to when she felt down—a nurse called Lola. Then, if possible, after confiding her woes to her close friend, she would spend time reading books about love that had happy endings. These novels were much sought after by the nurses; reading them was a way to relax. Other times, she would knit frantically in a kind of trance while staring into space. Initially, at the beginning of the Gallipoli campaign, when she had had a very bad day, Jill established a pattern that became her last resort: she would write down her thoughts in a diary.

Soon, every day was a bad day, and she made daily entries. It was a therapeutic outlet, one in which Jill could vent her sense of anger, hopelessness, disgust, and deep sorrow. She wrote bitter notes about the unspeakable suffering that she witnessed. She loathed those who perpetuated war. She tried to describe the misery, but words often failed this sweet young woman, and her tears stained the page. Sometimes, there was a black scratch and a smudge where she pushed so hard that the lead snapped and perforated the page.

Over time, the language in the diary became more bitter and exasperated as Jill questioned the rules under which she worked. It was her private release, because her job and her position did not allow such discussions to occur. Most of the time, her companions were nurses, doctors, and army officers—senior officers, mainly. The army camps that held the diggers were strictly out of bounds for nurses. The restrictions on nurses didn't stop there: within the hospitals, there was a clear and distinct separation of the ranks. A nurse didn't just sit down and have a chat with the senior sisters, ward charge-sisters and supervisors, or the lady matron. Discipline was strict: even minor misdemeanours were severely punished. Compared to those in public life, the rules governing nurses were very harsh.

CHAPTER SEVENTEEN

Jill's shift had finished. She had just completed a seventeen-hour stint containing one brief break. Taking stock of her day, she dismissed the bedlam and thought of Tag. It had been five-and-a-half hours since she'd left him, but he'd looked so done-in that Jill reckoned he would have been asleep in minutes.

She walked slowly to the quarters and bid goodnight to the duty officer. On the ground floor, in the laundry, Jill collected a pail of warm water for a wash and then plodded even more slowly up the stairs to her room. She quietly pushed the door open, put the pail down, and lit a candle. In the semi-darkness, she noticed a vacant bed. There was only one person in the room. She walked over to the other bed and said, 'Time to wake up.'

Tag stirred. It was 11.30 p.m. Jill had started at 6.00 a.m. that same day.

Jill spoke first.

'Hi, stranger. I'm having a wash, a half-hour's chat, and then a sleep. Okay?'

'Sure, mate.'

These were the first words that Tag had spoken to Jill all day — for months, in fact. She blew out the candle and there was quiet, interrupted only by a rustling of clothes, some small sighs and, finally, splashing water.

'Would you wash my back, Tag?'

He could just see Jill in the metal tub, as the broken light of the moon tried to force its way through the thin curtains. Jill had a towel covering her front. He gently took the washer and rubbed her back softly. Jill arched her back like Patch used to — Patch, the piebald rebel stagecoach horse that Tag had shod as an apprentice blacksmith over what seemed a lifetime ago. Her nostrils didn't quiver like the horse's did, but she did purr. Tag had tears in his eyes that Jill couldn't see. They gently rolled down his cheeks, and he glowed with a love that had the power of a sunrise. Her smell alerted his senses — those sharp senses that remembered things like a cold, frosty morning on the flat across from the cabin at Sheepstation Creek.

'Do you have a brush?' he asked.

Jill rose, dripping wet, and walked to the wardrobe. She put on a gown, lit the candle, and reached for her brush. Plopping on the floor with her back to Tag, her body between his legs, she threw her head back. Tag sat on the edge of the bed, and brushed and stroked her with the tenderness offered to a baby the first time you brush its hair. She flopped her arms over his legs and melted with pleasure.

'Tag, this is what I want. Someone who knows this life, but doesn't need to speak about it. This is so beautiful, Tag.'

Tears flowed even more freely from the tired soldier. A mixture of sadness and joy filled his soul. Tag had always been the quiet one. Ann, his mum, did all the talking when he was young. At school, he rarely spoke. Growing up, he spoke more to animals than humans. Later, at the blacksmith's, Bill the boss made enough noise for everyone. Then, his mates from home having signed up with him, Tag was always in the background. He was a listener.

After some time, he spoke.

'When Golly was killed, I went funny ... I didn't know

how to be with a dead mate. At home, when Dad died, it was okay—Mum took over. I thought there was some way you were supposed to be when someone dies. So I …'

He stopped. His emotions were on hold. That area of his being was too painful.

'Please go on, Tag.'

Flashes of Golly and Bucket, two of his best mates, and the trenches at Gallipoli were intruding freely in his mind. He wanted to speak, but didn't know what to say.

'It's okay, Tag. It truly is.'

'When Bucket died, it was too much. I couldn't cope. I wanted to hide and … I wanted to be with you Jill, not Mum … I wanted to be with you. I knew you would understand.'

Turning, Jill threw her arms around his belly. He lowered his chin onto her warm hair, and together they both swayed gently. Suddenly, the swell of love and affection towards each other was overwhelming. First, there were tears and rocking. Then, silence—a sweet, warm silence followed by a soft hum of joy and contentment.

'Tag, I'm so tired that I feel sick. When do you have to be back in camp?

'Tomorrow night. Yeah, ten o'clock tomorrow night … bugger it.'

'Got anything special on?'

'No way, mate—just this great sheila called Jill!'

Jill punched him on the arm.

'Sleep in Doreen's bed,' she said. 'I have to get up in four hours and go to work. I'll come back as soon as I can and see you. It will be early, then we can make plans.'

They embraced warmly. Jill wanted more, but knew this was not the time. It was 1.30 a.m. She was asleep in minutes, and was up again by 4.00 a.m. She kissed Tag tenderly and left, promising to return shortly.

Jill's plan required theft, cunning, a lie, and courage. She got up an hour early for a good reason. Rushing down the steps to the nurses' station, she informed the night supervisor that she'd come in early to help with the staff laundry. Nurses, like batmen, were expected to wash all the medical staffs' uniforms and gowns. Quickly, she filled an empty laundry bag, and headed for the washrooms. After soaking the bloodied gowns and uniforms, she went to the wards. By 6.00 a.m., she excused herself, returned to the laundry, and packed another bag. She headed for the nurses' quarters to collect further laundry. Then, leaping the stairs two at a time, she opened the door to her room. She greeted Tag with a brief hug.

'Get dressed, Tag—or, should I say, Captain Lakes of the Army Medical Corps.'

He held up the uniform and eyed it with suspicion.

'Where'd ya get this?'

'An officer's locker. It's the only way I could think of getting you in and out of here.'

'Hell, you'll get me hung,' Tag replied, with a huge grin on his face.

Jill explained the plan as he changed into the uniform.

'You look good, Tag—just like an officer. Leave your hat off. This is what's going to happen. I take you downstairs, the guard doesn't ask any questions, and I do the talking. Then you step out, with me walking behind. At the hospital, you leave me and go down to the officers' club, to be shaved and tidied up. I suggest you tell anyone who asks you that you're a veterinary surgeon on loan from … say, somewhere in Victoria. If asked, you should be able to bluff your way out of it. Book all your drinks down to Dr Harrows—he's an alcoholic, and wouldn't know the difference. Follow me.'

'Hell!' was Tag's only response.

Then, downstairs and at the front of the hospital, Jill stood to attention as she spoke to Captain Lakes.

'Enjoy your day in Cairo, sir ... Do as I say and we'll be fine, okay?'

'Sure, mate,' answered a somewhat wary Tag, cautiously glancing this way and that as if looking for snipers.

'Meet me here at 2.00 p.m. You will be my escort into town tonight, sir.'

To Tag's amazement, Jill then saluted him, bowed her head, and walked away briskly. He stood stunned, and walked out into the streets of Cairo with some hesitation. He put the hat on his head, looked down the long avenue, and felt that impersonating a bloody officer wasn't such a good move. He realised that he had no idea where the officers' club was located, and wasn't sure if he should visit it anyway. Then an idea popped into his head: he knew where the fellows hung out, so he might wander down there. The Hararbar was a popular watering hole-cum-pick-up place for the Aussies. Tag had been there before; in fact, he'd been kicked out by the military police just before the fun started. He had spent the rest of that leave locked up.

As he turned into the street that held the bar, he recognised the palm trees and a high fence surrounding the ancient building. Laughter, music, and merriment drifted out into the street. There was a guard in Arabic garb at the gateway. He stood to attention, and bowed and saluted all at once.

'You come for your men, sir.'

'No, just for a drink.'

'Drink? No good plurry place for officer man. You no don't drink here, sir.'

Tag frowned. The guard added, 'You a new doctor, sir. You should go to officer bar at club for drinking.'

It then dawned on Tag that his uniform displayed Medical Corps colours as well as a captain's rank.

'Thanks. Where's the bar for officers?'

Turning to another Arab, the guard muttered something in his own language, and a young man came forward.

'Sir, this is Harleeb. He will take you to officers' good bar and good mess, thank you. Good today to you, sir.'

Tag thanked the guard and shook the outstretched hand, not realising that the guard wanted a tip. He then forgot to return the salute and marched off following Harleeb. A short twenty-minute walk later, they were out the front of a palatial, two-storeyed ancient building. It was magnificent. Harleeb bowed, and again Tag shook the extended hand that asked for money. At the door was a suitably attired Indian gentleman with a huge moustache and a cultured voice. He saluted Tag.

'Captain, sir, what is being your pleasure, sir?'

'I'd like a shave, a haircut, a drink, and a quiet smoke, mate.'

The Indian gentleman raised one eyebrow at Tag's use of the word 'mate'.

'You are being an Australian doctor, sir.'

'A veterinary doctor.'

'And what is that, good captain, sir?'

'A doctor that looks after animals — in my case, horses.'

'Ah, captain, sir. What a villi good thing, sir.'

Tag was ushered into a large foyer, invited to sign the book, and then shown to the barbers. When he returned to the bar, another smart young man wearing a cummerbund invited Tag to sit down.

'I can take your hat, and what would sir like to drink?'

'A beer thanks, mate.'

'And your tab, sir?'

'Pardon?'

'What tab shall I put the drink on, sir?'

No answer. Another officer leant over, 'You have to book it up, old boy.'

Tag, red faced, racked his brain. Jill had told him about this.

'Oh shit, yeah—bloody Dr Harrows. Thanks, mate.'

The waiter, eyes wide open, stared at Tag in amazement. Never had he heard such language in the officers' bar.

'Villi good, sir.'

Tag enjoyed the beer; it was cool and soothing. He was sitting alone at a small table. Leaning back in the chair and looking around for the first time, he was amazed at the quiet in the room, even though it was almost half full. There was no loud noise or atmosphere. It seemed that the highly ranked officers dominated the conversations, and appeared to control the environment. Lower-ranked young officers laughed at jokes, but with no conviction. Some, he noticed—usually under the influence of alcohol—started to liven up the atmosphere. However, this was subdued easily by means of arched eyebrows and subtle coughs. Tag was curious. He couldn't help but notice that there was something missing, but what it was eluded him for the moment. Another officer came over and asked if he could sit at Tag's table. Tag nodded, and the man introduced himself as Peter Murphy—Captain Peter Murphy. Tag responded with 'Bill Lakes'.

'I see you're a doctor.'

'Yes, a doctor of animal husbandry. Not many of us over here—the horses get sick too, you know.' Tag gritted his teeth and immediately realised it was a dumb thing to say. Murphy just smiled.

'I'm from Adelaide—originally worked in a bank. I've only been here four weeks. I'm due to go to France with the Artillery. You sound like you've just come off the farm.'

Tag and Murphy prattled away for quite a while, then Tag asked, 'Is this your first time here, in the club?'

'No, old man. I've been here every night since I arrived. Swell place, you agree?'

'Is it always so bloody quiet?'

'What do you mean? This is the best mess I've been in—bloody Sydney was terrible. Count yourself lucky, old man; you can let your hair down in here.'

Then, like opening a curtain to a much-darkened room on a bright, sunny day, Tag realised he was seeing something hollow, even sad. There was no skylarking, no gambling, no swearing, no insults, and no fun. Even the waiters were men—there were no buxom wenches here. The fact that he could talk without shouting to Peter Murphy in a room of fifty men was amazing. It dawned on Tag that these officers had a tough job. To work with their men was fine. Good officers gained respect. However, to unwind, get pissed, stuff around, and finally to be put to bed in an alcoholic state was all part of the army that Tag understood. But this didn't happen in the officers' army. Here, a subtle protocol prevailed that created a stilted, awkward atmosphere. After only two hours, Tag wanted to leave, throw away the uniform, and plod around as Corporal Wardell. He turned to Captain Murphy.

'I have to go, captain, sir.'

Captain Murphy looked quizzically and then in a slightly disappointed way at Tag. Smiling, he said to Tag, 'I'm sorry about that. I was looking forward to a good chat and lunch. Might see you in France.'

Tag shook Murphy's hand, was handed his cap, and walked out into the busy street. With his fresh haircut and shave, he looked like an officer. Locals packed the footpaths, apart from soldiers dotted here and there. On the road were camels, carts, and several motorised vehicles. It was a bustle of noise and energy, with street-side cafés everywhere. They were places for meeting, talking, and drinking mint tea. Board games like backgammon and cards were popular, but no money changed hands as it did back in camp. There was no gambling in Egypt; Islamic law forbade such things.

Tag was thirsty, and noticed a drink-seller leaning on the trunk of a palm tree. Like many sights in this ancient city, the drink-seller, adorned in his traditional outfit, looked just as he would have hundreds of years before. Around his girth, a wide leather belt was fitted with beautifully jewelled glass-holders in which there were six glasses. Two huge, ornate, antique metal vessels hung over the man's shoulders, each of them containing traditional liquors: karkade, made from the flowers of the hibiscus tree, and the bittersweet tamarindi. He sang of his produce, beckoning buyers. On request, the seller poured a large drink and handed it to Tag. He sipped it warily, admiring the strong, heavy drink that left a pleasant taste in his mouth. He handed over some money.

'You like our drink, sir?'

'Very much.'

Then, after a pause, Tag asked, 'Where can I buy some jewellery?'

'You are wanting something for girl, sir?'

'Yes, someone very special.'

'I have brother that sells best jewellery in Cairo, sir.'

Waving his arms and chattering like a parrot in a fruit tree, the drink-seller led Tag down a narrow alleyway that opened onto a marketplace. They stopped, and an excited conversation made up of waving arms, grins, and hugs took place between the seller and another Arab man.

'This is my brother, Zahir. He will show you jewellery being for sir's special woman friend.'

The man bowed and invited Tag to sit.

'Coffee for sir?'

The two men sat and talked for ages. Tag was fascinated that Zahir and Harleeb could both speak English.

'It because we get work as servants in Englishman's mansion. Our family has been working for this family for long time.'

Tag enjoyed the company, and finally they got around to the matter of jewellery. Zahir spread out a large cloth roll of fine silk on the table. A collection of spectacular, delicate necklaces and rings sparkled in front of Tag's eyes. He had never seen anything like it before. Then an unusual piece caught his eye. It was a bracelet; to Tag, it looked like a very old bracelet. It was golden, and had what looked like blue star sapphires embedded at intervals. He held it up, spun it carefully, and admired the beauty of the stones and the artisanship. By now, several people had gathered, encouraging Tag to buy the bracelet.

'How much?'

'For you, sir, being a very special customer, six shillings English.'

Egyptian culture almost demanded that one should haggle and offer a ridiculous price in return. Then, after a series of heated bids, a fair price would be negotiated. However, Tag responded immediately.

'I'll take it.'

Zahir looked puzzled.

'You no want to bring it down, the money.'

'No.'

'Then you have it for five shilling, *ayah*.'

Tag took the bracelet and tried to imagine Jill's reaction when he presented it to her. Zahir, still curious, put his hand on Tag's shoulder.

'This girl, she being very special, I want for you to give her this shawl. It was made for by my mother, but she now pass on … Allah be praised.'

Tears welled in the man's eyes as he handed it to Tag.

'Thanks, mate. I'm sure my friend, who is a nurse, will treasure the gift.'

'A nurse, sir? Oh sir, what an honour. A nurse is a person who is like a mother. What a fortunate man you be.'

There were smiles all round. Zahir was happy, his brother indicating what a wonderful piece of jewellery Tag had purchased, and the small crowd just clapped. Since leaving Australia, this was the first time that Tag had become a temporary civilian. He was the only European in this marketplace, and the only person in uniform; the rest were Egyptians. He warmed to the two men, and asked about the small horse that stood across the narrow path, in the shade of the canvas awning that was Zahir's shop.

'Your pony has split hooves. Do you rasp him regularly?'

'What is rasp, sir?'

'You know, a tool—a sorta file. Ya rough 'em back and shape 'em so he doesn't trip or get foot-sore. It'll split if you don't trim the damn thing.'

'I only have him for two week. Soldier sell him—says he good horse.'

'He needs cleaning up, or he'll go lame. Who can get a file or rasp?'

'No, sir, but for what you mean, I have brother Jowl who can understand.'

So, in this short, one-day stay in Cairo, Tag found himself doing what he loved to do. Zahir lent him some robes, as horse-shoeing in an officer's uniform would not have been right. Tag trimmed the pony's hooves to perfection, doing it slowly so that Zahir could learn. He brushed the pony, spoke to it softly, and insisted that Zahir get some chaff or grain for it. Tag could see the brothers were keen to learn, and knew the horse would be well cared for. He trimmed its mane and plaited its tail—anything to make the animal look different, as Tag realised that it was a stolen horse. Donkeys and camels were the most common animals in Egypt.

It was a pleasant afternoon. Tag learned about Zahir's family, and visited their small dirt house. He drank coffee that tasted like sour mud, but was too polite to refuse. He tried to explain

Australia, the high country, and Swifts Creek. He told them about Jill, her job, and the hospital. They wanted to meet this woman.

'Let her wear my mother's shawl. She can be our guest. It would be an honour, captain, sir.'

Tag left Zahir's house with plenty of time up his sleeve. He wanted to visit Chatty, and to be early for Jill. He enjoyed the stroll through the streets with Zahir, who led him back to the main thoroughfare. It was Friday, and Tag wasn't ready for what was about to happen. It was the most important day of the week in Egypt, a predominantly Muslim country. At noon, Cairo halted. Vehicles stopped; carts became stationary; and mats, sheets, and cloths were put down on the roads, footpaths, and open spaces. So it began. Almost like clockwork, the people, with their shoes removed, knelt as one, and gently bowed forward in prayer. It was an overwhelming, magnificent sight. Tag, unsure what to do, moved quietly to one side and sat on a bench. The only real movement came from the goats: they meandered through the crowd, sniffed at the worshippers, and generally made a nuisance of themselves. This was such a stark contrast to Swifts Creek, where the only time that large crowds gathered with any enthusiasm was at the football finals. Then again, some Australians considered footy a religion.

As the crowds cleared and went about their business, Tag wandered towards the hospital. He was over an hour early. Upon entering, he headed for the amputation ward. Tag had built up the courage to visit Chatty, and walked straight down the steps of the ward. He removed his cap—to avoid salutes—and headed for Chatty, who was both thrilled and amazed to see Tag. He didn't salute, but his forehead was pitted with deep furrows that asked the obvious question: 'What's going on, you friggin' dag?'

Tag quietly explained Jill's cunning plan.

'You little beauty, mate. Hell, that is smart. What a bloody good woman!'

They yakked freely. Chatty mentioned that Tiger, three-parts pissed, had called in earlier that same day and blubbered drunken tears all over Chatty, and it had cheered him up no end. Tag, now more relaxed than on his first visit, talked freely and rolled a smoke for them both. Chatty's spirits had improved measurably. It was such a relief for him to find that Tiger and Tag were both alive. Fifty minutes of reminiscing, bawdy jokes, ragging, and bullshit followed. A lot of the old Chatty had returned. It was a wonderful healing tonic for both of them. Suddenly, Chatty burst out with some news.

'They're sending me home, mate. I go via England. Gotta spend some time in hospital — they're worried about me leg. Might lose it altogether, mate, at the friggin' hip, eh.'

'Hell, Chatty, ya slack prick, I reckon ya ready for another stint at the front.'

Chatty looked away. His lip trembled as he courageously tried to stay in character — the larrikin, the skylark, the dinky-di Australian, and the mate, all rolled into one. Under normal circumstances, Chatty fitted the bill. However, poor Chatty's circumstances were so far from normal that he had become a lost soul. His life and family were Tag and Tiger; he wanted to be with them. Part of his healing process had been the anticipation of having them visit him as often as they could. Then there was Jill: he loved her like a sister, although he knew very little about her and rarely saw her. The thought of going home excited and scared him. He was a sad, frightened man, with the odd grey hair already appearing on his scalp. After a pause, he looked at Tag with tears in his eyes.

'Tag, old mate, I'll be goin' in a few days. You keep ya friggin' head down. You're family now, mate. Just keep ya friggin' head down.'

The two men clumsily embraced, shook hands, and parted in less than five seconds. They had been together for nearly an hour. Tag could hear Chatty sobbing as he quickly walked away.

Tag paced up and down the foyer at the entrance. He carried a string bag in his right hand, containing the shawl that Zahir had given him for Jill. A soldier, visiting a wounded mate, threw him a loose salute. Tag turned to see whom the salute was for, then just winked at the bemused soldier. This had been happening all day. And then he heard, 'Hi, sir ...'

He threw his first salute. It was Jill, in full uniform. Tag glowed a warm greeting, and they walked down the steps and into the grounds. Tag walked in front and Jill followed; that was her place in the company of an officer. The two young people quietly walked out of the hospital compound. Once outside, they both burst into chatter. A fit of giggles followed, then Jill spoke.

'Let me take you by the arm. That's the proper way, you know. Besides, if I walk on your right, you won't have to salute. Then again, I would like to see you salute just once more, Captain Lakes!'

Jill again broke into a fit of giggles.

'I'm not saluting any bugger, ya cheeky blighter!'

Then, in a soft, serious voice, Tag turned to Jill and handed her the string bag.

'It's a shawl. It's beautiful. Oh, Tag, this is special. It looks very old.'

'A fine Egyptian man I met gave it to me; it was his mother's. I've brought you a present. Jill, let's find a café and I'll show you what it is.'

Jill dragged Tag excitedly towards a sidewalk café, and they quickly sat down.

'Coffee first.'

Tag was enjoying this. He went into the small shop, and ordered two cups and some biscuits—a toffee-like wafer, which was a delicacy in Egypt. He sat opposite Jill and tried to say something special.

'I like ya, mate. That's about the size of it! It's bloody great to have ya come out with me tonight. It's goin' be a real special bloody evening.'

'Thanks, Tag. That's nice.'

'I got ya some jewellery thing. I hope ya like it.'

Tag produced the small parcel in a coarse, papyrus-like paper. He took Jill's hand.

'I really hope ya like it.'

Jill's face shone like the sun through a foggy morning mist in the high country. She gasped, clutched the bracelet to her chest, kissed it, and wept.

'Tag, my sweet Tag, that's the most beautiful piece of jewellery I have ever seen in my life. Dear Tag, I knew you were a special person the first time I met you. Thank you.'

Jill leaned over and kissed Tag on the cheek. It was a polite kiss, one that was suitable for an officer. Then she whispered in his ear, 'Tag, I will give you the nicest kiss you've ever had when we're alone.'

Tag was lost for words. He beamed with love, and wanted to jump up and tell the nearest person how special Jill was to him. However, being a horse handler, he didn't have such courage. His voice went hoarse.

'I want you to meet a nice family. They're Egyptian, good people.'

Jill giggled. Tag's broken, emotional voice conveyed a vague rumble like a possum's. He coughed and repeated his request. Jill was thrilled; she was as excited as Tag. She couldn't have cared if he had asked her to go skinny-dipping in the Nile. Jill just wanted to be with her particular young man. Tag wanted to squeeze the daylights out of her.

They set off at a brisk pace, with Jill's arm hooked in Captain Lake's right arm.

Jill asked endless questions of Tag, and he, completely out

of character, answered freely, with enthusiasm and confidence. They were oblivious of other people on the footpath, and were quite breathless when Tag informed Jill that they had arrived at his new friend's abode.

Zahir's house was in a part of Cairo that, to a Westerner's eyes, looked like a slum. The narrow streets were only suitable for small donkey-carts and camels. The ancient, cobbled pathways meandered in every direction, occasionally opening out onto an area that held stalls or a small market. On the very edge of these streets, many of the buildings were two storeys high, all made from Nile river mud. There were goats roaming freely in the alleys, their young kids prancing, butting, and skipping in playful exuberance. By the attention and stares that Tag and Jill received, it appeared that not many foreigners ventured into this poorer part of Cairo. Children giggled; women hung from windows, calling to one another across the narrow alleyways; and men, squatting on their haunches, smoking, looked up from the dirt doorways with curiosity. Jill was amazed that Tag could remember how to find the dwelling. Finally, Tag stopped near the lean-to that housed the pony. He didn't have to knock, as there was no door; simply a curtain. He called, 'Zahir?'

The curtain parted, and a beaming, bearded Arab appeared.

'Captain, sir, and your good woman—please to bless our house with your presence.'

'Thank you, Zahir. This is my friend, Jill. Please call me Tag.'

Zahir bowed, and then, walking backwards, ushered the young couple into the lounge room. It was a large room, with sweet-smelling fragrances burning in earthenware containers. There were fresh riverbank flowers in a vase on a low table, and cushions were scattered on the floor. The dwelling had been in Zahir's family for centuries, and Zahir's parents, who owned the house, had continued the tradition by inviting Zahir and his wife to move in when they were first married. Several prayer mats hung from the wall, and goat and sheepskin rugs were scattered on the floor. Zahir was the first to speak.

'Jill, come and I will being to introduce you to the women.'

Jill followed Zahir, who parted the curtain, and they both walked into a room full of beaming smiles and silence. In the room were Zahir's mother-in-law, Fevall, his sister Juddiaan, and his wife, Peliah. Then he introduced Jill to his three children, Salliah, Bessrah, and Yonuuge. Zahir's father had died; Zahir was now the head of the house. In Muslim culture, the man was the absolute head of the house. If he had wished, Zahir could have had four wives, but this was no longer common in Egypt. A man's wife was required to be obedient. The mother, like all older Muslims, obtained more power and status as she aged. Consequently, his mother-in-law had status over all the family except Zahir. After making the introductions to the family, he turned to Jill without hesitation and said, 'You remain with my family while the men talk.'

He then turned on his heel and walked out. Fortunately for Jill, all of the family except for Peliah spoke broken English, as Egyptian schools had taught it for several years. Zahir invited Tag to sit down, and a fascinating evening began to unfold.

The men sat on the floor. The conversation was free flowing and light. Tag tried to explain Australia, his home, and his family as best he could.

'But what is bush?'

'What is jumping horse with baby in pouch called?'

The endless curiosity of Australian wildlife fascinated the Egyptian men. The banter about Australia's vastness and weird animals was conducted with a captive audience. Tag drew sketches, indicated relative sizes with his hands, and mimicked the kangaroo like an Aborigine at a corroboree. The men leant back in amazement, their arms held aloft.

'The kangaroo bigger than Mr Tag. Ooh, *ayah!*'

Then came the big question.

'What of your women, eh? You have no be in charge of, eh?'

'Their dress, Allah be praised; *ayah*, they look so naked … a beating would do … eh, Zahir?'

Tag was bewildered.

'And Jill, what about Jill?' asked Tag.

Silence … and then laughter.

'Hah, she pretty okay is what I say. Very bad to see ankle, eh.'

It was all good fun. Then, from the next room, came the sound of loud clapping and a penetrating female voice. The curtains parted, and the women brought in a meal on trays — sharply spiced delicate foods and a milk drink, along with grapes and dried fruit — and then returned to the other room. The men enjoyed the delicious meal, eaten to the accompaniment of constant chatter and a lot of arm-waving. After the room was cleared of dishes and bowls, Zahir suddenly jumped to his feet and clapped his hands loudly. The women shuffled in, and Jill, with several shawls around her neck, came in beaming. The scarves she was wearing were precious gifts from the women, a custom of greeting in Arab countries.

Zahir and his brother led all of the people into a courtyard outside. The brothers dashed in and out of the curtains, while some other men returned with either drum-like or strange-looking string instruments. It was very theatrical. After a short delay, other men appeared in flowing, bright, bloomer-like pants, and with vivid, long strips of bright silk material hung around their necks. Zahir stood solemnly and clapped. The others stood, bowed to him and their guests, and nodded in the direction of the women. After two sharp claps, the musicians sat down, and out of the apparently crude, roughly hewn instruments came hypnotic, soothing music. It started softly, and the colourfully dressed men swayed. Then, as it increased in tempo, the music appeared to enter the souls of the dancers. In this ancient, large quadrangle, with its sandstone walls and simple decorations, the men leapt into the air. Spinning and jumping in unison, they cried out with primitive shrieks and barks that copied the calls of ancient desert animals. All joining hands, twisting one way and then the other, they sang and yelled with joy.

The music slowed, the dancers returned to a trance-like swaying with their hands still joined in a circle, and then they stopped and started to clap slowly. Then, like a ball from a cannon, a new dancer leapt into the circle and stood in the centre while the men clapped faster. He jumped so high that a young man ran underneath. The dancer kicked and spun with his hands on his hips. The music reached fever pitch. The man flipped backwards and forwards, and then leapt out of the circle and disappeared. The music stopped.

The men sat beside their women. Zahir then spoke.

'For you, Mr Tag. For you—he is the best dancer in this village. For you, sir—for helping the horse. It will be good, the horse, *ayah?*'

Tag knew he should respond. He looked at the sky, which was a beautiful, soft red, like silk. He then looked at the floor. Tag didn't give speeches …

'That was beautiful. I have never seen men do anything as beautiful as that.'

He struggled, Jill took his hand, and Zahir frowned and then laughed. They all clapped.

'Thank you, thank you,' said Tag.

It had been a perfect evening, but Jill explained that, sadly, she and Tag had to leave early.

CHAPTER EIGHTEEN

IT WAS STILL twilight when they re-emerged among the busy sounds and bustle of the narrow walkways. Barely twenty yards from the front of Zahir's house, Jill quietly slipped her hand into Tag's. It was a precious moment in his life. They had touched before; however, this time a touch that transcended the physical flowed between the two young people. It produced a feeling of seeping, rich warmth and pleasant tingling, which humans crudely describe as love. Tag wanted the moment to last forever, and in a way it did. Such encounters pervade the spirit and soul of a being so deeply that they remain etched there for eternity. Softly, he gave Jill's hand a protective and reassuring squeeze. Jill lent her head towards Tag, and touched his shoulder.

The musty air of Egypt, with its spices, smoke, and animal smells, greeted Tag and Jill as they strolled. To date, the evening had been a grand social affair, a pleasant meeting of two different cultures. There were times during the evening that Tag and Jill's eyes had met in that large, warm courtyard. The response was a smile or warm affection. Nevertheless, as the evening had worn on, the glances became longer; the look, more intense. Tag was chuffed when Jill made the excuse that they had to leave early.

The narrow, winding passageways through this ancient land were a trek back in time. At one point, a mother goat and her two kids frolicked; then, standing tall on her hind legs, the goat attempted to drag a freshly washed sheet from a window above. Thump! An old steel container rattled around the passage, followed by a sharp burst of language. The nanny goat and the two kids dashed off. The abuse was indecipherable to Tag and Jill, but they both understood the message.

They walked very slowly. Jill was the first to speak.

'Tag, I had a wonderful evening. Thank you.'

'Me too ...'

'There's nowhere else I'd rather be, Tag. Not true — I'd love to be home, in the bush, away from here, just you and me.'

'Really?'

'Yes, Tag. I think you're the nicest person I've ever met.'

They had reached a low rock wall. Tag sat and pulled Jill down beside him. Slowly, he rolled a cigarette. The dark, moist tobacco that Zahir had given him had a deep, rich smell. With ease, Jill lent across and put her head on Tag's shoulder.

'I'm scared, Tag. I had a boyfriend at home in Benalla once. Mum wrote and said he was killed at Gallipoli. He wasn't a boyfriend, really ... I kissed him once. Tag, I'm scared of liking you. Every day I see fellas cry for their loved ones and families. Then, when I sit and try to forget what has happened on that day or any day, I strangely feel glad I'm alone. At times, I wish I had never met you.'

Poor Tag hung his head. He was overawed at having a girl like Jill. He didn't want to hear what she was saying. Then, surprisingly, he answered.

'Since I've lost Bucket and Golly, I avoid making new mates, just keep to myself, like. Even Chatty ... what a bloody mess. And Tiger—I'm too bloody scared to ask about Tiger after a stint. Of all of us, he should live. His mum needs him.'

He kicked at a rock. Tag's emotions were locked in; as with many young men, they would not come out. He clammed up, staring at nothing. However, his body language was powerful; his words, although limited, satisfied Jill. She didn't need profound explanations: Tag's silence and sad demeanour said it all. Both of their souls had been peppered with appalling, vivid visions and the muttered last words of dying young men, too many of whom they knew or respected.

For an hour, they walked and talked, mostly about Jill's family in Benalla and Tag's great love for horses. Just on dark, they stopped at a curbside coffee shop and had some strong coffee—a new treat for them both—sipping their cups and chattering like kookaburras at dawn. Then, talking and laughing at the same time, Jill suddenly stopped. She put a finger to her lips.

It was time to put the remainder of her plan into action—the plan she had devised back in her quarters many hours earlier with the emergence of Captain Lakes. It was the only part of the evening's outing she hadn't explained to Tag. This would take courage. She emptied her cup, and pulled at Tag's arm.

'Tag, we have some new material called moleskin. It would make perfect saddle blankets for the horses. It's soft but tough, and it washes well. Come and I'll show you.'

Tag frowned.

'Sure, but what's brought this on, mate?'

A HIGH WIRE fence surrounded the quartermaster's store, which was patrolled regularly. Medical supplies, food, and grog were but a few of the countless supplies located inside. A strong guard was a good idea—especially with those 'bloody Aussies around,' according to the general consensus of the British.

When they arrived at the army store, a young Welsh soldier was on duty. Jill turned to Tag. 'I'll do the talking,' she told him.

'Good evening, corporal. This is Captain Lakes, the army veterinary officer.'

The British soldier executed a rigid salute.

'Sir.'

To the guard's amazement, Tag's return salute was a very poor effort — a sort of wave with a grin.

'Lazy prat. Even the Aussie officers are slack,' the guard was to mutter later to his mates.

Jill added, 'We have come to look at the new moleskin blankets sent as hospital items. I have told Captain Lakes they would make ideal saddle blankets.'

'I have no idea where you would find such items, ma'am. I could call up the quartermaster.'

'No need. I know exactly where they are. Is building fourteen locked?'

'Sure, I'll get the key.'

It was almost dark when Jill turned the key and unlocked the door. There was just enough light to see their way about — it was a beautiful, orange, soft glow. Stars emerged for the first time. The twilight would linger for at least half an hour. Jill quickly went to the middle of the long row of shelves and took down two grey moleskin blankets.

'Business first,' she winked at Tag.

She then proceeded to lay them out on the floor. Tag, still bewildered by the goings-on of this young woman he thought he knew fairly well, was stunned by her next statement.

'This will be our bed for the next half-hour. Come.'

Gently, Jill pulled Tag down. She held his cheeks and brushed his eyebrows with her thumbs.

'Let my hair down,' Jill said as she reached inside her cotton carry-bag and produced a brush. Taking it, Tag started to draw Jill's golden brown hair into the air and then let it flow back onto her shoulders. She had her back to him. After a time, Jill slowly undid her cardigan and blouse, placing them beside her. Then the binding that held her breasts flat and in place was detached.

Jill sighed as Tag removed the wide, bandage-like length of cotton material and folded it before placing it on top of the other garments. She turned to face Tag. He briefly glanced down at the two pink breasts that rarely saw daylight. He was not embarrassed; he just felt awkward.

'It's okay, my sweet,' she said. 'This is our honeymoon.'

Leaning forward, she undid the buttons on his tunic and shirt. She slipped them off with the care of a nurse and the gentleness of an angel. Wrapping her arms over his shoulders, Jill kissed Tag softly on the neck. Her breasts were so soft, her nipples so hard. Tag gasped as he felt them touch his snow-white chest and tangle in his matted, bright-red chest hair. Jill kissed up along his neck and then nibbled her way with small bites until she reached his lips. They kissed with a warm joy that seemed to melt what few inhibitions both might have had. Tag slid his hand across Jill's back and pulled her tightly into him. She clung to his body, pushing sideways so they both fell gently onto the grey moleskin blankets. Together they removed all their clothing except for the undergarments. Jill, on her back, spoke first.

'Touch me, my sweet.'

He kissed Jill softly on the stomach. She purred like a well-fed kitten. With tense fingers, Jill ruffled Tag's rusty red hair. He continued to kiss her softly, moving up her body until he reached a soft, smooth breast. Taking the nipple between his teeth, he tickled the hard, protruding sultana-shaped delight with his tongue. Again, Jill just purred.

'Tag, I love you so dearly, so very dearly.'

Taking his hand, Jill slowly placed it under the band of her bloomers. Tag felt the soft, exciting pubic hair. He teased it tenderly. Creeping his fingers further under the cotton material, he felt the slight rise of the lower part of Jill's stomach. He inched his way until he felt an unfamiliar mould.

'That's my fluffy, Tag,' Jill sighed, with her eyes shut and humming softly. 'Take off my bloomers and explore my fluffy.'

Jill groaned with pure delight, brimming with love, desire, and primitive, overpowering sexual urges. After a while she sat up and, with just a little haste, removed Tag's white boxer undies. Panting, he pulled Jill towards him and held her as tightly as he possibly could. It was a wonderful union …

After a time, Tag withdrew and caressed Jill. It had been her first sexual encounter, and an air of awkwardness was starting to emerge. Jill reached into her cloth bag and took out some matches and a small candle. It was safe to light it between the shelves in the depths of the building. Jill knew she was bleeding a little. She took out a rolled-up flannel, wiped herself and then, with another flannel, reached to wipe Tag. Although not planned or intentional, the soft stroking of Tag's private parts had an almost immediate result.

'Holy Mother!' Jill squealed, who herself was still fully aroused; she was stunned by the strident leap of his organ back into full-alert life. She giggled and squeezed it with pleasure. Now it was his turn to groan. He shuddered and craned his head towards the heavens. Then, with no enticement from Jill, he again entered her. This time, Jill pushed with urgency and a primitive crudeness that expressed one desire—the coupling of two bodies to make one. A feeling of perfect togetherness flooded over them both. Their clinging grip on each other was so powerful that, momentarily, they were unable to breathe. Both were exhausted. Jill heaved a long sigh and mumbled about floating through the air.

How strange, in this land of death, sorrow, and tragedy, that this precious moment was given to them.

Slowly, they dressed each other. There were momentary pauses as each reached for a kiss or simply a touch. After inspecting each other's attire with the thoroughness of a matron or a sergeant major, both walked into the outside world. Tag had two blankets rolled up and tucked under his arm. With difficulty, they removed their broad smiles and resisted holding hands. Now came the hardest part: the resumption of their roles as the nurse and the officer. It was more difficult for Tag, of course, impersonating Captain Lakes, the reluctant officer. He marched with his head held high, Jill's arm threaded through his right arm. As they walked back through the compound gate, the new sentry threw a snappy salute. Almost forgetting to respond, Tag flopped a crude reply and struggled to get the smirk off his face.

CHAPTER NINETEEN

Tag returned to camp a different man, exhilarated after having been with Jill. He wanted the war to end today, marry Jill, return home, and show her off to his family before teatime. However, Tag was bothered: he felt the pain of unfulfilled love. He wanted so much to be with Jill, but realised that this was not possible and even that he might never see her again. The constant arrival of new faces into the battalion was a painful reminder to him of the hazards he faced. Since leaving Australia, almost half of his original company had been wounded or killed. In a way, he wished his time with Jill had been a fling or a bit of a flutter; but, sadly, this was not possible. They were soul mates, bound by a wonderful chemistry that had a force like gravity. It had been so simple before Jill. Before, only the deep sadness of remembering Bucket and Chatty was a daily intrusion that caused his eyes to mist over. Occasionally, he would think of Jill. However, the nightmare of Gallipoli, his memories of horror, and homesickness were always there. He missed the picturesque mountains of the Tambo Valley terribly.

Now, Jill added another dimension to his life. For the first time, thoughts of children and marriage flitted through his mind. Most importantly, he now had an overpowering desire to survive. In camp, he busied himself with his duties and the never-ending demands of the horses. Had it been just grooming and exercise, that would have been easy, and a joy. But the army didn't value these animals as farmers or delivery people did, having grown up dependent on horses for ploughing fields, snigging, travel, and companionship. Here, the horses relied on men like Tag to speak up on their behalf. The horses weren't given a night out. The army hadn't provided them with protection from the sun, the sand, and the solitude. That's when good men spoke up for them. Tag, and many like him who valued horses, considered it their duty to do so. It was a constant plea, as even a simple request for shade was scoffed at by the command. Fortunately, Tag now had allies — good men with rank like Glass Jaw Bond, now a sergeant major, who went into bat for him. Reluctantly, the command relented, and Tag, along with his helpers, gave the animals a much-improved life. As a result, the horses were stronger, healthier, and more settled.

By comparison to the horse, the soldier had occasional rest and recreation; alcohol (in abundance, where possible); and a voice with which to complain about and (hopefully) improve some of their conditions in camp. Nets were supplied to keep out the sand and the ever-present tiny, stinging insects as the men lay on their palliasses and tried to sleep, either in the searing heat of daylight or the freezing-cold desert chill of an evening. The evening winds were bitter. Many of the men volunteered for guard duty at night simply to keep moving, awake and rugged up.

IT HAD BEEN two weeks since Jill and Tag's special meeting. In that time, he hadn't heard from or seen her, and nothing much other than Jill occupied Tag's every thought. Tomorrow he would be on leave for two days. Tag was bursting with excitement and anticipation. He wanted time to speed up. He had his uniform laid out ready, his boots polished, and his kit packed. He even had his captain's uniform secreted away — in case it was needed.

Then, as so often happens in a war, the army had other plans. Tag became a number, a piece on a chessboard. Two hours before he was due to depart to Cairo to see Jill, he received an instruction: 'Report to the company commander.'

There would be no leave. Sadly, Tag was about to enter another horror zone.

On 14 July 1916, Corporal Tag Wardell reported to the company commander, Major J. O'Donnell, better known as 'The Boss'. The commander was a good man, and he had a lot of respect for Tag. Their last conversation a week before had been amusing. The major had tried to force Tag to accept promotion to sergeant; like so many, he had refused, believing it would alienate him from the lads. If the truth were known, the men felt that Tag was a natural leader and deserved rank. However, this meeting had nothing to do with promotion. The major wanted to simply give Tag the orders that had been specially written about the horse problem in France. He wanted to discuss the orders with Tag, gauge his reactions, and let him voice an opinion. The order was blunt, demanding, and to be carried out immediately. It was to change Tag's life dramatically — yet again. He entered the company commander's tent.

'Sit down, Tag.'

Tag sat warily. He knew that something was up.

'You okay now? Got a bit crook in Cairo, I hear.'

(Tag had been four hours late returning after his special time with Jill. He wasn't charged.)

'I'm fine, sir.'

'Tag, I have a big ask for you, young man. I want you to go to France with a new unit, attached to an infantry battalion. It's called the Horse Retrieval Unit or H.R.U. They want a good man urgently. What do you think, Tag?'

'Do I have a choice, sir?'

'No, but I respect you, young fella, and I want you to go there with your eyes wide open and realising what to expect. France is a total stuff-up. We are suffering horrendous casualties there, Tag. As well, the stretcher-bearers are struggling to retrieve the wounded. They have tried using horses, but two problems have emerged. Firstly, they are losing many animals bogged in the mud—don't know if you could do much about that. Secondly, a lot of the horses are shying and jibbing about returning to the field after they have experienced shelling.'

'Do you blame them?'

'No, but you will be able to help. That's important. Tag, there are too many soldiers dying of wounds in the field. Very bad for morale. Perhaps you can make a difference, young man. At least calm the horses—that's important.'

'When do I go, boss?'

'Tomorrow, to Fromelles in France. A bit of a mess, I believe, and you go early. Sorry, Tag. I'm sorry to lose you.'

'Hell, boss, I've just got myself a girl in Cairo. I'd like to see her first.'

'No, Tag, it's out of my control.'

The two men shook hands. They had been together for a long time. Tag put his hat on, saluted, turned, and strode out of the neat tent.

Early the next morning, he said his goodbyes to Tiger and some other mates. Tag was totally pissed off — at least, that was the message Tiger gave Jill about a week later. It was the first that Jill had heard of his abrupt departure. Distressed, she tried to find out some details about his posting. Was there an address or contact for him? Both questions drew a blank. Jill was distraught. At the very least, she wanted to stay in touch with her Tag by mail.

Tag hadn't even had time to write a letter before he left.

On his way to France, he spent most of the evening giving instructions to the two men posted with him. He had hoped that one of them would be Tiger. No such luck, but these two were fine horse handlers who had known Tag since that terrible trip over on the ship, eons ago; they had helped him with the horses at the time. He decided he would write to Jill as soon as he got to France.

TAG COULDN'T HAVE anticipated what he found in France. The idea of writing a letter to Jill was blasted out of his mind by the scenes around him of vast devastation, exhausted soldiers, and petrified horses — and this was at a staging station, a temporary aid post-cum-hospital, not the battlefield. The carnage in France was the same as at Gallipoli, but it took place over a greater area.

Tag soon found that the gossip about France had been right. It was a complete stuff-up, with death everywhere and many wounded being left unattended in the fields. There were endless stories of medics and stretcher-bearers trying to retrieve the fallen with horse-drawn field ambulances. Every memory was a repeat of yet another disaster. The fields in this part of France were strewn with rotting bodies and body parts; there were usually no burials, as the retrieval and medical services were unable to deal with the demand. No matter whom he spoke to — commanders, medics, or horse handlers — nothing appeared organised. More importantly for Tag, the condition of the horses was appalling, almost to the point of them having been the victims of wanton cruelty. These animals needed attention, or perhaps 'protection' was the better word. Tag would need all his skills and more.

He spent his first few days checking on the routines for the handling and caring of the horses. Next, along with a company commander from the H.R.U., Tag went on a foray to a holding paddock. It was very depressing. The horses, in their hundreds, were in the far corner, as far away from human contact and the war as possible. When Tag and his senior officer walked towards the animals, they bolted to another corner, snorting with fear. Many were weak and appeared full of worms from the scouring they had suffered. Then, to his amazement, Tag saw a rider appear. Cracking his whip, the rider herded the horses towards the yards. Many tried to career away in a frightened frenzy — the last place these animals wanted to go near was the yards, the rigging, and the harness pens. Soon, another rider appeared, also cracking a whip. Between them, the riders yarded two hundred of the three hundred horses into one of four such paddocks.

Tag shook his head. This would be a huge task. He enquired why the horses weren't stabled, why they were allowed to simply run as a mob, why there were no men tending to them. Yet every question, every query, was met with the same response: a shrug, a blank stare, a frown and then, finally, an insolent, even arrogant, reply that summed up the problem.

'They're only horses, Tag!'

Next, he visited the shoeing shed. It was huge, with forty-five smithies working in small stalls. Again, the sight that greeted Tag reminded him of Bill the bad-tempered bugger back in the Swifts Creek blacksmith shop. Here, in this long, low, stable-like barn, many a horse was the recipient of a sharp thump with a rasp to the ribs or a severe jerk on the halter. Few horses stood still; most snorted and flicked their tails with resentment. As if to add a sinister veil over the scene, a sour smell of liquid manure pervaded the shed. Tag was aghast at these sordid, putrid conditions. He noticed that some men had rags covering their noses. He wanted to intervene, but that would have to come later. He wandered to a far corner of the large shed and entered a small room. There he found a veterinarian pulling teeth from a panic-stricken horse. His first thought was, *How bizarre — tending to one horse's mouth while thousands need caring for.* However, after a formal introduction, Tag decided to approach the young man with a question.

'Excuse me, sir. Most of these horses seem in a poor state. Is it their food, their water, or maybe something else?'

'Has to be worms and food. The hay we have shipped here is poor quality. I have made the appropriate report.'

Suddenly, a voice from behind interrupted them. 'My God, it's the smithy from Swifts Creek. They said I'd find you here. Shit, it's good to see you.'

They shook hands vigorously. It was Sergeant Major Bond, Tag's old mate from Egypt. Tag flashed a rare smile. This was a pleasant surprise.

'Shit, I thought I'd gotten rid of ya for good. What are ya doin' here, sir?'

'Thought you could do with a hand, so I put the hard word on the boss. He sends his compliments. I arrived this morning.'

'And what good will ya be, ya useless banker? Sorry, I forgot—maybe ya could give these blokes some boxin' lessons, eh?'

Tag ducked as Bondy took a friendly swing at him. They laughed lightly, and swapped recent news of their mates. Sadly, Bondy had no news of Jill. He had heard though that, at long last—months since the troops had been evacuated from Gallipoli—the hospital was coping. This news, if not much else, pleased Tag.

It was lunchtime, so they left the shoeing shed and headed for the mess. Over the meal, they both got down to the serious business of the horses' welfare. After an hour's discussion, Tag made a suggestion.

'I'll get ya to call the horse handlers together in a few days. I've got a few things I need to say … might even have to make some notes and stuff. Might need your help, mate.'

Bondy agreed. He stood up, shook Tag's hand once more, and added, 'I'll catch you for a drink later at the mess, okay?'

Bondy left with a nod and a smile. For him, as for Tag, it had been one of the few highlights he had experienced since his arrival in France.

At the end of the day, Tag staggered to his tent, exhausted by the huge, endless task of somehow curtailing the horses' bewilderment. The poor animals were in a bad state, scared, scouring, and jibbing at returning to the fields. Once put in harness, most would rear, stamp the ground, and walk backwards in the traces when it was time for them to head off down the all-too-familiar road to hell.

Tag sat on his canvas stretcher, alone in his tent, and rolled a cigarette. He rested his head in his hands and tried to collect his thoughts. Suddenly, Jill's lovely smile appeared in his mind, and he quickly ruffled through his rucksack and grabbed some paper. He penned what became a long letter to her—ten pages expressing his gratitude, love, and hopes for the future—without lifting his head from the paper. He jogged to the quartermaster's store, and handed the unsealed letter to the sergeant. The censor would read it first; then it would be sealed and sent. Tag felt a brief moment of satisfaction.

Sadly, what Tag didn't know was that Jill and many of her work mates were being posted to England. The hospitals there were very short staffed, even more desperately so than in Egypt. Gallipoli was history. France was mayhem. Jill was due to sail two days after Tag landed in France.

LATER THAT SAME night, on his first break since having left Egypt, Tag joined Bondy at the boozer. After making a few introductions, both men just sat and listened to the chatter, which got louder and louder as alcohol loosened tongues. The talk was dominated by just one topic. Tag and Bondy were astonished, almost beyond belief, to hear the stories that these weary men told. Tag looked at Bondy several times with a deep frown on his face; Bondy simply shook his head quietly. There was no mistaking the tone of disgust in the soldiers' voices. These Aussies felt angry, almost rebellious, about the British, or 'the Tommies' as they called them.

As far as they were concerned, the British command had lost the ability to organise its troops. They told scores of stories to support this view. First of all, they claimed that many British officers were unable to connect with their soldiers and that they, in turn, were not like the Aussies, who fought as a team and generally got on with good officers. There appeared to be lines of distinct segregation within the Tommies—not only between the soldiers in the ranks and their immediate officers, but between the lower and higher echelons within the British command itself.

The blokes repeated what wounded diggers had told them about how communication from the British command to the senior field officers was vague, and often overruled and questioned. This meant that, before a move or attack, British support was again and again withheld when the diggers needed it. Chaos and indecisiveness prevailed, even at the top among the generals—the planning of troop advances often being questioned, called off, reinstated, and then cancelled. Yet, in the aftermath of battle, when questions were asked by the Aussie soldiers about what had happened, all they heard from their dejected officers was that, yet again, the Brits had decided not to turn up. It was truly a shock for Tag and Bondy to hear such criticism at the bottom of the line, down among the troops in the trenches.

These were not merely alcohol-fuelled opinions. It turned out that, indeed, few command decisions or battlefield engagements resulted in notable victories or even in ground being gained. More importantly, much criticism was levelled at the lack of clear decisions and the confusion that commonly prevailed at the scene of battles.

Opinions about all this at troop level were harsh. The consensus was that the command was failing, in a repeat of Gallipoli — there was a lack of coordination between the troops and artillery. At Gallipoli, there had been pauses and long breaks between barrages. Here, in France, it was almost never-ending. Breaks in artillery were measured in hours; sometimes, in minutes. Too often, confusion reigned when it came to the Allies' artillery. Meanwhile, the German artillery was bigger, went further, and devastated the entire countryside. The piercing blasts that came with the shells' detonations were heard even well back behind the lines. Like wild, intense thunder, the noise that went with fierce artillery barrages blasted the camps, causing tents to flap wildly and buildings to shudder, and scared those trying to sleep in hospital beds. It petrified the horses.

Artillery was almost a new weapon. Its ability to travel over many miles to its target, and the widespread devastation it caused, created chaos and led to logistical nightmares when it came time to withdraw troops and the wounded.

At the front, in the trenches, the Germans shelled the Australian troops before any battle began. By comparison, the supporting artillery for the Australian troops was often not only late, but was placed too far out or missed the right area. Allied communication from the front back to the guns was impossible due to noise, severed lines, or worse — the poor runners rarely made it with their suicidal dashes. However, there were other, more intractable problems. Those in charge of the guns had to deal with their coordinates being inaccurate, because of the poorly designed maps — or so the command said.

Repeatedly, the waiting Aussie troops would huddle together in pitifully shallow trenches — with all the mud, it was impossible to dig to any depth. They were scared and confused, pleadingly looking at officers as the time to rise and charge rarely matched the promised artillery barrage. All too often, these Aussies, awaiting the order to enter into a battle ahead somewhere, were blasted for up to fifteen minutes beforehand by Hun artillery, suffering appalling casualties. Then, when the order to advance was given, their own artillery would slaughter the diggers. Rarely was there accuracy, good timing, or coordination between the trenches and the artillery.

The very week that Tag arrived, Bondy had shown him an Australian report sent to the British command that highlighted the problem. A senior H.R.U. officer had told Bondy of the report with disgust, and had then handed it over. A promised British troop advance in support of a recent Australian push had simply not happened—suddenly cancelled from above for reasons that were never communicated or explained. Consequently, there was no wide charge, and the Allied artillery had fallen too short. The Australian assault had ended up on a small front of 150 yards, and the diggers had been easily picked off by the Germans.

Tag hoped that this was a one-off disaster. But, like a radio serial, it happened time after time. The report by the Australian command was one of many with similar themes.

MORALE WAS LOW in France. Tag was intrigued and bewildered by conversations he heard about the action on the battlefields. Yet it was a story he continually heard; like Gallipoli, France was a murderous disaster.

It staggered Tag to hear of the demands being placed on the medics. The figures that were bandied about within those first few days were terrible: from a series of combined battles, the Australian 5th Division lost 5533 men, of whom four hundred were taken prisoner, and a countless number lay out in that void between the combatants called no-man's-land. In those same actions or 'stints', the British lost 1547 soldiers; the Germans, 1500. It was no wonder that the medics couldn't cope.

Finally, in all of this turmoil, there was the gas. Delivered by screaming artillery shells, it spread quickly after the initial blast, and wreaked havoc. This silent killer maimed the men in terrible ways. The first symptoms were burning eyes, a raw throat, intense pain in the lungs, and tender, itching skin along with a burning sensation. The gas, which was difficult to detect, caused panic. It was hideous. Somehow, the men considered that using gas broke unwritten rules. This, more than anything else, caused the soldiers to hate the Hun.

CHAPTER TWENTY

No matter how well Tag's company commander, Jake O'Donnell, had described this new theatre of war, nothing could have prepared Tag adequately for France. His first trip into the fields with the horse-driven ambulances was hell. There were ten wagons, with two horses and two men per wagon. Tag was anxious, tense, and very attuned to the horses' behaviour. Soon he would have a sickening and gruesome distraction. For all his experience of war so far, this was a new reality for Tag. It was horrendous, unspeakable. The trenches were full of men—some waiting for the next advance, some wounded. As in Gallipoli, underneath them were the bodies of their dead comrades. Looking about, Tag estimated that it would take a week to retrieve the wounded … and they had, at the most, a day. Within thirty-two minutes, Tag's wagon was loaded, ready to return to the regimental aid post.

Their horse-drawn ambulance cart held twelve wounded men. With eight sitting up and four lying down, the four-wheeled cart was full. It was a large, canvas-covered wagon with a distinctive red cross painted on both sides. There were few medical supplies carried by the medics, as their priority was to get the wounded back to the temporary aid posts. Today, two strong bay horses stood harnessed to the wagon. Ahead of them was a two-hour journey, at the very least, to the aid post. Tobacco and cigarette papers shook in the hands of the frightened soldiers. Tag clicked his tongue and chanted the familiar 'Giddyup.'

That's when it happened ...

The cart was about to trudge off when, from over a small rise, a badly shaken, distraught digger came staggering over to them from the direction of the trenches. There were muddy tears smeared across his cheeks. He called out to Tag.

'Could you fit one more on, mate, please — me mate Locky?'

The digger was almost begging. His request sounded simple, but it wasn't.

Could Tag's team return briefly with a stretcher and go back to the area, to a bloke in a trench — his best mate?

Tag hesitated, and then obliged, not out of common sense or because he was obeying an order. The demeanour of this young man demanded Tag's response. So, with a stretcher and a bag of medical supplies, Tag and his infantry medic, Smithy, ventured back across the boggy sludge. Naturally, they couldn't run; at times, they were knee deep in mud.

Nevertheless, they struggled past the first trench, then across a mound, down a slight slope ... and, by God, there was another trench. Tag and the medic had no idea what they'd let themselves in for. It was sickening. Most of the soldiers were dead. There were few intact bodies ... just bits and pieces. The young digger leading them was most likely the only man in his platoon left alive or not badly wounded. He'd come to after having been knocked out, and kept muttering that only a few survivors had made it back, or maybe they'd been captured. Whatever the answer, the scene that greeted the retrieval team was horrific. It was almost too much for Tag and Smithy.

Where on earth would they find this bloke called Locky — his mate? Tag and the medic stood briefly, almost in disbelief. There were too many decisions to make, and too many wounded to cope with. It was an impossible task—a bad mistake. There were dozens needing attention after the earlier artillery barrage and brief assault. Tag and the medic had had no idea they were even there. There had been no indication from above, no order to venture in this direction to check out the area.

Tag could see why the poor bloke had called him. There were only dead and wounded left in the shallow trench.

Then a pitiful sound pierced the air. A soldier was calling out. Was that Locky? Then another called, and another. After much pointing and waving of arms, Tag finally came across the bloke's mate. Poor bastard … young Locky, who looked about fifteen, had had a leg completely blown away; as well, his chest gaped open, with several ribs exposed. Worse was to come. As the two tried to carry the badly wounded soldier back towards the cart, his mate became stuck in the mud and had to stop, exhausted. Then other men, with their own terrible wounds, called out, or tried to drag themselves or crawl towards them. Men begged for help, for water, for God's sake! Tag was aghast. He had never seen so many pleading eyes, never felt so guilty. They finally reached the wagon, and laid the wounded bloke on the floor with the other four. It was too crowded—a hopeless situation. The wagon got bogged twice on the way; it was too over-loaded. Almost by a miracle, they made it back to the aid post.

The entire event changed Tag. Gallipoli had been mayhem, but this was madness. In a matter of weeks, he became a man of even fewer words. Except around his horses … he still talked to them.

THAT FIRST TRIP established a pattern; only lime and mud gradually covered those left to die or already dead in the trenches. Disease, filth, and stench were rife. A comment from a medic who had been there long before Tag arrived summed up the horror of that first trip: 'The rats outnumber the men out here; the maggots outnumber the rats.'

There were cruel new unwritten rules — callous and heartless ones — for Tag and his medics to implement. They had an unenviable set of decisions to make: whom to rescue, and then, sadly, whom to leave behind. Always, they headed back to the aid stations with their wagons full to overflowing — but not too full, to avoid getting bogged. But who would make the decision to move off? Who was going to say, 'Shit, best we leave that poor bloke, eh?' Always, many wounded and dead had to be left where they lay, exposed to the elements.

This was their lot. Up to three times a day, these young men played God.

For Tag, the endless treks back into the battle zone were more than enough to cope with. Yet he had another responsibility: the horses around the camp. They, too, sensed the madness. Their conditions, appearance, and erratic behaviour were all too familiar. Cruelty and bullying was the preferred disciplinary method of dealing with them. Tag was disgusted by what he saw.

It was under these appalling circumstances that Tag had to bring about change and to improve the horses' welfare. He had seen enough of the battlefields to work out the problems that confronted the horses. Every day, as the horse-drawn carts headed towards the front lines from the crude hospital that had been improvised from buildings in the village, the animals behaved the same way. After harnessing the horses to the carts, the horse handlers and stretcher-bearers-cum-medics would encourage the edgy animals out towards the battlefront. But just to get any forward movement from them required constant whipping of their rumps or vicious slapping with the long reins. Cursing, yelling, and abuse were the norm.

When finally at the battlefront, the horses were spooked by

the endless cries for help and the screams of pain, and stood by as the medics went from one soldier to the next. However, if there was any shelling in the vicinity, the frightened horses would jolt the carts as they shied or jumped in fear. The handlers would try to stay near the animals to calm them; but, all too often, the horses would be left alone, as the handlers were needed to help the medics with their painstaking, risky task of lifting and carrying the wounded. Then, finally, there was the slow trip back to the aid post. Few ever made it without getting bogged at some stage. It was a major problem.

From the day he arrived in the first camp beside the hospital outpost, where there were over 450 horses stationed, Tag wanted to take control. He bided his time, covered all the areas that involved the horses, and then spoke to Bondy. It was time to talk to the soldiers responsible for the horses. As well, he asked Bondy to get as many of the senior rank along as possible. He knew that Bondy had not only high rank, but influence.

It was a large roll-up. Many were officers; others were sergeants, corporals, and section leaders who worked with the troops. They all sat to one side in chairs. Bondy had gathered the rest—all the handlers and the others who worked with the horses—and had made sure that the long smithies' shed had been scrubbed and swept clean. The men all sat on the ground, and Bondy spoke to them briefly. He then turned to the officers, snapped a salute, and turned to Tag.

When Tag went to address the men, all of them were quiet, and seemed quite keen to listen and learn. This surprised him a little. He didn't know that, prior to him arriving for his talk, all the men on the floor had been told by his old mate, Sergeant Major Bond, that this man was unique. At a special Orders Group of all the company and platoon commanders, Bondy had told the story of Tag taking control of the horses on the ship coming over. They were suitably impressed. Bondy was pleased;

that way, he knew all the men would hear the story, as orders from an O. Group were always passed on to all troops. At the end of that first O. Group, Bondy had added, 'What this man Tag says, goes — okay? He's the bloody best when it comes to horses. I've seen him prove it many times.'

This powerful message had filtered up into the officer lines as well as down to the lower ranks. By the time they were gathered in the shed, they were keen to listen.

Addressing the men for the first time, Tag and Bondy stood together. Tag tried to put the problem in plain English.

'Look here, ya dopey bastards, what's the point of whippin' the nags? It's bullshit. When ya were young and ya pissed the bed, did gettin' a floggin' stop ya from pissin' the friggin' thing again? No flamin' way — it made ya flamin' worse, didn't it?'

There were a few nods in response.

'It's the same with these flamin' horses, fellas. Lay off 'em. Get their confidence. Talk to 'em, a lot. Treat 'em like kids. Build up their trust in ya. Spoil 'em. Take 'em a surprise — a bit of carrot or somethin'. Then they'll do what ya want, I promise ya. Dunno about pissin' their bed, though — they still might do that.'

This ordinary joke got a few smirks. However, Tag's philosophy was greeted with many nods.

'In future, any prick caught floggin' a horse will have me to answer to. We might let you feel what it's like to get flogged — eh, Sergeant Major Bond?'

'Bloody oath, mate!'

That got a laugh. 'And I love floggin' dopey pricks — eh, Tag?', Bondy added.

Tag roared laughing. If only his mates could have been there to tell the story of when Tag had put Bondy on his arse. Then Tag unfolded a piece of paper, and looked at the men sternly. 'These are the new rules,' he said.

'Every platoon will be given sixty horses; two per man. You'll be allocated your own stall or stables, with time to water and feed them, and so on.

'You'll give every horse a name, record the name, and write down a weekly report of its health. When ya talk to this animal, it has a name, okay?

'Now's the new bit that some of ya might object to. From now on, ya gotta spend at least an hour a day with your nags when they're not in the wagons. With a halter, you'll walk them behind the paddocks, out towards those farms … as far away from this 'ere bloody war as ya can get.'

He paused. 'That all sound okay?'

Everywhere there were nods.

'When ya come back from the walk, you'll brush 'em for at least twenty minutes. A horse loves a brush. You'll lead your horses to the feed trough and stand there to make sure they get a decent meal. Some of these horses are bullies, and will scare off the timid nags.

'Talk to 'em, tell 'em a joke … might be the first time someone thought ya were funny.

'Ruffle their ears, scratch 'em around the tail. What will happen is that you'll have a new mate, and a good one at that!

'We're going to fence the current paddock into six smaller paddocks. The horses will only be herded into small groups of roughly one hundred. However, most of the time they'll be stabled, walked, brushed, fed, watered—all with a bloke leading 'em, okay?'

Tag stopped talking. He turned to Bondy 'That's enough for now, mate.'

Tag was exhausted. He wasn't the type to give talks or speeches. He quickly wondered if it made sense. Then Bondy spoke.

'Any questions?'

There was silence—an awkward silence. It was as if these men were aware of the problem, but no one had ever made a stand or cared enough. Then a man stood up.

'I'm from Bairnsdale, mate, down the road a bit. I heard about ya years ago. They reckoned ya were the best. All I can say is, *about bloody time*. I take my hat off to ya and the bloody army. Shit, yeah—fancy the bloody army doing this, eh?'

He lifted his hat. Slowly, they all lifted their hats; even some of the officers joined in.

The next day, the plan was implemented.

THE REGIMENTAL AID post-cum-hospital, which was three miles behind the frontlines, was an over-crowded, filthy mess—on a good day, Tag's team could only manage three round-trips. Just over a mile behind the hospital were the paddocks and tents of the horse handlers. Tag had now been in France for six weeks, and already a change was noticeable in the horses: the new rules were working. The scouring had almost ceased. The men stayed much longer with their horses; some even slept close to the animals under the stars in crude swags, as Tag did on most nights. Many of the names that the men chose for their horses were typically Australian: Bonkeye, The Farter, Dribbles, Wrinkle Bum, Sulky Sam, and Dumb One. Mind you, there was also Goldie Girl, Steel, and Tallboy. The men thoroughly enjoyed the endeavour, and continually talked to their horses. Now, their letters home mentioned a new friend that had a name and its own characteristics. The horses returned the attention with nudging, gentle nose-prodding, and affectionate rubs along the handler's back. At last, the initial horse problems faded away.

However, this welcome change was all too brief. Heavy rain had set in, yet again, and mud infiltrated everything. In the tents, their bedclothes and linen were chocolate brown from the wet, all-pervading earth. There were no floors in the tents; they were inches deep in mud. The rainfall in this area had been the heaviest ever recorded, as the incredibly boggy fields testified. Transportation on this flat, pristine, French farming battle-area was almost impossible for wheeled vehicles, and it was an exhausting foot-slog for the infantry. Trucks were useless on this terrain.

The killing, even greater than at Gallipoli, was horrendous, with casualties after each major battle regularly in the thousands. Most deaths and injuries were again due to shelling, although for different reasons here than in Gallipoli. In France, the soft, soupy soil made it almost impossible to dig adequate trenches. They ended up too shallow, which meant that the troops were continually exposed to the Hun's devastating artillery. The enemy's firepower was formidable, and its soldiers were well entrenched in fortified bunkers. Initially, the safest places during a barrage were inside the large holes that had already been created by incoming shells. The craters provided better protection than the soldiers' shallow trenches. However, even these came with a hidden danger. If the original shells contained gas, the potent chemical would seep into the lower ground — the trenches and the craters. Many young soldiers who were new to the front fell victim to this trap. In a panic when first confronted with artillery, they ran about desperately and leapt into the craters for safety, only to inhale lethal doses of the gas.

There was a distinct front, as at Gallipoli, but here the devastation continued well into the Allies' lines due to the Germans' bigger guns propelling their shells several miles into the Allies' territory. This meant that the wounded were to be found over a large area. However, the size of the German shells caused another problem. Due to an increase in rainfall, the huge mass and powerful blast of the shells churned the soppy earth into a porridge-like quagmire. This made the retrieval of the wounded for both the men and the horses an exhausting, pitiful task.

Unfortunately, the stretcher-bearers found it hard to keep their balance due to the mud and uneven ground. Deep holes created by the shells meant that many a deviation was needed on the slow trudge back to the carts. Often, the stretcher-bearers would fall while carrying a wounded digger. It was usually only after several falls and a lot of swearing that they reached the Red Cross cart. When it was fully loaded — or, usually, overloaded — it was the driver's turn to coax the horses through this quagmire. And, all too often, the cart became bogged. Before Tag's new rules came into effect, the horses would be flogged, so they would rear and churn the mud even more. Inevitably, the cart and horses would sink deeper, with the inevitable result — a bullet to the skull of the worn-out animal.

Now, new methods were tried. If a wagon started to struggle and sink, any of the wounded who were able to walk would be unloaded, and the retrieval team would attach ropes to the wagon and help pull it along. This sometimes worked, in which case the wagon would move on. But these soft patches of mud were hard to anticipate or see, and they were everywhere. If the worst came to the worst, and a wagon got bogged in one and refused to budge, all the wounded would be unloaded. Inevitably, one or both of the horses, now weakened by the ordeal, would be bogged to the belly. The horses would be unhitched, and sometimes a horse would be saved by this measure. Sadly, though, what usually happened was that, after desperate rescue attempts and much cursing, a rifle would be levelled at the horse's head, and the exhausted, pathetic animal would be shot. What else was there to do? It was inhumane to leave a horse there, with no hope of getting out of the mud, to die of exhaustion and starvation. The many dead horses and several dozen half-sunk wagons were constant reminders of the dangers for those who trekked along these familiar roads.

If only that was all that Tag had to contend with. Then came one final difficulty: the gas mask. It had been introduced to the horses just before Tag's arrival.

This bizarre-looking, cumbersome contraption—a crude attachment to the bridle—was essential for any horse that had to venture into the battlefield. But the horses loathed it. Admittedly, there had been some recent changes. It had been decided to remove the set of goggles originally issued; for some reason, they tended to fog up and restrict the horses' vision, and were rarely used. Now the mask was like a feedbag, covering the horse's mouth and nose, and reaching to just below its eyes, and was such a tight fit that it restricted the horse's breathing. Even quiet horses reared up in protest when they were presented with it. Others rubbed it against any surface they could make use of—often, the masks became dislodged when they were bashed persistently against a pole, post, or tree. Most horses just shook their heads in fear when their handlers approached them with a gas mask. Perhaps they were aware of the use to which this hideous apparatus was being put.

The masks were a recent addition to the animals' apparel after they had suffered a spate of huge losses in the fields. It had taken a while for the army to understand why poison gas could be a major problem for a cart-horse. Once they have had their fill of water and food, horses tend to like a nap—preferably in the shade. So it was that, in France, even when collecting the wounded in the fields after a stint, and being left standing for a period, the horse often reverted to this common habit. After a time, it gradually lowered its head as a way of dozing or having a quick snooze.

However, this behaviour had dire consequences in the aftermath of an artillery barrage that contained gas. The troops had learned to do two things immediately if they were exposed to any shelling that contained mustard gas: rush to higher ground and put on a gas mask, and return to lower ground.

But the horses, of course, were oblivious to this problem. The gas, which took a long time to dissipate, finally settled low to the ground—just above the height of a napping horse's lowered head. Without the benefit of a mask, the poor animal would quickly find itself overcome by the poison. After inhaling the gas, the horse would panic, and try to bolt from the area while still lugging the cart. Some would drop down on all fours, froth at the mouth, and shudder, their eyes balled in fear. Some died the same day, but even those that survived the gas were shot. It had to be that way, for they could be of no further use to the army.

How, though, could you get a horse to wear a gas mask? Realising that this was the most complex dilemma he had ever faced as a horse handler, Tag called a get-together with known horsemen within the ranks of the horse handlers at the camp. He wanted advice and opinions based on their experience to help find some answers. It took ages for him to craft a plan, but would it work? Yet again, Tag gathered the men and explained the try-out, and how it to put in place.

Over the next few days, Tag changed the horses' feed times. Then, after they finished feeding, some of the horses were masked and released, with the mask only removed when they had a drink several hours later. Then other groups of horses had the gas mask put on during the night, and it wasn't even removed the next morning while they were brushed. At random, horses were hitched to wagons, walked around the compound for an hour with the gas mask on, and then un-harnessed and let back into the paddocks without a mask. Gradually, the horses became calmer about the mask. The pattern of being harnessed, having the mask put on, and moving out towards the battlefront had been broken. There was no routine. Some horses now thought that the only way they could get a feed was to put on a mask. Others objected to the removal of the mask, as it meant they would miss out on being brushed.

Slowly, the problem disappeared. The horses allowed their handlers to put gas masks on them. The new method was simply a work of genius. It was an amazed Sergeant Major Bond, now an old friend, who turned to Tag one day.

'Tag, I think you're part 'orse, ya bastard. That, my boy, is bloody brilliant. They should give medals for stuff like this, ya know.'

'Bullshit, sarg.'

'One bloke reckons you're the Man from Snowy River.'

'What utter crap—though he did come from Omeo, they reckon. Anyhow, enough of the bullshit. Let's get on with it.'

'Yeah, ya stubborn bastard—look how many more wounded men are coming in, thanks to you.'

'Sure, mate. How's about we just stop the flamin' shellin', and bring them all in, eh —come to some friggin' arrangement like they did at Gallipoli, eh, sarg? Better still—just stop the friggin' shellin', full stop. Then we'd all be out of a job.'

Tag kicked at the ground. This was out of character; normally, he was a man of few words. After a brief silence, he added, 'Sorry, sarg, just pissed off.'

'Can't argue with that, mate. 'ow's the leg?'

Tag's old wound from the trench at Gallipoli was playing up. He now walked with a very pronounced limp.

'Still gives me curry, mate. Thought it had healed okay, but this mud caused it to fester.'

'Seen the doc?'

'Nah, just take a swig a rum to get me ta sleep.'

'Let me know if ya running short, mate.'

'Thanks, sarg.'

Rum was the army's answer to most small wounds, colds, sore throats, and minor illnesses. Rum was the answer for men with shell shock. Rum was given to the men on a stint, just before they went over the top—straight into the enemy's bullets, in most cases. There was always rum in the trenches.

For all Tag's training methods, gentle coercion, and infinite patience, there were still some horses who remained uncooperative and kept behaving erratically. They were a bundle of nerves — they refused the harness, baulked at any loud sounds, and were very difficult to handle. He knew that these animals needed to be retired, and sent away from the war. But, as that would never happen, Tag had to have them shot. This was such a frightful decision that even rum couldn't quell the pain of it. It went against everything that Tag believed about how animals should be treated.

After two months, the retrained horses' behaviour improved. Soldiers found them easier to harness; when presented with a gas mask, most of the animals lowered their heads and allowed it to slide over the bridle without any fuss. However, the major problem of horses getting bogged out in the fields had still not been solved. First, Tag tried keeping the horses on a well-worn, firm track as much as possible. The trouble, though, was that even well-worn tracks were still not reliable: overnight, heavy troop or machinery movements turned a road into a quagmire. This meant that the horse-drawn carts could only go so far, and stretcher-bearers had to travel much further carrying the wounded. Struggling to bring the wounded to the carts, the stretcher-bearers would become exhausted, and their constant falling-over was terrible for the wounded.

The next method tried was to have the horse take its empty cart onto the field; once there, the horse would be unhitched and led back to a firmer surface. Now using a very long rope attached to the cart, and with better traction from being on a firmer surface, a group of men along with the horses would then pull the cart back to the road. This was moderately successful. It was certainly much better than before, with fewer horses getting bogged. The new method meant that, at the most, three horses a week were flailed to exhaustion in the mud and then shot. Before, five horses a day were being shot while up to their flanks in the mire.

Now, more of the wounded diggers were getting back. However, a new dilemma quickly presented itself: as the fighting increased, there were even more casualties. The quandary of retrieval became more acute.

Because of the greater numbers of wounded, the army laid down some crude railway-type tracks to ferry the casualties to the receiving stations. Almost overnight, these narrow tracks and a railway-type cart, similar to those used in mining, found their way along the roads towards the edge of the battle. Pushed by soldiers along tracks that were packed with sandbags, the rail carts were a vast improvement. However, there were too few rail tracks, and much of the responsibility for retrieval still fell on the horses and their handlers. Then, as one might have guessed, artillery continually blasted the rails to oblivion.

Many suggestions were made—mostly by the handlers—to overcome the continuing problem of the horses getting mired in the mud. One idea that was tried was to fit cup-like leather platforms over the horses' shoes, using hooks, straps, and chains to tie them on. In 1912, Captain Scott had used this method to have ponies pull his team's equipment at the beginning of his journey to the South Pole. It had worked for Scott in the soft snow. Initially, it also appeared to work in France. However, mud is very different from snow. If the animal struggled, the leather platforms created even more suction, and the pitiable beast got bogged even more quickly. Next, Tag tried hessian wads or pads wrapped around the horses' hooves, but that also failed.

The rain continued, and the predicament remained. Then Tag came up with a superb but simple solution. He told the blokes that he felt totally pissed off with himself when the idea finally came into his head. He had seen the answer countless times in the bush back home—a simple sled used for carting fence posts, for taking hay into paddocks, or for moving very heavy objects too big to lift. In some countries, it was called a sleigh. At home, around Swifts Creek, farmers made the crude sled from a sheet of corrugated iron. However, it couldn't take a heavy load. More common was the sled made from the fork of a large tree. With the bottom part trimmed flat, and a timber platform built on top, a horse could just about lug a sled anywhere. They were very low to the ground. When fully loaded, a crowbar was jammed into the ground inside the fork and just in front of the load, and then the horse would move forward and pull the load off as it jammed against the crowbar. Until now, Tag had never thought of applying this idea in France.

Tag hunted up some wide, flat boards, and then a carpenter got to work on them. Using a drum of boiling water, he steamed a curve up at one end like a ski and, with the two boards bent to the same angle, built a frame over them. Then a light floor, measuring about four feet wide by eight feet long, covered the top. A trial run demonstrated that, with two chains hooked at the front, a horse could lug about six blokes over very soppy muck. The problem had been solved.

In the field, it was brilliant. The broad, flat timbers sat on top of the mud, so the sled slid easily on the slimy surface. Once they reached the carts further back, and transferred the wounded to them, the horse-drawn sleds would turn and head back for more. Then the carts would plod off to the aid posts. It was an ingenious idea; straight away, more wounded began to be brought in from every field. Admittedly, the receiving stations were overwhelmed even more, but the difference to the men's morale was immediate. There were fewer wounded being left to die, and horses rarely got bogged. For once, things went the right way. More importantly, only two horses were shot in the following month.

The senior command was impressed — so impressed that Tag

accepted the rank of staff sergeant. By now, he was an old digger. He trained new deputies: young men who, like himself, had been horsemen before the war. The army didn't interfere. At last, it had a more efficient ambulance service.

By now, two months after Tag's arrival, the front was a three-mile-wide stretch. Packed with tens of thousands of soldiers, it was a very crowded war zone. The Australians had lost over 23,000 men in the first seven weeks; in twelve days, the 2nd Australian Division lost almost seven thousand. The various battalions' numbers were, in most cases, reduced to hundreds. Some were completely gutted: the 48th battalion, for example, lost 600 of its 800 men. From April to December 1916, almost 90,000 Australian casualties would be reported on the western front.

By now, at least, a good system of training and handling the horses was in place. But, for Tag, who was in charge of the majority of Australian horses in this area of France, there were new challenges. Horses were becoming scarce: illness, stress, rest, and injuries were taking their toll. Now mules were arriving to replace the trusty nags, but Tag felt lost around them. The mules were very different. A mule looked like a horse, apart from its long ears and short, upright, thin mane. From the outset, the noise that came out its mouth was the main, noticeable difference — called a bray, it was a brazen, loud, deep, growling sound. If it felt unhappy, the mule heralded its displeasure by displaying quivering lips and holding its head high in the air. The braying would penetrate the unsympathetic ears of the nearby soldiers keeping company with their horses, and was not welcome. Most mules were wilful, uncooperative, and difficult to handle. And yet, the few that did work had as much, if not more, endurance and strength as the horses.

Most mules had real personalities: they showed a lot of

affection, and tended to bond even more strongly with their handlers than the horses did. Tag was intrigued by the animal. The mule reminded him of the worst horse he had ever handled, and the best. They were the opposite of horses—as different as a goat was to a sheep, or a beagle to a kelpie—and yet there were many parallels between them. However, most of them were stubborn and annoying. Tag, although perplexed, decided to apply his horse-training methods to the mule. It worked a treat: it turned out that the mule would only respond to affection, trust, and a calm atmosphere. It could sense a man with a mean streak. Given enough time and patience, Tag believed that the mule would become a valuable member of the team.

However, while the mule was a beautiful animal once you got to know it, it suffered from a physical handicap that no training or compassion could overcome. After their first trips out to the battle zone, the problem became very apparent, much to the handlers' disappointment. The mules' hooves were narrow, box-like tiny sticks, far smaller than the width of a horses' hooves. In the mud, the mule sank quickly, struggled, and tired rapidly, its extra strength being of little benefit. As a retrieval animal on the battlefield, the mule was a disaster. Yet again, out came the rifles to end the lives of exhausted, hopelessly bogged animals. The army acquired more horses.

The rain would not go away. The fields, once called bog holes, were now two feet of thick, soupy mud. Artillery guns now presented a problem that had never been envisaged. For the Allies, every round fired caused the artillery guns to sink a further two inches into the mud until the loading breech was eventually submerged to the point that the gun couldn't be fired. The gun would be out of action for at least four hours as it was dug out, gravel was put underneath it, and it was crudely realigned on the spot. No wonder the guns were inaccurate.

Then the troops, continually exposed to the soggy fields,

developed new health problems. A relatively new medical crisis emerged called 'trench feet'. This terrible condition caused soldiers' feet to soften to the point that they started to rot. The men, like the horses in the fields, were bogged and stuck in their trenches in the mud. Moving about and getting free of the mud was almost impossible; they could not sit or lie down. Many were forced to stand in the mud up to their knees, and they leant forward to sleep. Ablutions and all bodily functions were done on the spot. This, mixed with the decaying bodies of their mates, resulted in an appalling smell, and created a breeding ground for disease. Trench feet required attention straight away to avoid gangrene, which was becoming prevalent. The result was that troops were evacuated to have their toes and feet amputated. Many hundreds suffered from this disease.

Not surprisingly, soldiers at the front in France started to tire of the war and the conditions. Although it was yet to be revealed, yet another illness was afflicting the men—depression. Suffering from non-stop sleep deprivation, terrible conditions, the fear of dying, and the loss of their mates daily, many of them saw no future. All of this sowed the seeds for chronically low spirits.

As for Tag and his team, they were just coping. The system for handling the wounded had improved vastly. The hospitals were better organised, and a method was in place whereby the badly wounded were being put on trains and sent to Le Havre and then on to England.

YET AGAIN, TAG was called into a company commander's tent. Like his previous commander, this man had a high opinion of Tag. However, this time, there would be no discussions. Tag was off to yet another battlefield—one with more horse problems, and seemingly with no solutions. Reluctantly, Tag moved again. It was to be a devastating post for him.

It was midway through 1916. Within weeks, Tag found the demands on his teams at the new posting were relentless. They had to try to deal with an endless stream of wounded, more wounded, bodies, more bodies, bodies left behind … it was lunacy. He had gone five weeks without a break when an orderly at the crude tent hospital called Tag to one side.

'You're a hard bugger to keep track of, mate. Here, I believe this is for you.'

The worn envelope had followed Tag from Egypt to France, from one camp to another. It was from Jill, from England—his first letter in a long time. His frenzied, crazy life had given him little time for reflection, reminiscences, or letter writing. It was a very long, detailed letter. Out came the tobacco.

CHAPTER TWENTY-ONE

Whatever their experiences at Gallipoli, many diggers still referred to England as home. As young Australians, they had heard their parents talk of England as a place of castles, churches, and history — wonderful places to visit and to be impressed by. For Jill, though, England was a place of horrendous experiences. In her letter to Tag, she never mentioned the wonder or the splendour that had been emphasised during their schooling. She led a very demanding life that allowed no time for such adventures.

After having arrived in England from Egypt, it took only a short time for Jill to be valued as an experienced nurse. Her skills were good, and she put herself into an exhausting routine that left no time for sitting in silence and pondering on the realities of what she faced every day at the hospital. Initially, on her arrival, she mostly attended to severely wounded permanent or long-term patients, although there was also a ward set aside for those suffering from the effects of inhaling mustard gas. Then, after the long, wet, unseasonable rain in France, several new medical problems became major headaches for the staff in the English hospitals. The new condition called trench feet was creating havoc. The medical teams behind the front were unable to cope; patient numbers had reached epidemic proportions, with many soldiers having to be shipped directly to England. By the time most of them arrived, they required severe amputations, as gangrene had set in. Delay, which was unavoidable, led small problems to develop into major ones that required horrific amputations at the knee—or, in the worst cases, at the hip. And, of course, the more severe the amputation, the longer the rehabilitation; this meant that fewer beds were available for new patients. Nurses like Jill worked up to twenty-four hours without sleep.

However, for Jill and all the medical staff, the response of soldiers to their treatment was taking another direction—one that had the authorities baffled. Men were getting better after their treatment physically; but now, mentally, many were sliding into a dark abyss that confused those who tried to help them. Somehow, many men had lost the spirit to overcome sickness or confinement. In the wards, talking ceased. A well-healed wound no longer meant discharge from the hospital. Men stopped eating hearty meals: instead, they nibbled at it here and there, and then the plate was sent back with most of the food still on it. The patients slept long hours, and lost interest in hygiene, their personal appearance, and home. It was as if their lives held not much hope and no future for them. Once, the odd smile or a joke was a wonderful cure; now, men stared at nothing and reacted to very little.

At first, the army believed that this problem was a 'put on' by the men to stop them from being sent back to the field. However, this myth was quickly dispelled. Before this predicament had emerged, the pattern among the Australian casualties used to be that, if a patient was unable to cope with the gloom of the ward, he would plead with the staff to be sent back to France. At the time, when the staff heard such a request, they adjudged it as an indication that 'a change would be good for his health', and sent him back to the field hospital. From there, the soldier returned to his unit. It turned out, though, that this was disastrous.

After a brief respite in a French outpost hospital, the physically capable soldier became a blithering mess in no time—a nervous, shaking, crying, vague, absent-minded burden on his mates, the commanders, and the army. It didn't make sense, and the army didn't know what to do with him. Some of these pathetic soldiers returned to England, but most became a problem for the army by absconding, continually breaking the law, and living the life of an alcoholic.

Now, in Jill's hospital, fewer men were volunteering to return to the trenches once they were physically able to do so. The medical hierarchy responded to the gloom that swamped the patients in the only way they knew: the rum ration was increased. It made no difference. It wasn't that the authorities were ignorant of the behaviour; reports in the field after battles early in the war had hinted at a mental problem emerging, with some men described as having 'flipped', 'thrown a wobbly', or 'gone crazy'. At that time, such behaviour was ignored. Now, many displayed these symptoms. The authorities were lost, baffled by the dilemma as they entered these murky, uncharted waters of human behaviour.

By coincidence, there had been a documented case of this condition, which had been demonstrated after a terrible battle on Gallipoli. A soldier had simply walked from his trench back to the beach, and had started swimming out. When caught and questioned, he had stared vacantly, unsure of where he was, and then remembered: he was swimming home.

He was marched into the battalion commander's tent, a well-fortified command post further along the beach. Upon entering, the soldier didn't salute; he just kept on talking to his wife and children—the same behaviour he had displayed in the trenches for over a week. Here, in the headquarters, he still thought he was near home. He walked around, and called out to his missus and kids: he told them to get about their chores, and then told his wife what a tough day he had had in the shearing shed. The poor man, initially considered a hoaxer by the commanders, brought tears to all the senior officers present. Brief notes were taken, and the soldier was appointed as a batman (an officer's aide). He lasted a week, and then blew his own brains out. The incident stunned the command, temporarily, and then nothing happened. A dry report was written up, indicating that the case might be of value to the medical authorities. The report was shelved ... and gathered dust.

In Jill's hospital, the patients' low spirits had now become the major problem. It wasn't that the patients weren't receiving the best medical treatment available; in fact, the time taken for wounds to heal was improving, as a result of new techniques that had been introduced. The problem was the soldiers' souls. Their deep emotional inner being—the barometer of their *feelings*—was at freezing point. The men exhibited little or no humour, joy, anger, sadness, or caring. They had no will to do anything much.

It devastated Jill and the other nurses to witness this change in such young men. She had seen indications of it in Egypt, with a few men not coping, drifting back home in their minds to their past, talking as if their families were present. At the time, it terrified other soldiers to witness this madness, and many fellow nurses felt unable to cope with it. However, it was not common. At the time, Jill, like most staff, felt unable to help, and baffled by these terrible breakdowns.

Now, in England, it was everywhere, particularly after lights out. What was going on? What was this dark illness that was turning men into gibbering, wasted imbeciles? It was confronting, bewildering, and of deep concern to these dedicated carers. Sadly, for the nurses, most of the problems arose in the evenings, when the medical staff and other senior administrators had gone to bed. The quiet normally associated with the wards at night would disappear. With the lights out, men would call out names, rouse their kids to do errands, and call out to their wives or mothers. From other beds, there would be screams for everyone to duck. Piercing shrieks and crying abounded with the deepest heartfelt noises that Jill had ever heard. Bed sheets were soaked with sweat and, all too often, soiled. This dilemma only added to the men's problems: their dignity dissolved in front of their own eyes. Jill tried to give them affection, but how much could you give one person when there were hundreds in need? To further compound the problem, to be seen chatting to a patient would bring down the wrath of the medical staff; they considered it a time-wasting activity.

This combination of the battle-scarred soldiers' daylight silences and evening intrusions rattled the busy nurses. But how could they find a way to pacify the men, when the regulations clearly stated that bedside chitchat and personal attention were to be kept at a minimum? Out of desperation, Jill decided, against hospital policy, to concentrate on one man. His name was Jacko. In France, he had been a linesman.

His full name was Jack Bell, from the 7th Battalion, a man who had been responsible for maintaining communication lines between the battle trenches and the commanders at the rear. His medical history showed him as having been wounded twice. The first injury, not long after he arrived in France, had left him with a permanent limp and an eight-inch-long scar on his left leg. While he was in hospital in France, his battalion gained and lost one hundred yards of ground on two occasions. As he lay in bed during that last advance, or stunt, Jacko's mates felt the brunt of intense German shelling … there were many deaths. It was a shock to Jacko when he finally returned after a six-week stretch in a French hospital. However, he was back with his battalion and his best mate, Dicky. That was something. At the time, it was all Jacko wanted: simply being back with his mate satisfied his immediate needs. When they met, the first thing Dicky and Jacko did was to drink the week's supply of rum in a day. Somehow, they talked their way out of the resulting trouble.

Then it was back out again, lugging reels of wire and small metal boxes that held crude telephones. No sooner had they arrived at the second-last trench than the shelling began. Suddenly, all eyes turned to the signallers, Jacko and Dicky. A line had been severed—the line to the last trench. The boss called them up, and a brief discussion followed. They packed up their gear and then, the moment the artillery stopped, they both raced out to repair the severed lines, bent low, cursing, and hauling a heavy bag full of tools and short bundles of wire.

Unfortunately, the lull in the artillery was only brief. Jacko survived the shelling by pulling several dead bodies over himself, but his mate Dicky was killed. It was four hours before someone hauled Jacko back to the lines. He had a severe head injury, and there was no hospital in France capable of tending to his wounds. Jacko went from outpost, to aid post, to a railhead and, finally, by ship to England.

The medical staff at the London hospital were amazed that he had survived. He lost an ear in the surgery, which managed to remove most of the shrapnel and close up the gaping wound, and his wounds healed remarkably well after the operation. However, his spirits were low; very low. One of the few highlights of his day was a visit from a nurse called Jill Hunter … Sister Hunter.

JILL HAD DECIDED, behind the authorities' back, to give some of her precious time to Jack Bell. There was no particular motive, no explanation, for her selection. She had simply chosen Jacko the linesman because he was very depressed. Slowly, encouraged by Jill, he opened up, and started to tell her what his job in the battalion entailed. He made it sound easy when he described the task of laying cable from a circular hand-held reel as the troops advanced out of the trenches. But that was only because Jacko left out the grizzly bits. While the linesmen took the same risks as all the other diggers, there were subtle differences — and they were the reason that the blokes in the trenches held the linesmen in such high regard. If a line was severed or broken by shelling, it was the duty of the linesman to crawl out and fix it. In fact, the sooner he did this, the better: either immediately, or as soon as there was a lull, as no line meant that there were no communications. An operational line meant that the artillery got the directions they had to have, and that requests for vital supplies, ammunition, and medics got through. A broken line not only stopped the provision of supplies and up-to-date reports of the progress of battles; it also denied the soldiers any opportunity to warn others further back of the first signs of gas.

Having to repair cables in the field — often while hunched over the damaged lines, alone or with a mate — linesmen were frequently killed by snipers, who were aware of the reason for them ducking about like a bloody rabbit in no-man's-land, or just behind the trench from which the previous assault had been launched. The linesmen's job was almost a suicide mission. Fellow linesmen were very close; they had what was probably one of the strongest bonds on the scale of mateship. It was almost impossible for linesmen to survive a campaign without losing a mate, and this had been Jacko's lot.

Gradually, he filtered brief details of what had happened to him to Jill. She listened with almost disbelief to his tales. He had been with his battalion only five months, and now he was the only remaining linesman from his original platoon of thirty-two men. Slowly, he mentioned names like Smoky, Trokky, and Billy. All of them had been mates, and all of them were dead. He talked with hesitation about some of the scenes he'd witnessed, and the mayhem.

Jill wasn't sure if she was of any help to Jacko as, apart from holding his hand, she simply sat and listened. He still flicked his eyes continually around the room, checking for snipers. She had noted that he slept for the most part in brief naps of thirty to fifty minutes each. The only consolation for Jill, after several visits, was noticing that he was not getting worse emotionally and that he had had his first decent meal in weeks.

Jill not only persisted with Jacko, but she also spent some of her spare time with him after she finished work. He appreciated the extra attention, even though it seemed to make only a small difference to his well-being. Some nights, as she approached his bed, she would hear his repeated ramblings about his home, his wife, his job, and his family. Although she spoke very little, Jill told Jacko about Tag late one night. She didn't give him too much detail, except that she hadn't heard from Tag for months. Jacko smiled and nodded. Yet, somehow, Jill was aware that Jacko was skirting around an issue. Something was missing — something that affected many men. Her suspicion was confirmed the following evening when Jacko was talking quietly, in almost a whisper, leaning towards Jill. He was so quiet that she felt he was about to tell her something important. She leaned closer.

'Made a big decision today, Sis. I'm definitely going back to the mates.'

'You're what?'

'Going back, mate. I gotta. That's it.'

'But Jacko, you've done your bit. Rest up — take it easy.'

'I'd sooner be there than bludging in hospital, mate. I just wanna go. Poor flaming Dicky. Why poor flaming Dicky, Sis? The bastard was married and had two friggin' kids, poor prick. Damn the war. If I'd have fixed that damn line instead of lying there … Piss weak, you know … that's me. They could have stopped that artillery if I'd fixed that friggin' line. Sorry, Miss.'

He sobbed violently. That was a first.

For Jill, it was the missing link. He missed his world—his only world, where he knew mateship and a bond that was afforded few humans. Jill could not comprehend the statement. She tried to remain composed as she held Jacko tightly and patted his back. Then, either through wisdom or intuition, she uttered a powerful sentence.

'It wasn't your fault, Jacko—you did well. In fact, men around here reckon you linies are the tops. Dicky is at peace; he reckons you've done well, too, Jacko.'

'Bullshit.'

'Would I lie to you, Jacko?'

Jacko stayed in Jill's arms, sobbing for ages. Jill worried about the poor blighter. He stopped sobbing and turned again to Jill. He wanted her to contact his woman.

'I'm losing the plot, mate. Do us a favour and ask the missus to move back to her mum's joint. You know, Sis, it'd save the rent and bills and stuff. The old girl wouldn't mind.'

He gave Jill his home address.

Earlier, Jacko had told her that, before joining the army, he had worked on the roads, cleaning gutters. It was a council job, requiring a large straw broom and a wheelbarrow. 'A pretty steady job for a man with a couple of kids, don't ya reckon?' he'd said. Now, almost twelve months into the war, he had decided that his life was in the trenches, and that was that.

Jacko's request of Jill to write to his wife shocked her. She was very concerned about him. One legacy of his wounds was that he had lost his balance and was now only able to walk with the aid of a stick. Recently, he had stopped walking altogether. He told her, 'What's the point of walking? Me leg's jiggered, and it's no good for fixing a broken line or even wheeling a bloody barrow, if it came to that!'

He was becoming irrational. He swayed, started to shake, and kept sobbing. Jill held the sad man to her. Then, either because of exhaustion or some deeper reason, he fell asleep on her shoulder. Jill quietly laid Jacko back in his bed, covered his exhausted body, and walked slowly to her room in the nurses' quarters. She was worn out. Her feet ached; her whole body felt heavy and sluggish. This was no youthful, brisk walk. It was a walk that spoke of heavy duties; a walk that suggested she had few choices about where to go: the hospital, and her quarters. It was 2.30 a.m.; Jill had to be back on duty by 5.00 a.m. She had just used up her only night off for the week. Her supervisor had told her to finish at 6.00 p.m., suggesting, 'You look terrible, Sister Hunter. A good rest may help. I will stand in until the next shift arrives.'

Unbeknown to the supervisor, Jacko was Jill's priority.

Trudging up the steps to her dormitory and into her room, a very tired Jill lay on the bed fully clothed. For once, it was Jacko, and not Tag, who swamped her restless mind. His tears were the catalyst. A crying man is distressing for any woman, and Jacko's tears had etched themselves like a scar in Jill's soul. She eventually sobbed herself to sleep.

Agnes shook her awake at exactly 4.30 a.m. It was almost time for Jill to report for duty. Rushing about in an organised madness, Jill somehow managed to reach the ward in time while conforming to the strict dress code that required a starched collar and veil. In her rush to dress, she had grabbed a piece of dry toast; that would have to do her until lunch. Fortunately, she was early — a habit that most nurses displayed. To her surprise, Jacko stood at the doorway to her ward.

'Hi ya, gorgeous,' he said. 'I'm gunna get rid of this friggin' thing!'

He was waving his walking stick about. Then a person behind him spoke, loudly and angrily.

'Soldier, how dare you use such language!' It was the night supervisor, and she was not impressed.

'Sour-faced bitch, go and kiss a cactus.'

The supervisor had no idea what Jacko was implying, but guessed that it was rude. She turned to Jill.

'Sister Hunter, escort that soldier to his ward and report his behaviour!'

Jill turned to Jacko. 'This way, you jolly rude soldier,' she said.

Jill was rushing to get Jacko out of sight of the supervisor. He hobbled along rapidly, slamming his walking stick into the wooden floor with each swinging step. Back in the ward, she turned to him.

'What's happened, Jacko? You look like a hundred quid!'

'Dunno, Sis. Something happened the last time we spoke. Last bloody night I slept like a bloody angel. Hell, that felt good—bloody great! I'm putting in for home, Sis. No arsehole is gunna stop me from sweeping gutters. The bloody wheelbarrow will be a piece of cake; you bet my words on that! I reckon this stick and me's got about a month together at the most, then I'll throw the bloody thing away, eh. What's a bloody hop and a limp, mate? I'm bloody lucky I made it, eh.'

Jill grabbed Jacko and hugged him desperately. He dropped his stick and attempted a waltz of sorts.

'Never could dance much, mate!'

Jill laughed briefly and then she broke down completely. She sobbed and knelt on the floor, holding onto Jacko for support. He patted her on the head like a well-behaved dog, but with much more affection. Jacko ended up on the floor beside Jill.

'What's up, mate? Lost someone special?'

This was always the question when someone was distressed. Jill tried to talk, but tears were her body's preferred way of functioning at that moment. Jacko was concerned, as he admired Jill, and hoped he wasn't the cause of her distress.

'Does me swearing get ya down?'

Finally, wiping her eyes, Jill stood and helped Jacko to his feet. He frowned, and then Jill turned to him.

'I've just had my best moment in months. I've found someone—a handsome young man with a wide smile. His name's Jacko, and he's been hiding for months!'

Jill laughed, she hugged Jacko, and they started to waltz again. This time, they both sang a familiar song and laughed heartily. Others in the ward clapped, whistled, and joined in with the singing. Then a sharp voice pierced the air.

'Sister, report to my room immediately!'

It was the lady of the hospital, the matron—the one like the higher-ups in the army, who had all the power. Her glares made the entire ward go quiet. Jacko, still smiling, squeezed Jill's hand.

'Sorry, mate.'

He hopped off towards his bed, only using his stick every second step.

The matron's office was large, and painted in a cold, severe grey. Royalty and Florence Nightingale stared down from heavily framed portraits. Everything in the room was neat and orderly, to the point that it looked like the room was never used. The matron's desk, which was huge, was made of dull, hard oak. There was a solitary, formal chair near the desk, and a stool in front, but Jill was told to stand. In her mind were stories of nurses who had stood in this position, at attention, never to be let off lightly. At least she still had her moments with Jacko, his warm smile, his loving hug, and his spirit that had returned.

Jill stood nervously, her head bowed.

'Young lady, that sort of behaviour will not be tolerated anywhere in my hospital. Is that clear?'

'Yes, ma'am.'

'If there is a reason, it had better be a good one—or you will never nurse again, young woman.'

Jill absorbed this statement. She halted, took a breath, and lowered her head again. After all, it was not right to talk to a matron, even when invited to do so. All through her training, it had been drummed into her that, in the presence of such people, you lowered your head and accepted your punishment. A nurse had to be a living example of proper manners, deportment, demeanour, and subservience. All of this indoctrination rushed back into her mind. Then, mumbling another apology, she waited for the matron's decision.

'You will be given a week to organise your passage to Australia, and then moved to the trainees' lodgings. I will submit a report and forward it to the Australian command. Your work in the wards will cease immediately. Any questions?'

Jill was lost. Her heart screamed a response, but her head abided by the rules. The matron muttered something about responsibility, honour, and duty, as well as how deeply disappointed she was in Jill.

'You are a good nurse, but you leave me no choice. Dismissed!'

Jill turned, took a step, and then burst into tears. They weren't like tears that burst forth in response to a squashed thumb, or like those she shed regularly of an evening in her room. These tears were deep, rising up from her very soul. They had a heart-rending power like the forlorn cry of a dingo in the bush. The matron was moved. She walked over to Jill, and offered her something that wasn't in the thick book of regulations and rules.

'Take a seat, and tell me — tell me all.'

Softened by the act, Jill burst into voice.

'Well, ma'am, with your permission ...'

Jill told the matron Jacko's entire story as she knew it. She told of his experiences in the war, of his job as a linesman, of the admiration the other men had for his type, and of their deep respect for him. She talked about the loss of most of his mates, and about his wounds and the successful treatment of them. She explained how, physically, he was healed to the point that he had been almost ready to return to France, to his unit. Jill struggled as she tried to express her sadness and bewilderment at his emotional decline, and to explain her response—how she had flouted the non-involvement rule, and had started talking with Jacko properly and at length. Then Jill slowly explained Jacko's miraculous recovery, almost overnight, and what had happened when she had seen him the next day ... and she explained about the dancing.

Towards the end of her account, she started to cry bitterly. It was simply a cry for help—even a little would do. She cried not only for Jacko, but also for Chatty, and for ten other soldiers whose names she rattled off. She cried for her Tag, her sweet Tag. Now Jill lost all composure. She was gibbering, uttering brief, personal comments that made no sense to the woman in charge.

'Where is my Tag?' she demanded.

The matron struggled to remain composed. Between these two fine women, a long history of sadness, tiredness, and exhaustion had never been disclosed. They both had the same memories, like festering emotional wounds; and, like most, both women had struggled to keep them suppressed. The matron had witnessed this time after time in her nurses; it was what caused so many of them to go mad. Now it was time for the woman in charge to lower her head. For all Jill's ranting, she was unaware of how deeply she had touched the matron. Jill had hit a raw nerve in the lady of steel. Slowly, the matron's arm came up and circled Jill's shoulder. For Jill, it was a sign that she was permitted to cry—from her heart, in a tearing, heaving burst of exposure that would normally have been very private.

'It's okay, my sweet girl. I am so sorry. I wish I had never put on this uniform at times.'

Even though the matron understood Jill, especially her sadness and compassion, she couldn't see the vital role that Jill's empathy and counselling had played in helping Jacko recover. Jill had unlocked a chest of needs in the wounded man. It was what most wounded men and most soldiers needed done for them.

The answers were there. Like a riddle, they were there, waiting to be found in the personal, private attention she had given Jacko. Then again, Jill wasn't completely sure why Jacko had improved. Was it just because she had given him her valuable spare time? Had he simply wanted some company? There were too many puzzles for her to solve, and they were too close to her own problems. Her solution was simple: she hoped that these thoughts would just leave her alone and subside. Up until today, she had coped with a mounting sense of distress by working hard — very hard. Her only bouts of uncertainty would arise after work when she was alone, pondering the day that had just finished … and then tomorrow, and the future. Contemplating the future was not only difficult; there were times when it was utterly disheartening and demoralising. There had seemed to be no way out of the madness.

Now, alone in this large, hollow room with the matron, Jill was unwittingly displaying the same behaviour that Jacko had shown for months. She was caught up in a maelstrom of depression, guilt, anxiety, stress, and a despair born of hopelessness … and where was her Tag? Her inexpressible anguish and grief came out in the form of pitiful crying. In revealing her inner-most emotions, Jill was at the point of a breakdown. Had the matron remained as hardened as her training required, Jill would have suffered deeply. Somehow, though, there were powerful forces at work that day in the hospital. Now it was a different matron reassuring Jill, telling her that she was a wonderful, caring, professional nurse. She was speaking at length, and concluded with, 'And, like all good people of any age, you need to have this acknowledged every now and then. Sorry, putting it like that is stupid. I meant to say, I have been remiss. I have learned a lot today, Nurse Hunter.'

The matron beamed a soft, kind smile, offered Jill a seat, and then, to Jill's astonishment, asked about her home, her family, and her plans. They chatted for twenty minutes. The matron, who said her name was Grace, even told Jill a little about herself. It was another brief, perfect moment for Jill to cherish on this day. Finally, patting her hand, the matron smiled warmly.

'You run along, my girl. You are late for duty. Tell the supervisor I held you up with some private business.'

The fact that humans could suffer pain that was other than physical was to become a major problem for the matron. It was appearing in the nurses: they, too, were becoming sick regularly, but only displaying symptoms of tiredness and withdrawal. On some days, it was an effort for the poor souls to get out of bed. Then, the moment they were questioned, reprimanded, or accused, they broke down and sobbed for ages. They only ever expressed guilt or hopelessness for their lack of resilience — when pressed, most simply said that they were homesick. This was convenient for the supervisors, as it justified the usual response of, 'Just get on with it.'

Few nurses ever received the compassion bestowed on Jill. Instead, the pattern of broken-down nurses appearing before their supervisors every week became all too familiar. In the last month alone, the matron had sent thirteen young women suffering from deep emotional problems back to Australia. They hadn't had shrapnel blasted into their bodies, or gas sucked mysteriously into their lungs. There hadn't undergone amputations, or suffered the appalling physical pain of crude surgery in the field. As with the soldiers, this pain went much deeper. It was not treatable with a scalpel, a knife, or bandages. This illness warned the body: *Stop, rest, and get away from the mayhem. Your soul has had its fill of horror and sadness.* If this message was ignored, the body would close down. It would revert to a simpler form in which it coped once before in a world of childhood fantasies and dreams, of play and joy, of nurturing and shelter. The body might have looked perfectly healthy, but it was saying *I can't go on … I have no will or emotional energy left.*

Medical orthodoxy was of little help here; there was not much point in checking textbooks for information about emotional cures for war victims. There was only one acceptable response: one must simply soldier on, and ignore the signs of travail.

In England, in Jill's hospital — as in many other such institutions — the new illness started to take its toll on the nurses. Most were sent back to Australia, having already spent weeks convalescing in private quarters in England. Some showed the outward signs of shaking, crying, and the fear of being left alone, or uncertainty and insecurity in a crowded room.

Many soiled themselves, given the smallest fright. However, the saddest were those who simply shut down: they sat and stared, and faded away slowly. It was their way of blocking out the horror. Of course, the few who improved a little would volunteer their services to return to the wards. Like recovering soldiers, they felt duty bound to return to the madness and to share a part of the burden. However, it was quickly apparent that they were unable to resume their old duties. These nurses were fragile, shattered young women. Never again would they be able to relate to people their own age. Back home in Australia, what hope would these women have? They weren't heroes. Many would never marry; the few that did would marry returned soldiers. The result, often, would be two sad people unable to help or support one another.

Their brief youth had flashed past in an instant.

CHAPTER TWENTY-TWO

Jill was struggling. Her spirits were low. Her resolve to be strong in front of the patients was crumbling. The hospital was overflowing and barely functioning at a human level: care was brief, there was no individual attention, and compassion was a rare commodity. Wounded soldiers told her that the slaughter at Flanders and Ypres was inhumane. Just like after Gallipoli, dealing with the wounded in English hospitals on such a large scale was becoming logistically impossible. At every level, the war was a disaster. Rarely was there news to lift morale. Many staff read the newspapers looking for some words that might hint at an end in sight to the war. Yet the press continued with their emotionally charged headlines and news reports. The German spirit had been broken, apparently. Did this mean that the rest of them — the Allied forces — were okay?

Finally, Jill asked to be moved to another ward — anywhere that was away from the amputations. She was sent to the ward where the medical staff continually faced a hideous medical problem: gas, the hidden enemy. Initially, Jill felt a little relieved, even slightly spirited, now that she was away from the other ward.

Then something happened. One of Jill's patients was an army padre. He was a broken man; his story was similar to Jacko's, but different in a vital way. The padre had been wounded during an artillery barrage that had penetrated unexpectedly deeply into the lines. He had suffered from burns and shrapnel, and internal damage from gas; as well, his face was badly blistered and his hair had cooked onto his skull from the fire that had engulfed him. However, his physical wounds were only a minor part of the problems the man faced. It was his whole existence, his reason for being, his former deep commitment to religion and God that was the overwhelming focus of his heartbreaking sadness. At the outset of the war, he had been a man of the cloth, mingling among the wounded soldiers brought back to the medical posts in Cairo. He administered comfort and prayers to wounded men. Every Sunday, he held several services that the men seemed to appreciate. At the beginning of the Gallipoli campaign, the padre moved on to an army hospital in France. It was many miles from the front line ... two days away from Flanders.

Then, for whatever reason, he volunteered to go with the ambulance trucks to the nearest regimental aid post, much closer to the trenches. He had been there almost two weeks when, one day, while he was helping medics unload the severe cases, the post was shelled. It was the first time that shells had reached the Flanders receiving area. Few escaped the carnage, including the padre. Due to the severity of his wounds, he had been sent to England, to Jill's hospital. Since then, he had been recovering well. He still couldn't open his eyes—they remained under bandages—but he believed he could see. However, there was a deeper problem.

The padre's spirit was broken. It had happened during his time at Flanders, when the padre witnessed the morale of the troops seep away. Nothing seemed to lift their spirits. Rum and other crude antidotes were no answer; they only seemed to gain solace when they were back together with their mates after a battle. Most of what they experienced on the battlefield was meaningless to them in terms of tactical success or failure, or the part it played in the progress of the war. Their own survival and that of their mates was all that mattered, for that was their world. This started at battalion level. Each battalion had four companies; each company of roughly one hundred men were close; and the platoons, three to a company, were a very tight-knit bunch. This allegiance never went past battalion level. In fact, above that, there was intense rivalry. Anything beyond their battalion was a world of little interest to the soldiers.

The padre, normally attached to a battalion, was part of this family. Before the war and early in the conflict, his practice was to get to know many of his brethren. Then he asked to be near his men, and found himself at the nearest medical post behind the front lines. Quickly, he was moved into the first receiving wards, to attend to the spiritual needs of the wounded. He also planned to hold services for the staff and soldiers on Sundays. Just south of the aid post was a designated safe area, containing tents for sleeping, and a mess and cooking area. The front troops could have some breathing space here. It offered them a week's break before they had to go back into action — even longer if they had lost many men.

Little did this man of the cloth realise that he had walked through the gates of hell. The changes that the padre found with his new posting were almost beyond belief. After returning from the front lines, now well away from most of the sounds of war, men who were desperate for a rest stopped, sat, refused to attend small social events organised by the army, and simply stayed in their tents. Some didn't even turn up for the occasional mail-call. They simply drank together. The first time that the padre held a Sunday service, the large tent was almost empty. This came as a shock to him, as he had been used to having near-capacity services back at the main base. Now, this 'sticking together' by the soldiers in the rest area flowed into their shared religious nonobservance. Men stopped attending church services; religion was of little or no interest to the digger in the scheme of things. The padre had no choice but to stop his Sunday service. It shattered him.

Then, sadly, at this small outpost, in his receiving ward, looking after men from mainly his battalion, the padre came under extra, unbearable pressure. As if to destroy the poor man, the demands on the padre's time by the medical staff were impossible to fulfil. Men were dying continually: some, seconds apart; others lingered for too long. The padre was unqualified to deal with such horrors of war in the chaos of a crude field-outpost hospital. This was a new reality for him to face up to.

He found himself in a critical ward where a nod from the doctor indicated an imminent fatality. With robes and materials gathered for the last rites, the padre would dash towards a bed. But which bed? Sometimes, there was more than one digger dying at the same time. What was the padre to do? Administer a brief, panicked ceremony? The padre didn't know which call to respond to.

Suddenly, there would be a call from another bed, another ward … The padre quickly realised that it was *he* who had to decide who would die first. The busy doctor had already left. It was a hopeless dilemma, as most of the day there would be many soldiers needing to hear the words from him that opened the door to another world.

This man of the cloth's rituals became very curtailed, shortened to a few seconds. Like the nurses, he had to leave young men when they needed him most. He would quickly move to another soldier, hearing his name called yet again.

Every time the medical wagons arrived and dispensed their wounded, it meant mayhem for the padre as well. He pleaded for assistance, but the army ignored him. As far as it was concerned, that was the padre's lot at the front. But the carnage appalled him. He could not cope with what he saw. He had overwhelming and unending responsibilities to dozens of dying men crying for his presence.

Perhaps the gas and artillery that exploded in the squalid receiving area and wounded him seriously was a godsend — at least it got him away from his living hell. He had ended up in an English hospital … as a lost soul.

The padre's reduced appearance as a huddled-up, baby-like, frightened man, sucking the corner of his pillowcase, made Jill feel numb. She had never questioned God, religion, and the church. Surely, one of God's chosen would have the strength to survive. The whole experience frightened her. When Jill first met the padre, she was hesitant to attend to his personal needs. His being a Roman Catholic padre didn't help either, as Jill had grown up in a strict Irish–Catholic home. However, like so many people put on a pedestal, Jill soon found the man to be a kind, humble person who wanted his mum and liked to talk. He was incapable of assisting others, and instead was pleading for someone to comfort him. But Sister Hunter didn't have the time.

For Jill, the gas ward was now no different from the amputation ward. She was slowly losing her ability to cope with the pressure. Her old room-mate, Lola, her sweet friend who had always had the time to listen to her, and had always been there, was with her no longer. They had come over on the boat together, and had nursed together in Egypt. Lola had met Tag and thought the world of him. But Lola, the strong one, had contracted the flu — a new, virulent strain, which had just started to appear. It deprived her of much-needed strength, both physically and emotionally. Like so many nurses, Lola had tried to continue working. She wasn't to know that this was the worst thing she could have done. Her health deteriorated rapidly, and she unwittingly helped spread the disease through personal contact. Lola, the nurse who hugged and patted and held the hands of her patients, became Lola the carrier of influenza. Soldiers who normally would have recovered from their wounds were slain by its vicious attack on their respiratory systems.

Then Lola died.

JILL WAS CHANGING. Somehow, she had coped in Cairo; but now, after only five weeks in England, she was struggling to deal with her situation. She took Lola's death very badly. Now, she rarely spoke to or touched her patients. There was little comfort to be found in her workmates, either, as they themselves needed a strong shoulder to cry on. As a distraction, Jill turned to her last hope. Once again, she tried desperately to locate Tag. It had been ages since she had heard from him—since she had been in Egypt, in fact. She did everything she could to block out her wandering imagination, which played tricks on her as she dozed off to sleep. Despite herself, she would keep picturing a sickening scene of Tag's shattered body lying on a battlefield or, worse, him in a hospital bed, dying, wanting his Jill.

There had been a brief moment of hope when she had first arrived in London. Jill's original room-mate, Doreen, who was still in Cairo, forwarded to Jill the letter that Tag had sent there, including a brief covering note on the news from Egypt. But even the kindly action of sending on the letter turned out to be of no use in locating him. Jill answered Tag's letter immediately, unaware that he had already received another posting. The letter that Jill sent to his old address was returned automatically, as the army's mail system was failing. In any case, its priority was censorship, not keeping track of the whereabouts of its men.

All of this happened in a matter of weeks. Finally, in desperation, Jill wrote to Tag's mum, Mrs Ann Wardell, and mistakenly addressed it to Fish Creek. (As it happened, there was such a town in South Gippsland—a good four days' s horseride from Swifts Creek.) But Jill received no answer. Her conclusion was … well, she expected the worst. Jill assumed that Ann didn't have the strength to tell her the truth. But then again, Jill also knew that Tag rarely wrote home. She thought constantly of how she could contact her Tag, or at the very least get some news about him — whatever it was.

Then she remembered Chatty. Doreen had mentioned in her note that Chatty was on his way home. Of course — Chatty. Jill screamed aloud. *Chatty, Chatty, my sweet Chatty …*

She wrote him the briefest note in pencil:

Dear Chatty

Any news on Tag? I don't have his address and haven't heard from Ann, his mother in Fish Creek.

Love, Jill.

She addressed it to 'Mr Chatty Bills, Benambra, Victoria'. She remembered that Chatty had talked a lot about Benambra, and assumed that was where he lived.

Australia's postal service turned out to be better than the army's — Chatty got Jill's letter. When he opened it, he was chuffed. He didn't live in Benambra, although he had grown up there as a child. He was living at Ann's place, out in the stables with Tag's nags. Because Chatty was well known in the district, the local postman, Mr Kelly, re-directed the letter and delivered it personally. Admittedly, the old Chatty was pretty much under the weather when Mr Kelly bashed on Ann's back door. Ann grabbed the letter from him, and was thrilled: she thought it was from her Tag.

She anxiously took in the letter from the woman she had heard so much about. They both laughed about Fish Creek — for some reason, many people got Fish and Swifts mixed up. Then, just like Jill had, Ann assumed the worst. She hadn't heard from Tag for over a month. He never said much in his letters about France anyway. Ann could only gauge the war's progress from the newspapers reports, and they were depressing; even the press was struggling to treat the horrendous results from France positively. Ann, ever a clear thinker, immediately penned a letter to Jill. She told her what little news she had of Tag, and gave her Tag's latest address.

The mail was always slow, so it was many weeks before the mail call at the hospital saw Jill being handed a letter from Ann Wardell. Jill was curious when Ann's reply arrived, because there was a Swifts Creek return address on the back of the envelope. She, too, laughed when she saw the connection — she was positive that Tag had said Fish Creek. Quickly, she read the letter from Ann and let out a drawn-out sigh that had been building up for weeks. Then, immediately, Jill sat down and wrote a long letter to Tag. She started to jot down a few affectionates lines and to pass on some news; then, hesitating, she put down her indelible pencil, and thought deeply about Tag. A relationship during a war was, at best, a temporary affair. If one chose to be committed, any mail delivery could bring devastatingly bad news. But, for Jill, there was no path other than one of commitment. In her heart was a love for Tag that was as constant as sunrise. However, Jill also realised from bitter experience that the longer Tag was involved with the war, the lower were his chances of survival. She knew she might never see her Tag again.

Jill wanted to declare herself to Tag in an intimate way. She wanted to express every feeling she had for him, every thought, no matter how private. It didn't matter that Tag wasn't actually with her. She wanted to give herself totally to Tag—a decision never made lightly or without great desire by a woman. She started with a brief mention of Ann's letter. Then, for the first time, Jill expressed her deep love for Tag. She told him of his constant presence in her mind. She described their walk along the bank of the exotic Nile River, and wrote of the wonderful memories and joy of their times together, and the extent of her love for him.

Finally, she expressed her desire to share closeness with her Tag. Sex wasn't mentioned—that wouldn't have been proper, even for young adults from the country like Tag and Jill. However, what Jill wrote of was more beautiful, more intimate than just sex. She wrote of her obsession with the bracelet that Tag had bought at the bazaar. She adored it, and confided to Tag that it was her connection with him:

When I arrive back in my quarters after a day in the ward, I take the bracelet from its hiding place. Then, after admiring its beauty, I place it on the stool next to the tub I have just filled with warm water. Facing you (the bracelet), I get undressed and lower myself in the glorious warmth and talk to you as I wash my tired body. Turning, I close my eyes and I imagine you softly washing my back, my bottom and my legs. I turn and face you, the picture in my mind so clear, so perfect. I love your sweet shyness as you cover my breasts with the warm flannel and squeeze so tenderly. My belly, with its cute little button, and my pubic hair, you caress with sensitivity. Now it's my turn to be shy. Then quickly you dry me and I rug up, as this is a cold bloody place after Egypt! For ages, you brush my hair with such affection I glow like an open fire.

Then I go to bed and read by candle, just for a short while. For, of an evening when lying in bed, I think of you, my sweet. I am fresh and clean from the warm bath. I take the bracelet to bed. Slipping it under my nightie, I roll it tenderly over my breasts. They swell and go hard. The stones on the jewel excite my nipples when I rub them with its roughness. Then, slowly, I roll it softly around on my belly. It's so thrilling to feel you in this way, my sweet Tag. Eventually I place it between my legs, against my fluffy. The magic warmth of the bracelet makes my fluff throb and swell. It aches with desire and love. It is a most wonderful feeling, my sweet Tag. Then, satisfied with the sweet attention you have paid me, I close my eyes and go to sleep, my fluffy and belly flooding with warmth that I like to believe is a baby that you have just planted deep inside of me. I hope that I will dream of you; I usually do. It would be so breathtaking if you could get leave and come to England ...

Jill

Finally, Jill finished. The letter revealed the sweet, tender person that she was. Although she didn't know it, it was a beautiful, wonderful letter. Jill hesitated to send it. She wondered what the censor would do. What would Tag think of her? Then she realised that Tag would be thrilled. She turned for help in posting the letter to a young officer who lived in London and regularly escorted her to and from the nurses' quarters. He was quite happy to post it by civilian mail, where there was no censorship. Jill decided to leave off a return address on the envelope, only adding it to the bottom of the letter.

Writing and then posting the letter lifted Jill's spirits. She felt a purpose in her life that had been missing for ages. Then she read and re-read Ann's letter. Chatty had made it home; that was good news. Jill had made contact with Tag's mum; that was a good thing. Tag was alive; that was much more of a good thing.

Then, within days, Jill found herself yet again in the matron's office. It was so strange, given the letter she had written and posted to Tag. Jill was over four-and-a-half months pregnant.

'And who is the father, young lady?'

Jill explained everything that she wanted to reveal to the matron. Like Jill, this woman had been in Egypt. They shared a strange bond. Quickly, the matron's manner changed to one of sympathy and concern.

'You'll have to resign soon, as soon as the baby shows. What will you do then?'

'I will return home to Australia. I know the father's mother. She will help.'

'When do you think you will go?'

'I'm waiting for a letter, and then I will leave.'

Four-and-a-half months pregnant. Surely, a nurse of all people understood the reproductive system, and menstruation … but irregular periods for nurses were common. Stress and anxiety delayed the menstrual cycle, at times, for up to three months. Jill had never suspected anything until she had started to feel very ill in the morning. Then, within two weeks, it became obvious to her.

Jill's slightly enlarged stomach decided her future. Within a fortnight, she had set sail for home. Fortunately, the matron had organised a secluded cabin, and had confided in a few staff whom she felt could be trusted on the ship. It was, of course, an utter disgrace for a nurse to fall pregnant, so even Jill's official papers told a lie. She had received an honourable discharge, having suffered from anxiety and emotional problems.

CHAPTER TWENTY-THREE

Jill's letter galvanised Tag. He wanted to pack his belongings and head for England to join her. He reckoned he'd walk across the Channel if he had to. However, Tag was quickly brought back to earth — dry earth, and firm at last. The bloody rain had eased. He was at the point of exhaustion. Like nearly everybody caught up in the war, Tag had lost any sense of time. Rarely did the diggers know what day it was, let alone which month. Tag was aware that he had been away from home for what seemed a lifetime; in fact, it was almost two years since he had left Australia. It seemed like he was in another world — a world in which life was short, luck was important, and it was an achievement to make it through the day. Death was common, but never accepted. A dead mate's name would be mentioned briefly, but the conversation would move on quickly to the state of the horses, the mail, or when some leave might be snagged.

Receiving mail was wonderful, a channel to a dream: it provided a magic-carpet ride back to a land that had become almost a fantasy. Many soldiers who still had some spirit left felt the same, even if it was only on the basis of a dry letter from home that relayed news of the weather, local events, and family matters. Then, likewise, the soldiers' return letter from the battlefield would avoid the truth. Perhaps it was the threat of censorship, or simply that, even with loved ones, it was easier to ramble about nothing much than to write about how it really was. Hence, Jill's letter to Tag was unusual — a brief, warm delight that Tag treasured. He was impressed that Jill had arranged to send it by civilian mail.

That night, he sat on the wooden box beside his bed. A candle flame and a new moon provided the light. Often, at this time, he would repair harnesses or soften hardened leather equipment with beeswax, trying to undo the damage that the damp weather had done to their equipment. It was a never-ending job stitching broken straps, belts, and old rotten leather — so much so that, every night, a team of twenty-five handlers was rostered to work on harnesses. However, this night, Tag had a personal project: he was sewing a piece of canvas for a wallet. He waxed the last bit of thread carefully. This wallet wasn't for holding money — it was for Jill's letter. He decided it would be with him always. The wallet would protect it from his sweat, the weather, and dirt. Proudly, he slipped the precious letter into the canvas sleeve and placed it in his shirt pocket. Patting it softly, he smiled, and then laid back on his bed for some much needed sleep.

He hoped he wouldn't dream, for his dreams were vile and sordid, and never left the battlefield. An image of Jill had no hope of gate-crashing his endless bank of appalling memories.

IT WAS NOW August 1916. It was still dry; they were having warm weather. Tag brushed Noodles, a chestnut gelding from Roma in Queensland, for ages. Like most of the horses, Noodles showed signs that he seemed to know he was about to return to the place of loud noises, crying men, and rotting smells. Worse, and above all of this, Noodles wasn't fooled by the gas-mask routine. Fitting gas masks on the horses had been Tag's greatest challenge — and success. That was why Tag had this horse. He was a handful, a rebel, and a damn good horse. Few men could handle the high-spirited beast. Tag spoke to the young horse with affection and strength.

'You do well today, Noodles, and I'll throw in an extra basin of oats. Try not to shy if the shells start up, ol' fella. The wounded don't like being jolted about.'

Noodles nodded his head up and down, not acknowledging Tag's request, but thoroughly enjoying the scratch behind his ears that Tag applied with vigour and a feeling of larrikin fun. Carefully, Tag adjusted the traces around the horse's body, and then the cart was attached. The sleds were no longer in use, because of the drier weather and firmer soil. Tag unclipped the reins and then, adjusting the gas mask so it made a firm seal without being too tight, he continued to pat the tense animal. As with all carts heading out into the battlefield, there were two men on board. One was a medic; the other, a horse handler, or driver, as the army called him. Today, the medic, who was invariably known as Doc, was Dick Dando. Tag would be his offsider. Doc and Tag had done many trips together. Doc admired Tag's ability with the horses; similarly, Tag had nothing but respect and deep, heartfelt praise for Doc the medic. They had a tough, thankless job.

It was dawn when convoy of retrieval wagons headed out. There had been heavy shelling overnight, and both Tag and Doc knew that there would only be a brief respite while the soldiers on both sides had a quick meal. Usually, the carts tried to arrive at the front just on mealtime. There were eight carts in Tag's team. The going was slow. Every inch of the earth showed signs of gouging, or was churned like a ploughed paddock. After months of constant artillery, combined with the mud, the terrain had set like concrete. It looked like another planet, especially with horses and soldiers wearing gas masks, plodding into a landscape that had no intact trees left. In this once beautiful rural area, there was now no grass, no birds, and no beauty. Nevertheless, nature provided some survivors, even in this squalor. Rats thrived, as their food was plentiful, and maggots were always in plague proportions.

As Tag and Doc arrived at the battlefield, the devastation from the previous night's fighting became quickly apparent. There were many dead, and many more wounded. The carts quickly spread out, and medics gave their instructions, bringing the mayhem under a crude degree of control. Between them, the eight carts would hope to retrieve sixty wounded. It varied, though. If the stricken soldiers were able to sit up, the cart could usually take a dozen; if there were stretcher cases, six was the limit. During this time, as the medics and others attended the wounded, Tag and his driver mates would move among the dead bodies, removing their dog tags. It was better that they, rather than the men in the trenches, performed this task.

The dog tags—two discs, engraved with the digger's name, serial number, blood group, and religion—hung around the soldier's neck. Wearing dog tags became usual during the war. As few of these poor blighters would receive a funeral, a marked grave, or any other ceremony resembling a dignified burial, the collection of the tags was essential. The least the army could do was identify the dead. The procedure adopted was for one of the tags to be cut off and returned to the army, and for the other one to be left with the body, in the mouth. The plan was that, some time later, another party would identify the body, collect the remains, and return it for burial. In practice, though, this rarely happened.

The more that Tag's team spread out, the more they discovered that the overnight shelling had caused appalling injuries and death. Of the dead, few intact bodies were found; artillery had shredded the soldiers' torsos and limbs beyond description.

Tag reached the first body. It was badly lacerated from a massive shrapnel blast. In fact, it looked more like the remains of some animal after a pride of lions had attacked it, had their fill, and retired to the shade. Entangled in the flesh at the neck, Tag noticed the dog tags. He reached down and removed the young man's only claim to an identity. The poor, dead soldier had no head — no body, really. Tag wrapped both dog tags around his wrist, which was what he always did when he had to collect the set. It was the first thing he did, something he had learned to do instead of his previous practice of putting them in his pockets, as the result of a very distressing incident in camp some weeks back. After an exhausting day, he had undressed, thrown his pants in the laundry basket that would be collected that evening, and then lain down and gone to sleep. Next morning, in a panic when he realised what he'd done, he tried to trace the pants. But he had no luck. There was a fair chance that they and the tags had already been burnt, along with all the other bloody, stinking uniforms that had been handed in by the medics, stretcher-bearers, and drivers; their uniforms, stained with blood, dirt, and grime, were often beyond re-washing. He hunted for ages to try to find the dog tags, to no avail. It meant that another unknown soldier had been left behind, and it affected Tag deeply. He would in future wrap the tags around his wrist.

Now, looking down at the remains of the headless soldier, Tag fought back his emotions quickly. This was an acquired skill gained by most soldiers in battle. He said some quiet words of goodbye under his breath and, glancing at the metal tags, said, 'I'll see this gets home, Ross.' The dead man was Ross Johnson, a private soldier. What little remained of his body could have fitted into a coffin made for a newborn baby. Tag left the body. If there had been a head, he would have covered it with dignity.

After leaving the remains of Johnson, Tag heard Doc call out. He wanted Tag to take an injured soldier back to the cart. They would have to get a move on, as the shelling had started again, about a mile to the west. Tag humped the poor bloke piggyback-style. The soldier, who was suffering badly from having had both legs shattered, was making a whimpering sound of misery, pain, and shock. It was a common sound made by the wounded. They often shook uncontrollably, and inevitably asked for a cigarette. Tag asked the fella to hang on tight. Pausing at the back of the wagon, Tag wrapped the long reins that dangled over the backboard of the cart around his left wrist, just in case Noodles walked forward while he was struggling to get the soldier into the back of the cart. He bent over to roll the soldier onto the floor of the —

The blast was a blinding roar. There was a flash of heat, then an eardrum-shattering noise of screaming, whistling metal. The artillery had started again. In an instant, Doc Dando and the three other crews were blasted to pieces. Luckily, for Tag, bent over and struggling with the wounded man, it was the soldier on his back who shuddered as the shrapnel blasted the poor man's body. At once, Tag could sense his back and neck being set on fire as he was shunted with bone-breaking force into the tailgate of the cart. The impact crushed his head, and his right arm jammed into the railing. At the same instant, the terrified Noodles bolted frantically, his hooves tearing into the dry earth as he dashed away. The cart jolted, lurched, and wobbled along. With a loud crunch, one of the wheels smashed into a large rock. The cart reared, rolled, and slowly came down on its side. Luckily, there were no wounded inside — the soldier on Tag's back would have been the first.

Poor Noodles whinnied, thrashed about, and then collapsed. During its frenzied bolt, the horse had travelled about 150 yards. Tag, with the reins still wrapped around his wrist, had been dragged behind the rear of the cart across the uneven terrain. With his gas mask having been ripped away, Tag tried to jam his mouth shut as his lungs screamed in fiery pain; some shells contained gas. The left side of his face was burning with the intensity of hot, splattering fat on bare skin. The injury to his head was very serious, but Tag could only feel a burning sensation. His right arm had become entangled and twisted, and then it had snapped and become caught in a bundle of gas mask, webbing, and dog tags … Ross Johnson's dog tags. The cart had jarred, reared, and rolled sideways as it stopped. He tried to call out to Doc, but his mouth would not work.

Minutes — which took hours to pass — were all that was required to kill most of the men within fifty yards of where they had been hit. As it happened, Noodles had dragged Tag out of the range of the shells. Tag's other stroke of providence was the wind: a strong southerly wind blew the gas towards the enemy.

It was almost silent. Tag could hear men screaming in agony, but at least the shelling had stopped. He desperately tried to rub both eyes, but his left arm flopped loosely beside his body. Tag worked out that the arm was at a strange angle, perhaps badly broken. He tried to reach across with his right arm, only to be stopped by a sharp pain. He felt a long bone protruding out of this arm; it was sticking into his neck. The dog tags that had belonged to Private Ross Johnson were hooked in the protruding bone. He tried to untangle them with his teeth, but the pain was overwhelming and his mouth wouldn't work. Tag struggled to free his right arm, then fainted. He had been stripped of most of his clothes, his upper webbing, and his own dog tags by the rampaging gallop of the frightened horse, although his thick webbing belt had ensured that a part of his pants had stayed on. His back was red, raw, and bruised. Within no time, flies swarmed around him, landed, and started laying their eggs into his wounds. The numerous cuts quickly dried up with the dust and dirt and, fortunately, Tag was lying face down. Had the flies infected his macerated face, the result would have been fatal. After another brief struggle to untangle his arm, Tag lost all consciousness.

The letter from Jill, safely dry and protected by a canvas wallet, remained inside Tag's shredded shirt, fifty yards from his body. His dog tags, entangled in the shirt, were also fifty yards away. The cord had been severed during the mad dash of the crazed horse.

It was twenty-two hours after the shelling, just on dawn, when the body beside the cart was identified as that of Private Ross Johnson. The medic assumed the soldier was dead. Certainly, his head wound looked terrible. But when, suddenly, there was movement, he realised that the soldier wasn't dead—just very badly wounded. He appeared to be breathing in spasms. Quickly, the medic decided to have the soldier evacuated.

As he rolled the wounded man over, the new medic was surprised that the rats had not invaded the body. Others had warned him that this was common, and would be a shock when witnessed for the first time. These vermin worked frantically overnight on the wounded and dead. It was the reason that horses were shot immediately if they were wounded—rats were very partial to horseflesh.

The medic had been nervous about going out, having heard that all of the team who had gone out at dawn the day before had, most likely, been killed. He had only been in France for four weeks, and at the new camp just one day. He had never met Tag. When he had jumped up onto the cart with a new handler, waved goodbye to those at the aid post, and then been told in which direction to head, he braced himself for the worst. On arrival at the battlefront, his instructions were to move to the left.

It was when they were almost ready to leave with their first load that he'd spotted the body by itself, near the horse, beside the cart. He had jogged across, only to come across the repulsive sight of the poor horse, still hooked up in harness, on its side, with a neat bullet hole through its head. He had then moved quickly to the side of the cart. Although the body in the dirt had shown no signs of life, the new young medic had followed his training and had had a closer look.

During his brief appraisal, the medic had noticed the dog tags tangled in the soldier's broken right arm. *That's lucky*, he had thought. *Johnson must have been dragged some distance, seeing how his clothes have been ripped off him.*

Perhaps the dog tags had been hooked off by the sharp, protruding bone. But as to why Johnson had kept hold of the reins when the horse had bolted, the medic hadn't pondered; that's where his curiosity had stopped. Unfortunately, he didn't mention this small but important detail later, back at base.

Once he saw Private Johnson start to move, though, the young medic quickly strapped the useless left arm to the soldier's body. The right arm was badly broken, and was contained in a crude sling. The wounded digger was taking shallow, short breaths, and was unconscious. He had lost a lot of blood from the horrendous injury to the left side of his face. The soldier's body was a mess of deep cuts and large bruises, with bits of skin missing. Later, the medic was to comment that it was amazing that Johnson had lived, and lucky that he had still had his dog tags on him. Without them, he would have been unidentifiable. His shattered face was very swollen and distorted, and obscured by dirt caked with blood; no one would have recognised the man.

Carefully, Private Ross Johnson was placed into the medic's cart and finally delivered, along with six other suffering souls, to the outpost staging hospital for treatment. Initially, patient Ross Johnson, No. 37882, was left unattended—lying in the cart until morning—because his wounds were such that they would have tied up too many of the medical staff. This was a common practice. When things settled, if Johnson were still alive, there was a chance that he would receive treatment.

If he could have spoken, the soldier would have asked for a drink of water and then a smoke, and for the nurse of his choice—Jill. As it happened, he survived the night. After doing a brief check on him, the staff realised that Johnson needed major surgery and attention, and that the only way he could get it was by being moved further down the road to a better staging hospital. It was only an hour's drive in the Red Cross truck, but it was an unfortunate move, in some ways, for patient Johnson: had he stayed at the staging post, maybe one of the staff would have recognised the man, even though his face was badly mutilated.

SIX DAYS AFTER the artillery barrage that had caused so much havoc—and created patient Johnson—the nurse led the visitors into the cramped ward. The three men stood around the patient. Before they entered the room, the surgeon had informed them that the patient's stay with them would only be a brief one. They would send him to a base hospital and then onto England for specialist treatment. The surgeon also asked the visitors not to take too much time, and not to expect the young man to answer their questions, as he was unable to talk.

''Ow are ya, mate?' asked Peter Hajenko, a cobber who had been with Ross since training camp. Standing with Pete were John Henry and Bob Dent, all good mates of Ross Johnson. Together, they had only been in France for sixteen weeks, and already their original group of fifteen had been reduced to ten. Bob was visibly upset. Looking at his mate, all he could see was a left arm and shoulder, and a heavily bandaged right arm. The rest of the soldier's upper torso was covered in bandages.

Together, they assured their mate Ross that they would write to his parents and tell them he was on the mend. It was a brief visit. Outside, John (or Jug, as he was affectionately known) assured the others that Roscoe would pull through. 'No problems, he's as tough as nails, our Roscoe.'

The men left quietly. Their eyes were downcast; their steps were slow and measured. It was all too much. The young doctor watched Roscoe's mates as they moved away. He was concerned about Ross Johnson. Although there had been a slight improvement in the appearance of his external wounds, patient Johnson wasn't getting any better. The doctor felt it was time to send Ross Johnson to England. There was no theatre suitable to operate on the patient's shattered face in France. The doctor wrote a lengthy report, in which he also decided to mention the behaviour of patient Private Ross Johnson. It was most peculiar.

Report: Private Ross Johnson

Left arm: Has been examined and re-plastered. Minor break but severe lacerations and bruising. Left hand badly squashed. Recommend no movement for ten weeks. General arm condition: good, has movement already—full plaster to remain for six weeks.

Right arm: Severe breakage—needs further specialist examination.

Burns: Satisfactory progress, little secondary skin penetration, and possibly internal gas damage.

Eyes: Left: Burst pupil, will need removal; *Right*: Severe blistering. Still closed—requiring salt bathing and lanolin applications hourly. Unable to determine if sight is possible.

Facial fractures: Left jaw will require surgery to enable speech to have a chance of returning. Left eye socket has partial depression that will require specialist inspection to determine extent of damage.

Recommendation: Patient Johnson be transferred to England for above procedures.

Please note: Private Johnson displays bizarre behaviour when attempts are made to communicate with him by requesting leg movement. The patient thumps the bed with his free leg and attempts to grapple or kick the medical staff. Lately he has been more subdued, but in my opinion he is a violent patient, and if the pattern continues I would suggest restraints.

Dr S. Murphy

The doctor didn't realise that patient Johnson was going to get sicker—too sick to move anywhere.

THE EARLY FIRING of the enemy artillery had caught everyone unawares on Hell Heap Hill that terrible August night and day, and had caused carnage—six killed and sixteen badly wounded. The trenches, full of soldiers eating and waiting for orders, had taken several direct hits. Tag, who had remained conscious for two hours after the initial blasts, was the sole survivor from his team. As soon as the hospital and army command received the news that most of the soldiers, medics, and drivers up on the hill had suffered heavy casualties, they immediately ordered replacement medics and handlers—already exhausted from lack of sleep—to the front lines to retrieve any survivors.

Two new medics made up the team of twenty. After the first few carts returned, it became obvious that the staging hospital wasn't coping; even the resting tents were full. The wounded were placed out in the open, and the situation deteriorated every time another batch of carts arrived. Fortunately, each cart crew had an experienced driver who organised shade and a blanket for the wounded. Then one of these drivers returned, stepped straight down off his cart, and stumbled inside the aid post. He was the bearer of devastating news: he had spotted Tag and Noodles on the first return trip to the scene where the artillery had wreaked its havoc. Charlie Walker was his name, and the sad soldier was still shaking from the fright of having found Tag's body.

'He was lying face down, dead,' Charlie told his mates. 'I'd recognise that bloody red 'air anywhere. Poor bugger, his left arm was twisted up under his body. Poor little bastard was right near Noodles, his chestnut horse; somehow, he'd crawled or pushed himself for twenty feet to be near the horse. And that bloody Noodles, the mad bastard, was on his side, still in harness and still kicking. Tag loved that horse.'

A glance from Charlie at Tag had told him that this special man was dead—although Charlie had thought it strange that Tag and Noodles were alone, 150 yards away from all the other carts down near the original artillery barrage. When Charlie had walked over to glance at the body, he had recognised Noodles in an instant, and guessed that the man near the horse was Tag. Charlie had reeled back in shock. Tag was their leader, regardless of rank. He was their mentor, the man with the unique reputation of being able to talk to horses.

Charlie had also noticed that Tag's dog tags had been removed. *Some other bugger got 'em, I guess*, was his first thought. Naturally, Charlie assumed that Tag's dog tags had been taken by an earlier visitor, or maybe by a survivor from the trenches. He hadn't rolled Tag over to see if the other dog tag was in his mouth. He simply couldn't do that. Tag was dead, and that was that. Charlie hadn't had the strength to take a closer look.

There were blowflies crawling over the back of the body by the time Charlie had appeared on the scene. 'Poor bugger was as dead as a doornail,' he told the others later.

What Charlie didn't realise was that Tag's dog tags had been ripped off and left behind on the field, along with the precious letter from Jill that was still safely protected in its canvas wallet. Charlie didn't inspect the body closely. It was Noodles who had his attention: with the skin on its legs almost worn away, the horse was still bleeding badly from his frantic, kicking struggle. Charlie had no choice: he walked up and shot poor Noodles. He then turned and walked back to his own wagon, very shaken.

Tag was left behind. Charlie reckoned that, if time permitted, he would organise to go back and collect his mate and, 'bury him proper, like'. Deep down inside, though, Charlie was aware that that would never happen. Time was precious — too precious for burials.

Later, back in camp, when Charlie built up the courage and broke the news to the blokes in Tag's section, the reactions were stark.

'Hell, not Tag. No, not Tag. He was special.'

'Jesus, we need Tag. He was the only bloke who could calm the horses.'

'It's not flamin' fair. He was about to go to Blighty on leave, to see his Jill. Hell, hell … poor Jill.'

To his mates, Tag was dead. The fact that the dog tags had not been handed in — a detail overlooked in the grief and disbelief that followed — was soon forgotten. The entire unit was preoccupied by the need to send letters home, and to get Tag's belongings and private matters packed and forwarded to Swifts Creek.

The word had spread quickly. The men were saying very little. What was there to say? They never got used to death. Death … was that the right word? At any moment, they had to be able to deal with suddenly mutilated young bodies, and to try to help their hopelessly wounded mates. These young men, the survivors, were struggling to cope and remain strong. They were trying to support each other, and trying to comprehend the mayhem. Was that humanly possible? The horse handlers, like most of the diggers, were a bewildered group of miserable young men. All of them were very aware that they, too, were on death's shortlist.

At the staging hospital, Tag's second home away from his horses, they were shocked by the news of Tag's death. Tag was one of the few originals. Morale was already very low, but this was news about someone special having been taken from them. As if that wasn't enough, they had also just experienced the largest number of medics, handlers, and horses ever lost in a single night.

CHAPTER TWENTY-FOUR

It was late October 1917. Ann rocked in the same swaying motion that she had used with her sweet James all those years ago. But it was not a baby she had in her arms now; it was a brief note handed to her by the local policeman. The note offered no courtesies, consolations, or explanations other than that Tag had been 'killed in action'. Ann was shattered. For two days, she remained in another world, oblivious to requests or queries from family and friends. Her special Tag was gone. There were no details—he was just gone.

The first person she spoke to was Chatty. He had adopted Jess the beagle, and was scratching her belly when Ann appeared and told him the news. Chatty sat on the back step to Ann's house and stared at nothing, said nothing, and displayed little emotion. His eyes were full of tears; but, then again, they always were.

Chatty was a sick man. He drank heavily, but not at the pub. He drank alone in the dark out the back, near the stables that Tag had had built for his horses. Chatty's behaviour was frowned upon by most of the locals. They thought he was a lucky one—he'd made it home—so they offered little sympathy to a man who was missing half a leg and was now a drunk. Chatty still hadn't asked McCoy's at Omeo to make him a special extra-long boot. He was too embarrassed to do so. In any case, Chatty was rarely sober enough to have a sensible conversation with anyone.

He looked very old nowadays. What the locals didn't see or understand was what haunted Chatty. If he went to bed sober, which he did on odd occasions, appalling nightmares rotted his heart and brain. The deaths in the trenches, the cries of pain, and the pleas for food and water were re-enacted cruelly and destructively in poor Chatty's dreams. And now, he was starting to have visions of horror during the day as well. Several times a day, he would be overcome by shaking fits of fear and overwhelming sadness as the flashbacks and intrusions became more common. By now, his condition had a name: it was shell shock.

Ann was very good to Chatty. In her heart, she wished strongly that he would tell her a little about Gallipoli and the war. Innocently, she felt it would help her understand the bravery and courage of those who had died over there. However, like the rest of the men who returned, Chatty remained silent.

Once the news of Tag's death spread around Swifts Creek and the district, the church wanted to hold a memorial service for him. This was a kind gesture, but it received a polite refusal from Ann. She couldn't explain her reasons, but there was something missing or false in several army services she had been to. Perhaps it was Chatty. He came away from his first memorial service angry, and hurling oaths at the army, the politicians, and the bullshit.

'What a load of crap!'

Then again, Chatty was a fool, the town drunk, and a bludger. What else would you expect from him? Ann did the only thing that she thought was required: she wrote to Jill. Ann realised there was a strong possibility that Jill hadn't been told the news.

TAG'S FIRST RECOLLECTION was of being lifted into a cart—a medical cart—but it was a different voice he heard, not Doc's. Confused and disoriented, he tried to ask those around him what was going on; but, when he moved his jaw to speak, a pain of such overwhelming proportions seared through his face that he fainted. It was several days before he re-entered the world of the conscious. He guessed he was on an army stretcher, or maybe a bed. Tag was aware that he was in some trouble: he could barely move, as bandages covered most of his upper body, and he was in constant pain that was powerful although bearable. He assumed that the darkness was due to the bandages surrounding his face.

Tag could hear voices, demands, groans, and a lot of brisk movement all around him. He tried to attract somebody's attention. However, his mouth, throbbing with pain, refused to cooperate, and he couldn't get either of his arms to move. What was going on? Tag was bewildered. He twisted his head, only for a sharp pain to shoot through his entire body. He was vaguely aware that he was in a room, receiving treatment for whatever it was that was wrong with him. He tried to blink his eyes, but couldn't. The left side of his face felt weird, and nothing felt familiar on the left inside of his mouth. Suddenly, his lack of sight petrified him. It wasn't dark, but he couldn't see. The bandages couldn't be that thick, surely? He struggled to talk, but nothing came out; worse, his face repelled his efforts with a thumping pain, the like of which he had never experienced before. All he knew was that his swollen tongue indicated that the inside of his mouth was different and painful, and that somehow a new bone or hard thing had invaded one side of it. There was a tube or pipe there as well.

When finally he felt someone touching his body, Tag wriggled just a little to indicate that he was conscious. The stranger was Ken Hutton, an orderly who went by the name of Coppy.

'Say, mate, 'owya goin'? Me name's Coppy. Just gotta clean

up this little mess ya made last night. Feelin' a bit better, ya poor bugger? You're bloody lucky to be alive, I reckon. Crikey, ya were a mess when ya came in. Bloody terrible, mate. But we'll get ya spruced up in no time. Oh, I used to be a cop back in Melbourne before this flamin' war … that's why I gets called Coppy, eh.'

Then Tag heard another voice.

'Mind your language, orderly, and be quick about your work!' someone demanded. Was that a doctor?

'Yes, sir!' replied Coppy, with a sneer in his voice.

'Seeya, Ross.'

Those first few days in the hospital were painful, intrusive, and confusing for Tag; he was pushed, pulled, and poked, and often passed out from the pain. And there was something else that puzzled him mightily: those who attended him kept calling him 'Ross'. Maybe they'd made up a nickname for him. *Who knows?* Tag thought. He knew that the name 'Tag' was very unusual.

After five days, having gradually improved, Tag was told to expect some blokes for a visit. He waited for them eagerly. He was still in terrible pain, but in better spirits. He knew roughly what his injuries were, although he didn't quite understand the problem with his left eye. As far as he could work out, he would probably be able to see okay. They spoke in a funny language, those medical people, and Tag was frustrated that he couldn't ask any questions, either. Admittedly, he was bewildered the first time they re-dressed his face; he couldn't see or speak, although he had blurred vision. At least that was something.

When his visitors arrived, Tag initially thought that the three men were talking to someone who must have been beside him—some bloke called Ross or Roscoe—but no one was responding. That meant the voices were being directed towards him, but he had no idea what they were talking about, and the deep frown he made involuntarily caused him added pain. His curiosity deepened when they made jokes about the bandages

328

covering his ugly dial, and asked him how he managed to have a pee when both his arms were useless. Their laughter seemed affectionate. Then, when he felt them patting the bed as they left, he was completely bewildered. How could they think he was someone else? Everything was confusing. He had little or no recollection of what had happened on that early morning when he'd moved out to collect the wounded. He vaguely remembered heading out with Doc Dando and Noodles — or was it with Shadrack, the bay horse? That was all he could recall. Now, many days later, there were strangers talking to him.

Several days passed. Tag heard someone nearby. Struggling, Tag tried to attract his or her attention. Then a vaguely familiar voice spoke to him.

'Ya sleep a lot. And ya poor old gob's in a bad way, eh. We'll av' to get ya to nod or somethin' to talk to ya — okay, Roscoe?'

It was Coppy, the orderly. He was back on duty. Tag was stunned, not by the description of the injury to his mouth, but by the way everyone persisted in referring to him as Roscoe. He tried to shake his head, but the pain was excruciating. It was not only the pain that was restricting his movement, though; there was a large gathering of bandages criss-crossed around his head, neck, and upper body. The orderly could see Tag trying to respond. Knowing it was hopeless to expect him to shake his head, Coppy suggested, 'Just rock your left foot, mate — two for no, one for yes.'

Tag rocked his foot once. Even that was painful.

'Well done, mate. Do ya write with ya right hand?'

One rock …

'We'll get ya writing when the right arm's okay, mate.'

Coppy was to play a vital part in the restoration of Tag's sanity. He had common sense, or 'nous' as the Australians called it. He realised that Tag was distressed for some reason other than his horrendous wounds. Nevertheless, dealing with that was some time away. For the moment, Coppy detected that Tag was confused. He was right: depression was to set in as Tag's wounds started to heal.

After ten days of constant treatment, Tag's physical health started to improve. He still couldn't talk, but he was a fighter. He lashed out with a free leg at any member of staff who called him Ross. He started to ignore requests from staff to respond to their questions with a yes or no movement of his foot. He became the talk of the ward, to the point where his bizarre behaviour became the staff's main concern. They were contemplating strapping him to the bed, and then arranging for him to be sent to *that* hospital … for the mad ones.

Coppy never took part in these brief discussions. He would sit quietly, await orders to move a patient, and empty the bin from the surgery containing amputated limbs, or get the place cleaned up before the next intake. However, he was privy to the staffroom talk. It distressed him to hear the way they spoke of patient Johnson. For no specific reason, Coppy felt quite differently about him. He contemplated talking to one of the medical team; but then again, what would he know?

Then fate stepped in. Coppy was in Tag's ward, cleaning and replacing the bedpans. It was time for a fag when, suddenly, the ward runner appeared with the mail and gave it to Coppy. It was yet another of Coppy's endless duties to hand out the mail — and, in some cases, to read a letter out, as some patients were blind or, as in Tag's case, had their eyes covered continually. Since his arrival at the hospital, Tag had never received mail.

Accepting the bundle of string-tied letters, Coppy just kept glancing and nodding, acknowledging the recipient. Then, suddenly, he let out a yip — the same sound he made when he won at a poker game. He put all the letters except one to the side, and raced to Tag's bed in a very excited mood. Coppy had a letter from Ross Johnson's parents. He was sure that this would lift his patient's spirits. Strangely, though, when he explained about the letter, Tag rolled half-away from him. Coppy persisted. He started reading, 'Dear Ross — '

Before Coppy could continue, Tag tried to punch his own stomach with an open palm. This was followed by a low groan, as it caused Tag a lot of pain to hit his body. Half clutching his shirt with his left hand, he made a strange noise. Coppy was amazed — the letter was getting the opposite reaction to what he expected.

'What is it, mate? Ya don't want me to read the letter? Might upset ya, ya reckon, eh?'

Rock, rock. Tag moved his foot with as much energy as he could muster, and then lashed out with his leg, hoping to hit Coppy. Again, the pain almost caused him to faint. Normally, Coppy was required to report such deranged behaviour to the doctors. In fact, by now the doctors were receiving daily reports about Tag's moods. However, Coppy was curious. He had had many quiet, one-sided conversations with Tag, and such an instantaneous outburst confused the ex-policeman. He started to probe a little deeper, quizzing Tag about his family.

'Ya get on with ya parents, mate?'

One rock …

'That's confusing, mate. Ya mum?'

One rock …

'Ya dad?'

Rock, rock, rock … many times.

'Ya don't like ya dad?'

Rock …

'Ya do like ya dad?'

Rock …

'Somethin's friggin' wrong here, mate. You're not makin' sense! Is it the letter?'

Rock …

'Ya got me buggered.'

Coppy patted Tag softly on his left shoulder. Awkwardly, Tag half rolled, and was just able to reach out to grab Coppy's hand and squeeze it. His grip was very weak, as he had no movement in his fingers. But even though it hurt Tag to apply the squeeze, it carried a power of affection.

'I 'ave ta go now, mate. See ya later, okay?'

Tag felt relieved. He could tell that Coppy was not only confused, but curious as well.

The next morning on his rounds, the doctor stopped by Tag's bed.

'It might be time to move you on, Ross. We're thinking of sending you to the main hospital in the next few days. A letter will be sent to your family.'

Twisting and kicking, Tag was distressed. If only he could explain to the doctor that he wanted to stay near Coppy. He didn't want to leave — not just yet. He wanted Coppy. Although only the tiniest thread of hope connected the two men, Tag felt that his salvation rested with Coppy. He continued to pound the bed with his leg and rock his foot.

No, no, no.

The doctor — a worried and over-worked young man — left. Tag slid down in his bed and allowed the darkness of depression to eat away at him. There was no point to his life. He tried to refuse the broth or soup fed to him through a large rubber tube by waving it away with his weak left arm. He started to withdraw, to sleep twenty hours a day, and to ignore requests from staff.

A report describing his mood and behaviour was written. It would accompany him on his next journey, to the mad tent. He was not going to be sent to England — which was just as well, as his health was starting to deteriorate. And so, Tag was moved to another section of the medical hospital, to Tent D, where deranged men either died or returned to some form of normality. Here, the patients received little or no attention from the harassed, over-worked staff. Only the padre visited the mad tent.

Coppy was shocked and distressed when he learned of the decision to move Tag to Tent D. He still believed that, with the right help, Tag could get better. So he made a decision: whenever he was told to knock off, he would call by patient Johnson. He would visit his bed in the tent of despair, and spend a precious half-hour or so with this sad patient.

On his first visit, Coppy talked about some of the characters he had come across when he had been in the police force, who he had arrested or kicked in the bum and sent home. Tag would rock and sway with approval as Coppy waxed lyrical about the good old days in a sad, broken voice that indicated a yearning for that life to return. Coppy patted and squeezed Tag's knee during these conversations. Tag swung his left arm towards Coppy in an obvious sign of fondness, and in an indication that the arm was slowly getting better. But, most important of all, Coppy stopped calling him Ross. He simply referred to him as 'mate'.

TAG DIDN'T DIE. He got better, and managed to leave Tent D—thanks to cunning, deception, and help from an experienced hand like Coppy. In true Aussie fashion, it took a bit of paper shuffling, a lot of bullshit, and a forged signature. Four days after his move into that dark tent, Tag heard Coppy say to him, 'Time ta move on, mate, and I'm comin' with ya.'

Tag was perplexed. He had almost given up, even though he hadn't realised he was in Tent D. Nevertheless, he trusted this quiet man, Coppy. Perhaps there was a chance. This was all Tag wanted.

Finally, when the orderlies entered the tent with a stretcher for Tag, Coppy was by his side.

'We're off, mate. You friggin' ripper, ya tough, ugly prick. Now I have ta hold ya hand and all that bullshit. Hell, I'm pleased for ya, mate — over the flamin' moon, in fact! Get ya out of this hell 'ole. Best thing for ya, eh, you betcha!'

Tag patted Coppy's knee once. Coppy patted Tag and folded back the blankets. Overwhelmed, Tag reached out, patted Coppy, and then pulled him closer. He lifted his weak left arm and placed it around Coppy's neck, squeezing very gently. For the first time in a long time, Tag was happy.

Two German stretcher-bearers moved Tag from the mad tent to the Red Cross truck. Coppy gave orders that meant nothing to the Germans — they knew where to go anyhow. Tag sat up. With most of the bandages around his torso and neck no longer required, he looked a lot better. His right eye was uncovered, but he still had little sight. This didn't bother Tag, as it was improving slightly every day.

The German stretcher-bearers spoke in German, laughed, and carried Tag gently. They were just one group among many German prisoners of war who had been coopted to help with important jobs for the Allies away from the battlefield. As it turned out, they were good, honest workers, and were simply grateful for a feed and for the respect shown to them that allowed them to do such work. They caused no trouble, which was no surprise to the Aussies; ironically, there was a strange bond between these opposing soldiers, just as there had been with the Turks at Gallipoli.

The Germans helped Tag up into the truck, where he would be sitting beside Coppy. In fact, Tag was one of the few soldiers able to sit. By now, he could walk slowly in a shuffling manner. The terrible cuts and bruises on his legs were well on the mend. Most other patients had to lie in bunks, so that the truck was like a mobile bedroom. After ensuring that Tag was comfortable, one of the Germans gently patted Tag's shoulder and quietly whispered in German, '*Viel Gluck, mein Freund — moge Gott Diene Geneesung beeschleunigen.*' ('Good luck, my friend — God speed your recovery.')

Tag was reluctant to let go of the German. He only felt safe when he had hold of someone's shirt or hand. Although he was still unable to see clearly, he could detect light and dark with his right eye. He looked the German roughly in the eye; if it were possible, he would have said, 'Thanks, mate.'

Tag now knew that he had lost his left eye. Coppy had explained it to him in plain English the day before. Somehow, this was okay. It was also comforting for him to know that his left arm was getting stronger. By now, he was able to reach out, feel around, and identify his surrounds. His hand was becoming stronger, too; soon, he hoped he would have enough dexterity to write, even if it was with his left hand. He even believed that he would talk again — given time. In fact, Tag was in high spirits, the best he had felt since those dark days when he had first come to this hospital.

It was a slow, bumpy, four-hour trip to the hospital, but at least it was away from the noises of war. Coppy talked to Tag during the entire trip.

'Ya know, mate, I was proud to be an Aussie the other day. It was a bloody classic, eh! Some friggin' dumb British arseholes at the top tried to combine some of the Aussie battalions.'

'What bullshit!' a voice from a stretcher bellowed.

Coppy continued, 'Fair dinkum, mate, the numbers are so low in some of the boys' battalions that the dopey bastards in charge tried to put them all under the one battalion — combine them like, you know? Apparently, all hell broke lose. The blokes told them to shove the friggin' idea, the friggin' army, and the friggin' war, plus a few other things, fair up their friggin' arses. That was it. Oh, and the Aussies refused to friggin' fight! Friggin' beauties, mate. Fuck the British, and good on 'em!'

That brought cheers.

'No crap?' came an unfamiliar voice. It was a young Australian officer on another stretcher.

'Yep, the blokes in the battalions sorta went on strike, ya know. What a friggin' insult — a bloke from 22 Battalion being asked to become parta 18 Battalion. What a loada friggin' parrot's shit.'

'Yeah, I'd sooner join the priesthood than change my battalion!' said another bloke who was raised up on one elbow, smoking a fag. The young officer, with both legs missing, started to sing 'Waltzing Matilda', and they all joined in. Even Tag — although he made no discernible noise — rocked in tune.

How ignorant of the British. How could they believe that the Australians would swap badges and join another unit? The loyalty of the digger to his battalion was complete, and was never questioned. It was the core of that strange, unique bond called mateship. Right down to the platoons and sections, there was a club-like mentality. It was the basis of the digger's family — like a collective. It was no wonder that the decimated troops wanted to remain with their battalion, no matter how few of them were left. The final result of this embarrassment was amusing, but practical. The men in the battalion stayed with their battalion; and the battalions were joined together, but as distinct and separate entities. At battalion headquarters, seven flags flew, all at the same level, with no battalion being superior. The hierarchy called it the 'combined battalions unit'.

The diggers returned to their lines, went back to the trenches and the front, and sanity prevailed. The British were bewildered by the behaviour, but pleased that the matter hadn't got out of hand. Originally, they had the gall to describe the rebellion by the Aussies as 'desertion'.

The singing faded, but the banter in the ambulance continued. The best laugh came when Coppy took off his shirt and replaced it with one that had a sergeant's rank on it. It was all part of his plan—a very cunning plan.

Finally, the truck slowly stopped outside the chateau-cum-hospital. The wounded were ferried carefully into the wards, and Coppy led Tag by the hand towards the impressive building. He whistled and chatted away casually.

'Well, mate, this is the first stop. I believe they're gunna fix up ya right arm here, mate. Reckon you'll be here for a couple a weeks maybe. Anything ya want, mate?'

Tag tapped Coppy's side just the once.

'What, mate? What is it?'

Tag swung his left hand in a circular motion, indicating in a crude way that he wanted to write something. Coppy took ages to decipher the signal, and then he twigged. He quickly got Tag settled into a ward bed and then went off to find some writing material for him. Simple as the request might have seemed, Coppy struggled to find any useful writing tools. Finally, after passing by the sergeants' mess for a snack and a quick cuppa, he hit on an idea. A tray—a cooking tray, straight from the kitchen, but still covered in a light smear of fat—would be perfect for tracing out a few simple words with a finger.

Excitedly, Coppy headed back. He explained his idea to Tag and, as a result, the long, slow trek to find the real Tag began. It was difficult. First, Tag could never write very well at the best of times, as his schooling had belted out of him the writing ability that his natural left hand had possessed. Now, his tightly bound right arm was a useless limb, about to undergo an operation to have the bones rearranged and set. Nevertheless, Tag persisted.

When Tag finally mastered the use of the pointer finger of his left hand, only two or three words would fit in the tray. This made communication frustrating and extremely slow.

Tag practised for ages, using a rag that Coppy had given him to wipe over his early efforts. Finally, Coppy went to explore the hospital, leaving Tag alone to master his new skill. When he returned, Tag, who had been waiting anxiously, was keen to convey his first message to Coppy. He wanted to write about so many things, including the fact that he was starting to see properly again. When Coppy returned, he could see that Tag was ready. 'Okay, mate,' he said. 'Let 'er rip.'

Tag slowly rubbed his pointer finger over the tray. Crudely, it spelled out three words: *Tag not Ross.*

Coppy frowned at the scribble. He thought for a while and then said, 'I get it. Your nickname's Tag—is that right?'

For the first time, Tag gingerly tried to shake his head. It was barely noticeable, but then he managed to write, *No.*

Coppy got the message.

'Waddaya mean, mate? What's ya nickname?'

Slowly, and a little neater, Tag wrote, *Tag Wardell.*

'Stone the crows! That's weird, mate. Tag Wardell?'

With much smaller writing, he wrote, *My name Tag Wardell.*

'Bullshit. Ya 'avin' me on. Where ya from, mate?'

Coppy knew where Ross Johnson was from, as he had written a letter to his parents in Ringwood, Melbourne. Slowly, Tag's finger scrawled across the tray.

Swifts Creek.

'Hell!'

With pain, Tag nodded his head. Coppy went quiet. It was too much for him to digest quickly.

'Crikey, mate, what do I do?'

That was the question. What could Coppy do? He himself was at the hospital under false pretences, wearing false rank. He would be in deep shit if found out, and it could be messy for Tag, too. Coppy did what he thought was the smartest thing. He sat next to Tag and explained his plan.

'This is it, mate. I'm friggin' outta 'ere. I'll tell 'em I hit the piss back at the station and cleared off for a bit—I won't be the first, eh? I'll lose some pay, but stiff shit, eh? You, mate, or Tag, if that's right, you're on the road to recovery, ya friggin' ripper. I see ya name's down for England, mate. Friggin' beauty. You'll be off soon. Hell, that's good news. I've written a letter, and we'll put it in ya personal bag now, okay? It explains what ya wrote, and a lot of the things that'll help ya. In the meantime, ya have to stay as Ross Johnson. Got that?'

Tag nodded.

'Until ya talk. Shit, what a great fuckin' yarn, eh … I knew a bloke once who talked with a cookin' tray! Shit! Ya stay in touch, ya rotten bastard, after this is all over. I'll put my brother's name and address and details in ya pocket, too, okay? He'd be old enough to be a copper right now, just like me dad and me. He can't join the army, lost a finger on 'is right 'and as a kid … bloody trigger finger, the lucky sod. Anyhow, don't lose them letters, ya useless prick. Meantime, I'll write to him and explain I might be lying low for a time. If they find me out, I could go for desertion, jail, and stuff — that means I can't write, eh? Fuck 'em, that's all I say.'

Coppy left, and managed to hitch a ride back to his base. He was elated — not only with finding out who Tag really was, but because, for once, now that he thought about it, a poor bugger with no name had had a win. In his work, Coppy had seen other cases of mistaken identity. Someone would go missing for three days after a stint, and the army would report him as dead. Often, the guesswork turned out to be accurate. Other times, they'd find a body with no dog tags … or dog tags and no body … or a badly wounded bloke with no dog tags, and no idea who he was. Again, the solution was to play the guessing game. Usually for the badly wounded, the identity problem was sorted out when the soldier's health improved. But what about a poor, badly wounded bloke who got found with his voice box burnt out, blinded, and with no identity? Coppy had seen a case like this once before, and that poor bloke had died. Perhaps this was what had stirred Coppy's curiosity when it came to Tag. During the war, identifying the body and doing the necessary paperwork was always behind—miles behind, even months behind. This sometimes led to devastating mistakes being made; and then, back in Australia, there'd be a knock on the door: 'Sorry, madam ...'

CHAPTER TWENTY-FIVE

Tag's recovery after surgery in the London hospital was relatively rapid. He started to talk, albeit in a slurred and barely coherent way, as the effort was still very painful. He practised and practised his writing. His eyesight returned to normal, although his lack of depth perception frustrated him: with only one eye, he had to guess distance, depth, and size. He would reach for a cup of tea and be two inches too short. He had great difficulty hanging up a hat or pulling a light cord. And as for reaching down, he was hopeless. If Tag dropped something on the floor, he preferred to crawl around and pick up the object; otherwise, if he tried to get it from a standing position, he would have to give up — fortunately, in a fit of giggles most of the time — after lurching endlessly in the general direction of the floor. Walking about was not a problem, though, until he had to go up or down steps or a slope.

'Went arse over head again' was how he explained his countless bruises and bumps to the nurses. But still he practised his walking every day, and finally managed to negotiate steps and stairs while using his one eye. He started to eat solids carefully, and chewed his first piece of fruit slowly after having been in England for only six weeks. By now, everyone was calling him Tag. Most thought it was a nickname, although it bore no resemblance to Johnson. His energy returned and, for the first time since he'd been shipped over, he allowed other thoughts to engage his mind. He started to ask questions.

'Do you know where Jill Hunter, the nurse, might be? She works in a hospital hereabouts somewhere.'

'I'll make some enquiries, Tag, but no promises. Okay?'

'She's of average height, very pretty, with brown hair. She comes from Benalla in Victoria.'

The request drew a blank after a week of asking around.

Then came the hardest problem to deal with. Tag asked to speak to an army officer, someone from outside the hospital.

'It's a matter of urgency, Sister … a personal matter.'

A matter of urgency indeed. Poor Tag had waited for what seemed a lifetime until he could see, and talk fairly clearly, and write very crudely. This was going to be tough.

Finally, a Captain Charles Healy of the British Army Survey Corps stood beside Tag's bed.

'What's so important, young man? I have a busy schedule.'

'Well, the thing is, I'm not the soldier they think I am, sir. There's been a mistake.'

Tag handed over the letter that Coppy had written. As the captain's eyes scanned down the page, the frown on his forehead got deeper. Quietly, he folded the letter and handed it back to Tag.

'This is remarkable, if it's true. What's been the hold-up? Something's not right here — you've taken a jolly long time act on this. Are you sure this is all true?' Captain Healy said, offering no compassion or concern.

The comment almost brought a burst of anger from Tag. He felt like lashing out with his left arm — at least now it was capable of packing a decent punch. Instead, under his breath, he mumbled, 'Friggin' Tommy Pratt.' Then he took a long, slow, careful breath.

'Positive, sir. I can give you my name, rank, number, unit, and postings—or my commanders' names, what they smoke, and how often they wipe their arse, if you like.'

That was the longest sentence Tag had spoken for ages.

Not amused, the officer took out a pencil and pad.

'Damn cheeky lot, you Australians. Let's hear what you've got, then.'

Within two days, Ross Johnson was dead and Tag had been reincarnated. Tag's memory became clearer to the point where he recalled removing the poor bloke's dog tags from his headless body. Tag was relieved, and pondered over what he should do next. Although hospitalised, he still wanted to find Jill, write to Ann, and maybe contact Johnson's family. The matter of Ross Johnson consumed him. He felt as if, in some way, he had cheated the man's parents. He asked to see Captain Healy again. The captain was there early the next morning.

'Could I tell Ross's family, mate? I believe I'll be sent home soon. Or at least could I write and tell 'em what's happened? No gory details, but ya know what I mean, mate?'

'It is "Sir" not "mate", Staff Sergeant Wardell. I'll have to ask my superiors.'

'Fuck 'em, mate. Can't we work this out ourselves—do it proper like? Ya don't want a friggin' copper knocking on ya door. Mum wrote to me about that ages ago. It's friggin' wrong, mate, fair dinkum!'

'Okay, I'll think about it.'

'Thanks, mate … Sir.'

Next came the matter of Jill. It had been three weeks since his first real enquiry, and he'd heard nothing. He explained what he could to the captain. Mind you, he had very few details about her—no full name, address, or rank, and he couldn't even remember the hospital where Jill worked when she'd written her last letter to him.

Captain Healy returned. He had found out the hospital where Jill had worked, although apparently she had since moved on somewhere; there were no further details. However, in the matter of Ross Johnson, the captain had done well. He placed an official-looking envelope on Tag's lap.

'It's all organised, Tag.'

'You bloody beauty, mate.'

'Now pay attention. Take this letter—it is sealed and signed by a high official ... me! When you get to Australia, you must have a policeman accompany you when you first visit the Johnsons. After that, ask the policeman to have a copy sent to the army. I will write also, but well after you have gone.'

The captain removed his hat, and bowed his head in a gesture best described as a silent tribute. He finally spoke again.

'That's it.'

Tag's shook Captain Healy's hand with his left hand.

'You've done the right thing, mate, believe me. Thanks. I've just heard I'm off to Australia in ten days' time. I'll be bloody glad to get home, mate, I can tell ya. With a bit a luck, me sheila's gone home, too. If ya can't find her anywhere, that's a possibility, eh? Bloody hope so.'

Captain Healy stared at the one-eyed man with a badly mangled right arm that would only bend at right angles. The young officer tried to fathom what he had been through, this young man, Tag—what with this dreadful war, and the incredible business of the mistaken identity. Captain Healy had never left England. He had a degree, and worked in mapping and surveillance. He threw his officer's cap onto a nearby chair, and sat on the edge of Tag's bed.

'Tell me about the war, mate—your war. Tell me all about it.'

An hour later, a very tired and much older and wiser Captain Healy got up to leave.

'You take care, mate.' He winked at Tag through misted eyes as he left.

THE TRIP ON the ship home was uneventful. Tag practised reaching for things, hanging clothes on a line, and walked and walked. Because his right arm would only bend to ninety degrees, he had to learn to do up buttons and buckle up his belt one handed. His right hand was fine; it was just that the arm had lost most of its inward movement. He had written to his mum two weeks earlier. It was just a brief note that ended with, 'I'm okay now. Put the kettle on, Mum.'

He also left a letter for Jill with one of the nursing sisters in the hospital, in case they found her.

The ship berthed in Melbourne on a Monday. Within ten hours of disembarking, Tag had his discharge papers signed. He spent the night at Watsonia barracks, and the following morning he caught the train from Flinders Street to Ringwood. After a long, steady walk, he entered the front office of the local police station. Unsure as to how to go about this unusual task, he asked what turned out to be a smart question.

'Excuse me, mate. Any of your coppers ex-army?'

Overhearing the query, someone with a Scottish accent spoke up from further back in the office.

'Who wants to know?'

The policeman came forward, glanced at Tag in his khaki uniform, and said, 'How can I help?'

The old policeman was Jock Roy. He had seen war in Africa; the ribbons on his coat gave it away.

An hour later, they both left the station. Senior Constable Roy insisted that Tag calls him Jock. It was only a fifteen-minute walk, as the Johnsons lived in Wilana Street, only a few blocks away, but it would take Tag half an hour. Jock stopped regularly for a break, once rolling a cigarette for Tag. As they sat, he quietly asked where Tag had seen action. The answers made Jock shake his lowered head.

On arrival at the Johnsons, Senior Constable Roy knocked on the front door, and introduced himself and Tag. Briefly, he explained the reason for their visit. Tag took off his hat, bowed, and asked whether he could come in. There were no more pleasantries. Tag had rehearsed many times in his mind how he would approach this awkward meeting, but now his plans went out the window. The moment they reached the lounge room, he thrust the envelope towards the worried mother.

'I have a letter I'd like you to read. I haven't read it, but I know it contains sad news about Ross,' he said.

Dear Mr and Mrs Johnson,

It is my sad duty to inform you that your son Ross has been killed in action in France. Unfortunately, this notification is very late. Ross died bravely many months ago, but the young man who gave you this letter was mistaken for Ross. Consequently, you received several reports about his being wounded and his imminent recovery. No doubt, some of Ross's mates wrote as well. They all believe he had survived. Tag, the young man with this letter, will explain what happened. It is terribly sad and my heartfelt condolences go out to you.

The young soldier who gave you the letter is a fine young man. He has experienced war at its worst. He, like your son, has suffered. I deeply admire what he wanted to do in meeting you. I have nothing but the highest respect for him. I consider him a good mate.

Sincerely,

Captain Charles Healy

Mrs Johnson cried for ten minutes. She left the room, returned, and started to offer them a cup of tea, but the moment her lips parted she again burst into tears. She sat, jammed her hands holding the wet handkerchief between her thighs, leant forward, and rocked. It was a dismal, bleak sight for the two men. For the soldier, Tag, it was another side to war that he would normally never have seen. But Jock sat sternly. He always sat sternly — more than anything else, he hated this task. A further awkward ten minutes passed. Finally, Mrs Johson remarked, 'Tom will be home in an hour. What will I tell him?'

'Would you like me to stay?' offered Tag.

'Thank you, young man. And, please, just tell me how it happened.'

Jock and Tag left after tea that evening. Tom Johnson was silent most of the time. Tag's description of events was only brief, but the way he held himself and his constant pauses had such a powerful effect that Jock the policeman started to cry bitterly. Tag didn't offer opinions or arguments. He told them what he had seen, although it was a heavily censored version. He didn't hint at how he felt. He didn't need to — it was obvious from looking at him and listening to him.

That night, he slept at Jock's house. The next morning, Tag was offered a generous breakfast of bacon and eggs. During the meal, he reached inside his pocket and took out the other letter that Coppy had written, which explained in much more detail than Captain Healy had about Tag's ordeal. Obviously moved after reading it, Jock promised to locate Coppy's brother, if possible, and to put him in touch with Tag.

Jock and Tag talked like brothers for ages. It wasn't war talk, but it came with that special bond from war that allows men to reach out, to show emotion and deep trust. Admittedly, Jock did most of the talking.

Then it was time for Tag to leave.

'If you're ever down this way, there's always a bed, laddie,' Jock told him.

They shook hands, and then Jock came out with a most unexpected statement. 'That damn pirate patch over your missing eye, tighten up the cord or something, me boy. Whenever it flaps up and down in the wind, it scares the living daylights out of people, lad.'

Tag smiled, promised he would do something about it, and then shook Jock's hand again.

'Thanks, Jock,' he said.

He turned and walked down the two steps outside the Roys' front porch without hesitation. After spending the night at the Watsonia barracks, he would head for home tomorrow.

IT WAS THREE months before a very pregnant Jill arrived unannounced at Ann Wardell's front door. The two women said nothing. Then, after a moment of staring at her, Ann spoke.

'Jill?'

Jill broke down and sobbed uncontrollably. Ann turned and walked into the kitchen, sobbing loudly herself. Chatty, who'd been having a fag out the back, rushed in.

'Jill? Oh hell. Jill? Oh hell.'

Chatty hugged Jill with overwhelming affection.

Jill smiled and looked at Ann. 'Yes, I'm Jill, and this is your grandchild,' she said, patting her bulging stomach.

Ann walked outside. Chatty scratched his head, looked at Jill, and added, 'She'll be right, mate. She'll come round, you betcha.'

Jill didn't put down her small case of belongings. She sat down, exhausted, with the case on her lap, and confusion flowing into her being. This was her only hope — Ann and Chatty, then Tag. This was what had kept her going. It had kept her from losing her baby when the ship had hit terrible weather across the

Bight and she had been hospitalised for three days. Without her dream, what would she do? Chatty spoke.

'She's been doing it tough, mate, you know — what with Tag and friggin' Bucket and poor Golly.'

Jill froze. She dropped her bag and walked out the back.

'You don't know, do you?' said Ann, her sad face pale and drawn. 'It's been months. I don't have any details ...'

No SOONER HAD Jill arrived, it seemed, than so did her baby. Baby Wardell was born screaming, with red hair like his father. Jill had managed well, and Ann was by her side every minute of the way. He was born at 2.00 a.m., with a hint of a ginger complexion and powerful lungs. The *Omeo Standard* announced that 'Mr Tag Wardell (deceased) and Mrs Jill Wardell were the proud parents of a baby boy, Greg ...' The name Greg had come via Chatty. He told Jill about Tag and Tiger when they left the trenches at Gallipoli and his comment to Jill was 'That's what I said to Golly, just as we were about to leave: "My first kid, I'm gonna call him Greg, mate, after you."'

It was a rare moment of joy for the household. Jill had lived with Ann from that first day. To counter the gossip and the guessing games, Ann had come up with a little white lie about Tag and Jill's marriage. As it happened, many months earlier, the kind matron in England had given Jill a ring as she departed and had said, 'Wear it always, and never explain.'

Consequently, on the ship and at Swifts Creek, Jill had been greeted with soft smiles and sympathetic nods, and before the due date she received many bundles of baby clothes and necessities. Since Jill had arrived, Chatty had curbed his drinking a little and had started to help in the butter factory. It was hard, at first, for Chatty to leave the Wardell stables, which had been his home since returning. He moved into a tent behind the butter factory. At least he had the support of Lilly, his mum. She had been wonderful from the day that Chatty had arrived in Swifts Creek. She visited the stables every day, snuck him some money, and never asked him difficult questions like all the other nosey buggers.

Jill had warmed to Lilly straight away. She told Ann one day, 'It's as if she knows without being told.'

'That's Lilly — she's special. It's wonderful to see her with Chatty,' Ann replied.

'Is she Aboriginal?'

'Yes, that's what makes her special. Lilly senses things. She knows every person she's seen in Swifts Creek intimately, even though most of them ignore her. Of all people, Lilly has been my friend.'

Ann paused.

'I miss her laughter the most. I commented on this once to Lilly, and she said it had gone with her boys to the war, to give them strength.'

Then Tag's letter arrived. It wasn't delivered, as they usually were, to the accompaniment of a sharp rap on the door by a distressed local constable with his hat removed, fidgeting with nervous tension, dreading the task of delivering sad news to anxious parents. Tag's letter came in the normal post. It arrived at the Swifts Creek post office via the old seven-seater mailcar that had taken the boys away so long ago. As always, there was a small gathering of locals outside the post office by the time the mailcar left, bound for Tongio and then Omeo. They chatted away while, inside, the pigeonholes were filled with mail. Then Des Kelly, the postman, unlocked the door, and the locals filtered in.

Ann recognised the handwriting straight off, though it was a little untidy, even smudged. *Must have taken a while to get here*, she thought. A cold shudder ran through her body, as that first thought warned her of sorrow and even more grief to come. She felt certain that the letter had arrived very, very late. It must have been written a long time ago — before Tag's death.

She didn't know what to do, as colliding thoughts rushed into her mind. *Tell Jill. No, read it and then maybe tell Jill. Chatty, sweet Chatty — he's cut down on the grog since Jill's arrival. Poor Chatty, he never mentions the boys anymore … and I don't want him back on the grog. If I tell Jill, Chatty will know something's up — they're very close.*

Ann walked across the dirt road and sat on the edge of the water trough out the front of Sandy's store, clutching the letter to her chest. A soft hand touched her shoulder. It was Lilly, Chatty's mum. She sat down, held Ann's hand, and looked her in the eye.

'Today, me Chatty boy said he wanted ta move back ta 'is room. I's coming up to tell ya. That's all I wanted — me boy back in our 'ouse. Such a special day, eh? Tell Jill, too. She'll be so happy when ya tell 'er. Today's a relly good day, I know this. Yeah, relly special.'

Ann showed Lilly the letter, adding, 'It's from Tag. I don't know what to do, Lilly.'

'You read it to me and we talk about that. It come today — means it could be a good letter.'

Ann tore open the envelope.

Dear Mum,

Don't know how to write this, but I'm alive and kicking. There was a mix-up with me and another poor bloke and you got the wrong story. He was killed, and I copped a few injuries. Lost an eye, other ones OK. Main thing is I am on my way home. Leaving in ten days. I'm okay now. Put the kettle on, mum.

Love Tag

Lilly nodded as she hugged Ann to her body. Tears flowed down their cheeks. Old Mrs Carroll stopped by, took Ann's free hand and Lilly's arm, and simply said, 'Come, I'll take you home.'

BABY GREG was several months old when Tag stepped down from the mailcar at Swifts Creek.

CHAPTER TWENTY-SIX

Tag had kept himself very busy on the long voyage from England to Melbourne, treating the time as if he were in training for a sporting event. He had walked around the ship, and walked some more. He had practised lifting the heavy bag that contained his entire army possessions. He had kept throwing a pair of rolled-up socks into the air, trying to catch them — that was hard, but he had improved until almost perfect. He had simply wanted some of his strength and dexterity back.

He had kept to himself on board, but it was rare for him to sit and allow his thoughts to wander. He hadn't even given much thought to coming home, apart from hoping that he'd find out what had happened to Jill, and looking forward to seeing his mum and Chatty again. He was longing to pat Jess, the beagle, and Dimble, the horse, and he was already planning a trip to the old log cabin on Sheepstation Creek, and maybe up into the Angoras. No way would a dicky bloody arm stop him from riding a horse; as for blacksmithing again, his right arm would let him know about that.

He had only given Bucket and Golly's family a fleeting thought one morning on the ship while enjoying a beautiful sunrise. He shuddered at even contemplating the prospect of seeing them. Sadly, this part of his mind only came alive as he slept. In the vile, dark world of slumber, every terrible scene he had ever witnessed was re-enacted. The lads would be there — Golly, Bucket, Chatty, and Tiger — particularly Tiger. Tiger was always lost in the desert, calling out for Tag. It was a bad omen, and often caused Tag to jolt awake in a wet bed, smelling of fear and urine.

Now, finally on his way to Swifts Creek, looking out the train window at Pakenham as it passed cows wandering away from the dairy after their morning milking, he had only one thing on his mind: Mr and Mrs Johnson. That get-together had affected Tag deeply. He continually questioned his decision to be the bearer of their bad news. How naive of him: in trying to do a good turn, he had received in return an emotional message equivalent to a solid smack on the nose. At the time, he could see plainly that, in the briefest of moments, he had witnessed a family disintegrate and dissolve into two individuals. Both the Johnsons had reeled into a state of overwhelming anguish. They felt helpless, but he could see that their grief was solitary; they could offer no support to each other. They were a mother and a father, each alone in a world of despair. Earlier, twelve months before the news of Ross had arrived, they had had another boy killed at Gallipoli. Now, neither of their boys was alive.

Leaning on his chin, looking out the open window as smoke from the steam train's funnel wafted into the cabin, Tag stared blankly at some of the finest farming country in Australia. Already in his mind he was deciding that, when he got home, he would stay at home. Yes, it would just be him, his mum, and the animals. He so much wanted to see his animals.

BETWEEN THEM, ANN and Jill had worked out when Tag was due to arrive, but they were three days out in their calculations. Or, more accurately, Tag's visit to the Johnsons had caused an unexpected delay. Each day, for almost a week, they would walk to the post office around midday—all in their best attire, including baby Greg—and await the arrival of the mailcar. Ann had told the Bankses and the Elliots about the news of Tag's survival, but they decided against greeting him on his arrival. As it was, a small crowd was there every day: Lilly, Chatty, Old Bill, Sid, Sally Sandy, Ann's mum, Phyllis with two kids, and Albert and Tiger's mum, along with a few other locals with fond memories of Tag.

Then, in the distance, a car appeared. It had to be the mailcar; the Omeo Highway through Swifts Creek was lucky to host four cars a day. As the dust settled and Tag stepped down from the old Hudson, the onlookers didn't clap or cheer. Most stepped back, aghast at the sight of this frail man wearing a patch where there would normally be an eye. His deformed face tried to present a lop-sided grin, but didn't bear looking at for too long, as the locals would put it later that night. However, Jill and Chatty both rushed forward with enthusiasm. The sight of a one-eyed man was common to them both. Then, just as Chatty went to shake Tag's hand and Jill clapped in delight, Ann rushed at her son and hugged him tightly.

Tag showed little or no emotion. Next, Jill stepped forward. They both stared at each other. He knew her, but he didn't; it was his Jill, but it wasn't. For Tag, this woman looked weary, much older, and very tired. For Jill, the sight of Tag was upsetting. It wasn't the missing eye that troubled her, but he was hunched over, he was going bald, and he had lost a considerable amount of weight. They went to shake hands, and then Jill grabbed Tag and held him for a long time. Nothing was said between them until, finally, Jill commented, 'Here's our new baby, Greg.'

Baby Greg beamed a beautiful smile on cue, as if rehearsed. Tag said nothing. This was all too much for him.

Quickly, the crowd dispersed, and those who had stayed

behind walked quietly up the hill to Ann's house. Tag and Chatty almost rubbed shoulders all the way; Lilly held Chatty's hand; and Jill and Ann walked arm in arm. Then, as the front wire-gate closed behind them, there suddenly appeared a frantic, crazed, desperate beagle named Jess. She tried to jump, spin, lick, bark, run about, and wag her tail vigorously, all at the same time. Tag was overjoyed. He knelt down, scratching the excited dog on the belly as she lay on her back. It was then that Jill noticed something wrong with Tag's arm. He had on long sleeves, so there was no visible scaring. Nevertheless, his restricted movement was obvious to a nurse. Once in the kitchen, Ann stoked the stove and slid the kettle into the middle.

Then Tag spoke for the first time. 'Is Dimble about?' he asked.

'Out the back, mate,' Chatty said. 'Come on, I'll show ya.'

Once out the back, Tag produced his second lop-sided, wide smile for the day. Dimble had come trotting down the hill the moment he heard the squeak of the hinges on the back gate. Tag put his right arm around the horse's lowered neck, and held Dimble very tight. The horse rubbed Tag's shin, nibbled at his army boots, and blurted soft humming noises.

'I've missed ya so much, mate. I've told many a horse all about ya. Ya goin' okay, mate?'

Dimble answered with a fond push. In the past, Tag must have received a thousand such pushes from this sulky pony. The horse's eyes sparkled.

After a time, both men wandered back inside. Tag felt distressed. He wanted to be alone with just one person. Should it be Ann, Jill, or Chatty?

Then Lilly spoke.

'I think we oughta leave 'em together a bit.'

She was looking in Jill's direction.

'How's about the rest of us go out the front, on the veranda for a bit, eh?'

They were together and alone. Jill, holding baby Greg, coughed lightly and then spoke.

'I'm still at a loss, Tag. We all thought you were dead. We only got your letter a week-or-so back. It's been really strange — it was such a horrible thing, what happened. Just when we were sort of coping, the letter came. I hate the mail; most people do. They write to their boys in the hope they'll read it and write back. That rarely happens. Sorry, I'm jabbering. It's just that I wanted to say that Chatty reckons your mum was shattered when she read that note the policeman handed over, saying you'd been killed in action. Why do they say that? It's so official, cold … sorry, Tag.'

Jill was struggling. Tag was silent. She continued, 'I've only been here a short while. Greg was born here. I found out I was pregnant in London. He's your baby, Tag. One get-together, and I fell pregnant. How about that?'

She paused, as he was hardly listening.

'Are you okay?

Tag looked down. This wasn't home — apart from Dimble, Chatty, and Jess. His mum looked worn-out and weary. Jill had changed considerably. Of the people who'd come to meet him, none spoke or smiled. Phyllis had stayed all of two minutes and then rushed off. The town was different, somehow. Now he was a dad. Where was the home he had left behind?

His left hand shielded his eye as he lowered his head. All of a sudden, Jill recognised the same Tag she had seen outside the hospital at Cairo after his visit to Chatty. At the time, it was a world that few humans — other than nurses and soldiers — had ever entered. Now, finally back home, he was lost again. Jill sensed that there was more to it than him just being home.

'Tag, tell me, please tell me. Say something. All I can say is I missed you so much when you went away … and then, and then, after I got here, I tried to forget you.'

She started to sob.

Tag wanted to leave, and he wanted to stay. He wanted to say something, but he couldn't think of anything that made any sense.

'Sorry, Jill. I'm sorta lost. I do like the baby, Greg, though. What a great name—funny, but that's what I wanted to call my first kid.'

'Do you want to hold him for a bit?'

Gingerly, Tag took the little boy. Greg's tiny arm swung and gently slapped Tag's cheek. In the process, the eye patch was ripped off.

'What a good job. Gosh, that's healed well.'

Tag gave Jill a steady look. Her statement was like a magic key, like a small miracle. That was what he wanted to hear. That was the Jill he remembered—the nurse, that great girl from Benalla who, during those many hours they had spent together so long ago, offered him such wisdom and comfort, and passion. He remembered the caring, devoted nurse who was always concerned for others, and always seemed so grateful that she'd found someone who would let her just talk, and then talk some more about the pitiable blokes in the palace hospital wanting nothing more than her company.

Tag held Greg close to his chest, rose, and then sat beside Jill on the couch.

'I had a pretty bad time in Melbourne, Jill. I visited the bloke's parents—the bloke who was alive but dead, the bloke who was me. Shit, it was hard. They didn't know he was dead, and I … I tried to say …'

Tag was lost. He stared at nothing. It wasn't a familiar stare—that stonewalling look of belligerence, or cowardice, attributed to many a man over the ages when it came to delicate matters. Tag had a look that, in time, people came to recognise and call 'the thousand-yard stare.' It was a strange stare—the look of a hollow, blank human being when faced with matters of the heart. People could pick it from afar, and would then nod to each other, knowing that they were looking at a returned man.

Tag's eyes were puffy, red, and wet with tears. His face looked so tired, so old, and so sad.

'Can't say much more about that … it's good ya here, though. Yeah, real good.'

Tag tried to smile. As his tight lips arched to perform that difficult task, they quivered instead, and he let out a heart-rending low moan. He shook uncontrollably as Jill's outstretched arms encircled her baby, Greg—and her Tag.

Two years had passed; the war had ended. Tag had improved a little in terms of being sociable. More importantly, he was still improving. His first attempt at leaving the front gate of the Wardell house, about a month after getting home and catching up with a couple of his old friends, had been a complete disaster. He had decided on a visit to Bill and Sid at the old blacksmith's shop, where Jack Murey was the head farrier. The men had stopped work on seeing Tag walking towards the shop. Old Bill had spotted him—with only a slight limp now—and Jess, the happy, prancing beagle, by his side.

Bill called to the others. They all came out, and Tag met the new apprentice. There were handshakes all round, the warmest of smiles offered, and many comments of 'So good ta see ya, mate'. But none of this gave Tag the strength to cope with what was about to happen. They all wanted to talk at once—such were the powerful feelings these men had towards him. Bill was quite emotional; to avoid the embarrassment of tears, he turned and suggested he go out the back and put the billy on. His eyes were very red when he called them all in for a cuppa. The conversations went from cars to mine closures to rogue horses, and then to reminiscences about Patch, the piebald.

'Still in harness, and no trouble to shoe. I reckon 'e looks round for ya every time 'e's 'ere,' Sid said.

The men all laughed. Tag, whose continuing silence didn't bother them, nodded and smiled. With the cuppa finished, Bill spoke up.

'Yer comin' back, mate? We could do with a spare smithy.'

Tag raised his eyebrow. It wasn't the reason for the visit, but occasionally he had tossed the idea around in his head. He spoke up for the first time.

'Could be,' he said. 'We'll see, eh?'

Tag followed the men into the workshop and took a seat on a bag of chaff. What happened next was the talk of the town for the next few days. Not only did Tag jump after the first hammer blow hit the anvil, but he ducked, crawled around behind the chaff bags and hid, shaking. The hammers kept pounding as the men concentrated on their task—each blow of the heavy hammer had to be accurate. The sharp clang as the tool hit the anvil was so loud that most smithies were deaf by retirement age. Bill had put his hammer down, about to coke up the furnace, when he spotted Tag's boots sticking out behind the chaff bags.

He rushed towards Tag, but stopped dead as he came face to face with a staring eye that radiated total fear. He turned and, waving his arms, ran around and got the men to stop working. They looked at Bill with frowns until his shaking finger pointed out Tag for them. As they approached, the smell of soupy human shit hit their nostrils. What to do? Sid knelt down.

'We'll get a jinker and run ya 'ome, mate.'

Tag didn't nod; he shook. The distressed, cheerless men lifted Tag into the jinker. Bill sat beside Tag and held his hand; the others, along with Jess, walked quietly behind as the cart headed for the Wardells' house. It was like a funeral procession.

There wasn't a lot of activity at Sidley and Cooper's blacksmith shop that day. There were just many quiet conversations and cuppas, and they all knocked off early. Ann went and visited Bill Cooper at his home several hours later. Bill was most grateful, although he didn't ask any of the hundreds of questions that were pounding in his head.

Remedies to improve the emotional health of returned soldiers didn't exist in the 1920s. Many relied on alcohol. That might have helped the soldier, but not his family. His mates, in many cases, were his only support.

ANN ANSWERED THE knock at the door. There stood Coppy, the kind orderly who had enabled Tag to reclaim his identity — he had knocked very softly on the Wardells' front door. Tag recognised Coppy's voice, rushed to the front door alongside Ann, and then just stood and looked in amazement. Characteristically, Coppy's first comment was a smart-alec remark.

'Changed that stupid bloody name yet, or do I still 'ave ta call ya Tag?'

They hugged, patted each other's backs, and sucked in the delight of the moment. In no time, their jumbled, excited talking, swearing, and laughter had Ann, Jill, Chatty, and Golly all standing and staring.

'Coppy!' shouted Tag, not realising that he had never explained the importance of Coppy to those present. Typically, Coppy did all the talking. After many tears, gasps of wonder, and cries of amazement, things settled down. Coppy was treated as an honoured guest, and spent a week at the Wardells. He loved them, the Swifts Creek township, and the powerful, small group of people he met who surrounded Tag with love and support.

In no time, he left the police force and moved up from Melbourne to Swifts Creek. Greg, or Golly junior, was now five.

He was a beautiful young redheaded boy, swamped with love and affection from all Tag's friends and family. After spending one night at the Junction Pub, Coppy set up permanent residence in Tag's old stables.

Coppy was a good man. Many echoed that sentiment. However, the day he walked into the Wardell kitchen waving a sheet of paper, he became a hero. It was a letter from his brother, a policeman in Melbourne. With the help of old Jock Roy, they had found Tiger: he was locked up in the Dandenong police station. Other details accompanied the letter. Apparently, Tiger had become a senior man in the Light Horse, and then there was a mention of Beersheba—and that was about it. Quickly, after Coppy read the letter to the excited listeners in the kitchen, they made plans to rescue Tiger.

It was hardly a formidable team that Coppy assembled—his brother, Jock Roy; Jill; Tag, with his one eye; and Chatty, with his one leg—but they were determined.

When they got to the Dandenong police station, it turned out that the local police had to be convinced that Tiger was safe to be let out on the streets. One of them read out a lengthy report to the gathered group of friends from Swifts Creek, and it was not good news. Tiger had a record of drinking to excess, brawling, fighting, and using foul language in drunken rages over the supposed ignorance about the war of those at home in Australia.

Coppy did all the talking. Things became tense when a policeman mentioned, 'He's donged some bastard for trying to take away his bag—so happens it was a copper.'

It didn't sound good. 'He carries this damn army bag everywhere with him. Touch it, or try to take it off him, and he goes berserk! Mind you, he's always happy to show us the contents.'

The policeman raised his eyebrows, looked away, and continued.

'Inside, it has a couple of cards. He hands them over and just points. On them is his name and other important stuff, but no address … it's like he can't talk at times.'

The policeman stopped. Tag was about to say something, but instead just shook his head. Chatty put his arm around Tag's shoulder, murmuring, 'That's the Tiger we knew at school.'

The policeman went on.

'It's also got his baccy and a bit of moleskin cloth in it—someone told us Tiger reckons it was part of his last saddle blanket—and a long bunch of hair, part of a mane off a horse called Sandy or something. It's all a bit strange, we reckon.'

Silence descended. There were quiet, sad looks, until finally Coppy spoke.

'We'll keep an eye on him—we promise ya, Jack. We'll take him back up the bush, home to his mum. These blokes 'ere all know him real well.'

Of course, Coppy knew the policeman in charge from his earlier days as a junior officer. The police huddled into a small circle, and a brief meeting took place. Then Jack spoke.

'OK, mate. He's all yours.'

A miserable-looking, scrawny Tiger emerged from the cells clutching a small army canvas bag. He looked like street beggar. He had a mad stare about him that reinforced exactly what the police had said—try to touch this bag and you're dead! His anger towards the police was apparent as he jerked and twisted while they pushed him towards the front office. He snarled as he faced the wooden floor. Then Tiger heard a familiar voice. Looking up, he spotted Chatty and then Tag. He dropped to his knees, and a scream pierced the air. Slowly, he fell down completely, sobbing as his knees came up into his stomach. He dropped the canvas bag—that was a first. The police were stunned. Jill quickly walked forward and knelt down. She lifted his head onto her lap as Tag and Chatty squatted on either side of him. He tried to call out, 'T-t-t-t-agg!'

His behaviour was dreadful, pitiable. Much earlier, on arriving at Ringwood, before even heading to Dandenong, Jock, who had visited Tiger, had warned them, 'He's a friggin' wreck, poor sod. Lord help me, 'e should've 'ad some 'elp—not locked up, for Christ sake!' However, no amount of warnings or descriptions could have prepared them for this.

It took twenty long, painful minutes to get Tiger to his feet and to calm him. He was like a puppy as the gang surrounded him. He patted their shoulders, hugged Jill, and shook their hands several times. Then they all laughed and cried together. Like a little boy surrounded by a stack of presents on Christmas day, Tiger was chuffed.

When he got home, the gang never left his side. Together, they visited his mum, and then they moved him into the stables with Coppy. Jill took him his meals, and Tag kept the alcohol supply up. Chatty stayed all day, every day. He only went home when Lilly called for him.

Gradually, Tiger calmed down, gained confidence, and slowed his alcohol consumption. Although he rarely went home, his mother visited him every day. He put on some weight, started to shave every day, and ate the evening meal with the gang in the kitchen. After six months, he spent a lot more time in the house, in the lounge after tea, and started to join in. His stuttering had diasappeared, just as it had all those years ago when he was with his boyhood mates. Then, one evening, he came in with a tuft of ginger mane.

'This 'ere belonged to Sandy. Ya would 'ave loved 'im, Tag … 'e was such a good mate … 'e got shot, fell badly under me … poor ol' bastard.'

He looked at Ann.

'Just wondering if ya 'ad a jar or somethin'?'

Ann produced a small glass container, and Sandy found a new

home on the mantelpiece over the Wardell fireplace. It was a special evening — one of the first times that Tiger not only spoke at length, along with the others, but also reminisced about the good times. Some of the stories were about what had happened while on leave in the army, but most were about their boyhood. Over the next few nights, these enjoyable conversations sowed the seeds of an idea for a re-enactment of an old adventure. Tiger made the suggestion, adding that he had a plan. After he explained the reason, their curiosity led to a feeling of excitement.

THE TRIP TO the Dargo high plains took a long time to organise. For months, the lads talked about and worked out ways for all of them to do it. They would need horses, a tent, and an apparatus of sorts to tie Chatty to the saddle. Jill and Coppy would come along as well, as both were competent riders. Then came some good but disappointing news: Jill was pregnant. Overnight, in the minds of the men, Jill changed from one of the gang to a frail, delicate, mother-to-be who needed wrapping in cotton wool. Now, allowing Jill to ride a horse was out of the question. No amount of protests from her or Ann would change the men's minds.

The next plan involved a separate car trip to the high plains for Jill and Coppy, who was the only one with a driver's licence. Luckily, the Elliots offered their vehicle; a car-cum-delivery truck, it would be ideal. The remainder of the party would still travel by horse. It would be a special trip, which they were all looking forward to in a strange way. It was going to be a repeat of the out-of-the-ordinary outing they'd had all those years before during the school holidays. They'd follow the same route this time, via the old log cabin and Mount Baldhead … except now in a somewhat smaller group, and for a different reason.

The date was set. The car was loaded up with extra fuel, a very detailed map, tyres, food, and camping gear—perhaps even some cotton wool. Jill and Coppy had quite a send-off from the locals. The horsemen had left two days earlier. Surprisingly, Jess, now a very old and frail beagle, didn't hesitate to follow or lead. She knew where they were heading, the moment that they reached the top of the Angoras.

THE CAMP FIRE crackled as the friends sat close together under the vivid, clear evening sky. Shooting stars and the southern lights were putting on a fine show. Jess, showing her age, was very content. With a full belly, and Tag to cuddle up to, she was feeling complete beagle bliss. Dimble had just come along for the ride. He had plodded along behind the riders without even having to wear a bridle. Almost twenty-three years old now, he nodded off to sleep regularly, whether it was day or night.

For Coppy and Jill, it was a first. They sat quietly, in awe of the cosmic display. Chatty, with a stringy-bark crutch under his arm, had just returned from attending to a call of nature in the nearby bush. He felt proud to have been able to ride all the way with one leg. He sat near his mates, and Tiger turned to him.

'Ya didn't lace the camp oven with wombat turd this time, mate.'

They all laughed.

Chatty explained the joke to Jill and Coppy, adding, 'That was a great meal, Tag.'

Tag was the reluctant cook. It was his turn. Then it was Tiger's job to do the dishes. The men took it in turns to perform all the duties, except for Coppy, who was the guest. As for Jill, she was treated almost like royalty. Golly junior had stayed home (after much protest) with Gran. Ann hadn't objected, of course.

'Bloody dampers weren't as good as Golly's, but they'll do, eh!' Tiger said.

'You mean *ayah!*' said Chatty, remembering Cairo, and grunting as he sat down.

'Velly good, *ayah!*'

They all laughed softly. There was so much laughing to catch up on. It was the first time that this group had been alone together.

Dawn on the Dargo high plains was greeted by three happy kookaburras. The group stretched, groaned, grunted, and rolled back the canvas. Jill was jammed somewhere in the middle near Tiger, or was it Tag? In no time, Chatty had the fire going, and Tiger was straining the tadpoles and wrigglies out of the water. Tag, of course, was attending to the horses. Dimble was first. Coppy, tentatively given the task of making the first brew, didn't dare put a foot wrong. All he had ever heard about his skills was that they were bloody hopeless, like those of all bloody city-ites.

As the group sat and sipped their mugs of billy tea, their sighs said it all. A sigh covers most emotions, except greed or anger. By now, in this group of special people who had been mellowed by their experience of war, both greed and anger were absent. For the horsemen, this was their first morning after having made the long, wearying trek up from the old log cabin on Sheepstation Creek—the cabin that was once again filled with wombat holes, and whose stringy-bark roof had caved in. It was a unique trip.

Once breakfast was over, Tiger awkwardly delved into his canvas army bag and produced his tobacco tin—the same tin that had been issued to him years ago at Gallipoli. It was intact, with a good lid. Carefully, he unrolled the tin, which was still wrapped in a piece of khaki material.

It did not contain what used to be the standard issue of one cake of tobacco. Instead, it was full of dirt. Tiger had kept this tin with care—from the day they had left that trench, that tunnel, that mound, and those two bayonets at Gallipoli.

They stood in a small, tight semi-circle around the waterhole on the Dargo high plains.

'Rest in peace, fellas.'

'Yeah.'

They all echoed the sentiment as Tiger gently threw the dirt over the water.

ACKNOWLEDGEMENTS

Old Jack Campbell or the horses: that was a hard choice when I had to decide the subject of the dedication for this novel. Although much of the story of *Tag* is based on old Jack's experiences and reminiscences, other parts are fiction. The story of the horses, however, is true. Only one of them returned to Australia after World War I.

Old Jack was a loner, a World War I veteran who owned the farm at the top of Connor's Hill, just up from the tiny town of Ensay, Victoria. I was a young boy when I first saw him, wearing a strange patch over his eye. I recall asking Mum what had happened to him.

On leaving school and then starting a job on a farm at Ensay, I soon got to know the likeable old fella. I have many memories of him; his humour, his simple farming methods, and his affection towards his stock come readily to mind. I was struck by how, as I rode my horse to work every Monday, I would see several very old horses in one of his paddocks. Most farmers would have sent them off to market, for pet food and a few bob. Not old Jack, though: those old nags would spend their last days in the shade enjoying retirement. He loved them.

A sense of curiosity, various comments I came to hear, and some papers that came my way in 2002 aroused my inquisitiveness about Jack's service in World War I. I then decided to find out a little more about the man. From Bairnsdale to Broadmeadows, from Melbourne to King George Sound, a story started to unfold. I knew that the poor treatment of horses on the ships and in Egypt would have riled the likes of Jack and others from the high country, and then I came across documents which revealed that the army brought about changes in its horse-handling procedures. Surely, I thought, men like Jack Campbell would have been involved. Then I followed the Gallipoli campaign and the tragic day of the first armistice — such a bizarre event. Finally, my research took me on to France and the mayhem of mud and the distressed, scouring horses. It became disturbing reading as I delved deeper into the history of the horses.

I kept thorough notes. This was a story I had to tell — the horses, and old Jack and his ilk deserved nothing less. By late 2004, I had the story of *Tag* well underway.

During my investigations, I found the writing and thorough research of Patsy Adam-Smith to be the most valuable. She led me down paths that opened my eyes to the journals and diaries of returned men. As well, a line in one of her books about the lot of a nurse turned my inquiries in a totally new direction. I have always had sympathy for the army nurse after attending the opening of their memorial in Canberra several years back, followed by the honour of meeting Nurse Vivian Bullwinkle, a hero from World War II. However, my reading also revealed the almost draconian treatment of those women in hospitals during World War I. Some of the effects that this treatment had on them emotionally stunned me. Whether it was the long hours, the pressure of work, or their prison-like living quarters, I felt this needed highlighting in my story. Therefore, Tag had to have a girlfriend.

Finally, I read many of the *Omeo Standard* newspapers from the late 1800s to the early 1920s to get a feel for the Omeo area of that era and the experiences of its returning soldiers; I found them very informative. My account was also broadened by being able to read *Bairnsdale's Changed Men: a community's impression of its servicemen*, Shaun Mason's 2001 thesis for his honours degree at the University of Melbourne. His sources included local court documents, a history of the Bairnsdale shire, and the local newspaper, the *Bairnsdale Advertiser*. This material both directed and enabled me to acquire a better understanding of the returned men of World War I.

I read many journals and diaries. One in particular, given to me by my old school teacher Mr Les O'Brien, who I mention fondly in *The View from Connor's Hill*, was very insightful. The family had turned the diary into a self-published book.

I would also like to thank sincerely Max Prendergast, who has been involved with my last two books; his corrections and advice have been most welcome. Henry Rosenbloom, my publisher at Scribe, is now a good friend. His literary skills and my passion for telling the story have combined to produce what I hope is a realistic account of those starry-eyed young men and frightened horses who went off to war—'the war to end all wars'.

Doug Treasure, Ron Connelly—a horseman with vast experience—Blake Hollands, and many other high-country men offered advice and experience. As well, the staff at the State Library in Melbourne, and Ian Jackson and staff at the Canberra War Memorial, all deserve thanks.

For photographs, and other details of the background to *Tag*, readers can visit my web page at barryheard.com.au. It contains photographs of horses wearing gas masks, the medical carts, and other unusual material from World War I, as well as a photograph of Sidley and Coopers Blacksmith shop (1900), the old log cabin, and many other historical images from that era, including of the Dargo high plains.